RESISTANCE

PATRICIA DIXON

BLOODHOUND
— BOOKS —

Print ISBN 978-1-913419-81-3

ALSO BY PATRICIA DIXON

WOMEN'S FICTION

They Don't Know

THE DESTINY SERIES

Rosie and Ruby

Anna

Tilly

Grace

Destiny

PSYCHOLOGICAL THRILLERS

Over My Shoulder

The Secrets of Tenley House

#MeToo

Liars (co-authored with Anita Waller)

For the women who stayed behind and kept the home fires burning, and those who toiled the land and fed a nation, who grafted in factories day and night, or donned a uniform while others nursed the troops. For those who risked it all and by the light of the moon, the female agents who jumped into the dark abyss and occupied territory, whose life expectancy was an average of six weeks. To all the women who did their bit, shining a brave beacon of love and hope and strength so that women like me could be free, this is my salute to you.

To La Résistance, the brave Maquis, who fought for France, for liberté. The day I read Guy Môquet's letter in La Musée de la Résistance, it touched my heart and stayed with me. This story is inspired by the tragic events that occurred in Châteaubriant in 1941.

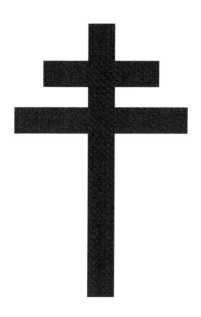

PROLOGUE

ARMISTICE DAY, NOVEMBER 2020, FRANCE

M aude paused for a moment, needing time to gather her thoughts and as tradition had begun to dictate, have a little chat with Dottie. It was something she did most days but only when they were alone.

Today was going to be special and one that caused Maude to feel slightly tremulous but excited nonetheless. Silently making her way to the corner of the room her eyes fell upon the smiling face of her grandmother and in a heartbeat, calm was restored. It had always been the way.

Whatever trial or tribulation befell Maude, a quiet chat with Dottie did the trick. It usually came in the form of wise words, sometimes a firm but well-meant rebuke, or silence accompanied by one of her penetrating stares. If, on the other hand, salacious village gossip was the topic of the day, they would have a chuckle at another's expense and Dottie would pronounce that she knew all along that he, or she, or they, were not to be trusted. On the other hand, those she deemed as harmless scoundrels would be invited round for drinks and delicately interrogated until they gave up the next juicy instalment.

Reaching forward, Maude's fingers gently touched the face

of her dear grandmother whose portrait hung in one of the alcoves. It wasn't the prime position she deserved or would have requested, but the chimney breast wall was out of the question. The smoke from the fire below would damage the paint and anyway, Dottie couldn't always have her own way, not anymore.

In a similar way Maude's greatest desire could never be granted, to have one last conversation with her gran, to hear her voice again and not have to imagine what she would say or do. Maude would forever feel robbed of that moment so instead, she clung on to all the precious times they had shared.

Yes, one could say that conversing with a painting of your dead grandmother was a small step towards insanity, but it gave her great comfort and sometimes Maude sensed that Dottie was still around. A scent on the breeze, forest wildflowers, or was it Femme de Rochas and Gauloises, her grandmothers non-negotiable scent and cigarette of choice?

No wonder Maude could trick herself into believing Dottie was there, when her spirit-essence lingered, and her voice echoed around the corridors and rooms. She could still hear its steely determination or languish in the velvet kiss of kind words when they mattered. Oh, and her infectious laugh, that bubbled from deep within and then gurgled into a smoker's cough.

Curiously, Maude's fingertips would sometimes tingle, remembering the feel of Dottie's peach-soft skin, enhanced by the powder and rouge she religiously applied each day. Perhaps it was Maude's own artistic tendencies that were to blame for the trickery, transcribing themselves so fluidly, images and memories becoming words, sounds and feelings.

Nevertheless, Maude still gained immense pleasure from her painting of Dottie that had been a labour of love, portraying a vibrant young woman in every sense of the word.

Set on the edge of a small French village, with field upon field of rural countryside as a distant backdrop, red-headed

Dottie was pictured shielding her eyes from the sun in what could be interpreted as a salute, smiling into a camera lens, almost laughing at something the photographer had said. Maude knew exactly what it was because the photo, that eventually became oil on canvas, was part of family history. In a shutter speed moment on a late summer's day, as she rested against the trunk of a gnarled oak, Dottie had let down her guard and allowed herself to be happy, carefree even.

She was so pretty then, just a young girl who had yet to grow into her beauty but due to circumstance, had already become a woman and seen things, done things, knew things that should have been saved for later, or never at all.

Despite her surroundings, amidst the daily struggles of war and tyranny, in a world dominated by men, Dottie exuded confidence and even through the medium of paint, you could sense it as well as see it.

With her bare legs outstretched and crossed at the ankle, utility lace-up shoes dampening any hope of glamour, she wore a dull grey skirt that Maude knew Dottie had hated, but at least it covered her muddy knees. Her favourite white blouse, speckled with flowers, was faded and worn at the collar, one odd button, but Dottie still stood out. The painting didn't betray the honesty of the original scene that had been retold slightly by the artist. It was a mere misdirection and a private glimpse of a glorious and sometimes inglorious past that had faded into history, remembered faithfully once a year, lest anyone forgot.

Today was different. The first time Dottie wouldn't be here to pay her respects in the year she'd made her century, something she saw as a personal victory and nothing to do with any assistance from the quacks. Maude was sure her gran would have loved a telegram from the Queen, but she'd forbidden anyone to request one. With Dottie it could always go either way.

Nevertheless, at long last, seventy-five years since VE Day, Dottie and her comrades, those brave souls who spent so much time in the shadows, waiting underground or camouflaged in mountains and forests would have their moment in the spotlight, a place where they would shine. Their faces would be matched to names, a love story woven from fact would be told, the bones of the dead raised from the dust, standing tall, together. They would be made real once again.

Recognising the swell of returning nerves and knowing there were no guests around, Maude took the opportunity to have a few words with her gran.

'Now then, Dottie, I'm off to pay my respects and then we will have the grand unveiling so don't be late, and wear your best dress, and your specs. I know you've been peeping and looking over my shoulder because you never could bear to be surprised, so try to look pleased when you see the finished result, if you haven't already. And make sure you bring everyone, I want them all there. This is their day too. It's not all about you.'

Despite her attempt at humour, Maude was forced to swallow down the blob of emotion that was obstructing her throat, unable to prevent her eyes misting over. She was being soppy and received a silent chiding from Dottie which at least brought a smile and allowed Maude time to pull herself together.

What would people think if they saw a perfectly sane, thirty-six-year-old, talking to a painting of a man and woman who never, ever answered back? Shaking her head, Maude placed a kiss on her fingertip and transferred it to the face of Dottie and then the handsome companion seated by her side, the true love of her grandmother's life.

Turning, she removed the book that lay on the coffee table and placed it inside her bag. It was a gift, signed and dedicated to someone special. Then she pulled on her gloves and straightened her back before heading towards the door. As she passed, Maude acknowledged another of her works, one that hung in the opposite alcove. It was a portrait of her very own namesake to which she gave a quick wink and a wave before leaving the room.

Outside, after closing the large wooden door of La Babinais, her grand *maison de maître*, Maude made her way down the path and through the gate, stopping briefly as she always did to admire the plaque attached to the post. It was a golden, shiny statement, a symbol of her freedom and proof, not that she really needed any, that thanks to Dottie she was living the dream in a place that had meant so much to both of them. It read:

Mademoiselle Maude Mansfield
Propriétaire
École d'Art

When Dottie bought the house for Maude, it, as with most things, came with a condition or two. The first was that Dottie would be allowed to live there until her death and not be shuffled off to a home or the loony bin.

Much to everyone's amusement, her imminent demise had been on the cards for years and was frequently used as a ploy to gain her own way. Yet against her own odds, Dottie somehow clung on to life, stubbornly resisting death just like she resisted anything that wasn't to her liking.

The second condition was that Maude converted part of the square, double-fronted house with its high ceilings and four rooms on each floor, into a school of art and painting retreat. She was to carve out an independent life, follow her dream, sell her work and continue making a name for herself. Naturally

Maude agreed to both, once again happy to be stage managed by Grandma Dottie.

Closing the gate, tucking her scarf further inside her coat, Maude did up another button to fend off the chill of the blustery November morning. At least it wasn't raining. Today didn't deserve a deluge. Each year Maude prayed that the grey clouds, like those bearing down above her head, burdened with the weight of tears, wouldn't weep. Instead they would remain strong, brave and steadfast. Then, at the hour of remembrance, the winter sun would break through allowing the souls in heaven to peep through a crack and shine their bright, silvery light on those left behind.

Making her way towards the centre of the village, Maude nodded politely to the locals who too were heading for the service. It took only minutes to arrive and as she passed through the iron gates of the walled cemetery, the first face she sought was that of the *maire*, Gabriel. She couldn't help herself, not anymore. The slight nod of his head told Maude he'd been watching for her too, as did the look in his eyes before he quickly turned away. Their affair, that began with a coming together of minds and shared interest, had evolved. Maude had no idea where it was heading but for now it was better like this, safer, avoiding scandal or distress. Gabriel was already positioned by the memorial and preparing for the service, his wife by his side. This observation irritated Maude immensely and the woman's dour presence was something she resolved to firmly ignore for the remainder of the day.

Instead, Maude focused on the cenotaph. It was engraved with the names of the fallen from the village and surrounding areas and each would be read out during the service. The ritual was always the same, a sombre moment shared, a time to reflect, but since the passing of Dottie, Maude was ever more unsettled, disappointed in fact.

Even though she had not died for France, Dottie had taken her last breath in the country she had always secretly loved the most, in a little village that she could finally call home. But it was more than that. Maude's brave and indomitable grandmother had once fought on this soil, almost two tumultuous years of risking her life every day, experiencing fear and heartbreak, love and loss.

Maude understood why Dottie's name would never be called out, but it was the omission of her memory, her service and dedication to duty that rankled. And there was something else. Almost to the last, Dottie had fought for and believed in justice, righting a wrong, serving revenge stone cold, laying the past to rest. She'd solved a mystery that had rocked her and others to the core. This and one of her final acts, borne in some ways of retribution, brought her freedom and acceptance. It allowed her to come back home for good.

Dottie never believed in taking the path of least resistance and for most of her life, seemed to take great pleasure in doing the opposite, refusing to be tamed or trussed. For this reason, once Dottie had been laid to rest in the village graveyard by the side of her great love, Maude had decided that somehow, some way, her grandmother would be remembered, not just in her memoirs. With the help of Gabriel and after many months and hours together, time well spent in many ways, they gathered everything they needed. Now, with the blessing of the commune and after the service of remembrance, Maude's tribute to her grandmother and her comrades would be revealed.

It was time. The Tricolor blew in the wind while the bugler played his sad lament. Gabriel began his speech, bringing the carved names back to life, if only in memory. And as they were remembered one by one, Maude touched the antique ring on her finger, and her heart swelled with pride for the young English girl who looked like a mouse but had the heart of a lion.

Placing a hand on her bag, Maude smiled. The book inside, written by an adoring granddaughter, told of an unassuming waitress who enlisted at the start of the war, then became an SOE operative, and after being dropped into France in the dead of night became a courier for the Historian Network, a trusted member of the Resistance, proud fighter with the Maquis and loyal supporter of the Free French.

Her family called her Dorothy 'Dottie' Tanner, the villagers knew her as Yvette Giroux, but in London, her code name was Nadine.

1

DOTTIE'S PARTY

LONDON, 2005

Dottie sipped her gin and lemonade while silently thanking goodness that the birthday song and candle blowing palaver was over with. She wanted to relax, enjoy a quiet drink and a huge slice of chocolate cake.

The private room above their favourite Italian restaurant was teeming with guests, some of them Dottie didn't know from Adam, others she vaguely recalled from weddings and funerals and various family endurance tests. Ragtag remnants of her life. Two step-children, one ex-husband who was pickled as usual, a sprinkling of cousins, God only knew how many times removed, neighbours, and her daughter's churchy lot. Had she the patience, Dottie could have named them all because even though most days she couldn't find her specs or her slippers, she clung on to her perspicacity, a word Dottie loved and was worth twenty-three points in Scrabble.

Still, Dottie had no idea why Jean, her daughter, had invited so many people and she bloody well hoped she was paying the bill because the birthday girl had no intention of doing so. A quiet celebration with friends was what Dottie had asked for. An evening of 'Guess the Dubious Family Member' was what she got. Dottie bloody hated her birthday and for a very good reason.

In a rare moment of humility Dottie thought, *Bless Jean.* Maybe she was being a churlish and ungrateful old biddy, after all, she was luckier than most. Not only that, her daughter meant well and did her best, despite being in a permanent state of fluster. For this reason, Dottie would be sure to thank Jean the next time she bustled by *and*, just to be on the safe side, appear to be suitably grateful for at least a month. Her daughter would no doubt ask a hundred times if Dottie had enjoyed her unsurprising eighty-fifth birthday bash because it was the same with everything – days out, Christmas, even bloody mealtimes when you were expected to rave about some under- or over-cooked faddy concoction.

Jean had always been a bit of an attention-seeker with a cloying need for praise and appreciation. Dottie had always found it very tiresome. In fact, Jean could be tiresome in general, not that mother would ever say that of daughter – out loud anyway. In return Jean openly blamed all her failures and foibles, the absence of an alcoholic father most of all, on her mother.

In some respects, Dottie accepted the blame, after all nobody was perfect, even her. But despite minor irritations she did love Jean and was grateful for her devotion, sometimes. This reminded Dottie not to let on that she had known all about the party. You didn't need to be a spy to work it out and this was not a time for point scoring. Although Dottie thought she did deserve an accolade for looking astounded by the bloody annoying party poppers and the cries of 'surprise'. Dottie was glad she'd had her wavy bob recoloured and styled, her Rita Hayworth red needed a bit of help these days. For an old trooper she scrubbed up quite well.

With a shake of the head, she noted that Jean was presently

fulfilled in her role as hostess, carving up cake and wrapping it in pink serviettes, while her husband Ralph dutifully loaded them onto a tray. *Good old Ralph*, thought Dottie who smiled, then turned her attention from Mr Under-the-Thumb to someone infinitely more interesting who was seated by her side. It was her oldest, marvellously still alive (just like her) favourite and adored friend.

'Konstantin, pour me some vodka. Now I've done my duty to Jean I feel like getting outrageously tipsy especially as I managed not to dribble all over the cake when I blew out the inferno. Thank God I plucked my whiskers.'

Dottie slid her glass containing the gin dregs to one side and watched as Konstantin poured a shot of clear liquid which she then raised in a Russian toast. '*Nah zda rovh yeh.*'

'Cheers,' replied Konstantin, raising his glass before downing the shot, 'and *s dnem rozhdeniya.*'

This was their tradition, harking back to the days when they'd met and his first ever 'happy birthday' toast to Dottie, just like the bunch of wild flowers that lay on the table before them.

Dottie downed her shot and didn't flicker as the vodka burned its path down her throat, then pushed her glass forward for a top-up, before quizzing Konstantin.

'So, you old fox, what tricks have you been up to lately? I need you to tell me something thrilling and wicked and, of course, totally secret.'

At this Konstantin chuckled and pulled at the point of his gingery-white beard with one hand, meeting her misty green eyes in challenge, his similarly misty blue ones shielded by his spectacles. 'Now, now, my little Zaya, you know the rules, ladies first.'

Dottie laughed out loud and tapped his hand. She loved to be called Zaya, little rabbit, it had for many, many years been

Konstantin's private term of endearment and one he'd given her in France when they first met.

'Stop it right now... you know full well I have nothing of interest to tell you apart from who cheats at poker nights and steals books from the library, oh, but here's something. I'm sure the chap who lives three doors down on the opposite side of our road, you know, the house with the permanently closed blinds and the big red door, well I'm convinced he pays for a prostitute twice a week.' Dottie waited for a reaction then tutted when none was forthcoming.

'I knew it. Unless he's in the Cabinet or a minor royal, that will be of no interest to you whatsoever, will it? Now, come on, it's your turn. Off you go.'

'Ah, Zaya, you know me too well, but your information is duly noted. After all we never know who lives in our midst, do we?'

Dottie returned his wicked grin. 'We certainly don't but stop stalling, a trade is a trade.'

'Well actually I do have something you might find of use, but I will expect great favours in return... as usual.' The grey-haired Lenin lookalike raised a wispy eyebrow.

It was their secret game, trading useless, trivial information for reward. In their younger days Dottie had played along, knowing that Konstantin wasn't always looking for fun, more hopeful that with persistence she would capitulate, be turned and pass on some very useful snippets from her job at the MOD. Dottie had no interest in espionage, those days were gone but she still enjoyed being pursued, and absolutely adored caviar and vodka even more.

Tapping her fingers on the table as Konstantin waited for her answer, she feigned a moment of consideration then put him out of his misery. 'Okay, it's a deal. Pie, mash and liquor on me. Usual place. So come on, it'd better be good.'

'Are you sitting comfortably?' Konstantin's body shifted as he stared into the crowded restaurant, as if casually commenting on the meal they had just eaten or the weather, speaking in an almost theatrical whisper, his Russian accent more pronounced.

Dottie gave a nod, smiling at the question, one he'd first asked her sixty years before.

'Then I will begin. It has come to my attention that later this evening, perhaps in the next few moments, someone is going to drop a rather large bomb.'

'Dear God, where?' This was not what Dottie was expecting and her hand whipped to her chest, stilling a fast-beating heart.

'Here, in this very room.' Konstantin was sounding more mysterious by the second.

Dottie instantly relaxed and felt a bit of a fool because if that were the case, Konstantin would be outside, watching the smoke from inside a diplomatic car at a very safe distance.

Dottie was, however, intrigued. 'Konstantin, be serious, what on earth do you mean?'

Slowly, he turned to face her and there it was. The wicked grin and twinkle in his eyes she knew so well. He had something, she was sure. He was also enjoying getting one over on her and that meant only one thing; she wasn't going to like it.

'If my observations are correct, the young man by the bar, wearing the blue shirt that is clearly irritating his perspiring neck.' Konstantin nodded and smiled when Dottie followed his direction.

She gasped. 'Lachlan. Maude's boyfriend. Is that who you mean?'

A jerk of the head then Konstantin continued. 'The very same. Now, earlier, when I visited the men's room, I came across young Lachlan muttering at his reflection in the mirror, perhaps reciting some lines. Before departing, he took a moment to check inside the telltale black box he had secreted in his pocket.'

Dottie's hand flew to her neck. 'No, he can't be, please tell me you are winding me up, Konstantin. My Maudie's only twenty-one and hasn't even finished at The Slade. No, he can't, I won't allow it. She's is far too young to be engaged especially to that idiot.'

Grabbing her empty shot glass, she slammed it back down on the table, doubly irritated. Hearing the rumble of laughter from Konstantin, she tutted in response, then asked, 'What can we do, Konstantin, please, this is not remotely funny. I know, let's have him deported, can you do that?'

'Not to Australia, that boat sailed many moons ago and the Gulags are all booked up this time of year, so, my little Zaya, you may just have to let Maude make her own mistakes and maybe, if we are lucky, she will say no.'

Dottie was enraged. How could she have not known, or spotted that the long streak of useless Australian... beer, was going to propose? Her eyes locked on to Lachlan. At this precise moment, perhaps somehow warned of an incoming missile by his inner defence system, he appeared to shake off nerves and straighten his back before pushing away from the bar he was propping up.

'Here we go,' said Konstantin.

'On no,' said Dottie as she tracked Lachlan's pathway through the crowd.

Marching purposefully towards Maude who was helping her mother give out cake, not bothering to excuse his interruption, Lachlan grabbed her hand and pulled her towards the small square of dance floor. Maude stood, looking bemused, but when Lachlan clapped his hands and asked for quiet, the room quickly fell to a hush. Dottie could do no more than watch as the colour simultaneously drained from poor Maude's face. She knew.

By Dottie's side, Konstantin lifted the bottle of vodka and

filled two shot glasses, sliding one of them over. Reaching out, Dottie took the glass and while Jean and Ralph and the crowd looked on, Lachlan got down on one knee and Dottie downed her shot.

The guests were leaving in interminably slow dribs and drabs, and Dottie wished they would hurry so that she could go home and sleep off the vodka and maybe, when she woke up in the morning, Lachlan and his ridiculous proposal would be nothing but a terrible nightmare.

Poor Maude. Dottie knew her granddaughter was avoiding the inevitable chat, ever since she'd approached the table with Lachlan to receive congratulations. While Dottie's response was polite but muted to say the least, Uncle Konki, Maude's nickname for Konstantin ever since she had been a baby and unable to pronounce his name, was full of flourish and dramatic kissing.

Dottie tutted and erased the memory, then began impatiently tapping her feet. Konstantin had already left in the company of his minder who stood out like a sore thumb amongst the partygoers. She wished she'd asked them to take her home, perhaps a drive in a bulletproof car would've been prudent because once she told Maude exactly what she thought, shots might be fired.

Dottie was exhausted and not to mention quite tiddly, already wearing her coat and checking she had everything in her handbag when she felt a body slide onto the chair by her side. Tentatively, Maude took her hand.

'Are you cross with me, Gran?'

A smile, quite genuine. 'No, my darling, not at all. You did exactly as I would have expected and didn't make a scene by rejecting such a ridiculous proposal. There was no need for a fuss or to send your mother into a meltdown, so well done. Now, all you have to do is work out how to let him down gently.'

At this point Dottie fixed Maude with a stare and waited for her granddaughter to drag her eyes away from the diamond ring on her left hand. When Maude finally found the courage to meet her grandmother's gaze, Dottie's next question sounded more like a fact.

'I take it you *are* going to let him down, one way or another.'

At this Maude paled. Her fair skin was almost ashen while her smudged eyeliner made her look quite tragic. 'I don't know, I think so, I might... but how? It will break his heart and for some reason he's got it into his head it's what I wanted.'

'And is it?' Dottie thought she might as well ask the blatantly bloody obvious question.

'NO, not marriage. But he'd mentioned going to Australia when I graduate and I thought it would be fun, you know, an experience, and loads of my friends have been. Somehow he's took that to the extreme and wants to go the whole hog and settle down there.'

Dottie was horrified. 'Settle... there! Why on earth would anyone want to do that? Dear God, Maude, have you lost your mind? You're doing so well, think of your career and not just that, I'd never see you if you lived on the other side of the blasted world. And who knows how long I've got left? I am eighty-five, you know! We need to make the most of our time together. Remember, we have big plans for our last hurrah.'

'Gran, stop making out you're going to pop your clogs every five minutes, and I know exactly how old you are because I stuck the blooming candles on the cake. Now listen, I said yes to getting married, not to moving to Australia so don't panic and anyway, we could have a long engagement... years and years maybe. We haven't talked it through properly so just let the dust settle and please, don't make a scene, not tonight. Mum's worked really hard on your party so don't spoil it.'

Dottie huffed. 'And what does *she* think about having her daughter spirited away and her career ruined before it's even started?'

Maude sighed and let go of Dottie's hands then rubbed her temples, eyes closed as she spoke. 'I haven't mentioned that part to her yet. I only found out after the proposal when Lachlan blurted out his idea... seriously, I think he's either homesick or lost the plot so again, do not say anything to Mum and Dad about Australia.'

At this Dottie's head whipped around. 'Did he know, that father of yours, was he asked for permission to marry you?'

Maude shook her head. 'Apparently, Lachlan decided on the spur of the moment and bought the ring earlier today, so Dad had no idea at all. And that's all a bit old-fashioned don't you think... asking permission?'

Dottie just raised her eyebrows at this, wanting to agree without condoning Lachlan's actions. She chose silence.

Maude made another attempt to smooth things over. 'Look, Gran, let's leave it for tonight. I can tell you're tired, and you and Uncle Konki drank far too much vodka, *again*.'

There was no response to her gentle admonishment from Dottie, so Maude ploughed on. 'We should both sleep on it. Lachlan is going to Amsterdam with some of his friends so we can have a few special days together, just you and me. We can talk properly then. Is that a deal?'

Dottie felt tears prick at the corner of her eyes. She felt dreadful now, and it had nothing to do with vodka or tiredness. She loved her little Maude more than anyone in the world. But, if Lachlan did turn out to be the love of Maude's life, and Dottie still seriously hoped the Barista from Billabong wasn't, then she had ruined a very special evening in her precious granddaughter's life.

And then there was Maude's engagement ring. Dottie was no snob, never had been and never would be, but it was run-of-the-mill, not the special piece of vintage jewellery Dottie had guarded as fiercely as her own heart. The ring had always been destined for her granddaughter and Dottie had kept it safe since the war. Her hope had been that when Maude found 'the one', she would wear it as a symbol, of many things, really. Partly in honour of the past, but mostly as a testament to friendship, loyalty and love, three elements so important in life and marriage. Gathering her emotions, Dottie took Maude's hand in hers and as Lachlan approached, spoke softly.

'I'm sorry, Maude, I'm being a selfish old grump again and I hope I haven't spoilt tonight for you, so will you forgive me?'

Clearly responding to a less brusque approach, Dottie saw Maude brighten and smile. 'Of course I do, you big dafty. I know it's because you love me. Now come here and give me a hug.'

After they embraced, Dottie bade Maude a fond farewell and even managed not to grimace when Lachlan came over and pecked her on the cheek. Watching them walk away, her scowl quickly returned as did Jean, to gather Dottie up and ferry her home.

During the ride to Hackney, the birthday girl feigned exhaustion and yawned from the back of the car, nodding in all the right places as Jean asked on a scale of one to ten how surprised she'd been – replying with a ten when she really meant zero. She also kept Maude's secret and didn't swear when Ralph went too fast over a speed bump. Dottie did, however, resolve that one way or another, come hell or high water, she was going to rid their family of Lachlan and as a consequence, save dear, precious Maude from him, herself and Australia.

2

VE DAY CELEBRATIONS

LONDON, 2005

I t had been an odd day that had plunged Dottie into what everyone always described as 'one of her funny moods' so she was now holed up in the parlour watching the BBC News. In the other room the young ones sang along to a concert that was taking place in Trafalgar Square to celebrate the 60th Anniversary of VE Day.

That said it all really, referring to her fifty-five-year-old daughter as a 'young one' meant Dottie really was feeling her age and on a downward spiral. She needed to drag herself back up the slippery slope before she ended up covered from head to toe in maudlin mud.

The only way to do this was to dissemble the factors that had conspired against her and she began with the easy one, her nemesis, Lachlan. The sight of him grated on her nerves, even more when he opened his mouth. He was a loud, obnoxious ignoramus and the epitome of all the negative stereotypes imaginable. Bruce, in his *Crocodile Dundee* hat, putting a shrimp on the barbie, swigging a can of lager and asking his Sheila to bring another tinny. His existence on the earth and his supposed adoration of Maude drove Dottie to distraction and had

Konstantin been willing, she'd have paid whatever price to have Lachlan shipped home in a container. It was quite possible, she knew that.

There was time yet though. It was only May so she needn't panic. Who knew what would happen between now and December? Maude would graduate in June and intended working up until Christmas to earn enough for her fare to Australia. Once there, the intrepid pair were going backpacking, Lachlan regaling the sights they would see and what fun they were going to have. Dottie simply seethed and bided her time, hoping and praying Maude would stay put, find a job and take on more commissions, maybe hold an exhibition, own her own gallery. The sky was the limit if she would only set her heart and mind to it. Feeling mild panic setting in, Dottie muttered, 'Be patient, give him some rope.'

Her attention was drawn back to the television and a news report about the 60th celebrations. Dottie watched the footage she'd seen umpteen times that day. The Beeb, like all news channels, was painfully repetitive, like the rerun of Prince Charles placing a wreath at the Cenotaph. The clip had been edited so she was unable to scan the crowd, curious to see if she recognised anyone amongst the dignitaries in attendance. The old guard of civil servants, MPs past and present, whoever was still hanging on to life or hankering after their glory days inside the hallowed corridors of Whitehall.

It was the same on Remembrance Day, where in years gone by she'd weathered the cold to pay her respects but nowadays preferred to stay at home. From wherever she watched, it was impossible not to feel, remember, and shed a tear. In Dottie's case her memories were of a different war to the brave survivors who marched by wearing their medals. Hers had been a secret battle and one that still waged, but not with an invading army. This conflict took place within. The faces of those who had passed through her life had dug in, hiding in the trenches of her heart.

One face that was guaranteed to ignite a spark had been there in the crowd today and when she saw it, Dottie allowed a moment of indulgence, the ripple effect causing a flurry of buried memories to resurface. Hugh Grosvenor-Townshend rattled her cage whenever his face popped up on a talk show, a news interview, in the paper or the back-cover of one of his books. She'd never bought one, just taken a peep then replaced it, sometimes mischievously moving it to the front of the display. It was her way of repaying a favour or two.

It was odd that even though Hugh remained on the periphery of her life, not quite in the shadows because he wasn't a man of mystery, the mere sight of him could knock her world off its axis. He was a scar on her brain, a star in the movie of a life she had sought to forget but hankered after in equal measure, depending on her mood. Poor Hugh, he had no idea how much his existence pained her especially when he'd been such a help.

Ever since the end of the war he'd remained constant, always willing to make a call, drop a hint or name, point her in the right direction. They weren't close friends and confidantes in the Konstantin way, more acquaintances that enjoyed one another's company if their paths crossed, usually at a function, private dinner or celebration, or through their work. Maybe that was down to Hugh's awkwardness; he'd always been rather shy and self-conscious. Over the years, while the scars left by pubescent acne had faded, his slight stammer hadn't. Dottie could always see past his disfigurement and impediment, but others couldn't.

She had been sad when he couldn't attend her party, a flare up of gout and his war wound still gave him gyp. It would have been fun for the three of them to get together again and

Konstantin did enjoy sparring with Hugh, the communist versus the capitalist.

Maude always referred to their friendship as a love triangle and teased Dottie mercilessly that both men had always been in love with her, vying for attention, this and their constant one-upmanship was all the evidence she required. Dottie simply batted away Maude's comments while admitting to herself that there could have been some truth in them. But their friendship had outlasted all of Dottie's husbands and for this she was glad. And anyway, she felt sorry for Hugh.

Revered amongst his peers, he was a highly regarded expert on post-war politics, a respected commentator whose opinion was sought after especially around election time. He'd received a knighthood and later a seat in the House of Lords and despite rejecting calls for him to stand in various safe seats, he'd been a trusted advisor to the PM and Cabinet.

Dottie admired Hugh immensely for his reluctance to trade on a reputation as a WW2 agent and as with most aspects of his life, he preferred to protect his privacy. She had visited his beautiful home for dinners and cocktails, the last two occasions on the arm of her fourth husband, the first for a charity fundraiser and the second, the wake of Hugh's wife, Lady Townshend.

Childless, she imagined him lonely in his house in Belgravia, another world from her own modest home in Hackney. Then again, the three-bedroomed terrace with an attic, cellar and decent back garden, a stone's throw away from her parent's café on Broadway Market had turned out to be a nice little nest egg.

Who'd have thought that the run-down home she and her first husband had regarded as a stepping-stone and bought for hundreds would now be worth just short of a million pounds? From the first time she saw it, Dottie had loved the house that stood forlornly in a dilapidated row. It had miraculously remained unscathed by bombs, in a working-class, East End suburb that was now classed as gentrified; full of olive bars, gastropubs, fancy florists and delicatessens selling Lord knows what to up-and-coming Londoners.

Dottie often congratulated herself not only on her invest-ment, but managing to keep hold of it during three divorces, no mean feat but she always enjoyed a challenge and apart from one, she regarded each sorry affair as a marital endurance test.

The house had been worth fighting for though. Mémère Delphine had taught her that, wise words from a much-missed grandmother ingrained in Dottie's brain. It wasn't just *her* home; it was also for Maude and nobody was going to take it away. Jean and Ralph were doing nicely and would benefit from Dottie's substantial savings, amassed from a juicy settlement from husband number four and a couple of tip-offs from Hugh that she'd passed on to her broker. And if Morris, Dottie's third husband, didn't drink away his savings, Jean, who was the only good thing to come from that marriage, would be quite comfort-able in her old age.

But Maude was the true apple of Dottie's eye and had been living with her in Hackney for the past three years while she studied at The Slade. From being a teenager, Maude had spent more time with Dottie than with her parents, preferring the vibrancy and diversity of Hackney to Jean's home in Hounslow.

Some of Maude's best paintings had been inspired by street scenes, or the once very unlikely Regent's Canal that was no longer a dumping ground or drug dealer's paradise. Dottie loved Maude's portraits the best because she had the knack of catching a look, the glint of an eye, capturing a face and moment then suspending it in time and gouache. Maude had potential, she could do anything, Dottie believed in her.

Where Maude was concerned, Dottie's cheque book and door were always open, and over the years, this had caused many stand-offs between mother and grandmother. Jean said that it was wrong to live life vicariously through a child and that Dottie was to refrain from manipulating Maude for her own ends, something she vehemently denied.

Dottie insisted there was absolutely nothing wrong with encouragement, Maude *should* learn to ski, and drive, and abseil. If she wanted to look like Daisy the cow, there was no reason why Maude couldn't have ridiculous false eyelashes or various parts of her body pierced. The tattoos remained a closely guarded secret between them both, for now.

On the subject of Maude moving in permanently, Dottie wasn't getting any younger, so it was nice to have some company in her big old house, especially with so many dodgy dealers and muggers about. This was usually the point when Jean would remind Dottie that according to untold legend, she was a fearless secret agent, trained to kill. Therefore, a spotty fifteen-year-old mugger shouldn't really cause her too many problems, should it? Not only that, Jean insisted Dottie's house was more secure than the Bank of England, no doubt to protect her arsenal of wartime weaponry and secret documents. At this Dottie merely huffed and tried to look mysterious, with no intention of refuting or confirming Jean's sarcastic suspicions.

Things were about to change though and unless Dottie could throw a spanner in the works, Maude would be swapping urban living with Grandma for a bloody mobile home and sand in her knickers. Putting down the *Radio Times*, Dottie tutted her irritation. The droning of the BBC wasn't helping her mood either, so she stood and switched off the television before approaching the writing bureau in the alcove. Here, she cast her eyes over the rogue's gallery of photographs that adorned the top.

Only her favourite people made the grade. Maude was there, obviously. A chubby three-year-old in her frilly Selfridge's birthday frock, bought by Grandma Dottie. Jean and Ralph on their wedding day were included, more to keep the peace than anything. Then there was wonderful George and his dog Eddie. Oh, how he loved that animal, Eddie the Beagle. Had George not died they'd be enjoying their twilight years together, but Dottie pushed that thought right to the back of her mind. Going within an inch of such a dreadful time would only send her further into despair.

Next her gaze fell upon her mum and dad, *mama et papa*, her terms of endearment for them. They were pictured standing outside their café, looking proud as punch. Mama was wearing her white pinny and Dad had his arm around her shoulder, they were so in love. It had taken decades to be able to look at any photograph of them and not shed a tear or feel that swell of despair at the back of her throat. Today both threatened to make a comeback.

And then there was Mémère. Just the sight of her stern face and scraped back hair knotted into a bun always made Dottie chuckle because in reality, the demeanour was a facade. Her grandmother's habitual attire of black high-necked dress with thick stockings and hobnailed boots gave the impression of a life-hardened black widow. So too did her posture and pose, sitting in her straight back chair, staring right into the camera, challenging it almost. But that was how Mémère lived her life, revelling in her resistance and defiance of anything that was alien to her, unbending and unyielding. Delphine Charvet had been, by her own testimony, dragged across la Manche against her will to live amongst pie-eating atheists, so from the moment her feet touched British soil, she rarely spoke anything but French. Her obstinacy and intelligence served Dottie well. Yet in the middle she was soft, kindness ran to her core while her brusque and matriarchal tendencies kept her amused and the family on their toes. It was one of Mémère's little quirks, borne from the old ways of tough love and was the reason Dottie had adored her.

The last photograph, well, that was always a challenge and when she chose to meet it, would bring joy or pain. Sometimes it brought irritation because it was incomplete, a word she hated, maybe a reflection of her life. Dottie had often toyed with the idea of putting it away, slipping it inside the drawer, but the burden of loyalty to the past forbade her to do so.

The black-and-white image was of a young woman leaning against a tree, the Loire countryside sprawling in the distance. She was shielding her eyes from the sun, smiling into a camera lens, holding in laughter at something the photographer had said. That woman was her, aged twenty-three and already she was weary, had seen and felt so much, too much.

Most days Dottie averted her eyes, but her mood had swung and today it sought indulgence so in a rare moment she gave in. In doing so, she experienced the most overwhelming feeling of loss, not just from the photo but her life. Bizarre as it seemed, she could often imagine him there by her side and as if invoking a spirit, Dottie felt her left arm tingle, as though touched gently by the essence of the past.

On the day the photo was taken, he'd been there too. Vincent. His rolled-up shirt sleeve caressing her bare skin, the warmth from his body pressed against hers, the faint odour of sweat mingling with wine on his breath. If she looked downwards there would be dirty fingernails, strong calloused hands resting on a rifle that lay across long legs covered by worn, woollen trousers, almost threadbare at the knee.

Even though she sensed his presence, Dottie never looked sideways. The profile of the man, missing from the photo but not from her psyche, the one she had never stopped loving, wouldn't really be there. But how she longed to touch his dark hair that swept back from an angular face, trace the firm jaw and straight nose. Oh, and those full lips, that sometimes smiled, rare like the sun on a winter's day and in stolen moments kissed hers with a passion stronger than life.

In the same way he was missing from the photograph, he was missing from her world too, one he had fought for, believed in. What good would it do to search for a ghost? Instead she had trained her heart and head to be strong, not long for the impossible. Therefore, Dottie never said his name out loud, never told anyone their story, and never, ever looked to her left.

Taking the photograph, Dottie moved to the window, holding the frame to her chest and looked onto the deserted street outside. Apart from the fancy cars and the permit signs, it was the same as always. Bricks and mortar, concrete foundations, the cobbled section of road merging with neat black tarmac. It was the residents who had changed, swishing in like waves on sand, swooshing out again, moving on with their lives. Holocaust survivors, refugees and migrants from every corner of the globe had all traversed the high street. Their footfall was an invisible imprint on their journey towards a better life. Nowadays, rather than worn soles, well-heeled footwear left their mark.

She too had left her footprint on another land, one that she had never found the courage to revisit and instead skirted its borders, holidaying anywhere but there, defiantly resisting the longing to see it one more time. Stubbornly refusing to admit she missed that life, one of meaning, despite its danger and heartbreak it had been the greatest battle of all.

But something had changed since her birthday, or was it these blasted celebrations? Who would have thought that she, Dorothy Tanner, at her ripe old age would again know fear, let alone admit to it? But it was true, although this fear was not of death or torture, it was of defeat. She had fought all her life for independence, a right to choose and most of all not to be swallowed whole by melancholy. What was the point in hankering for the past, wishing to make amends, knowing she could not? Instead she had forged ahead. Searching, and even now she wasn't sure what for.

A moped scooting along the street, its screeching engine heralding the imminent delivery of pizza, cut through the relative quiet of the day, jolting Dottie back into the here and now. After replacing the photograph without another glance, she returned to the sofa and clicked on the television.

In the room next door, while Maude and Lachlan sang along to the concert, Dottie could hear Jean and Ralph clattering about in the kitchen preparing dinner. While she waited to be called, Dottie watched more newsreels, footage gathered from around the world of the celebrations to commemorate sixty years since the guns fell silent.

President Chirac arrived at the Arc de Triomphe and laid a wreath at the Tomb of the Unknown Soldier and then the camera cut to a rural churchyard in France where the community were out in force, the Tricolor flying high. It could have been anywhere amongst the swathes of villages or towns but there was something about the scene that gave Dottie goosebumps and the hairs on the back of her neck tickled.

In a quiet graveyard, in a village so similar to the one on television, some of her friends had been laid to rest. They'd been rounded up by the Gestapo, questioned, tortured and executed. Dottie hadn't had the chance to say goodbye before their lives had been cruelly taken away, she'd had to flee. But not going back to pay her respects was definitely down to her. Had she been cowardly? Never, ever. Or was her determination to bury the past just that, convincing herself nothing would be gained from returning to France, to Renazé? Had she been running away for all these years?

Slowly, like the rising of the sun, her strange mood lifted, and Dottie realised what the nagging voice inside her head was trying to tell her, had probably been doing so for years. True to form, instead of listening to her heart and obeying a head determined to do things its own way, she had fought the enemy within herself. She had resisted. *Oh, you stupid woman, so much time has been wasted. Why haven't you realised sooner?*

Well no more. For once, finally, she was going to break the rules and obey her heart. Her head was already in the process of capitulating because Dottie knew exactly what to do. It was time to go back to France where she would face the past, pay her respects and say goodbye. And best of all, even though she didn't know it yet, Maude was going with her.

3

MAUDE

HACKNEY, LONDON, 2005

Maude zipped her suitcase closed before heaving it off the bed and pulling it towards the door. Checking her watch, she saw there was over an hour before she had to meet Lachlan for dinner. After the relief at having time to spare, she felt the splash of another wave, this time flooding her with apprehension. It wasn't going to be a fun date.

Lachlan was already put out that Maude had agreed to accompany her gran to France, but the double whammy of an open-ended trip had unsettled him no end. *How would she be able to afford the fare to Australia if she didn't work through the summer? He'd hoped to move into her gran's so they could save on rent, it made sense especially as Maude paid nothing.* He should've known he was barking right up the wrong tree on that score. Dottie's house was a man-free zone, never mind allowing the unwanted 'grandson-in-law-to-be' a foot in the door.

No matter how Maude pitched the trip as a once-in-a-life-time-memory-fest, Lachlan wasn't having any of it and had just about stopped short of forbidding her to go. Pride was the only thing that prevented him from begging, she knew that. Still, Maude was immensely relieved he'd not been that stupid – she didn't want to lose total respect for him. But what had troubled her was that for a moment, she'd kind of hoped he would put his foot down. Not so she'd capitulate, forced to choose between Lachlan and her gran, but so she could tell him to piss off. Maude knew that was a bad sign.

London in August was humid, and Maude was already exhausted from the mere thought of her farewell dinner with Lachlan. After pulling up the sash window she found solace in her rattan chair and a cuddle from Taily, her battered, patched-up childhood toy. The squint-eyed monkey had been with her forever and as she flicked his long tail back and forth, a habit that had seen her through many a temper tantrum or the moments before sleep, Maude looked around her bedroom.

Her gran's house was a large Victorian terrace, cavernous inside and gave them both plenty of space to do their own thing. It was well-maintained by their jolly cleaner, Vanya, who came in three times a week to whistle while she worked and drive Dottie mad. Maude's mum, Jean, said it was extravagant, employing a cleaner, but according to Dottie it was a necessity, especially as she'd always worked in Whitehall and housework had never been high on her agenda.

Maude's bedroom was a veritable time capsule, a personally collated museum containing all her treasures. Whenever friends had entered the room, it hit them in the eye, like a migraine; swirling colours and an attack on the senses. Along with the aroma of patchouli, Maude's favourite, there was an unmistakable aura of times gone by, dimensions overlapping and coming together. Like the naff seventies peacock chair she sat in, and her post-war mahogany bed and furniture, apparently all carried across from her great-grandparents' café. The daisy print duvet set from Asda and far too many scatter cushions were probably the most modern things on show. The walls were still decorated with white anaglypta, but they provided a good setting for her favourite paintings.

The bookshelves told an orderly tale of her childhood; weekend and holiday sleepovers when her gran would read bedtime stories seated in the creaky rattan chair. It was a ritual that began with Beatrix Potter then on to Enid Blyton and later, Jacqueline Wilson who guided Maude through her early teens. After that she'd swapped books for magazines but it quickly became clear where her attention lay. Art.

The cast iron fireplace had been there since the house was built but now held an assortment of candles not lumps of coal. Apart from the varnished floorboards on which lay a huge rainbow coloured rug she'd bought down on the market, nothing had changed but that's how Maude liked it. Her bedroom was her space and she insisted it remained exactly as it was. It brought her great comfort.

Maude's thoughts were drawn back to her upcoming trip, not to France but the one on the horizon, to Australia. Lachlan already had most of the money for his airfare and had suggested Maude drop a hint to her gran, if not a gift maybe a loan, then they could get off sooner. At this Maude had bridled and reminded Lachlan that nobody in their family got a free ride and where Dottie was concerned, you stood on your own two feet.

This wasn't strictly true of course because if anyone could break the rules when the fancy took her it was Dottie. Maude knew her gran could be a contradiction at the best of times and was all for tradition when it suited her. Dottie would have cancelled her birthday forever if she'd had her own way. She loved Christmas and Mothering Sunday, loathed Bonfire Night and the hooligans with their air bombs, adored hot cross buns at Easter and wild flowers, and she disliked Sunday lunch which she preferred on a Monday. She couldn't be doing with the palaver of New Year so was in bed by 10pm, and never wore black for funerals because that was just bloody depressing. In most areas of her life, Dottie made her own rules and expected others to follow them, or leave her out of the equation.

Maude sighed and sat Taily on her knee then regarded his face. His monkey whiskers were long gone as was his drawn-on mouth but he could still answer back, he was magic.

'What to do eh, Taily? Can you fast forward time for me... so that I've been to dinner and I'm back home with you and Gran? I've run out of words for Lachlan and no matter what he says, I'm going to France and I'm not asking anyone for the air fare to Oz. I'll get there under my own steam or I won't go at all.'

Nothing. Obviously Taily was in a huff because he didn't want her to go to Oz either. A little voice whispered in her ear, *but do you want to go, do you really*? Maude ignored it because as much as the proposal niggled her, the idea of seeing a new land, painting under the stars or dipping her feet in the Indian Ocean would be marvellous. So what was the problem?

'I do love Lachlan, you know...'

Taily clearly didn't believe her, or care.

'Okay you're right. It's not that mad, desperate kind of star-struck love you see at the cinema or read about in books but that's because I'm not a silly girl anymore. I'm a grown-up, almost a graduate, an artist.'

Taily's button eyes looked bored.

'I really wish he'd not proposed though, but please don't tell Gran I said that. I can't bear her to be right, *again*.'

Taily gave a wicked smile.

'He's spoilt everything, hasn't he? Taken the fun out of an adventure by making it all grown-up and serious and I'm not ready for that yet. I know I'm not.' Taily seemed to perk up at this point.

'What can I do though? I want to go travelling and I'd feel

safe with Lachlan, and it'd be nice to meet his family but I cringe when I think of him introducing me as his fiancée, the bloody idiot.'

Taily agreed.

'So, my little friend, it looks like I've got two options. I could tell him it's all off, the engagement, then there'll be a big drama and I just know he'll be moody for the whole trip. Or I could weather the storm tonight, go to France with Gran and see how he is when I get back... and it's not like we're going to get married in Oz, or he's arranging a surprise wedding because I'd want my family there. He wouldn't do that, would he?'

Taily definitely raised an imaginary eyebrow at that comment.

Maude sighed and hugged him to her. Wedging the monkey underneath her chin she closed her eyes and relaxed into the cushions, her peacock chair folding its wings around her. Why did everything have to be a bloody battle? It had always been the same, her mum fighting with her gran over all sorts but mainly Maude and now, with Lachlan thrown into the mix it would only get worse. Her mum was thrilled at the idea of a wedding, Dottie clearly hated it and the fact her only granddaughter was heading for the other side of the world threatened to send her over the edge.

Heavy eyelids accompanied a yawn, so Maude pulled the throw over her and Taily, plumping cushions before she felt settled. Thoughts floated back to her date with Lachlan. They were going for street food, nothing fancy, so that meant she could have a nap, chuck on a clean T-shirt and off she'd go. This time tomorrow she'd be on her way to France with Gran and they could have an adventure of their own. It was the next few hours that would be tricky.

Whenever she thought of the trip to the Loire and basically, down memory lane, it caused a little flutter in Maude's chest and that was nice, reminding her of when she was little. During school holidays they would go for spur of the moment days out, usually decided on over breakfast. Within the hour they'd be on the Tube to Victoria Bus Station, or Paddington and here, she and Dottie would pick from one of the destinations on the board. They'd been all over; days at the seaside, or to another city, or a castle, whatever they fancied.

And when Dottie had asked Maude to accompany her to France she'd also dangled the carrot of indulgence and opportunity, an all-expenses-paid jolly and the chance to paint and learn a bit about her heritage. How could anyone resist?

There was so much Maude didn't know about Dottie's work during the war, snippets really. Even Uncle Konki was cagey but then again, his whole life was a mystery and he loved to tease and speak in riddles, quoting Russian proverbs with a twinkle in his eye. He had a faded scar that ran from the corner of his eye, along his cheek, and when she was little she would sit on his knee and trace the line with her finger. No matter how many times she asked how he got it, the stories were varied, a duel with a bear, a sword fight with a Tzar, she still didn't know the truth. Him and Dottie were as bad as each other with their half-stories and stubborn ways. But apart from their lives of covert mystery, recently there was something different about her gran. Maude had noticed it since the VE Day celebrations. She seemed a bit far away, like she was working through a problem that only she could solve.

That was Dottie all over. Independent and stubborn, she could tear a strip off you with a look never mind a verbal assault, but then she could be cuddly and kind, fiercely protective, and wickedly funny. She sometimes wondered why her mum had struggled to get on with Dottie because Maude had her figured out from being a child. It was simple. With Dottie you had to give and take, pick your battles wisely and know when to stand firm or capitulate gracefully.

Like the time when she was about seven and Dottie collected her from school. Maude's best friend Desiree called her parents and grandparents by their first names and on the way home, she told her gran all about it. Dottie said it was a wonderful idea because if she was honest, the word 'Gran' always made her sound old. After they bought ice-lollies from the van and made their way to the park, Dottie made a suggestion.

'I've had an idea, let's ditch boring old "Gran" and instead I'll be your Dottie, won't that be fun?'

Maude sucked the juice out of her strawberry lolly before answering. 'No. I like calling you Gran, that's what you are, my gran. My mum is my mum, not Jean, and Dad is Dad, not Ralph. That's how I like it.'

'I know that, darling, but it's just a word so why don't we be all hip and trendy, like Desiree's family?'

The conversation went downhill from there.

'Because you're not hip and trendy, that's why.'

Dottie stalled for a second, rooted to the spot on the path before retaliating. 'What do you mean, not trendy? I am, look.' Dottie motioned to her well-cut Marc Jacobs suit. 'I'll have you know everyone thinks I'm very stylish.'

'Yep, you are. I love that you always dress up and wear nice make-up and pointy high shoes and I'm glad you're not a hippy like her grandma and I don't want you to be. I want you to be Gran, my boring old gran who wears smart clothes and smells nice. Not like a cat.'

Diverted for a moment from the main crux of the conversation Dottie asked, 'A cat... who smells like a cat?'

At this Maude rolled her eyes and took a huge suck of her lolly. 'Desiree's family all smell of cats because they have about...' Maude started to count on her fingers, 'More than ten anyway and when you go to their house they are everywhere and you get covered in hairs, and it smells funny too. They have poo boxes in the kitchen.'

'The cats?'

'Yes, Gran, not Desiree and her family, obviously.'

'Mmm, I thought so. But I saw her grandma once, at the summer fair and she had a lovely floaty dress on... don't you think I'd suit one?'

Maude was horrified and it must have shown on her face because Dottie seemed to mimic her reaction.

'Gran, are you mad? You'd look like you were wearing your nightie! And do you know Desiree's mum sometimes walks to school barefoot, so if you ever dare show me up like that I will divorce you straight away, I mean it.'

They had both come to a standstill at the gate to the playground and faced each other off, Maude looking determined, Dottie had that stubborn look, and then her lips began to smile and her eyes crinkled.

'Okay, I promise. No bare feet or nighties and I will allow you to call me Gran, but only because it's you! Now off you go and bag that swing before someone else gets it. Here, pass me your cardigan and satchel... hurry up, run.'

With that, Maude flung her belongings into Dottie's outstretched hands and raced to the swings, her long limbs easily beating the others who vied for the prize. Once she had claimed it Maude got on with the business of swinging towards the sky, keeping an eye on her gran just in case she wanted to go wild and decided to take off her clothes and swim in the pond... that really would scare the ducks!

It was a battle Maude remembered well over something as small as a name, but a skirmish nonetheless. The only other ones were over tinned prunes and custard – it wasn't happening – and Maude's refusal to allow her gran to accompany her to the family planning clinic to get the pill. Yes, it had been Dottie's suggestion and a prudent precaution when Maude started at the local technical college, but who in their right mind takes their gran?

Smiling, Maude snuggled down under the blanket and felt herself drifting off. The sun shining through her open window warmed her face and the people on the street provided background noise.

Taily in the meantime rested under her neck and kept one beady eye on the clock, watching the minutes tick by. And had she not been fast asleep, Maude would have spotted that the silent monkey wore a wicked smile.

4

DOTTIE AND MAUDE – SUMMER HOLIDAY

2005

It had all gone quite smoothly so far and Dottie had hired a nice, comfy four-by-four because no way were they travelling in Maude's old bone shaker, then the Eurotunnel had been booked along with a chic boutique hotel off The Champs Elysée.

Once Maude's graduation was done and dusted, and her photograph placed on top of the bureau, they'd set off, leaving London and Lachlan behind. To be fair and although it pained her slightly, Dottie had to admit he'd been gracious and encouraging in the face of guile, but really, what could he do with the impendence of her demise? Nobody would forgive him if he'd kicked up a fuss and then Dottie had kicked the bucket.

Maude was busy rummaging through the carrier bag of snacks, convinced she'd packed two mango smoothies that had mysteriously been replaced with two cans of gin and tonic. Dottie meanwhile was people watching from the passenger seat.

'Maude, do stop rustling, you've probably left them in the fridge at home. Drink the water instead. It's much better for you than those ridiculously overpriced bottles of mashed fruit.'

'Yes, I know that but I was really looking forward to them... Bugger.'

At this Dottie merely raised an eyebrow and smiled. It amused her when Maude swore because she tried really hard not to, whereas Dottie loved a good burst of profanity when the need arose.

'You know what being in this shuttle makes me think of?'

Maude ceased rustling and asked, 'No, amaze me.'

'A big silver suppository shooting up someone's ar...'

'Gran, stop. Honestly where does your head go sometimes? Here, have some chocolate, anything to shut you up.' Maude was laughing as she passed Dottie a bar of Dairy Milk.

'Okay, then it's a silver bullet. Does that sound better?' Dottie began making rustling noises of her own as Maude cracked the seal on a bottle of water.

'Much.'

After two chunks of chocolate, the silence was broken by a question about her bête noire. 'So, has he forgiven you then... for almost standing him up?'

Maude huffed. 'Just about, but Lachlan can take sulking to the next level when he wants and last night was no exception. I was dead to the world when he rang and to be honest, I probably could have stayed asleep there all night. I'm sure that bedroom drugs me, or was it you? I seem to remember you made me a cup of tea before I went upstairs, and I wouldn't put it past you.'

At this Dottie smiled and winked. But seeing as they were trapped in the silver bullet, she thought it might be a good time to have a subtle word in her granddaughter's ear. 'Well, my darling, it's little things like sulking that one hopes to tame, that turn into mammoth issues once the honeymoon is over. And I speak from experience, as you know.'

'Mmm, well I have no intention of becoming Lachlan's therapist or life coach and for the record, grandmother dearest, for the foreseeable future I have no intention of going on honeymoon.'

Dottie shrugged. 'So you keep saying but from where I'm sitting I suspect your fiancé has life all mapped out for you, which is why he kicked up a fuss about this trip. So mark my words, learn from my mistakes, otherwise my suffering will have been for nothing.'

This time Maude really did roll her eyes so far back they nearly disappeared inside her head. 'Well actually, Gran, seeing as you have never actually told me of this deep suffering you endured on my behalf, I have no way of avoiding it, do I?'

'You do know. I was married four times; to a man I hardly knew, then to one who was taken away too soon, a useless drunk and finally to a cheat. There, what more do you need to know?'

Maude swivelled in her seat and after a sip of warmish water, gave her gran an incredulous look. 'Seriously, you expect me to base my future on one sentence that you've repeated verbatim all my life? Sorry, Gran, but if you expect me to take your advice then you'll have to give me more than that.'

Dottie could feel Maude's eyes boring holes. This trip was an opportunity to relive the memories and a life she'd locked away so maybe, with thirty minutes or so left before they arrived at the Eurostar Terminal, it was time to fill in the gaps she'd purposely left blank for years.

'Okay then, so what do you want to know?'

Maude looked a bit taken aback by this and sat straighter in her seat. 'What they were like, where you met, what went wrong, why you tried marriage out four times and then gave up... whatever you want to tell me really.'

A dramatic sigh preceded Dottie's mild capitulation. 'All right, if you insist. And anyway, I'd rather talk about them now, than when we're in France. They're part of afterwards, Post-War

Me. Or perhaps Wartime Me played a hand in what happened when I went home, back to England. Mmm, that's quite an interesting way of looking at it.'

'Gran, focus. Just start with Roberto, your first husband, the one who took the photo of you that's in the parlour at home. You said he was a war reporter, that's all I know.'

Dottie was startled by Maude's interruption, lost already in her memories. 'Oh yes, Roberto. He was a nice man, ambitious and I bear no serious grudge against him at all. It was a shame really that we parted company, but I believe in fate and it had other ideas for us.'

Maude tutted loudly. 'Gran, the beginning...'

'Oh yes, sorry, darling, I do tend to wander, don't I? Right, I shall do my best to focus so in the words of your Uncle Konki, are you sitting comfortably?' A nod from Maude. 'Then I shall begin.'

Dottie never thought she would see Roberto again after the war, in fact she hadn't thought about him at all since the day he took the photo of her. He was such a colourful character though, a free spirit who went where the wind or his next hitch took him. Roberto was impetuous and principled, and after escaping political repression in Hungary had made his way to Paris and enrolled at college where he studied photography. The Nazi invasion provided fascinating subject matter, but it was too dangerous to stay in the city, so he fled again, south.

Avoiding forced labour, he hooked up with the resistance movement that was quickly gaining momentum. He fitted in well with the communists, aristocrats, students, farmers, academics, liberals, and anarchists of the Maquis. Roberto flowed with the tide, moving amongst the units, gathering images of the fighters who lived in the hills and mountains, risking his life to get close to life or death, seeing the battle through the lens of a camera. His photographs appeared in subversive publications, read by the more passive resisters but his images appealed, he had an eye, and he was brave.

When pressure began to mount on the Nazis, the Allies closing in, Roberto made his way north, towards the beleaguered coastal towns along the Atlantic Wall. Along the route he joined with the Historian Network and it was here he met a young woman he knew only as Yvette. Roberto was only with them for two days before moving on, but had promised that once all the madness was over, if he was ever in London, he would look her up.

Roberto remained in France for a while, moving back to Paris where his photographs were in huge demand. Following the Armistice and the wild celebrations on VE Day, national fervour whipped up another wave for him to ride but once it hit the shore, he needed a new challenge and, on a whim, he headed for London. Here his reputation and portfolio secured him a job on Fleet Street. It was twelve months before he thought of looking Yvette up and all he had to go on was that her parents lived in Hackney and their shop was on the high street, named after one of the most famous places in the world, Broadway.

When Dottie alighted the number nine bus that evening, after a long day in the stuffy offices at Whitehall she had no idea who would be waiting for her. She found Roberto eating pie, surrounded by locals who wanted to know all about his daring adventures in France. In her mum and grandmother's case, the big question was how this dark-haired, swarthy young man with the film star eyes and curious accent knew their Dottie, and why did he call her Yvette?

. . .

Maude hadn't taken her eyes off Dottie the whole time and surprisingly hadn't interrupted either. 'So, there you go, that's how I met him. His main objective was to deliver the photo he'd taken of me. He'd had it printed and put in a frame, the one at home.'

Maude sounded eager. 'But what happened next, did you fall in love straight away? I've seen photos of him on your wedding day and he is very dishy.'

'No, I didn't fall in love with him straight away, I never fell in love with Roberto at all and I doubt he really loved me. But we got caught up in it all, that post-war euphoria, being free, liberated and young. After the things we had seen, horrors that the lady sitting next to me on the bus could never imagine or the annoying pipe-smoking clerk who polluted our office with his ignorance and presence, would never believe. Maybe we went a little bit wild.

'Roberto knew so many wonderful and interesting people; war correspondents, writers, actors and actresses, musicians... the list was endless. So we partied and drank but deep down I knew I was trying to erase the terrible sadness in here.' Dottie touched her chest.

'I thought by blocking it all out, that I wouldn't miss France, and the men and women from my village. It left a mark on me, my Resistance, and my comrades were like family and I missed them, and I missed my life. I yearned for Renazé, the little village I'd called home.'

Dottie looked in the visor mirror, and noted her make-up was still in place, no sign of tears. That was good. The visor flipped up with a snapping sound.

'My parents thought Roberto was the bee's knees, everyone did, from the customers in the café, my doe-eyed colleagues, the barman in the local pub and his bosses at the news agency. He was a rising star, travelling back and forth to the Allied-occupied zones, his photographic journalism in great demand. Roberto proposed to me in a smoky pub, New Year's Eve, 1948, a few minutes after Big Ben chimed. It wasn't a great romantic gesture but somewhere in between clinking our glasses of whisky and a kiss, he said, "Hey, let's get married," and I said, "Okay, why not". It really was as simple as that.'

'But it's a huge thing, and you always seem so independent and I can't imagine you getting married on a whim.'

'Well I did, and I don't regret it, not one bit. You see I'd been away for almost two years. I left my family in limbo, with no idea where I was or if they would be the next ones to open the door to the telegram boy. My mum was beside herself with happiness when Roberto asked for my dad's permission. I can see from the expression on your Modern Milly face that the idea is alien to you, it is to me now, but back then I didn't care. My marriage told my mum that the days of worry were over. Her little girl had come home and was staying put. Life would go back to normal.

'We had a town hall wedding, a reception and knees-up in the café and after a honeymoon night in The Strand Palace hotel, we returned to a surprise. Mum and Dad gave us the deposit for a house and the key to the door of a property two minutes away. Roberto and I went straight over and had a look and by the following day, the ball was rolling. I was a married woman, career woman I may add, with a handsome roving reporter for a husband and after a while I convinced myself that I could do it. I could be normal, a good wife, and as a reward my heart would stop aching and eventually those damn pictures in my head would fade.'

Maude asked the obvious. 'So what went wrong?'

A sigh. 'We'd been jogging along happily for seven months, it was summer, July, and Roberto met me from work so we decided to walk to St James's Park. It only takes four minutes, I know this because the girls and I used to go there for our lunch and be back at our desks at one, prompt.

'We held hands and chatted, but I sensed Roberto was agitated. I had no idea that there were only four minutes left. That's how long it took to basically end a marriage to a man I didn't really love.'

Maude said nothing, instead fiddled with the flip-top lid of her bottle.

'He'd been offered a job with *Time* magazine in New York. There was an apartment thrown in with his generous wage and other benefits that I can't even remember now, oh yes, there was a rooftop pool and terrace for the residents, and a concierge on the door. Poor Roberto was animated and overjoyed. He was going to the land of opportunity and had already been commissioned to photograph the NATO negotiations when they began. We had a one-way ticket to paradise.'

'And what did you say?'

'I asked him what I would do all day, while he was clicking away, doing his dream job in his dream city. He told me I wouldn't have to do anything, apart from shop and look fantastic. He behaved like he'd found the pot at the end of the rainbow. I wanted to push him in the lake.'

'Yep, that's more like my gran.'

'The whole scene, his animated face, his excited pacing, the picture he painted of the promised land meant nothing to me. It was actually like an epiphany. Okay, so I didn't have the most scintillating job, overseeing supply movements to military bases, but it was my job, that I got up to go to every morning. I had my own desk with my nameplate, and an extension number. People knew who I was and what I did, and no way was I giving it up to spend my days lounging on a roof terrace, gossiping with other wives.'

Maude took another sip of water. 'I can actually picture the scene and I sort of know what happened next... how did you tell him?'

'I didn't straight away, because as much as I knew in my heart that I wouldn't go, I felt he deserved a period of grace, to believe I had given it due consideration and not dismissed it and him out of hand. That's what I was doing really. I was letting him go and truthfully, Maude, I didn't care.'

'That's very civilised of you, Gran, letting him down lightly.'

Dottie harrumphed. 'He sulked immediately because I hadn't jumped for joy so the ride home on the bus was somewhat subdued. I told him I needed to get my head around it all. He told me we'd be going at the end of the month. Three weeks away.'

'Blood... blooming heck! That was a bit quick.'

Dottie folded up the chocolate that lay in her lap, it was getting warm and she'd gone off it now. 'The best way to describe it was like a rush of blood to the head. How dare he presume that I'd simply throw away everything to follow his dream? I'd survived so much during the war. I wasn't just his wife, I was a woman who'd jumped out of a plane into the blackest sky, then gone undercover, fighting a war far from home. I'd hidden in the dark, smelling of forests and fox shit. I risked my life, felt fear, loved, lost, cried. I was more than his wife and I would not be shuffled off to play house.'

'Did you tell him that?'

'No, I didn't because he should have known, or at least had the decency, the wherewithal to see things from my point of view, after all, he'd met me in France, he knew what I did. My life there was not a total secret. I just preferred not to talk about it.' Dottie passed the bar of chocolate to Maude who placed it in the carrier bag.

'I stayed up all night after he'd gone to bed, probably exhausted from trying to persuade me. By the time the milkman was doing his rounds I'd got it all straight in my head. Over breakfast I told him that there was no way I could leave my parents. Mémère Delphine was becoming frail and after being away from home for so long I felt duty bound to stay close by. I pitched it as a simple choice, duty over love. I omitted to say what I really felt, that the choice was my self-respect or marriage. Like I said, Roberto was let down lightly and had a ready prepared line to feed anyone who asked why his marriage had failed.'

'So it was all quite amicable, what happened next?'

'We parted as friends which I suppose was all we were, but as you young things say nowadays, with benefits.'

'Gran!'

A roll of the eyes from Dottie, then more. 'Roberto booked a flight, he went a few days later and to soften the blow we both made easy-to-break promises and bold statements that made saying goodbye easier, less awkward. He would try to come back regularly, and he wanted me to visit for holidays and who knew, I might fall in love with New York. In other circumstances maybe I would have been bitten by the big apple. It sounded like a fantastic place. I wasn't completely ignorant to its charms. We did keep in touch, for many years actually, even after we divorced. I was always extremely proud of him and subscribed to *Time* magazine, scouring the pages for one of his articles. He was an outstanding photojournalist and a happy part of my life. A chapter at least.'

The last comment received a raised eyebrow from Maude. 'But what did your parents say, were they disappointed?'

'No, not really. They'd lived through the war without their daughter and didn't want to lose her again. I kept the house once we were divorced and continued to live around the corner from the shop. We were all happy. Simple.'

'Well, that's something at least.' Maude checked her watch.

'We've got fifteen minutes before we arrive so I reckon that's plenty of time for the next instalment so come on, now I've finally got you to open up let's get on with it.'

Dottie huffed. 'Oh, Maude, do we have to? I'm exhausted from all this talking. Let's listen to the radio instead.'

The look Maude gave her grandmother indicated that Radio 4 was not going to be an option so sucking in air, then exhaling loudly to demonstrate her dissatisfaction, Dottie moved the story on to the next bittersweet point in her life. George.

5

DOTTIE AND THE HUSBANDS

2005

This was going to be a tricky one because the story of Dottie and George didn't end well, and for reasons that Dottie didn't feel able to expand on, not at that moment. The truth of how George died was a secret well buried, the circumstances still haunted her like the pain he'd suffered, both of them tormented but in different ways. Maybe she would never tell anyone what happened, what good would it do?

Maude, as always, was impatient and had plenty of questions. 'So come on, tell me all about Jazzy George. Husband Number Two.'

The comment lightened her mood and made Dottie chuckle, knowing the nickname was a result of Maude's childhood fascination with old photos and ferreting through the suitcase that contained them. She used to think that in the 'olden days' everything was really black and white and then suddenly someone coloured in the world. It had taken a while for it to sink into six-year-old Maude's head that the people in the monotone images actually led colourful lives. But at any time, the mention of George always inspired such a conflicting range of emotions and to combat the worst, Dottie tried hard to picture him at his piano in the club, playing jazz.

'There's not much to tell really because he left the world far too soon, but who knows, had the scourge of cancer not ruined everything we might have been happy, perhaps we could have made it.'

'But did you love George? Please tell me it wasn't like with Roberto.'

Dottie squinted at Maude. 'Ooh you are such a romantic, Maudie, and I do hate to disappoint you so I will say that in this case, I loved being his wife, I really did. George let me be me and I let him be him. He was a night owl who lived for music. He stayed out late, smoked and drank too much, didn't realise he had to take care of himself. I left early for work, cycled whenever I could, ate vegetables. We had different sets of friends whose circles crossed spectrums now and then. The house was always full of music, he was a fabulous cook and made glorious food. We rubbed along and sailed our ships that most days would pass on the landing, but we were very happy.'

At this Maude smiled.

Dottie felt suddenly wistful. 'It makes me sad sometimes, that I'll never know if we might have had a happy ending. I like to believe we would.'

'You said he died of cancer, that's so sad. And what happened to Eddie the Beagle?'

'Oh, Eddie plodded on for years, but he preferred our cleaner, Elsa, to me. So when he started to pine for George I felt bad leaving him alone all day, so she gradually adopted him. He'd still come with her while she cleaned and would lie in his bed in the kitchen, I couldn't bear to throw it out, and then Eddie would go home with Elsa. It made me happy that he was happy.'

Dottie didn't want to dwell on George for too long so moved the conversation along.

'And then there was Morris, your grandfather. All I can say in my defence is there had been a three-year drought on the man front and I must have been bored. Whatever it was, I took my eye off the ball. After George I'd convinced myself that I didn't need anyone. I liked living alone. I thrived on the notion that I wasn't like the other women in my office who couldn't wait to meet a handsome chap and escape the drudgery of work. I didn't see my life that way.'

Maude made a point. 'Thing is, Gran, not everyone yearns for the big career, we all want different things.'

'Oh, I know that, but it irritated me so much, that during the war years women shouldered the burden while men went away and fought. We worked the land, in munitions factories, joined the army, doing whatever men did before the war. Women showed the world that they could do it too, or at least have a damn good try. They stepped up to the mark. I couldn't believe that after everything they had achieved and endured, for some of my colleagues and friends, marriage became their main aim.'

'Yes, but some people want to settle down and have a family, there's nothing wrong with that.' Maude sounded indignant.

'I agree, Maude. However, I preferred to have a choice and alternatives, not fit into a neat box. I'd already decided after George that I wasn't prepared to conform. Not in a radical polit-ical way, it was more of a personal choice. Marriage definitely wasn't for me, so I made it my mission to work my way up the career ladder. The woman I had been, the special agent trained to do all sorts, wasn't prepared to capitulate and resign herself to a desk in the corner. Instead I chose to resist. I was good at that.'

Maude folded her arms across her chest and looked slightly confused. 'So, with all this resolve and a great big fire in your belly, why on earth did you marry Granddad? And when are you going to tell me about your secret service life? You keep dropping hints and mentioning places, you promised you'd explain.'

A loud tut and a huff came before a revelation. 'When I'm good and ready, Little Miss Impatient and in answer to the marriage question, I married Morris because I got pregnant with your mother. Once again I found myself trotting up those bloody registry office steps.'

'And what did your parents and Delphine think of all this? Surely in those days it was a bit unusual, you know, to have so many husbands.'

'Ha, you make me sound like a black widow or man-eater, which I certainly wasn't. I was having their grandchild; my family were overjoyed, and after all it wasn't my fault that circumstances had curtailed the previous two unions. As far as they were concerned Morris was a good catch and this time it'd all work out.'

'That went well then.'

Dottie tittered at that remark. 'Well nobody can say I didn't try. Eight years I put up with that bloody man and for the last four it was for the sake of your mum, otherwise he'd have been down the road long before that. Why I even looked twice at him I will never know. Actually, that's wrong because before he acquired the purple-nosed, permanently pickled look, he was very handsome. But an accountant, I ask you? At least he'd resisted the lure of the family business because the thought of marrying a funeral director...' Dottie grimaced and shuddered.

'Like I said, I think I lost my mind and paid the price for sex, literally.'

When she looked over Maude was laughing but trying to hide it with her hand.

'Gran, stop, that's my granddad you're talking about and there is a thing as too much information. But how did you meet in the first place? And was it his drinking that ended it? Mum hates talking about her childhood. It's like she brushes it under the carpet.'

'Oh well that's your mother all over. What she doesn't like or can't deal with she just ignores and I'm fully aware of how disappointed she was with me in particular, that's why she was hell-bent on being the complete opposite.

'But back to Morris, before I get diverted. It began because he worked for my dad's accountants and I met him when I dropped the books off. It ended when he couldn't even be trusted to watch over your mum while I was at work. He'd been sacked for being drunk so I became the breadwinner. He decided to make some chips for tea and then passed out while they cooked. He set the kitchen on fire and could've burned the house down had Jean not smelt smoke. I was horrified when I came home to find the fire brigade there. My dad had a fit and punched Morris on the nose. Then when he got up off the pavement, I told him to go to his parents and stay there. Forever. That was that.'

Maude sucked in a breath. 'Flipping heck. Mum never mentioned a fire, but she did say that it was a messy divorce, lots of arguing about the house. Is that why you still don't get on?'

Dottie shook her head. 'He gets on my nerves. That's why we don't get on. That man is a whisky soaked waste of space. If he'd done something about it, joined AA, or stood on his own two feet and not kept them under his parent's table then I'd have had a bit of respect for him, but he didn't. Instead he tried to take half my house and unbelievably wanted custody of your mum, as if. Hugh sorted all the legal stuff out and got one of his old school chums to represent me in court where he wiped the floor with Morris and his solicitor. Nobody was going to take away my home. Mémère Delphine once told me a story about fighting for what is yours, and I never forgot it.'

'What story?'

'I'll tell you another day, I promise.' Dottie wanted to wind up the whole annoying husband issue.

'If that's what you want. But back to Mum and Granddad Morris, they have a good relationship despite his obvious faults, so I don't understand why it wasn't the same for you. It's not like you did anything wrong so why are you and Mum always at loggerheads even if it's all done in a very polite and non-confrontational kind of way?'

Dottie raised her eyebrows at this. 'That's very observant of you, Maude, and you're right, we've always danced around each other I suppose, but I do love her, for all of her faults.'

It was Maude's turn to raise her eyebrows. 'Aw, Mum's lovely, she's just not as domineering as you so maybe she wanted a quiet, battle-free life.'

Chuckling, Dottie agreed. 'How very diplomatic... and yes I am domineering but somebody had to be sensible and keep it all together. Don't forget the early sixties weren't used to single mothers and career girls. The *Good Housekeeping* version of the fifties was ingrained and where women's independence was concerned, they'd shoved the forties into a drawer marked "best forgotten". That's how I felt anyway.'

Dottie folded her arms and could feel a bad mood coming on, but thought it best to get the trip down memory lane over with. 'Your mother had a good life. I provided for her while Morris went from one job to the next. The only reason he has money these days is because he inherited the family firm. Thank goodness people keep dying otherwise he'd be bloody destitute.'

At this Maude made a 'Brrrr' sound and shivered. Dottie agreed, it gave her the creeps too, which was why they rarely mentioned it.

'Yes, he saw Jean now and then and did the superhero daddy thing, but it was me who paid the mortgage and for her school trips and holidays. Every single year I took her away and no matter where we went, I could tell she hated it, or me, or both. While I was proud of being the single mum by the pool, surrounded by beach ball batting families, Jean wanted to fit in, be like them. She was the only one in her class with divorced parents. I could tell she cringed when her friends came for tea and her father wouldn't breeze in from work and get out his pipe and slippers. Instead there was just me, drinking G&T and grilling fish fingers.'

Maude smiled. 'That's how I remember you too, cooking my tea in your work suit, those kitten heel slippers with the fluffy front and drinking naughty water. That's what you called G&T.'

Dottie shrugged. 'Well your mum hated it. I tried hard to show her an example, pass on some of my resilience and independence. I took her to work so she would understand what I did, who the person who paid the bills was. I *so* wanted her to be proud of me. I was the one who helped with homework, who hoped her school reports would say she excelled at something or showed an interest in at least one subject. But Jean seemed to delight in being average. And no matter how hard I tried, I was always her biggest disappointment so I gave up egging her on, or chastising her, whichever way you want to look at it. The last thing I wanted on my list of faults was "pushy mother". Instead, I made sure she was happy, whatever that meant in Jean World, and that she never did without. Then I let her make her own way and mistakes.'

'At least you weren't at loggerheads and gave in gracefully, that says to me that you were sensible, still loving her but in your own way.'

Dottie shrugged the compliment off, Maude continued.

'When she talks about her childhood she's never nasty, you know. It's more matter of fact, a sort of "that's how it was" attitude. She doesn't come across as unhappy at all and Mum loved being with Granddad Tommy and Granny Paulette, she told me. And she loved Delphine too.'

At this Dottie brightened. 'Oh yes, your mum loved being at the café, we all did. It was one of those places that buzzed with warmth and activity and your mum would be there as much as she could. Straight after school and whenever I had to work late, she'd stay over. And she won't know this but when she began working there I was so proud. On her first day I watched from across the street as she waited tables and served behind the counter. It was like looking at myself because I used to be happy there too, working with my parents, laughing with the regulars so I understood why she liked it so much.'

'Were you cross when Mum married so young?'

'No, not at all. I expected it really and I could see she was happy, radiant in fact. Jean wanted to create everything she felt she'd missed out on and who was I to deny her that? I paid for her wedding because "you-know-who" had lost his job again but I was pleased too, for many reasons. I hoped it would make up for what I'd been unable to give her, even if it was in the form of a silk dress and a dream wedding. I was proud to hand over the cheque that paid for it all and even though I would've loved to walk her down the aisle, I bowed graciously to tradition and kept my fingers crossed that Morris managed a straight line.'

'And did he?'

'On the way down yes, but I spotted him taking a swig from his hip flask during the signing of the register so going back up was another matter. The vicar wasn't amused.'

'Well I hope you've enjoyed being a grandma a bit more than being a mum. You and I have always been best friends, haven't we?'

Dottie's heart flipped at this and she was eager to make a point. 'My darling Maude, you have been a total joy ever since the moment I saw you, surely you know that?'

'Course I do. I was only teasing.'

When an unexpected cloud settled on Dottie, she knew why. The only way to blow it away was by braving the deluge that accompanied it. 'She is brave, you know, your mum, brave and strong and a fighter. I saw it first-hand when she had her miscarriages. My heart broke for my child. I couldn't give her the one thing she wanted more than anything, but it was the only time she ever let me hold her and comfort her. For a little while, each time, she let me be her mummy and wipe away her tears. She needed me and it felt so good.'

Dottie swallowed the lump in her throat. 'Whenever she found out she was pregnant I prayed so hard that it would be okay, then cursed and railed when it wasn't, so you can understand the joy I felt when you were born. Not for me, for my daughter. And as much as I can be a grumpy old goat, I adore your dad and I am truly happy that he married your mum. I do not begrudge them one moment together.'

Maude reached over and held Dottie's hand for a second. 'I wish we'd had this conversation before, Gran, and I think you should tell Mum all this. I bet she has no idea you feel this way.'

Dottie shook her head. 'I'd like to think that she knows I love her, without me having to put it into words. Anyway, you can tell her on my behalf but for now I'll stick to driving her nuts. I'm good at that and I enjoy it.'

Maude gave Dottie the squinty-eyed look. 'Do you realise that in some ways you and Mum are similar and that maybe, your stubborn ways and fondness for resistance rubbed off on her. While you were bucking the trend and determined to be an independent woman, Mum stood her ground with you and refused to let you mould her. She chose her own path, regardless of what was expected of her.'

A smile cracked Dottie's face that had previously been focused on Maude and her erudite appraisal. 'Well, there you go then, my work here is done. You and your mother have turned out fine with me steering the ship and providing solid foundations, what more could two children ask for?'

When Maude caught Dottie's wink, she returned it with a tap on the arm. 'Gran, you are such a wind-up merchant. Right, be serious for a minute because we are at husband number four and I'm dying to know what he did to upset you.'

Dottie was feeling weary from her meanderings and noting the time, decided to close the conversation down quickly.

'Ah, William. There's not much to say, really. After your grandfather I properly swore off men unless they were taking me to dinner, the theatre or the ballet, on all-expenses-paid holidays, had a home of their own and no desire or need of a wife.'

'So what happened to flying the flag for women's lib and paying your own way?' Maude smirked.

'I enjoyed independence, Maude, but I wasn't bloody stupid! If someone wanted the pleasure of my company that was fine and yes, I could pay for my own ticket to Barbados but if a wealthy chap wanted to treat me, who was I to refuse? And anyway, it's only demeaning if you repay generosity with sex. I didn't. I had sex because I wanted to, not because I couldn't afford to go on holiday without dropping my knickers.'

'Dear God, Gran, enough!' Maude slapped her hand against her forehead.

Howling with laughter Dottie forced out some facts before Maude disowned her. 'I'm putting this debacle down to a mid-life crisis and a mutually agreeable but decent proposition. I met William through Hugh. They were colleagues at the Home Office where William worked as an advisor. We'd enjoyed some lovely evenings together and had grown quite close. He was articulate, interesting and I accompanied him to many dinners and functions. I had no idea his feelings for me had deepened so his proposal came as a shock. In the moments where I sat open-mouthed and grappled for words, he took the opportunity to assure me that our marriage would be nothing like my others.

'I have to say his pitch was excellent. He would remain at his apartment in Kensington, I would keep my house. William admired my job and wouldn't dream of asking me to give it up. We were a good match. I would look good on his arm. He would look good on mine.'

Maude interrupted. 'And he cheated.'

'Yes. I had my suspicions and raised them with Konstantin. He brought me the proof in a brown envelope. The pictures inside, prostitutes at William's private club, were not part of the deal. My handsome divorce settlement was.'

Maude puffed. 'Bloody hell, Gran. There's a book in there somewhere.'

'I do hope so, but enough of my tawdry past. Let's focus on the here and now. We'll be there soon, and I want us to have that holiday feeling, in fact, find Cliff Richard on that ipop thing of yours and we can have a sing-song.'

Again, Maude roared with laughter. 'It's an iPod, and your wish is my command, Mrs Flibbertigibbet. Hold on.'

Maude picked up her phone and searched for the song as Dottie looked on. That was one chapter in the story of her life done and dusted. Even if the only people that read it were Maude and Jean, it would be enough. At least once it was told, they would know more about who Dottie really was, what she had done, and why.

6

DOTTIE AND MAUDE – ROAD TRIP

FRANCE, 2005

Dottie was riding shotgun as Maude referred to it and while she had enjoyed their whistle-stop tour of Paris, was glad to leave the city behind them and finally be heading south. So far, the journey hadn't been the least bit stressful mostly due to Maude doing all the hard work, but she seemed happy enough taking what she thought was control.

With the trauma of the Boulevard Périphérique behind them, they were now taking the A11 towards Angers and Dottie could see from her posture and facial expression that Maude was more relaxed. She couldn't see her eyes as they were covered by sunglasses to counteract the glare of a bright July day, but at least her brow wasn't quite as damp as earlier, although her fringe still stuck to her forehead. Despite this, Dottie thought Maude looked very French, her dark-brown hair, cut into a short bob, framed a heart-shaped face that with a bit of luck would take on a golden glow during their trip. Maude erred on the side of pale and could look a bit wishy-washy especially during the winter when she was holed up inside her studio, but a few days painting outside in the fresh air would do her the world of good.

The autoroute stretched ahead and the pace of the traffic

had slowed considerably when Maude wound down her window a touch, then asked Dottie a question. 'So, my little travelling buddy, are you looking forward to your road trip down memory lane? I absolutely loved Paris, but I have to admit I'm glad that box is ticked, aren't you?'

Dottie was listening to Maude and trying to open the tin of travel sweets, twisting and prising the lid.

'Maybe once you take out the landmarks most cities are the same, full of rude, pushy people or someone trying to flog you a cheap souvenir.'

Dottie nodded her agreement then gestured towards the dashboard. 'Still didn't stop you from buying the Eiffel Tower, did it?' The tiny plastic statue was attached to the key fob and jiggled as they drove.

'Hey, don't diss my souvenir, I love it and Mum will love hers, too.' Maude had bought a bigger flashing statue for her mum. It was pure kitsch.

Dottie laughed. 'Do you think? Where on earth will she put it? It's huge compared to yours.'

Maude shrugged. 'In the downstairs loo, probably. And you didn't answer my question about how you feel about going back to Renazé. I wonder if there will be anyone there you recognise? Maybe we could look up some of the names you remember and see if we can find them or their families.'

Dottie remained silent, deep in thought because this very idea had been buzzing around her head for weeks. It would have been easy to do a spot of research, contact the *maire* who, in any town or village, was an excellent starting point for most issues. But for now, she preferred to simply look and wander, be anonymous.

'And you promised that once we left Paris, you'd tell me all about your time here in the war otherwise I won't understand it properly. I'd like to look at it from your eyes, not through tourist goggles and seeing as you've been so blooming secretive all these years, I think it's about time you explained.'

Still Dottie held her tongue. Not because she didn't agree with Maude; more because she wasn't really sure where to start. Instead she let her granddaughter soldier on, cajoling her into sharing a story she had the fullest intention of telling, when she was ready.

'After all, I did let you talk me into leaving my fiancé, although I do think Mum was a bit relieved you didn't ask her to come with you. The actual thought of you two stuck in a car for longer than it takes to get to the supermarket makes my eyes water.' Maude chuckled at her own observation.

At this Dottie responded. 'It's not like I dragged you kicking and screaming, did I? Anyway, we won't be gone forever and I'm sure Lachlan will manage just fine, camping on Henman Hill. Fancy him liking tennis. I thought it was all rugby and cricket over there.'

'Dottie, I wish you'd stop generalising about Australians, one of these days you'll get arrested by the PC police, I mean it.'

Dottie huffed and looked out of the window, reading the graffiti on a concrete bridge and not for the first time wondering how they managed to dangle upside down and spray paint with such accuracy and flair.

Maude persisted. 'And stop changing the subject. I'm up to speed with the husbands so why don't you start right at the beginning, with my great-grandparents. You've only ever told me about the café and Broadway Market. It's my heritage and if you think about it, their story brought us here.'

Silence ensued. Dottie knew that Maude knew the score. Plant the seed, wait for it to grow then when, and only when Dottie was ready, would she pluck whatever bloom sprung from her mind. Checking the map and speedo, she estimated that they had over two hours before they reached their hotel and as the road meandered into the distance, Dottie succumbed to the inevitable *and* the stupidity of making a promise, especially to Maude.

'I suppose it would be sensible to tell you how it started, not the war because you *should* know all about that from school at the very least. You're right though, it began right here in France when my dad went on a day trip to St Malo and met my mum. He said it was love at first sight.'

Maude interrupted. 'Maybe we should have started our trip there, not Paris, or could we go now, is it far?'

Dottie reached out and placed her hand on Maude's leg in order to silence her. 'Don't worry it's all in hand, and on the itinerary.'

Maude glanced over quickly. 'But you said that apart from visiting Renazé and Nantes we would play it by ear, see where the fancy took us, no firm plans.'

'That's correct. I want to be free to go where my memory takes me, not march around chateaus and museums like I'm on an organised coach tour. It's all up here, Maude.' Dottie tapped her forehead. 'Pictures, faces, places, words. They're all jumbled in a pile and I need to sort through them, lay them out in some kind of order which is why I have to take it a step at a time. Do you understand?'

Maude nodded and this time it was she who squeezed Dottie's hand.

'My parents are part of the story, so is St Malo, at the beginning and end, which is why I'm saving it till last, if we go there at all.'

Another squeeze from Maude, and then a question. 'I understand, I really do... it's like an onion and you have to remove a layer at a time. Are you sure you want to talk about it though? I feel bad now for pressing you. We could just go and look at things, like the camera-clicking sightseers back home.'

Dottie shook her head. 'No, no. Like you said, this is part of your history too, and your mum's. I think I owe it to her to explain why I've been cantankerous and a proverbial pain in the arse since the poor woman popped out of the womb. First though, I have to work it out for myself and as they say, lay a few ghosts to rest.'

'Okay, if you're sure. I'll try to remember everything then I can tell Mum whenever we get home... that's if you do intend on letting me go home and not holding me hostage forever, or until Lachlan gets fed up of waiting for me to come to my senses.'

Dottie inclined her head slightly and regarded Maude who was smiling, sunglass-covered eyes firmly fixed on the road.

'Whatever do you mean by that? Of course, you'll be going home, eventually, and I'm sure Lachlan will be waiting when you get there, of *that* I have no doubt.' Sometimes Dottie just couldn't contain her sarcasm. It had a will of its own.

Maude sounded unconvinced. 'Mmm... we'll see. I'm onto you, Dottie Tanner, even though you think I'm a pushover.'

'I think nothing of the sort. You're just a sweet, kind-hearted girl who adores her gran and is devoted to making her twilight years as happy as possible.'

'Twilight zone, more like.' Maude sniggered.

Dottie allowed herself to laugh at that. 'Anyway, less of the cheek and back to your devotion and our pilgrimage. So that you don't forget anything and one day, when I'm gone, your mother can read her family history, you're going to write down everything I tell you. And it might come in quite handy if I go gaga, then at least I'll know who I am.'

When Maude responded she sounded shocked and a bit put out. 'Write it all down, are you being serious?'

'Yes, of course I am. You can write it in the journal.'

'Gran, what blood... blooming journal?'

Sighing loudly, Dottie answered in her exasperated tone, the one usually reserved for Jean. 'In the bloody journal I bought for you. It's in my case along with some lovely new pens and a brand-new box of gouache, nice ones by the way, my treat.'

Maude didn't respond immediately, instead she made a huffing noise, then a snorty laugh as she shook her head and concentrated on the road. 'Okay, fine. I will write down whatever you tell me, so it'd better be damn good.'

Dottie smiled then adjusted her seat belt which was rubbing her neck. 'Excellent, that's settled then. You'll need to catch up and make notes about the husbands. We can't leave them out, which is a shame where Morris and William are concerned.'

'Well it's a good job I have a decent memory, isn't it?'

'Mmm, if you say so. Right let's focus on this life of mine... I know, let me tell you about London and the start of the war.' Dottie paused while Maude listened to the satnav and took a turning onto a quieter road.

Once they joined the flow of traffic she continued. 'I want you to picture your great-grand-parents' café not how it is now with its fancy neon sign and all the vibrant colours of the rainbow passing by, but like in the photos at home. Not completely black and white, maybe with just a hint of colour here and there.'

Dottie saw Maude nod. 'Remember it was wartime, in the thick of the Blitz and rationing, and for the life of me I can't remember it any other way than a smudge of muted colours. Utility clothing, uniforms everywhere, dark navies, khaki browns and air force blues, sandbags and dust, the blackest of blacked-out nights. There was colour, of course there was, splashes here and there, the union flag, Dad's tomatoes and vegetables he grew on the allotment, the flowers in Hyde Park that popped up regardless of what fell from the sky, like bright dollops of defiance.

'Between the sepia we tried our best and even nature kept up appearances. We made do and mended, transforming our old summer dresses, putting beetroot juice on our lips and boot polish and spit on our eyelashes yet still, for me the city was always grey. I desperately wanted it to light up again. I wanted to light up too, feel hope, not resignation and the tinge of fear when the siren sounded. I wanted to fight back. I can feel it now, you know, here, deep inside.' Dottie touched her chest.

'It was like anger brewing but not yet formed, or panic, yes that's a good way to describe it, a suffocating sense of frustration at our situation. Not just for Britain but for the whole world that was being infested by the Nazi regime. I had to do something. That's why I joined up and found myself in the hallowed halls of the War Office.'

Dottie took a breath, surprised by the passion that overcame her. Taking a moment, she was grateful for Maude's silence. This was where the journal would begin, with a young woman on the brink of her greatest adventure. Dottie could almost touch the scene in her head, the kitchen above the café, a letter, her father pacing the worn lino and the unrelenting tears of her dear mother.

7

MAMAN, PAPA ET MÉMÈRE DELPHINE

Tommy Tanner took a break from wearing a hole in the floor and pulled another ciggie from his packet of Park Drive, lighting it quickly before taking what looked like a long, life-saving drag. The enormous swirling puff of smoke that he exhaled reassured Dottie that he wasn't going to die anytime soon. Once he'd imbibed some strength, Tommy took position behind his wife, Paulette, who was sitting at the kitchen table, sobbing into her handkerchief while on the other side sat Mémère Delphine.

The living accommodation above the café was usually warm and enticing but tonight it felt sombre, a shadow cast upon it. The kitchen-cum-living-room was where they all gathered for meals or to discuss the day's events, seated around the long, scrubbed pine table with its mismatched chairs collected one by one from the second-hand stall on the market.

During the winter months the fire in the kitchen grate welcomed you in and they spent many happy times, or since the outbreak of war, worrying ones, seated on the battered old sofa and chairs as they listened to the radio. The three bedrooms along the corridor were in darkness, their windows blacked out as were those where they sat. Despite the roaring fire, the meal of stew and potatoes they'd mopped up with bread and the hum of the radio, the current atmosphere belied the ambience of the room.

While her parents were visibly distressed, Dottie's grand-mother appeared quite unmoved by the scene, understanding everything, saying nothing, but that was her way. Only when she had something of value to offer and a suitable moment arose in which to impart her erudite words would she interject so until then, Dottie knew Delphine would keep her counsel.

She was thankful though, that at least one member of her family was being sensible because as far as Dottie was concerned, the other two were completely overreacting to her news.

Tommy eventually cut through the silence, patting Paulette's shoulder in between puffs and soothing words. 'Now, now, love, don't take on so. There's no need to get into a state. Our girl's just taking a little trip, ain't you, Dot? And it don't mean she'll be in any danger, they might just have her doing a bit of typing, like she does now. Nothing to worry about at all.'

When her father gave her the nod, obviously encouraging her to fib to her mum, Dottie stood firm. This was no time for pussy-footing about. It was wartime and she was doing her bit, so *no way* was her thrilling opportunity being dampened down or likened to a day at bloody Margate.

'Dad, stop it, it's not fair on Mum and anyway, I don't know what's going to happen, none of us do in this bleedin' war. But what I do know is I want to go. No, actually, I am going, I have to.' Dottie took a moment to glance at her mémère, who remained impassive and merely sipped her coffee.

Expecting no immediate assistance there, Dottie softened and approached her mother, kneeling before her and then taking her trembling hand.

'Maman, Mum, please stop crying and listen.' Dottie frequently alternated how she addressed Paulette, borne from avoiding being teased by her friends in public yet in private, she enjoyed speaking in her mother's tongue.

'It's going to be fun and I'll get to see somewhere new. You've always wanted me to travel so now I am, and I bet wherever I'm going, it will be lovely this time of year.' Dottie already knew it was Scotland but wasn't allowed to say and had no idea what April in the Highlands would be like.

'There won't be any air raids and look at it like this, it's probably more dangerous working in a munitions factory or White-hall. Please cheer up, Maman. I thought you'd be proud.' Dottie stroked Paulette's hand and waited for the tears to subside.

Wiping her own face, Paulette then took Dottie's in the palm of her hands, stroking flushed cheeks with her thumbs. '*Ma précieuse fille*, I have only ever wanted the very best for you, I promise this with all my heart, but still I cannot bear the thought of you going away, to a strange place and for what? I do not understand why you are going. Everywhere is dangerous and I need you here with me otherwise my heart will break, I know it.'

'But, Mum, I have to do my bit, like everyone. I've been specially selected, me, Dottie Tanner from the East End, who'd have thought it?' Dottie placed her hand on her chest and willed her mother to understand. 'This is my chance to make a difference and I can honestly say that typing notes for the War Office, day in, day out, doesn't really feel like I am.'

While Paulette mulled over her daughter's words, Delphine chose to speak. For the most part, Dottie's grandmother spoke in French but tonight she surprised them all and chose English albeit it with a strong accent. Maybe it was for Tommy's benefit, so he could understand everything not just the odd dry insult or comical French phrase, or perhaps on that day, at that moment in time, it would make them all listen, really listen.

'Paulette, Thomas, stop this at once. Do you not understand what is happening a few hundred miles from our door?' She swept her arm towards an invisible enemy, her voice dropping to a hiss. 'Do you not feel the breath of the Nazis on your neck? Hear their boots marching closer while poison pours from their minds. Soon it will wash into the sea and onto these shores and if it does,' Delphine pointed at them in turn, 'what you call your homeland will be invaded by sewer rats, just like they are crawling all over mine.'

Pausing as if to gather her thoughts and let the previous ones settle, Delphine eyed each person gathered around the table. Dottie was totally enthralled while her parents looked sheepish, her mother especially.

'Do you ever wonder who lives in my beautiful family home now? Do you remember where my son, your brother is?' She directed this at Paulette. 'I'll tell you who, the Gestapo, I'll tell you where, in Germany. Our dear Bernard is forced to work for that scum, or face death in a camp. My brother was too old to go but has been evicted from our family home and faces a firing squad if he dares to defy the invaders of my beautiful St Malo.'

Delphine's shocking words educed a gasp from Paulette and sorrowful looks from the others.

'I read the newspapers, I listen to Mr Churchill on the radio and this war is not going our way so there must be a united effort to rid the world of this...' Delphine paused, as if searching for her words, 'despicable scourge.'

Paulette's voice, when she found it, was laced with exasperation and no small measure of determination. 'But, Maman she is just a girl... what can she do that will make such a difference? We need more guns and soldiers, planes and bombs and the help of our allies. War should be fought by men not women.

What can Dottie do, look at her, this tiny thing, and why must she go away when there are jobs she can do here?'

The sound of Delphine's palm as it slapped the table caused all three members of the Tanner family to jump and the teacups to jiggle in their saucers. 'Enough of this nonsense, Paulette, and shame on you. My granddaughter is not just a girl. She is a woman with a brain in her head and a spirit that you could never hope to possess. All over this country and in France there are women fighting their own battle. Like in the last war they will struggle to feed their children, but hold up their heads when really, they want to weep tears of great sadness. They do not give in to the threat of invasion. No, they are doing what they can. There are women *everywhere*, young and old, working on the land or through the night in factories, making ships, bombs and bullets, parachutes and planes, side by side while the fear of another air raid hangs over them. At this very moment, women toil in field hospitals and aboard ships, tending the wounded and dying, far away from home and probably in terrible, terrible conditions, seeing things they will never forget. And you ask why?'

The fury in Delphine's face was in stark contrast to the look of shame on that of her daughter whereas her granddaughter wore one of pure admiration. Delphine wasn't finished just yet though.

'Dottie, please come and sit by me for a moment and leave your maman to her tears and conscience, there are things I need to say to you and if it does not distress her too much, my daughter may listen. Thomas, could you please bring the wine?'

Doing as he was bidden Tommy shuffled off to the pantry while Dottie moved to Delphine's side. Once the wine was poured for all of them and Paulette, suitably chastised, accepted her glass and took a fortifying gulp, the Tanner's listened to what the true leader of their clan had to say.

Addressing her daughter first in a softer manner, Delphine forgave Paulette. 'I do understand the fear in your heart because I too had to let a precious child go. You forget, Paulette, that I have already lived through a war that saw millions of young men go to battle and their deaths. One of them was your oldest brother, my first born, Serge. He is now one of God's angels.'

At this Paulette nodded as she reached for her mother's fingers, wrapping them in her own briefly until Delphine pulled them away as she straightened in her chair and continued.

'Sacrifice comes in many forms, as does bravery but none of us should seek to better another or hold up our pain as a trophy to that end. But we can understand, we must, because by respecting each other, our fears and trials, our mistakes and regrets, we can learn. I had to let Serge go. He was three days past eighteen. I watched him march from our village with the other young men, his friends since they were children. My husband, your papa led the way, his head held high. Some of them came back, Serge did not. You all know this. The day he went away I had no choice, all I could do, all any of us could do was wear our fear with pride and hold it up like a beacon, shining a light on those brave men, hoping it would guide them home.'

Everyone around the table nodded, the sombre mood deepening.

'Paulette, do you not remember how the women of France came together? Three million farmers were fighting at the front so who brought in the harvest? We did. Once again women must rise up no matter how much our hearts are breaking.' Delphine smiled kindly at her daughter then took a sip of wine. All eyes were on her.

'You also know that I left my home in St Malo and came here with you, but you don't understand the real reason why. It was time to make another sacrifice, this time for my youngest son, for Bernard and his family. Yes, I was bitter, like very bad wine because the farm had been my life, but there was no room for two women in the kitchen, not when one of them was Sandrine. I knew we would never be friends; enemies, yes. I would have made a worthy adversary and perhaps enjoyed myself too much, but Bernard did not deserve that, he is a good man. This is why I left him to run the farm and be the man of the house not a plaything that wife and mother could fight over, pulling his loyalty and affection this way and that. By leaving my beloved home and country I allowed him his pride, something he needed in the face of Sandrine.'

'But, Maman, you caused such a fuss when we brought you here. You made me feel like I'd forced you to come, saying I would need you in a strange land.' Paulette looked perplexed.

Delphine shrugged. 'You did need me, everyone needs their maman especially when babies arrive, and I knew there was one inside your belly even though you didn't say. Why do you think I capitulated when Thomas asked for your hand? Pah, do you think I am a fool? I could not let you come alone to this land of beefy monarchists and anyway, you would have missed me too much, I know this. Or am I wrong, and all my years of sacrifice were for nothing?'

A hint of a crease at the corner of Delphine's eye told Dottie she was playing with them, lightening the mood a touch. Her mother, as always, took the bait.

'Of course, I am grateful, Maman, we all are, aren't we?' Paulette had flushed crimson, no doubt at the mention of her pre-marital state.

Thomas remained silent but shuffled uncomfortably, avoiding Delphine's gaze as she spoke.

'Well, thank you and in the interest of *cordialité*, I feel I should apologise and confess. You see at first, I was angry and confused and so, so homesick and I took it out on you. That was wrong so I wish to say sorry and *hope* to be forgiven.' Delphine pinned Paulette with a stare.

'Of course, you are forgiven, Maman, isn't she, Tommy?' Paulette looked to her husband, eyes round as though willing him to agree.

Tommy smiled and fiddled for his packet of Park Drive. 'Course you are, Delphie, and anyways, it wouldn't have been the same without you to keep us in line, that's for sure.'

Delphine nodded her acceptance while Dottie smiled; knowing that despite her commands and the odd Gallic curse, deep down, Mémère adored her dad, darning his socks, starching his collars, making his favourite *galettes*, and most of all allowing him to marry her only daughter. And after all, he was the only person that got away with calling her Delphie.

In the silence, Tommy took a drag of his cigarette then asked a question of his own. 'But why, in all these bleedin' years have you refused to speak English, to me anyways? That's the first time we've ever had a proper conversation. And I know you talk to that lot down at the church because none of them can *parlez Francais*, ain't that the truth.' Tommy took another drag and just like his wife and daughter, waited for the answer.

'Because I am stubborn. I am not afraid to admit this, and it was a way of holding on to who I am, my identity. Keeping the flame alive perhaps and anyway, how would I amuse myself, calling you *une lavette* would be no fun if you knew what I was saying.' Delphine winked at Tommy who was none the wiser.

Coming to his rescue of sorts, Paulette sounded cross. 'It means lazy, my darling, which you are not, is he, Maman?'

Delphine shook her head. 'Of course not, I am teasing you, but perhaps it was *ma métier*, my job, to teach you at least a few phrases, not like our darling Dottie. She has been the very best student of all.' Delphine reached out and stroked Dottie's face, pushing a lock of auburn hair from her sea-green eyes.

Thomas chuckled and flicked his ash in the tray. 'You're a card you are, Delphie, but I wouldn't have you any other way, and that's the truth.'

Feeling the tension in the room ease slightly, it was Dottie's turn to speak. 'Thank you, Mémère, if it hadn't been for you teaching me French and being the most stubborn person I have ever met, I wouldn't have got the job at the War Office in the first place.'

At this Delphine looked pleased.

'But it seems to me you have given up so much for others, I'd like to know if you could go back in time, what would you have done differently?'

Delphine huffed, then made a face as though she was considering her answer. 'Not so much, because really I had a good life. Before I met your grandfather, I lived in a beautiful maison de maître overlooking the bay of St Malo. My parents were well educated as was I, fluent in English and eager to become a teacher, perhaps at a school for young ladies. I was all set to go to Paris where I would study the arts, something regarded as avant-garde by many. But I was lucky to have parents who supported my dreams, my mother especially. She loved to paint and sing, her knowledge of literature was astounding and my fall from grace hurt her more than anyone. But I do not regret throwing it all away for a farmer's son, how could I reject a love like ours, or that of my beautiful children?' A glance towards Paulette then she continued.

'There were hard times, the saddest times, joyful and wonderful times too and for these I am thankful. Of course, I sometimes wondered "what if", but not too often, not enough to make me restless. There is only one thing that has troubled me that I could do nothing about.'

Once again, all eyes focused on Delphine.

'The way women were treated by the French government

was so unfair. We wanted, as you say "to do our bit" but times and convention were always against us and what we were permitted to do was quickly swept under the carpet after the war. Doors were closed on a glimpse of independence, the tables turned in the most cruel and unjust manner. Then, when my parents died, my brother took everything. I should have questioned the unfairness of the situation, put up a fight, shown some resistance. If I had a wish now, apart from an end to the war, it would be for women like you, Dottie, to be treated fairly and equally. That is all.'

Delphine sipped her wine and as Dottie swallowed down a ball of what felt like anger and hurt, she noticed her grandmother looked tired and somewhat lost.

'Well I promise that I'm going to make you proud, Mémère, no matter what it is they have me do, even if it's only staying up day and night typing notes. Somehow, I will do my bit and prove that we can be just as useful as men and hold our own, they won't know what's hit them.' Dottie leant over and engulfed Delphine in a hug then looked across the table and asked her mother a question.

'Mama, do you understand a bit better now why I have to go? I don't want to make you sad and scared but it's important so please, will you give me your blessing?' Dottie clung on to Delphine and willed Paulette to smile, say yes, and let her go.

'Of course, I understand. I am blessed to know two wonderful women, who are braver and stronger than I could ever hope to be, so I promise, I will not let you down. I will hold up my love and shine it so brightly that you find your way back home to us. And I will be proud, Dottie, of you and all the women everywhere who stand together, side by side, hand in hand.'

Paulette reached across the table and took her daughters hand in hers, to have it covered by Delphine's and once he'd wiped a tear from his eyes, Tommy's huge palm rested on top of all three.

In the silence of the blackened room, as the grandfather clock ticked and the candle flickered, Dottie silently recited Mr Churchill's words, the ones she had seen in the secret notes she had typed, a transcript of an order given directly to the leader of a new and secret organisation. They were going to 'set Europe ablaze' and the words alone had started a fire in her heart. And unbeknown to her beloved family, she'd decided there and then to put her name forward so if she passed the tests and made the grades, she, Dorothy Tanner, an ordinary girl from the East End, was going to be a part of it.

8

GHOSTS

CHÂTEAUBRIANT, FRANCE, 2005

Maude was sitting cross-legged on the end of Dottie's bed, her brow knotted in concentration as she wrote down everything she remembered from the earlier car-confessionals. Her pen was bobbing up and down while Dottie was beginning to get restless. It had been a long day and she was looking forward to dinner, however, Maude had insisted on making notes.

Propped up against her pillows, Dottie luxuriated in her surroundings and congratulated herself on choosing their hotel well. Their twin room was modern and elegant within the converted stone grain warehouse, an inconsequential building that during the war Dottie would have passed many times, never knowing that one day she would be a guest within its contemporary walls. There had been so much she hadn't known then, as she'd cycled through the streets on her way to a rendezvous, skirting patrols and risking her life for what was hidden beneath the bread in her pannier.

Dottie allowed a smile as she observed Maude who was almost the same age she had been back then. Regardless of the fact she had made it home in one piece, her dear mama's torch guiding the way, Dottie would never ever let Maude walk into the lion's den, of that she was sure. How the tables turned, hindsight bringing with it a glimmer of wisdom and the pain of understanding.

Had Dottie not been a tough old boot she would have wept there and then for Maman Paulette because now she got it, the desperate almost consuming desire to keep your child safe. What she had failed to grasp, maybe stubbornly refused to even consider, was a mother's innate love, bundled up with fear and hopes and the terror of never seeing your precious child again. On that night in the kitchen as Paulette had wept, she had regarded her twenty-one-year-old daughter as just that. Dottie hadn't comprehended it then, but she did now.

The past was definitely creeping up on her, like a benevolent spirit seeking to enlighten and remind. In its own way the ghost of days gone by had already begun to sway Dottie, taking her hand and gently pulling her off the course she had set. After the war years, riddled with fear and uncertainty, Dottie had embraced the beckoning future, following the signpost that pointed to self-preservation, resolutely sticking to the path.

Dottie gave a silent tut. This trip was supposed to be a practical way of ticking some boxes, doing the right thing in her inimitable no-nonsense way, not sending her soft. The last thing she wanted was to have regrets and should her body pack in any time soon, Dottie couldn't bear to be trapped inside it, tormented by a fully functioning brain. That would be worse than the opposite. Anyway, she had planned for either eventuality but at the moment, her demise was way down the list. There was life in this contrary old dog yet.

To that end, knowing that wounds would be opened before they could heal again, Dottie had mentally prepared for the trip, or so she'd thought. What she hadn't expected was the urge she had to wipe her mother's tears, to say she was sorry, that had been a complete surprise. Dottie hoped there wouldn't be any more tears, but it was raking over the past that had done it, however lightly. And this was only the start.

As they'd entered the town earlier that day, the essence of a latter-day scene, set in the kitchen above the shop, careered headlong into the present. Slowly, she began recognising landmarks and buildings, solid bricks and mortar, stubborn memorials holding on to their secrets, guardians of history. It had been like a sensory explosion, a time bomb going off in Dottie's mind. For this reason, she thought it might be prudent to proceed with caution and watch out for landmines. It was imperative she survived the trip to France, the second time around.

Shuffling slightly to adjust her position, disturbing Maude momentarily, Dottie hoped the little scribbler would hurry up then they could have a nice G&T and watch some television, or maybe listen to the radio. Maude continued in her task, Dottie remained unquenched.

It was too quiet in the room and gave the mind time to wander, daring her to rub shoulders with ghosts who, alerted to her return, were gathering in the corners of Dottie's memory, not quite uninvited guests, more unexpected or unfashionably early. She'd sensed them as they arrived in the town, standing sentry, saluting her as she passed by.

Once they had checked into the hotel in the centre of Châteaubriant, Maude and Dottie had enjoyed a relaxed lunch in the restaurant and then spent the rest of the afternoon reading in the small garden at the rear. Dottie hadn't wanted to take a stroll like Maude suggested. She'd done a bit too much in Paris, not that she would admit it so instead, blamed it on the heat of the afternoon and the need to gather her thoughts before they embarked on their pilgrimage.

This was partly true because as they had driven through the outer suburbs, nothing had seemed familiar, the landscape contradicting the images Dottie had held for so long. She hadn't expected the sprawling housing estates and a large retail park that seemed to go on forever, where restaurants and shops lined the carriageway and camouflaged the older medieval heart of the town. It had been stupid really, considering how the city in which she lived had changed but for some reason, she'd expected the past to have stood still, as though waiting for her return.

It was as they neared the centre that the hairs began to prickle on her arms, recognising instantly the train station, such an important place in her memory. Next, the Gothic spire of Église Saint-Nicolas rose above the rooftops and speared the cloudless blue sky. The imposing church still standing proud and firm, almost as defiant as the residents that had once flocked through its doors to receive blessings and in some cases, safe haven. But it was the sight of the Hotel de Ville that flipped Dottie's stomach.

The office of the present *maire*, with its creamy walls bathed in midday sun, three Tricolor flags flying high and gently fluttering in the breeze looked serene, a symbol of La Republique, a place of authority. Dottie's memory flashed back to forlorn grey walls wearing a shroud of shame. If a building could hang its head, then all those years ago, beneath the flags bearing the Nazi swastika, the windows of the occupied *maire* could not bear to look the townspeople in the eye.

Seeing it again, and yes, feeling the evil that had once emanated from the hub of such a fearsome regime had been a shock to the system. Perhaps that was why Dottie had preferred to retreat inside the hotel and take things one step at a time.

．　．　．

Maude closed her journal and clicked the top of her pen, signalling, much to Dottie's delight, that her jottings were complete.

'Right then, I think that's everything. Shall I read it out to you?' Maude unfolded her legs accompanied by a pained expression.

'Dear God, no! The last thing I want is to hear it all again. Just get me a drink before I die of thirst, and I don't mean water.'

Maude rolled her eyes and chucked the journal onto the eiderdown. 'Oh, flipping heck, my bones have seized up... hold on while I limber up.' Maude rubbed her shins vigorously. 'So what's it to be, a glass of red or a G&T?'

'I'll have one of each, and some of those nice nutty snacks they left for us and then we can order room service. I don't fancy going down to the restaurant again. Is that okay?'

'Yes, room service is fine although I did spot a kebab shop as we drove in... dare we sneak one up to the room later?'

At this Dottie brightened. 'Oh yes, lets. I haven't had one in ages and I'm sure nobody will notice as long as you're quick and don't take the lift, they'll make it pong.'

They both giggled and Dottie rubbed her hands together with glee as she watched Maude prepare their drinks. This was so much fun, being here with her granddaughter, girls together and for a second, she wondered if they should have brought Jean. The notion was swiftly banished because vegetarians and kebabs were not conducive to enjoying one's guilty pleasures or listening to the hoo-ha when you broke hotel rules. No, they were right to leave Jean at home. Dottie's conscience was therefore swiftly and thoroughly appeased.

Maude carried the drinks over, placing the glasses on the bedside table before going back for her own. 'Shuffle over, big bum, and make room.' Relaxing against the plump pillows she took a sip and closed her eyes.

 relaxed and enjoyed the tranquillity, not in the
oy the hum of traffic beyond the windows or the
ner guests as they walked along the corridor. She'd
d the bustle of the city or a town, as long as she had a
bub⌐⌐ ⌐ retreat to now and then, so when Maude popped it by
asking a question, Dottie couldn't contain a sigh.

'You know what I love? The way the French say my name, in
fact I love the accent and how everything sounds so much more
romantic when they speak English... but then again, you just
chatter on like a local yokel so there's no need.'

'Well, forgive me for saying so, Maude, but if you'd tried a bit
harder at school and not been so stubborn then you'd be fluent
by now. I did try to teach you, remember.'

Maude swivelled sideways. 'I know, it's one of my regrets and
I do wish I'd listened especially now we are here. I feel a bit
disloyal to Paulette and Delphine, never mind you!'

Reaching over Dottie patted Maude's leg. 'Please don't feel
that way, you are far too young to have regrets and I shouldn't
complain. I wanted you to be a free spirit, didn't I? Lord knows I
encouraged you enough and if I'm honest I was very conflicted,
you know, with the desire to respect my heritage versus the pain
of speaking a language that reminded me of what I'd lost and
left behind.'

'Oh, Gran, that's so sad. I didn't know you felt like that but
I'm starting to realise there are lots of things I don't understand
and I'm a bit worried all this is going to upset you.' Maude
wrapped her arm through her grandmother's and snuggled
closer.

Dottie gave a reassuring reply. 'There's no need to worry, I
promise.'

Maude took a sip of wine then rested her head on Dottie's
shoulder. 'Okay, then can I ask you something?'

'You can always ask me anything you want, you know that, whether I'll answer is another matter. You know that too.'

Maude tutted. 'Mmm, I do. The thing is... I get the feeling that when you were here, there was someone special, someone you miss, or are you referring to your comrades in the Maquis when you mention loss?'

Dottie felt her body stiffen if only for a second, then she bent over and pecked Maude on the side of the head. 'You are very perceptive, dear, and yes I did, in fact I lost two people who I loved dearly but in very different ways. And then there were my friends, the other fighters, such brave young men and women who were betrayed...'

Dottie's voice cracked causing Maude to sit up straight, quickly placing her glass on the table before hugging Dottie tight. 'I'm sorry, Gran, I didn't mean to upset you, let's talk about something else.'

Dottie managed to raise her arm from beneath the bear hug and patted Maude gently. 'No need to apologise, it's all coming back to me in such a rush and it seems that now I've opened the proverbial floodgates I can't stop the tide of...' Dottie touched her heart, 'hurt and longing, and anger I suppose. But I want you to hear it, from me, my way, and not necessarily what we did as a movement. You can get films and books about the Resistance from anywhere, and I would hope they taught you all about the war at school. They did, didn't they?'

Maude nodded. 'Yes, some, but not in depth and in a way that I could relate to it, like you say, I know more from the telly and Remembrance Day. That's when it really hits home.'

Dottie bristled. 'Well that's simply not good enough and annoyingly, beyond my control. But for me, it goes much deeper than history lessons, Maudie, and I have this tremendous urge for you to know what it was like then, for a young woman. I was around the age you are now, sent off to another country where the life expectancy of an agent was six weeks, that's if I survived the parachute drop.'

Maude gasped. 'No way, seriously?'

Dottie merely nodded. 'You see it changed me, what I saw and did, losing people in the cruellest of ways and even though I will never apologise for my actions during that time, or for the person I became afterwards, I'd like you out of anyone to understand.'

'I'd be honoured to listen, Gran, and I must write everything down, I get that now. Then I can keep it forever and show my kids, too.'

Dottie smiled. 'Well that would be lovely, to know that everyone's names are never forgotten. That would make me very happy.'

Maude released her grip and gave Dottie a kiss on the cheek. 'Well I can't wait to hear about it all, especially you jumping out of a plane, seriously that's epic.'

Laughing, Dottie untangled herself and took a gulp of her gin and once she was more relaxed, decided to lighten the mood. 'I'll tell you what *will* be epic, a kebab. All this chattering has given me an appetite so get a wiggle on. You can pretend you're an agent who has to get two giant packages past the Boche sentries on reception, I'll keep lookout.'

Maude laughed and swung her legs off the bed then saluted as she stood. 'Mission accepted... my treat.'

Dottie watched as Maude searched for her shoes that as usual had been flung into separate corners of the room. Finally located, as was her shoulder bag, Maude set off for the kebab van with strict orders to get plenty of hot sauce and a portion of frites if they had them. When the door to the room finally closed, Dottie flopped against her pillow. She needed a little chat, this time with herself.

.   .   .

Two humongous kebabs eaten and the bag containing the offending containers deposited in a bin on the corridor below, Dottie and Maude were in their beds and preparing to settle down. The window was open slightly to allow in some air while the curtains were partially drawn, leaving a crack of light that streamed into the room, casting a silver beam onto the carpet.

They had stayed well away from any maudlin reminiscences while they ate, however, bowing to her own advice, given earlier while Maude was out, Dottie resolved to start as she meant to go on.

She had spent a lifetime resisting but it was time to face a simple fact. Dottie had to surrender, otherwise what was the point in returning to France? In the grand scheme, maybe it would be a good thing, to let it wash over her. After all, she'd felt so alive back then despite the prospect of capture, torture and death. Another fact that loomed large was her age, maybe she was nearing the end or could rumble on for years, so in that case perhaps an injection of nostalgia would invigorate her. It was worth a try.

Looking over to the shape of her granddaughter who was unusually quiet, she asked, 'Are you sleepy, Maude?' Dottie hoped the answer would be no.

A yawn preceded the reply. 'My eyes are but my blood is full of spices and seems determined to keep my brain awake, why? Don't tell me you want to read. It's really late, you know.'

'No, I don't, but I do want to tell you a little story before we set off on our tour tomorrow... it's about your name.'

Another yawn. 'But I know that story. You were vexed because Granddad insisted on calling Mum after his mother, and you absolutely hated the name Jean, so when I was born you guilted Mum into calling me Maude. Then, at the christening party, when the vicar asked where Maude came from, you confessed it was the name of your first pet, a Jack Russell.

Mum went ballistic that I was named after a dog. It still cracks me up, the thought of poor Mum's face when you told her. You are so mean, Gran, but in a wicked way.'

Maude was laughing out loud and so was Dottie who, once she'd wiped her eyes, decided to set the record straight.

'Well actually, the truth is you're not named after a dog... really, as if I'd do that.'

At this, Maude sat up and turned on the bedside light, causing them both to shield their eyes for a moment.

'Seriously... so who am I named after?'

Dottie sighed. 'Just turn off that blasted light and I'll explain.' There was a click then partial darkness. 'You, my dear grandchild, are named after a precious friend, someone I absolutely adored and idolised. Her name was Lady Mary Eliza Balfour, Maude to her friends and I'm proud and honoured to say that I was one of them. She was beautiful, clever, refined, mad as a box of frogs, loyal and brave, and a day hasn't gone by when I haven't thought about her and what happened.'

'Oh, Gran, she sounds... wonderful. Were you a bit in love with her, it sounds like you were?'

Dottie smiled into the darkness and wiped away a tear. 'Oh yes, totally smitten but not in the way you mean, but then again everyone loved her, it was impossible not to. Now shush while I tell you all about her, I'll get to what happened in my own good time.'

Dottie glanced over as Maude shuffled and turned on her side, her hands were tucked under her pillow. Aware now of being under close scrutiny, Dottie remained where she was, lying under the duvet, staring at the ceiling, travelling through the darkness, back in time, to her first meeting with Maude.

9

MAUDE

THE SCOTTISH HIGHLANDS, 1942

Dottie thought she had never been so cold in all her life as she was bounced around in the back of an army truck, clinging on for dear life as they trundled along winding lanes that were peppered with holes, no, craters. There were five women in total huddled inside and sitting well away from the open back, while up front next to the driver, was a sullen-faced sergeant who had barked orders at them from the second he appeared on the station platform. Not being able to hear his voice or see his scowl was the only upside of being in the back of a bone shaker. Focusing on keeping her suitcase wedged between her knees, Dottie grasped on to anything that kept her body firmly in place on the wooden seat.

It was early April but the northern hemisphere clearly hadn't received the memo that it was time to warm up and Dottie deeply regretted her choice of clothing because it was no match for the bitter temperature and howling wind that chilled the air further. A quick glance at her companions told her they had all made the same mistake but then again, with rationing and mostly utility clothing to choose from, none of them were likely to arrive prepared for a hike up Everest.

Dottie wondered if the others had the same leaden feeling in their hearts as she, or an apple-sized lump in their throats or a voice in their head that kept saying, 'What have you done?' Dottie did not dare think of her mum who, since that night around the table had been stoical and selfless. Even so, Paulette's voice had been a touch too cheerful as she helped Dottie pack and choose a travelling outfit. She'd been beyond grateful for her mum's bravery because it helped bolster her own flagging enthusiasm, or maybe it was just nerves and sentimentality getting in the way.

As she fussed with the clothes brush, Paulette had told Dottie she looked perfect in her two-piece, almost mustard-yellow suit, and black court shoes she wore for work, polished up so they shone. Her dad had bought her a tan leather suitcase, brand new, far too big really because inside all she had was her clothing as specified, no personal effects were allowed.

The pain of leaving her family was still raw and stung like her frozen toes and feet. Dottie had refused to let them accompany her to the station and instead said goodbye at the door of the café. Her dad with his wobbly bottom lip, her mum unable to speak while her face drowned in tears and Delphine, skin ashen, lips set in a stiff line, her ice-blue eyes bright and focused. After she had kissed her parents, Dottie clung to her grand-mother's bony frame that despite its outward frailty afforded a vice-like grip, spindly arms wrapped tightly around her.

When she finally let go, Delphine whispered in Dottie's ear. 'I am so proud of you my brave, brave girl. Never forget how much we love you. Come home to us soon, we will be waiting.'

How Dottie had made it to the bus stop without looking back she would never know but once she had boarded the number nine and knew she was out of sight, the shaking subsided as did the tears that welled. Telling herself this was the start of a great adventure, Dottie had spent the rest of the journey staring out of the window, trying not to imagine what was ahead of her or how they were coping at home. They were sad she'd miss her twenty-second birthday the following month, but it was just a day. This was war and just like the thousands of men who had said goodbye to their loved ones and faced the unknown, she was determined to face whatever was thrown at her.

After the jeep rattled over a cattle grid then thankfully came to an abrupt halt, they alighted one by one, all of them landing in a quaggy puddle, mud splattering their stockings. When it was her turn, Dottie sighed, ignoring the squelch, more relieved to be stood and in one piece as she took in her surroundings.

Encompassed by pine forest, she would have been completely disorientated had she not known from the station sign that they were in Aviemore, the mighty Cairngorms that rose in the distance confirming her Highland location. Before her was Glenmore House, its name carved into the sandstone above the doorway of the huge Victorian hunting lodge. With whitewashed walls and pointed apexes, the sash windows like watchful eyes looking over the vast estate, guarding what was to be her home for the months ahead.

The sergeant in charge had lost none of his bluster during the journey and it was clear he was starting as he meant to go on, ordering everyone to gather their belongings, form a line, two by two, and make their way inside. The women obeyed and walked briskly, as did Dottie who was glad to be out of the biting wind that carried a hint of icy rain.

There had been no time to chat to anyone on the station platform and Dottie found it ironic that five women had made such a long and solitary train journey when in fact they could have helped each other pass the time. But when you were told to tell no one who you were or where you were going, it was hardly surprising that silence had been Dottie's only friend.

There had been a few swear words and yelps, the odd, 'Are you okay?' during the truck ride to the lodge but once inside, still wearing looks of bewilderment, the women remained silent. The wood-panelled entrance hall with a wide uncarpeted staircase was lit by wall lamps that glowed in the fading light and here, the sergeant ordered them to wait for further instructions then left them alone, the sound of his boots pounding the floorboards as he marched off.

Dottie sensed everyone was relieved by his absence as they took the opportunity to warm up in front of an open fire, a small comfort in a very strange place. Within minutes, pinched white faces and fingers soon looked rosier and wind whipped lips loosened, as one by one, they introduced themselves.

The boldest of them was a stocky brunette who had turned her back to the fire but kept her arms behind her back, hands facing the roaring flames. She reminded Dottie of a tweed-clad schoolteacher as she spoke in a broad Yorkshire accent.

'Well, he were a right bundle of laughs, weren't he? The miserable old get. Thank God he's buggered off. Let's hope it's the last we see of him. I'm Penny by the way, Penny Perkins and I'm from Leeds. Where are you lot from?'

There were mutterings of hello then a well-spoken voice from the left drew everyone's attention to a petite blonde with flushed cheeks, who raised her hand as she spoke. 'My name's Camilla Ludlow and I'm from Winchester, very nice to meet you all.'

Dottie went next and then it was the turn of the two women on either side of Penny. The first stepped forward as she introduced herself as Ivy Doyle from Glasgow, her accent strong and her voice just as bold which made Dottie feel quite envious of her assumed confidence. She was followed by the remaining member of their group.

'Hello, I'm Lily Duncan and I hail from Hampshire, Portsmouth to be precise.'

There was no shaking of hands or anything formal, but it seemed to have broken the ice as Penny wondered if they'd be fed and Camilla said she desperately needed the loo. Their chatter was interrupted by the arrival of two uniformed women carrying clipboards and any noise in the room quickly petered out.

The first to speak was a stern-looking woman with piercing blue eyes, who stood almost to attention as she addressed them. Her smudge brown uniform, similar to the one Dottie used to wear for work added to her air of authority.

'Good evening, ladies. My name is Captain Walsh, and this is Sergeant Morgan and we will be looking after you during your time here. I'm sure you're tired after your respective journeys so once I have shown you to your quarters, dinner will be served in the dining room which is situated down that corridor to your right.' Heads swivelled and nodded. 'Seven o'clock prompt. Cook doesn't cater for dilly-dallies. Breakfast tomorrow will also be at seven, you will have your first briefing at eight in the conference room, the blue door to your left.' All eyes followed her finger then rested back on her face. 'Now, please follow Sergeant Morgan who will allocate your rooms. Save any questions for tomorrow when I'm sure most will be answered accordingly.' With this she stepped to the side and nodded to her deputy who spun in her polished black shoes and headed upstairs.

Hurriedly picking up their suitcases, everyone followed. Dottie, keeping up the rear, still wasn't sure if this was the start of a great adventure or a terrible dream. There were so many thoughts racing about in her head that were searching for reassurance. The women seemed friendly enough, and although the captain was quite abrupt, she wasn't fearsome or unkind. Like the officers in Whitehall.

Maybe it was something Dottie would have to get used to, like that strange feeling in her chest, a deep hole that ached whenever she thought of home. She did manage a smile though, when she glanced at the four sets of legs in front of her, all splattered with mud, wearing shoes that were in dire need of a bloody good scrub.

At the top of the first landing the sergeant halted and tapped on the first door of the corridor. 'Doyle, Ludlow, you're in here.'

Both women looked unsure of whether to enter or wait.

'Well don't just stand there. Get inside and unpack otherwise you'll miss dinner and you'll need to change, we have certain standards to maintain.' A cursory glance at their shoes gave them the hint.

At this both women nodded, first at the sergeant and then at the other women. Ivy chanced a quick wave as Camilla turned the handle and then both disappeared inside the room.

'Right, Perkins and Duncan, you're just down here.'

They all followed along the rather gloomy corridor, their footsteps muffled by a worn floral carpet that might once have been blue. The walls held no cheer either, the bottom halves covered with slate grey Lincrusta made slightly less depressing by the faded, peeling Victorian flock hung above the dado rail.

When they stopped outside their room, Penny and Lily scurried inside without a by your leave, obviously heeding Sergeant Morgan's previous instructions. This left just Dottie, roomless and partnerless.

Sergeant Morgan rested her clipboard against her chest as she set off again. 'Right, off we go. You're up here, Tanner.'

It occurred to Dottie that had it not been 1942, she might have been starring in a dreary Gothic novel, and as they climbed another set of stairs not only was she dreading sleeping alone in a huge strange house, images of Rebecca began to haunt her.

On the next landing there were four more doors much closer together which indicated to Dottie that the rooms would be far smaller, and she would be on her own. When Sergeant Morgan rested outside the first and inclined her head, Dottie sucked in a breath and without waiting to be told to scrub her shoes and not to be late, twisted the door handle.

Sergeant Morgan, however, clearly enjoyed the last word and was beginning to sound like a broken record. 'Your room-mate arrived earlier this afternoon, but I'll leave you to introduce yourself. Remember, seven sharp, smarten up.'

And with that she ticked the sheet of paper on the clipboard before walking briskly back the way she came. Overcome with shyness, Dottie hovered, her hand had already half turned the knob so all she had to do was twist and enter. Not only had she never stayed away from home, she had also never shared a room in her life so her previous trepidation was now replaced by the desire for solitude. There was nothing for it because whoever was inside would think she was odd, hovering in the corridor so taking a sharp breath inwards, Dottie pushed open the door.

For a moment she was enveloped in a smoky haze and then assailed by a heavenly scent that mingled with the tobacco fumes. Before she had time to get her bearings her attention was drawn to one of the beds placed under the eaves and there, lay a vision of complete loveliness.

Dottie gazed at what she could only describe as Hollywood screen siren, dressed in what looked like pale green silk, the folds of the tea dress draped across the eiderdown. Lounging elegantly, flicking through a magazine while the other hand held a cigarette holder, the goddess immediately looked up and when her eyes alighted on Dottie, red lips smiled while the English rose face took on a delighted expression. Then came the voice, deep and plummy, yet animated and friendly all at once. Jumping from the bed, the goddess strode over and held out her hand as she spoke.

'Oh, thank goodness... I was beginning to think I'd been abandoned in this little nest and I can't bear to be alone but here you are, my lovely room-mate, at last. I'm Mary Balfour, by the way, Maude to my friends and you are...?'

'Dorothy Tanner, but everyone calls me Dottie.' As they shook hands Dottie was aware of Maude's long elegant fingers wrapped around hers, a delicate hand that felt light as a feather, skin like velvet, pale enough to expose blue veins.

'Well, then Dottie it is, and I know we are going to be firm friends and have a riot even though we are trapped in Northanger Abbey in the middle of God knows where. Now, let me help you unpack and then we can go downstairs for dinner, I'm famished, aren't you?'

Dottie followed as Maude chatted on.

'I bagged the bed nearest the window so I could have a sneaky puff during the night, but I don't mind swapping and look, I saved you oodles of space in the wardrobe.' Maude glided over and pulled open the door which was almost full of clothes which she swept to one side, the wire hangers screeching as they made room. 'This is such a lark, just like being back at school, now where shall we start? Here, you pass your things and I'll hang them up.'

Dottie allowed Maude to take her suitcase which she plopped onto the bed, and as the buckles were undone and belongings unfolded and stashed away, any nerves that lingered were replaced by a tiny bubble of excitement.

Maude wanted to know 'everything' about Dottie and where she came from and was beside herself to be in the company of a real-life East Ender. By the time they'd located the bathroom and followed orders to scrub up, and Maude had squirted the heavenly scent of Femme de Rochas all over Dottie, it was time for dinner. As they headed downstairs, Maude linked her arm through Dottie's and chattered away about handsome men in uniform and the whereabouts of the local pub, you'd have thought they were in a hotel, not a Special Operations Executive training camp.

Brushing all thoughts of what was to come aside, Dottie focused on Maude and the aroma of food that lured them to the dining room. Tomorrow was another day, one where she hoped to telephone her parents and let them know she had arrived safely. Beyond that everything else was a fog, an adventure waiting to happen, a whole new exciting stage in Dottie's life and the best part, her new friend the goddess would be along for the ride.

10

KILLER TANNER

CHÂTEAUBRIANT, FRANCE, 2005

Dottie was in the almost deserted dining room, waiting for Maude when she finally came down for breakfast, fresh-faced but with tired eyes. Her cheesecloth dress flowed as she rushed towards the table, the little bells that dangled from the multitude of bracelets on her wrist tinkled with each stride.

'Sorry, Gran, I was out for the count and didn't even hear you get up... you should've given me a nudge.' Maude took her place opposite and poured a cup of coffee.

'It's fine, we had a late night and you looked too peaceful to disturb but my, you do snore! I think I may need some earplugs.' Dottie dipped her croissant in her hot chocolate and ignored the incredulous look on Maude's face.

'Me! Are you joking? I thought there was a camel hiding under your bed at one point. I even considered smothering you with my pillow. Honestly, Gran, you should hear yourself.' Maude chose a pain au chocolat and took a huge bite.

'I do not snore; you must've been dreaming. Now, I hope you haven't forgotten what I told you last night, it was a lot to take in, but the most important part comes next: the training and how intensive it was. And then there's Maude. You'll understand the bond we formed and why it was so hard when we had to say goodbye. She was such a special person.' Dottie eyed Maude who was mid-chew and unable to respond immediately so nodded instead.

Taking a sip of coffee, Maude washed down the pastry and then replied. 'Yep, it's all in here,' a tap of the head, 'and later when I get time, I'll write it down so don't worry.'

'Good, just ask if anything is a bit hazy.'

There was a pause in the conversation, long enough to indicate to Dottie that her thoughtful-looking granddaughter had a question and she was working out how to ask it. 'Come on, spit it out, I know that look.'

Maude met Dottie's eyes. 'Well, not only do you snore, you talk in your sleep, too, and last night I heard you muttering a name... Vincent. Is he someone important in your story because I've never heard you mention him before?'

Hearing his name spoken out loud after all this time caused Dottie to catch her breath, annoyed by the tremor in her own voice as she answered. 'He's the other person who I loved and lost, Vincent was the leader of our cell and he was murdered like the others.'

'Oh, Gran, I'm sorry. Trust me and my big mouth.' Maude reached over and for a second or two their fingers entwined until Dottie broke the spell.

'Don't apologise, Maude, I'm fine and I will explain all about Vincent, but for now I'm going to get some more of those little pastries, back in a tick.'

When she returned, Dottie was relieved that Maude had taken the hint and moved on to another subject.

'It really touched me, you know, what you said about Great-great-grandma Delphine and Great-grandma Paulette. I wish I'd known them. And all those soldiers going off to war, they were so brave but women were too, and then there were ones who stayed behind and, to use your phrase, kept the home fires burning, they were all courageous but in different ways. I'm starting to get that now.'

Maude fiddled with a packet of butter then began peeling away the foil lid. 'And I can't imagine how heartbreaking it was, watching your loved one go and then getting on with it at home. You were so young when you joined up, and then set off for Scotland. It must have been tough, plus you missed your parents and had no idea where you'd be sent. I am completely in awe of you, I really am.'

'I thought you'd *always* been in awe of me.' Dottie couldn't resist teasing.

Maude sighed. 'Yes, that's true but now you're like superwoman status, not just an awesome gran. Satisfied?'

Dottie smiled and nodded, then ripped open a roll and spread it with the butter that Maude had opened, then a dollop of jam. 'Yes, I am. Now eat your breakfast. I want to go back to Renazé and on the way I'll explain how I ended up there. I hope it's not changed too much, and I recognise things. Châteaubriant is virtually the same in the centre but the rest, it's like another world.'

'I'm sure there will be bits and bobs that jog your memory, and I'll take lots of photos too so we can make an album of the trip. I might even be able to use them for my work.'

Dottie poured more coffee. 'You and your photos, but that would be lovely, a nice keepsake. Now hurry up. It's almost lunchtime.'

At this Maude rolled her eyes and grabbed a croissant. 'Gran, it's not even ten, stop being a stress head. We've got loads of time and I want to enjoy our holiday, have a bit of a chill if you even know what that is.'

'Of course I do, I'm not a fossil yet.'

'I know, tell me a bit more about you and Maude, and SOE

training. There's nobody about. I'll get some more coffee and then you can get cracking.'

Dottie chuckled. She couldn't help being eager, even though she felt slightly nervous too. But she was here now at last, a grown woman, not a naïve young girl. That's how she saw herself back then. A girl who'd never been away from her parents, thrust into a strange world and with an innocence that belied the skills she had learned in a relatively short space of time. Dottie had been prepared to risk her life and, thankfully, at the time was oblivious that most agents survived only six weeks, some less.

There were so many things she wanted to tell Maude, supposed wisdom she needed to impart. What was the point in it all, the mistakes and sacrifices, if someone couldn't learn from them and the only way to do that was to talk, explain, unburden oneself? Triumphs were all well and good, they set examples too, but so did the dark side of life. She so wanted Maude to be proud, stand tall, stride out, be herself for a while before joining her life to another. Maybe if she could give her granddaughter an insight into what those who had gone before had endured, then going forward it would embolden her, keep that fire alive in her belly. Maude wasn't shy by any means, she was talented, intelligent, kind, funny and an all-round lovely young woman, but that's what worried Dottie. Was Maude too nice, too malleable, and too easily led? She had great potential to succeed or would she settle for an easy option, Lachlan to be precise?

Maude returned with a full pot of coffee and some cereal which she proceeded to drown in milk.

'Right, I'm ready... come on, Killer Tanner, tell me all about secret agent training, I'm all ears.' Maude spooned cereal into her mouth and waited.

'Okay, I suppose I'd better get it over and done with. What I'm going to tell you might come as a shock in places, but as I explain what I learned and then what I did, I promise to be truthful. It's up to you if you judge me or not. I can't ask or expect you not to. What I did was of my own free will, just like your opinions are your own. Do we understand each other?'

Maude, wide-eyed and with a mouth full of muesli, nodded her agreement.

Dottie took a deep breath and prepared for another round of unburdening. But she had survived a wartime France riddled with danger, for almost two years, then lived through peacetime only to find herself back where it all began. And just like last time, she would have to buckle up, take a breath and dive into her memories, and face her fears head on.

11

MAUDE AND THE TANNERS

LONDON, NEW YEAR'S EVE 1942

Dottie's eyes were drooping as she listened to *Workers Playtime* on the Home Service, the fire in the grate fending off the chill while opposite, Delphine concentrated on darning socks.

It was such a pleasure to be home, and had she been allowed, Dottie would've gone downstairs to help in the café just so she could spend more time with her parents because every second counted, it really did. Instead they had insisted she rest, she was too thin and looked tired, and the bruises on her legs were a sight for sore eyes, something that had raised many questions around the kitchen table, none of them she was able to answer. How could she tell them where she'd been or what she'd been taught? Part of Dottie wanted to explain because she was sure they'd be in awe of their little sparrow while the other part knew it would scare them to death. They didn't deserve that or for their heads to be filled with images while she was away, and that was another thing, for how long.

When she said goodbye to them in two days' time, Dottie had no idea when she'd be back. They had been told to report to an address in the West End, a holding house where they would be given their code names and final orders before being moved to a forwarding base in Sussex, then dropped into France. It was the culmination of months of gruelling training that had begun on their first full day in Scotland, where the skills she had learned were designed to keep her alive or end the lives of others.

The journey from Scotland to the New Forest had seemed to last forever, but Dottie and Maude both agreed that their new billet was much nicer and a whole lot warmer than the chilly Highlands. Hidden in the grounds of a country estate, the cottage had been their home for the past two months and compared to the rigours of Glenmore House and then a stint at Ringway Airport in Cheshire for parachute training, it was a doddle.

Basically, they'd lived in a make-believe world. F-Section was solely for agents being sent to France where they would work behind enemy lines. The intense training prepared them for a clandestine life, learning a range of techniques so they could operate in the field, communicate with other networks and London. Consequently, Dottie and Maude were adept at making imprints of keys, picking locks, and more than capable of burglary. Hopefully, the skills they'd learned to complement their training in Scotland would keep them alive and prevent them from making stupid mistakes that would mark them out as agents. It was the simplest of things that could get you killed, like asking for black coffee or looking the wrong way when you crossed the road. They had to think and act French which was why from the moment they arrived on the estate, that was the spoken language at all times, even in private.

It would have been easy to break the rules but others had done so, up in Scotland, and the consequence of that was failing the course and being sent to the cooler, another mausoleum on another isolated estate in the Highlands. According to rumour, that's where you would remain for the duration of the war, so that all Glenmore's secrets and training methods would be secure. Dottie and Maude had agreed, in French, that they hadn't come all this way and achieved so much to get packed off to a Highland hotel for losers, regardless of the three decent meals a day and stunning scenery.

Parachute training had been the least arduous, for Dottie anyway. Even though they'd practised over and over, she was getting used to being bawled out, maybe she had perforated eardrums or something but a daily beasting was water off a duck's back.

It was hard to believe she was the girl who used to blub if she was told off and sent to the back of the class by the teacher, Mrs Hitchen. This new Dottie had recently jumped from a static balloon and then an aeroplane, 400 feet above Tatton Park in Cheshire, just about missing the lake and landing with a wallop into a field of surprised-looking sheep. Or that she'd endured and survived a mock interrogation, been strip-searched and kicked, handcuffed, had her face slapped, her hair pulled and the verbal abuse... Mrs Hitchen was a pussycat in comparison.

The hardest part of training without a doubt had been in Scotland where Dottie had faced her toughest challenges both mentally and physically, thrown in at the deep end like all the others, men and women alike.

Conversely, she'd relished that aspect, being pitted against the men, and had striven to hold her own. It had occurred to her during survival training that out there in the wilderness, when you were cold, wet, starving and alone that gender didn't matter. The person that survived would be the one who found shelter, could light a fire and catch, kill and prepare a rabbit, and if they could navigate their way back to the starting point first, it was a bonus. Dottie carried this theory throughout her training.

Even weapon handling allowed her to excel, it was a skill that allowed her to hit the target well, same with the art of sabotage. She could set a charge and knew how to demolish a building or blow up a bridge or railway line with explosives as well as the man in line beside her. Dottie could move with stealth, plan escape routes, read a map, use Morse code, and she truly believed she could kill.

This had been the highest hurdle to jump. Dottie had worried that physically, one on one, she might fail. Their burly instructor, an ex-police officer recruited from Hong Kong and an expert in martial arts and hand-to-hand combat convinced her otherwise. Dottie now knew how to kill silently with a stroke of the blade, and that when using her firearm, the double tap method of elbow resting on hip, aim, fire two shots, should always be used by the agent. Clean, quick and sure.

It had been hard but in between the exhaustion were moments so magic, ones where they laughed till they cried, that she would remember forever and the spell was always cast by Maude.

The bedroom was filled with smoke as Dottie and Maude lay on their beds covered in mud, aching all over, too tired to speak, just about able to drag on their cigarettes while they rested weary bones.

Dottie to Maude: 'I'm starving, aren't you?'

'Mmm... but I cannot get off this bed, darling, I simply can't. I will just have to starve to death right here on this yucky eiderdown rather than face the bathtub again... scatter my ashes on the roses, won't you?'

Dottie giggled then yelped. Her stomach muscles, no, every bloody muscle in her whole body was pulled and sore. 'You are so dramatic, Maudie... you really are. I know, why don't we have a stand-up wash, we could just scrub the bits that show and have a bath tomorrow. It's only mud and nobody will know especially if we wear slacks.'

A pale arm flopped over the edge of the bed, a delicate hand dangled while a dramatic groan escaped from Maude's lips. 'Oh, darling, it's simply too much trouble so could you please just strip me off, chuck a bucket of water on me and wash me down with the sponge because I really don't have the energy.'

Dottie chuckled and then tried to cajole Maude. 'Ivy told me that it's haggis for dinner and someone got their hands on two bottles of malt, and it's jam roly-poly for pud–'

'Perhaps I might just make it down... if there's whisky.'

'And you might win at gin rummy again. That Hugh chap was most put out the other night, I've not seen him since, that's how upset he was.'

At this Maude became revitalised and flipped onto her side to face Dottie, a wicked grin spread across her face. 'Yes, I really got his goat, didn't I? Good, odious man. I think he must have passed the training and been sent on. I hope that's the last we see of him.'

Dottie turned to face Maude but winced as she did so, in real pain. 'I felt sorry for him. He had quite a bad stammer and his skin, the poor man must have had terrible acne when he was young. His face is covered with scars and it still looks quite sore.'

Maude made a sort of humming noise but didn't add to Dottie's observations.

'Why don't you like him? You didn't say you knew him.'

'Oh I don't, never met the man in my life but my gramps knows of his family, the Townshends. They have connections with the new money lot apparently, something to do with the *Daily Mail*. I forget the ghastly details. But Gramps is never wrong, and I'll have you know he was right about the king and that Simpson woman.'

'Well there you go then, can't argue with Gramps, but I thought you said you weren't a snob!'

'I'm not, darling, truly, but I just wasn't keen on him, call it intuition. His eyes were on you every time I looked over, and he's too quiet, shifty.'

'Get off with you, he was not looking, and maybe that's what they look for in male agents, the silent type.'

Again, another noise from Maude, this time a tut.

Dottie began taking off her woollen socks that ponged a bit but would last another day. 'I'd call it only knowing half a story. My mum does that all the time, comes home with a bit of a tale then makes the rest up... anyway, my tummy is rumbling and Lord knows what they have in store for us tomorrow so let's make a move.'

Maude yawned loudly. 'You slave driver, heave me up then and I'll raid the wardrobe and find something for us to wear. If I get tiddly later just throw me in bed as I am. I can get rather silly when I drink whisky, you know.'

'Yes, Maude, I know. It was me who coaxed you down from the table last week when you went all Vera Lynn on us. Now move, I mean it.' Dottie held out her hand and hauled Maude off the bed, then marvelled at how spritely and rejuvenated she'd become.

It was a good thing though because Maude's spirit and *joie de vivre* was infectious and everyone in their group adored her. Sometimes Dottie felt like a jealous schoolgirl, craving all Maude's attention, not wanting to share her with the others at mealtimes or when they lounged in the sitting room, listening to records. She'd even been jealous when one of the men, Gregory, had asked Maude to dance, which was silly really. But Dottie had never met anyone as wonderful and for however long they were together, she wanted Maude all to herself.

Two months later, the women were given their next set of

orders. Dottie had felt the ball of tension unravel when her name was called out; then after Ivy, Penny and Lily, she heard Captain Walsh call out Maude's. Camilla hadn't come down for breakfast and when they went back to their rooms later, her bed was made, and she was gone. All of them suspected she was bound for the cooler.

Only Lily went with them to the New Forest; Penny and Ivy went their separate ways, neither mentioning where they were heading to finish their training, all of them aware they were being tested at every stage and one slip up would seal their fate. You didn't really know who the friendly lady seated opposite was. The one who bounced her baby on her knee and asked you where you'd been and where you were off to. Or the man who asked for a light and then offered to take down your suitcase who was simply being kind, but then followed close behind and was still there when you came out of the ladies' toilets.

They said tearful goodbyes at Paddington Station, promising to meet again afterwards. As far as Dottie was concerned, she meant every word, even though none of them could be taken for granted.

Beaulieu was beautiful though and at least Dottie could actually say she'd seen a bit more of England, if only to herself. They'd all been allowed leave for Christmas Day, the war didn't stop for festivities and they were required at the holding flat on January the second. Here, they would be given clothing and footwear that had been donated by refugees or meticulously tailored in the French style, with labels and buttons, collars and cuffs, soles that were exactly as a seamstress or cobbler in France would have made them, nothing was left to chance. Their new identities would be revealed, and they would be provided with false papers, a cover story and a code name to be used in communications with London. The final addition to their kit would be a set of two pills, the L suicide pill, kept in a rubber cover and a Benzedrine pill to keep you awake.

All they had to do then was wait to be moved to the forwarding base and then when the moon was full and weather conditions suitable, the agents would be dropped into France and their new life would begin.

Dottie had succumbed to the heat from the fire and was starting to nod off, dribbling slightly on the cushion that she'd rested upon. Mémère Delphine, noticing she was awake, smiled and went to rise.

'Ah, the sleeping babe awakes, I will make coffee.'

Jumping up, Dottie protested. '*Non, Mémère, je vais le faire.*' It came so naturally now, something so simple as saying as 'I'll do it', slipped out in French. She was beginning to think and dream in her second language which in a way was a good thing.

Delphine watched her as she put the kettle on the stove to boil then returned to the hearth. Dottie could tell her grandmother wanted to chat.

'Dottie, you seem so different since you came home, distant perhaps, and definitely more assured. I can see it in the way you walk and hold yourself, and you are alert but then so tired. Is there anything you would like to talk about, things that you cannot say to your parents? You know I will listen and not panic, not outwardly anyway, perhaps a little inside.' Delphine gave Dottie a warm smile then waited.

'Oh, Mémère, there are so many things I want to tell you but can't and won't, because the last thing I want to do is worry you, but thank you for asking.'

Delphine nodded slowly. 'I understand and for your

thoughtfulness, I thank you. But I would like to say a few words, while I can, if I may?'

Dottie swallowed and forced down emotion, it was good practice. 'Of course, Mémère.'

Wasting no time Delphine began. 'I do not want you to respond, just listen. I think I know where you are going, to France, and I suspect it is to aid the Maquis, or spy. Either is dangerous, and this fills my own heart with terror, while yours is truly brave, that of a lion.'

'Oh, Mémère, I'm definitely not a lion despite what you would like to believe, I'm no braver than any of the men who have gone to fight so shush, you will only upset yourself.'

'No, I must say what is in here.' Delphine touched her chest. 'What you are going to do, wherever they send you, I will be thinking of my wonderful granddaughter every minute. My prayers are all I have to keep you safe, but I will say them so many times a day God will be tired of hearing my voice. You will be fighting for *liberté*, for peace and for the future and I am so proud of you, my child, so very, very proud.'

They parted from their embrace at the sound of footsteps on the stairs and the door to the corridor opening. Dottie flicked away a tear and pecked Delphine on the cheek, as the animated voice of her mum drew nearer.

'Oh, she will be so pleased to see you, here, come inside.' Paulette appeared first and before she even had time to introduce their guest, Maude was in the room.

'Ta-da! Surprise.' Maude flung open her arms and struck a pose, a huge red grin cutting her face in half.

'Maude, what on earth are you doing here? I thought you were staying with your parents.' Dottie rushed over to greet her friend and found herself swaddled in fur and assailed by her heavenly scent.

'Oh, darling, believe me, one week at Glum Hall is quite

enough for anyone so I'm booked in at the Ritz with some chums and thought, I know, who would I most like to see the New Year in with, and it was you! So here I am. I hope I'm not intruding.'

At this Paulette interceded. 'Of course not, we are honoured to have you. Dottie has told us so much about you so please, sit, I will make coffee.'

'Oh, thank you, dear Paulette. I have been longing to meet you all, and, Mémère, how marvellous to see you at last.' Maude stretched out her arms and rushed over to Delphine and kissed her in the accepted French way, on each cheek.

Dottie watched with amusement as Maude began to charm the birds from the trees, slipping off her fur and flinging it over the back of the battered sofa before flopping down opposite Delphine, warming her hands by the fire as she chattered away in French about the silly taxi driver who asked her three times if she was sure she'd got the right address and that she couldn't wait to go back downstairs and try some pie and mash.

'Oh, that reminds me.' Maude jumped up then ran down the corridor and came back struggling with a suitcase that appeared rather heavy. 'Here, I come bearing gifts.'

Maude heaved it upwards and deposited it on the kitchen table, just as Tommy blustered into the room. 'Thought I'd pop up and see how you are, I've left little Tina minding the shop for a minute.'

'Well you're just in time, Tommy, because I have something you might like in here...' Maude had undone the buckles and flipped the catch to reveal, much to everyone's delight, what looked to be the contents of the Glum Hall larder and cellar.

After passing Tommy a rather dusty bottle of whisky, Maude presented Delphine with one containing wine that made Mémère's eyebrows raise and put a beaming smile on her face. Paulette received chocolate truffles in a box so fancy that Dottie knew it would never be thrown away, and after that came a whole ham, a perfectly round wheel of cheese, three jars of preserves and, wrapped in brown paper, a string of sausages.

'There, that should keep you going... I didn't chance the eggs, even I'm not that silly.'

Dottie spoke up, voicing what she imagined was on all their minds. 'But, Maude, won't your mum wonder where all her food's gone? She'll have a fit, surely.'

At this Maude flapped her hand and raised one eyebrow. 'Dottie, my mother has only been to the kitchen at Glum Hall once in her life, shortly after she married my father. She got lost and had to be taken back upstairs by the butler and has never been back since. My secret is safe and anyway, I rather enjoyed my clandestine foraging, you could call it extra homework.' Maude winked at Dottie then turned away.

'Now, where were we? Oh yes... pie and mash. Come along, Tommy, I want a huge portion, Dottie's told me all about how delicious it is.' And with that she linked his arm and they headed downstairs, leaving Paulette to admire her box from Fortnum and Mason and Delphine to caress the bottle of Margaux, while Dottie chuckled and began to stash their hoard of food in the larder.

It was to be one of the best New Year's ever. Maude had no intention of heading up west to be with her chums, she'd done that so many times before. Instead she insisted on spending the evening with the Tanners and experiencing a real East End knees-up which began in the local pub and finished above the shop. Once the neighbours headed home and the kitchen was tidied, tipsy Tommy was helped to bed by Paulette after which Delphine bade everyone goodnight. Dottie and Maude then squashed into her bed, top and tail, exhausted in the darkness.

Realising that she had only one more night at home before she would be on her way again, Dottie felt as though she never wanted the night to end. Maude yawned very loudly, fidgeting in the bed, her cold feet against Dottie's arm.

Quickly losing the battle against sleep and as her eyes began to droop, a thought popped into her head and without thinking, she asked a question. 'Maudie, are you scared, you know, about going to France?'

Dottie waited for a glib retort, one that she was sure would lift her heart and wash away the fear she'd kept hidden inside. There was silence, just two heartbeats, and Maude replied.

'Absolutely and utterly terrified, darling.'

12

TOUR DE DOTTIE

FRANCE, 2005

Maude and Dottie sat in subdued silence at the end of a long dusty lane and surveyed the farm and sprawling fields filled with chickens. This was it, Tante Helene's farm, Dottie's home during the war. Aunt, or Tante, was what she'd called the kindly woman who had taken care of her, a fellow member of the Maquis. It had hardly changed at all, the *longère* farmhouse was still intact and exactly as she'd remembered, but the metal outbuildings were new and the sign at the end of the lane told them it was a free range egg farm, but the surname on the letterbox told them that Tante Helene's family were gone.

During the twenty-minute journey from Châteaubriant to Renazé, Maude had listened while Dottie continued her story about how she had ended up here, her French home.

'Did you not keep in touch after the war?'

Dottie answered. 'I sent one letter when I got back to England, after I heard about the executions, but I never had a reply. She may have received it, or it could have got lost in the mayhem, who knows. There was no point trying to fathom it. I tried to blank it all out because there was nothing I could do, Tante Helene was in the past. They were all gone. With hindsight and in modern-day terms I think I was in shock and behaved accordingly.'

Maude reached over and placed her hand on her gran's leg. 'I could go and ask at the farm if you like, and see if they know anything about Tante Helene.'

'No, let's leave it for now. We can head off into the village and take a look there. Let's just go for a drive and if I spot something, I'll point it out. Today I'd like to get my bearings rather than come face to face with anyone. Does that sound feeble?'

Maude shook her head vigorously. 'No, not at all. We'll call this the Tour de Dottie, like the bike race but at a more sedentary pace. But as we drive, perhaps you could tell me some more about your life here, like your work with the Resistance, or do you prefer to call it the Maquis? Then I can imagine it all as we go.'

'Of course, I'd like that. And to me it's Maquis. Oh, and sometimes we called the Germans the Boche, they had alternative names for us, I assure you.' Dottie then pointed to the map that lay on her lap. 'Look, if we follow this road, we can circumnavigate all the villages around here, drive in, take a look and then on to the next. We can save the churchyard until last, or another day. I have no idea who will be buried there or where to find them so think I'll need to work up to that.'

Maude started the engine. 'No problem and I see your ordinance skills are intact. Right, you point me in the right direction and tell me a story about an awesome woman called Yvette who cycled everywhere to deliver secret messages. I bet you were fit as a fiddle.'

'Oh, I was! And in the summer brown as a berry, well my face, arms and legs were. I spent almost every day outside, helping Tante Helene in the garden or as you say, cycling for miles into the forest taking supplies, picking up messages, delivering incendiaries, fuses, dynamite, whatever was needed. It was the same in winter, but slippery, raining a lot and I was much paler.'

'So, you were a bit of a farmer then, did you grow all your own food? Was there rationing here in France too?'

'Oh yes, in fact here it was stricter than at home in England. Don't forget the Germans were in control of the north and pulling the strings of the Vichy Government in the south. You'd imagine that living in the countryside there'd be an abundance of food but the bulk of meat and other supplies went to the Boche, so we were stretched even further. Many country dwellers grew their own produce but with the men away there was nobody to farm the huge swathes of land and again, women took up the mantle.'

'But where were the men, did they join the army?'

'Those who were fit and of the right age were enrolled into Service du Travail Obligatoire, forced labour to you and I. If you refused, a prison camp awaited so many French citizens found themselves transported. Sometimes they went to Germany where they had to work on munitions or build planes, lay railway lines or whatever they were told to do. Many refused so before they were arrested, they fled and joined the partisan cause.'

'Oh, I see. That's who the Resistance were, and the ones you told me about, like Roberto. I get it now. So, were you hungry all the time?'

'Yes, I suppose we were, but we adapted. Tante Helene kept chickens so we always had eggs, and then rabbits.'

'For eating!'

'Yes, Maude, we didn't cuddle them in those days.' Dottie rolled her eyes.

'Oh, I don't think I could have eaten one.'

'You'd be surprised what you'll eat when you are hungry, but

I won't go down the offal route. But cow's head stew was and still is considered a delicacy...'

'Gran!'

'Sorry, I forget you have a weak stomach. Have I told you about the ersatz coffee? Oh, that was dreadful, Maude. They made it from acorns and chickpeas or sometimes chicory and roasted barley and we always drank it black because dairy products were rationed. People were inventive though and once, Tante Helene made some soap from caustic soda, resin from pine trees, and boiled cows' feet. Those were the days, you know, tough but we survived.'

'Mmm, I bet that soap smelt delightful and was so gentle on your skin. Did you have ration cards and coupons like in England?'

'Yes, and that was one of the things the Maquis would regularly target in raids on Town Halls. Don't get me wrong, the farmers and silent resistors made sure our groups were fed, but the coupons came in handy and it was a kick in the balls for the Boche.'

Maude laughed. 'Yep, there she is. Little Miss Prim and Proper.'

'I'm saying it like it is. I remember at weekends city dwellers would come by train to see if they could buy food from the farmers and one of our group, little Polo, would take the rabbits in a basket to the market at Châteaubriant and they'd be snapped up in minutes.'

'Gran, can we just skip the rabbits, please?'

Dottie was prevented from answering when Maude's phone began to ring inside her bag. The loud tut which escaped her lips brought a smile to Dottie's face.

'Shall I get that for you, Maudie?'

'No, it'll be Lachlan again. I bloody told him not to ring on my mobile, it'll cost a fortune. Why can't he wait till I get to a phone box like we agreed? If Mum can do it so can he.'

'He's just crazy in love, that's all.'

'Don't be sarky.'

Again, Dottie smirked. 'Just remember, when you go to live in Australia you'll have to get used to eating horrible things. I've seen that programme with Ant and Dec and they eat some queer stuff over there, witchetty grubs, kangaroo bits, cute fluffy koala burgers...'

'Gran, stop talking rubbish, that's just a game show and I am not going to live there, okay? I'm going for a holiday. That. Is. All.'

The phone chirped into life again much to Dottie's glee.

'If you say so... Uh-oh, he's being very persistent today. Perhaps I should turn it off, if it's annoying you.' Dottie tried not to smile or sound too eager.

'Just put it on silent, he'll take the huff if he knows I've switched it off. Oh look, here's the village.'

A hush fell on the car as Maude slowly traversed the quiet streets and Dottie focused on the houses that skirted the centre, none of them at all familiar but as they continued, the architecture changed. After passing the well-tended gardens and houses of similar modern designs, older, squat, higgledy-piggledy rows of bumpy walled terraces came into view. The roofs sloped and bowed in tiled waves, one joining onto the other, the windows were small and square, the doorways low and no doubt requiring the householder to stoop before entering. The elm lined road curved into a bend, obscuring the route ahead but Dottie already knew what to expect. On the rue des Poses, to the left would be Café des Amis, *let it be there, let it be there*, and opposite the row of shops, the *boulangerie* and *boucherie*, and then the cobbled market square where in summer the baskets of produce would be sheltered by the trees. On the other side would be the *chambre d'hotes*, the little hotel owned by Polo's Tante Elise and a few paces along, the church: Église Saint Denis.

Dottie held her breath and her skin prickled. 'Oh my.'

Maude slowed the car and pulled to the side of the road. They both sat in silence for a second or two and took in the scene until Maude asked a question.

'Is it how you remembered, Gran?'

Swallowing, Dottie looked on through misty eyes. 'It's like I've never been away.'

They were in the graveyard of Saint Denis. As many tend to be, it was a peaceful place, at the rear of the church where rows and rows of crooked headstones and engraved slabs edged parallel pathways. At times, during their meandering along the white gravel that crunched underfoot, they had been shaded by twisted oaks and the gable end of the church. But it was nearing midday and becoming clear that searching for names that Dottie recognised, and one in particular that she knew well, was not going to be a simple task.

On the way into the churchyard they had passed the hotel and on closer inspection she realised that it had fallen into disrepair and part of the grounds were cordoned off by tape, a bulldozer lying idle signified major works were underway. She wondered if it was still occupied and what had happened to Tante Elise and her daughters, the aunt and cousins of little Polo, but the mere thought of his and their fate had cast a shadow which Dottie swiftly stepped away from.

They could have popped into the *tabac* across the road to ask, or perhaps made enquiries with the lady who was talking to a gentleman, seated in his wheelchair opposite the hotel but instead Dottie walked on, *there's plenty of time, take it slowly.*

Maude stopped at the end of a path, a few paces away from Dottie, and placed her hands on her hips.

'Look, there's a bench. Let's have a sit down. It's getting a bit hot now, Gran, and even I'm knackered from wandering up and down so you must be too.'

Dottie followed in silence and it wasn't until she plonked herself down beside Maude that she answered.

'You're right, it's shaping up to be a scorcher so let's take a few minutes here and relax. Not that I've done much apart from sit on my bottom and natter on. You're a good girl you are, for indulging me.' Dottie took Maude's hand in hers.

'It's been a pleasure, Gran, and I'm loving having you all to myself and hearing your stories. But don't you find it a bit depressing, you know, being here?'

'I always find graveyards very relaxing. I often visit George, you know, when the mood takes me.'

Maude twisted slightly to look at Dottie. 'Do you? Well fancy that. You're a dark horse, Gran, that's for sure.'

Dottie chuckled. 'Oh yes, we have lovely chats and I take my transistor and play him some jazz. I always feel cheered up afterwards.'

Neither spoke after that, instead they let the sun warm their faces and the breeze tickle their hair, accompanied by birdsong, and then the engine of what sounded like a digger revving into action.

'Was it always this quiet in the village? I imagine it was a lovely place to live apart from having the Germans swarming everywhere.' Maude closed her eyes and tilted her head towards the sky.

'You know the funny thing is, that when I was here, I didn't see it like that, you know, how it is now; a tourist spot where thousands of people come for holidays. To me it was a strange place, full of even stranger people, the Boche not the French. I'd been catapulted into a war zone and thrust into a world of espionage. Can you imagine it? A young girl – I was barely a woman back then, if I'm honest – who'd been brought up in the capital, surrounded by smog and bricks and noise turning up in a place like this.' Dottie gestured to nowhere in particular.

'Before training I'd never been away from home, the furthest I'd travelled was in a charabanc to Margate for a day at the seaside. And here I was, staying with a woman who I called aunty, who I'd never seen before in my life, where I fed chickens, watered vegetables and delivered sticks of dynamite and couriered downed airmen and other evaders to safety. When I look back, even though I know I did it, I honestly can't believe that little Dottie Tanner from the pie and mash shop was a special operative, in the middle of nowhere, alone, homesick... oh, and a virgin.'

At this Maude's head spun to the side. 'Gran! Did I really need to know that?'

Dottie chortled. 'I'm only trying to give you an idea of how I was then, so you can grasp the enormity of what women like me did.'

'Okay, I get you. So while we're here in the middle of nowhere, in a moderately creepy graveyard with only our bony buddies for company, why don't you carry on from where you left off, when you and Maude were ready to come to France. I'm sure this lot haven't heard a good story for a while.'

Dottie tapped Maude's wrist but appreciated her humour, sometimes it got you through the worst situations. 'I suppose you're right. I'll explain a bit more and then we'll head off and get some lunch.'

'Deal.' Maude gave Dottie the thumbs up.

'Okay, so once again, if you're sitting comfortably, then I will begin.'

13

INTO THE ABYSS
FRANCE, 1943

They had waited for days at the holding site, the moon needed to be full before the pilots would risk flying across the channel and dropping their cargo in France. Agents, or 'Joes' as the pilots called them, were flown in Lysanders into France or dropped from a Halifax bomber. Moon Squadrons, in every sense of the term. The Germans were swarming along the Atlantic Wall, making things difficult for the British flotillas that also used the short distance from Dartmouth to ferry supplies, agents and evaders back and forth, landing on the northern coast of Brittany.

Dottie had steeled herself before saying goodbye to her family, and in the end dealt with it like one of their role plays at the Beaulieu training camp. She was up, dressed and ready to go when her parents and Delphine came into the kitchen and you'd have thought she was off to the office at Whitehall, not saying what could be her last goodbye. After swift kisses, firm hugs and a cheerio, Dottie left her mum to her tears and Delphine to rattle the kettle on the grate, her dad caught like a rabbit in headlights as she bit her lip and took the stairs two at a time. Never looking back.

Maude was waiting at the flat after returning to the Ritz, tactfully giving Dottie one last night at home with her kin. Here, they were kitted out and given their code names, forged identity papers and cover stories. Dottie quite liked her new name, Yvette Giroux, previously resident in Paris, the orphaned niece of widowed Madame Helene Noury who had kindly taken her in. Maude became socialite Estelle Sable, relocated from Corsica, ex-wife of recently deceased Baron Sable. They would be met by the Maquis on the ground and moved to their new locations which would be revealed after the drop.

The night before they left, Dottie and Maude lay side by side on the single bed, staring at the moon through their shared bedroom window. It was January the twenty-first, absolutely perishing outside and not much better in, hence the need for warmth and comfort.

'I wish that full moon would bugger off. It's Burn's Night at the weekend and we'll miss out on the haggis, I got quite a taste for it in Scotland.' Maude was her usual forthright self.

Dottie attempted a laugh and barely managed a smile, but it would have been wasted in the darkness. 'I think you liked the whisky more, but I know what you mean. I've spent days watching the sky, waiting for it to be our turn and this time tomorrow we'll be up there, waiting to jump. I don't know if I can do it, you know, not now it's actually here.'

'Of course you can because I'm not bloody well yomping across France on my own so if I go first, don't you dare let me down, and if you dither at the edge I'll give you a push. That'll do it.'

Dottie felt ridiculously grateful for that. 'Will you promise you'll chuck me out? And I promise if you go first, I'll not let you down, I'll be right behind you.'

'Good woman, that's what I like to hear and yes, I promise.'

Dottie had another question. 'Why are you always so

bleedin' brave? I wish I could be like you, Maudie, I really do. You've got me through these last few months, and I don't know how I'm going to cope without you. You're the best friend I've ever had, you know that?'

There was silence and Dottie began to feel a little stupid, perhaps she'd gone too far, after all, Maude was from the jolly hockey sticks, stiff upper lip and off to boarding school brigade.

Maude's voice was soft. 'Do you know, that's the nicest thing anyone has ever said to me.'

Dottie nudged Maude. 'Getaway with you. I bet your posh chums say nice things all the time, you're lovely, you are.'

Maude shook her head in the darkness. 'No, really, I mean it. That's why I'm so grateful I got billeted with you because for the first time ever I feel like have a true friend, who's taken me as I am, not because of who I am, or who my parents are. The night I stayed with your family was one of my happiest memories and I shall hold it in my heart forever. Nearly all my happy times have been with you.'

Dottie didn't know what to say because this was the first time ever that Maude had shown her heart. She was kind to a fault, generous and caring, contrasted with a wicked wit that complemented her sometimes acerbic observations.

'Well when this is all over, you can come and stay forever, or whenever you like. They fell in love with you straight off, just like I have. You're special, Maudie, don't ever forget that.'

Maude reached out and Dottie reciprocated, holding her hand tightly.

'Do you really mean that, Dottie Doolittle?'

'Yes, I do, all of it.'

When she heard a sniff, Dottie's heart plummeted and instinctively she let go of Maude's hand and took her sobbing friend in her arms. 'Oh, Maudie, please don't cry, you have to be the tough one, you must be. Whatever is the matter?'

The tears continued for a while and when they ceased, Dottie felt Maude wipe her eyes and with her usual aplomb, she sniffed and took a breath, the stiff upper lip returning.

'Oh, it's just me being silly, I'm fine now, I promise. This blasted war is turning me into a softie, and we can't have that, can we? Now we should get some sleep, it could be the last decent night's kip we'll get for a while.'

'Are you sure you're all right, Maude? It's not fair that I expect you to carry me all the time and we all have our moments. You know you can tell me anything, don't you?'

If Dottie could have seen Maude's face, she knew her eyes were open, staring at the ceiling, weighing up her options, her face deadpan giving nothing away. She'd seen the look before, guarded, wary then boom, she'd be like a firework, going off in any direction to avoid opening up, the moment lost.

'Yes, Dottie, I know that I can tell you anything, I trust you. Don't worry, I truly am okay.'

Not satisfied, Dottie decided to test her. 'Okay, then tell me your code name.'

Silence. 'Why do you want to know that? We're not supposed to say, you know the rules.'

'It's a test. How much we trust each other, you tell me yours and I'll tell you mine and we will never speak of it again but at least while we are over there, if we hear it, we will know it's each other.'

Another silence but this time just for a second. 'Simone.'

Dottie smiled, it was a nice name, then replied. 'Nadine.'

Maude spoke next. 'Go to sleep, Dottie, tomorrow is a big day.'

Obeying the super brave and sensible one, Dottie did as she was told but before she closed her eyes, she once again took Maude's hand in hers, then by the light of the moon, side by side they slept.

. . .

126

Dottie's body absorbed the rumble of the engine and the vibration of the creaking metal interior of the Halifax bomber, as it cut through the clouds en route to the sky over occupied France. She had no idea that the noise of the engine would one day forever invade her dreams and herald the beginning of her nightmares, where the faces opposite and to her side, of Maude and another male agent would lose their skin and appear as hollowed out skeletons.

She was uncomfortable, her civilian clothes squashed underneath her jumpsuit and her insides felt warm from the hot toddy of rum they had just been given, a tradition before the drop. Then the fuselage was opened and a gaping hole appeared, a rush of air, bitterly cold, whooshed in. Next, they stood, a moment to glance at Maude, no words, and then the static line was hitched onto the chute, the sergeant making a show that it was attached, a gesture meant to reassure. Then the red light. Dottie was first. She sat, only 500 feet above ground, just like she'd been trained, her legs dangling over the edge of the hole, mind and body on autopilot now. Fear had taken a back seat, pride combined with reckless inevitability fuelled much needed adrenalin, because she had to jump.

Dottie knew that Maude was by her side, waiting to take her turn, then quiet as the engines were cut to slow the plane, not silence because the wind still whistled past. GREEN LIGHT, like the eyes of a monster, JUMP.

The free fall into the dark abyss, the earth hurtling towards you, then the jolt of the chute opening, and euphoria. Then after the relief came fear, the landing came in seconds, the prayers came faster, *Let there not be a lookout, no machine guns, a clear spot, no trees... please God...* and then she hit the earth, her brain shook inside her skull from the impact as Dottie's body made contact with the earth.

Winded, she lay still, waiting for the pain of a broken bone but there was nothing more than a dull ache that she knew would soon ease. Her battered brain still functioned and urged her on, so she gathered her parachute and as she did so, heard the sound of another body making contact with the earth – Maude – followed by the other nameless agent. Above them the plane was already heading home, the distant sound of its engine the background music to Dottie's opening scene. She'd made it, the abyss hadn't swallowed her whole, machine guns hadn't pummelled her skin, the ground hadn't snuffed out her life. She was there, in the dead of night, in the occupied zone of Nazi controlled France.

They used the small shovels attached to their legs and buried the parachutes and jumpsuits, then using a torch, followed the map and compass, heading south-west, walking for ten kilometres through soggy fields, climbing hedges, edging sleepy rural hamlets until they reached the outskirts of what they all prayed was the village of Pontivy, and once they'd located the church of Saint Pierre, rested against its walls and waited in silence for dawn to break. Dottie slept at some point, only for minutes at a time, her head resting on Maude's shoulder while the nameless agent kept lookout.

Dottie heard every bird in the surrounding trees sing its morning song and wondered how they could sound so cheerful on what she was convinced was the coldest January morning ever. Yet it was a beautiful scene, one Dottie would never forget, of fields and valleys stretching into the distance, gilded by rolling silver mist set aglow by the peachy-gold hue of the rising sun.

When she heard the whistle, three short sharp sounds, Dottie knew it wasn't one of her feathered friends and nudged Maude and her now sleeping secret agent. It was hard to spot them at first, the figures in the trees that lined the farmer's field, but as they approached, moving quickly through the mist,

Dottie was filled with a sense of wonderment and relief. They were real, not just mythical, mysterious men whose tales of bravery filtered back to England, they were there and she was about to join the fight alongside the Free French, the Maquis, la Résistance.

They exchanged code words and once assured of the others' validity, Dottie and Maude said goodbye to their fellow agent there and then. He left with one of the guides who mentioned only that they were heading north to Paris, and neither Dottie nor Maude asked anything more. Their own guide introduced himself as Robin and whether that was his real name or not, Dottie didn't care because from that moment, she was Yvette and Maude became Estelle.

They walked for another few kilometres to a farmyard where a flat back truck containing coal was waiting.

'This is how you will travel, underneath the coal. It is a good way to get you as close as possible, it has worked many times before. At the safe house you will be able to get cleaned up.' Robin signalled that they should board the truck. 'At this time in the morning we should not meet any patrols, but we must go now.'

There was a section to the side of the bed of the truck that had been scraped aside and a blanket to which Robin nodded. 'Lie down and I will cover you with these sacks and then the coal.' He pulled four or five from the side panel and held them up. 'You will still be able to breathe, don't worry, it is only one layer to camouflage you, now hurry.'

Yvette and Estelle silently did as they were told and lay flat but as Robin flung the sacking on top of them and began to shovel on the ebony rocks, an English voice as clear as cut crystal spoke from beneath.

'Well, if only Mummy could see me now!'

Had Yvette not laughed, she would most definitely have

cried.

They said goodbye less than six hours later. Perhaps it was the heightened sense of urgency and being in the company of surly men of few words that forced them both to reign in whatever they were feeling on the inside and put on a show. Yvette wasn't too sure who for, but it did the trick. And she knew where Estelle was going, Nantes, and for some reason it made her feel better. Yvette was going to a village near Châteaubriant. If they were stopped and managed to escape, each knew where to head.

They stood in a farmyard, outside a smallholding that appeared to be abandoned but which had enough meagre and ancient facilities to keep someone sheltered and alive. That was the only thing they knew about where they were, it smelt of manure and wood smoke, and it was drizzly and grey and cold.

'Now you take care, on the journey and always. Don't get cocky either, remember who and where you are, stay focused.' Yvette could hear herself talking and couldn't quite believe she was the one giving advice.

'And you believe in yourself, you are brave...' Estelle fell silent, her eyes awash with tears as she grasped Yvette's hands and squeezed tightly.

Unused to seeing Estelle like this, Yvette had to take up the slack. 'I will. I promise. I'll see you soon, one day, I know it.'

An impatient voice intruded. One of the watchful men who had turned up at the farm. 'Come, the guide will not wait, hurry we must go.'

With that, Estelle gave a quick nod and Yvette did the same and watched as her friend turned and hurried through the open gate and out of sight.

Two hours later, Robin delivered Yvette to her new home, an isolated farm on the outskirts of Renazé village. Here, Tante

Helene made her feel immediately welcome with a meal of bread and eggs, washed down by the worst coffee Yvette had ever tasted, before showing her to her bedroom.

As she looked around the clean but sparse room, containing a chest of drawers on which stood a bowl, jug and mirror, and a wooden chair beside a single bed, Yvette didn't dare picture her family so far away, and allowed only a second to imagine Estelle in a bourgeois apartment in Nantes. Exhaustion, both mental and physical, engulfed her, preventing any more thought or movement. All she knew, as her body flopped onto the creaky bed that swayed slightly when she moved, was that it had begun; a new life. She was part of the fight.

14

THE HISTORIANS

RENAZÉ, FRANCE, 2005

By the time they'd wandered back to the car, the Café des Amis was already full, so they abandoned their plan to eat there and headed off in search of an alternative. The village had a one-way system and as they passed by the cobbled square, not only did Dottie notice the workmen at the hotel securing the site, but also the chap in the wheelchair who had been seated opposite being wheeled away by who she presumed was his carer. It had always been the same, nothing had changed because even during the war everything stopped for lunch, no matter how meagre it was.

Dottie watched them make their way along the pathway while Maude loitered outside the car, texting a message to Lachlan who either couldn't read or follow basic verbal instructions. That man was a pest and severely tested Dottie's patience even when he was hundreds of miles away. Every time Maude's phone buzzed it reminded Dottie of an annoying fly that she'd like to splatter on the windscreen. Bloody men, they were such a hindrance unless you found the right one, and no matter how much Jean pleaded Lachlan's case or Maude rolled her eyes, Dottie knew he was wrong for her granddaughter.

Maude finally stopped jabbing at her phone, returned to the car and started the engine. Whether she sensed something was wrong, or was merely trying to break the silence, her next question set Dottie's mind racing once more.

'So, Supergran, what's our next move? I really don't fancy wandering around any more graveyards and let's face it, from what I've seen, every single village has one so it'll take forever.'

Dottie puffed. 'I know, but I did a bit of research online and I believe that the *maire*'s office holds records of where people from their communes are buried so perhaps we should make an appointment with Renazé's head honcho. He should be able to help and might even pull a few strings with the others in the area.'

'Good thinking, Batwoman. We'll need to write a list of all the names you remember, how many Resistance members were there?'

'In France, thousands, with more spread throughout the rest of Europe and Poland. In our group there were eight of us who worked closely together, plus a radio operator, a recruiter and someone who arranged surveillance and other operations, but for raids we would sometimes join with others. Did I tell you what it was called, our network?'

Through the corner of her eye, Dottie saw Maude shake her head.

'Historian, I always liked it and wondered how they chose it, anyway, we were part of the Shelburne Line that moved evaders through France and back to England, along with all the other bits and bobs we got up to.'

'It sounds so exciting, Gran, never mind jumping out of a plane, all this espionage and the camaraderie too.'

'Yes, but for the most part I lived a life of fear, with some wonderful moments scattered amongst the bad.'

'What were you scared of most?'

'That's easy, being captured. I got it into my head that I could handle death, but not torture or living with the knowledge I'd given away secrets. That truly terrified me for the whole time.'

Even though the air conditioning in the car could be glacial, having all the windows closed sometimes made Dottie feel claustrophobic so she wound down the window and relished the feel of the breeze on her face.

'The thing was, there were so many people moving through France from all walks of life and all over the place, Spain, Poland, Russia, there was simply no way of checking everyone out. When I handed my identity papers to a German soldier, how was he going to find out if I really was an orphan from Paris? For all he knew I could have been the Pope's sister from Pompeii. The only way he'd know is if he checked the serial number on my identity card. So there was always an element of risk. We had to trust strangers, take apart their stories to the best of our abilities when they turned up without papers. Had they really lost them, or had them destroyed when their boat capsized at sea, or were they infiltrators, hoping to wheedle their way in?'

'I see what you mean. So you had to rely on instinct.'

A sigh. 'Yes, we did, and unfortunately sometimes it was a mistake and the Maquis paid the price.'

'That's awful... but I can see you're getting a bit maudlin, that blooming churchyard didn't help, so on a lighter note, you haven't told me about how you met Uncle Konki. And when you're ready I'd love to know about Vincent, but not the gory details, okay? Just be tactful and remember I'm your grand-daughter.'

They were entering another village, the narrow streets empty of pedestrians, the blinds on the bread shop pulled down, the flashing green cross on the *pharmacie* grey and dull.

Dottie laughed at that, grateful for Maude's ability to lift the mood. 'Oh, you are such a prude, Maude, but I'll try to remember. Oh look... there's a little bistro, let's go in there and once we're settled, I'll tell you about Vincent. Pull over and we'll peep in.'

Maude did as she was told and they both peered through the window.

Dottie gave a little clap. 'Marvellous. There's a few empty tables so park up. I'm famished.'

As they made their way towards the bistro, Dottie was looking forward to a large glass of white wine, no, she'd order a bottle. Not for Dutch courage, because she was ready now to talk about Vincent. After looking away for so long and turning down the volume, she wanted to describe him, see his face in her mind's eye and hear his voice and laughter in her ear. And today, she would drink white wine with him and be happy, like she did the very first time they met.

15

YVETTE AND VINCENT

RENAZÉ, 1943

Yvette watched for patches of ice as she freewheeled down the hill, her hair coming loose from underneath her beret, a fiery tangled mess that she would have to tidy before she saw Vincent. Her nose ran from the cold of a December day and apart from her legs, the rest of her body was warmed by exercise. It had done her good though, the trip to Châteaubriant, even if it was a good hour and a half there and back. She hadn't slept well again, the same nightmare coming back to haunt her and no matter how exhausted she was after a day on the farm or riding for kilometres to make a delivery, the abyss waited patiently.

The road began to straighten out and Yvette pedalled, a steady pace so as not to exert herself too much because she didn't want to arrive in the forest all sweaty and smelly. It was hard enough keeping up appearances as it was, wearing second-hand clothes that frankly had seen better eras never mind days, and the last of her stockings were irreparable so bare legs were the norm, tanned during the summer, goose-bumped under her trousers during the winter. She was becoming weather-beaten. This thought troubled Yvette slightly and her poor, wind exposed face was probably ageing with each turn of the pedal.

In the countryside it hardly mattered, but she tried hard to keep up appearances with a hint of make-up, a touch of rouge on the lips and cheeks. Back at home and in French cities and towns, women were encouraged to look the best they possibly could. Everyone knew Hitler abhorred women who wore make-up or painted their nails, so it was a small act of defiance, annoying Adolf.

How different she looked from her city days before the war, especially when she and her friends would get all dressed up and go down to the Pally on a Saturday night. What would her friends and parents say if they could see her now, masquerading as a simple country girl? That thought was immediately squashed because she couldn't bear the swell of homesickness that enveloped her like a wave, washing her out, leaving her feeling isolated and vulnerable, stupid maybe. Had she not realised that this is how it would be, hundreds of miles away from home, away from her loved ones, for who knew how long?

No, she hadn't, not really. That was the truth. When Yvette looked at the person in the mirror, she saw that her summer sun-kissed skin and nose scattered with freckles had been replaced by winter ruddy, red cheeks. She also saw sad green eyes that looked away quickly, not prepared to countenance the reality that lay behind her defiant facade.

Yvette was scared most days, really. When she saw the German patrol move through the village, two grey pillars of stone marching along the streets, occasionally hammering on doors to randomly check the inhabitants were obeying the 8pm curfew. Or when, as today, she delivered her missive, destined for Rennes and the printing presses of a clandestine group who produced propaganda leaflets. Paperwork was easier to conceal than most things she couriered and could be folded and hidden inside her clothes, but her heart still raced whenever she was stopped at a checkpoint. And her mind, it never stopped thinking, preparing, noting. Surveillance was another of her jobs, to report back anything she saw or was told, the smallest snippet could be useful.

But the true fear came from the mere notion of being exposed, and it happened frequently; agents were captured or betrayed and Yvette lived in trepidation of that moment. Not that she wasn't brave, she knew that now, and told herself if she could jump out of a plane into a blanket of ebony, watching the moonlit earth hurtle towards her, she could face the Nazi torture chamber. But could she?

Forcing her mind elsewhere, she rested instead on Estelle and again her chest constricted. What was that phrase she'd learned at school, 'parting is such sweet sorrow'? At the time she had no idea at all what the English teacher had been droning on about, but she did now. Saying goodbye to her family and then to Estelle had been the hardest thing of all. But now she had Vincent and amidst the maelstrom of apprehension, at least they had snatched moments, hours and once almost a whole day, of happiness.

Being in love was not how she imagined it to be, not in this climate of fear, but in some ways the days of longing in between their reunions fuelled the passion when they were able to meet. No wonder they had grabbed their moment, once both of them realised they felt the same way. Yvette felt herself blush, not recognising the well-brought up woman who made love in a field of maize to a man she'd only just met, but this was the war, and since the moment she'd laid eyes on Vincent, she wanted only to be with him.

The day she met Vincent, Tante Helene had drawn a map that Yvette studied carefully, memorising the route to the camp hidden deep in the forest. There had been a late visitor the previous evening; the little boy named Polo had passed a note to Yvette, his voice a shy mutter as he told her she was to take it to the Maquis and make contact with Radio Londres. Then he bounded off like a whippet after a rabbit.

The co-ordinates, written on a folded piece of paper concealed within her bra, giving the location of a fuel dump in Angers, scratched her skin as she cycled along the dusty lanes on that February morning. It was to be her first encounter with the local Maquis, made up of men from the surrounding villages who had fled rather than work for the Germans. If she was stopped, the food was for her grandfather who was chopping wood in the forest and she had a fifty–fifty chance of being believed.

It was cold on the roads, the biting Atlantic wind whipped across the fields and stung her face but once she took the first lane that seemed to go on for kilometres and kilometres, the sparse hedges that lined the route afforded her some respite. Focusing on the forest up ahead that was so vast that its border to the left and right seemed endless, she imagined the scrawled map that Tante Helene had eventually thrown on to the fire and destroyed.

Soon, Yvette found herself cycling under a canopy of green as the scent of pine invaded her nostrils and the tyres crunched as she rode. She tried not to feel nervous, but she was worried that she'd go the wrong way and be lost forever in an ever dark-ening, rather eerie setting. After a further ten minutes she reached the clearing, and Yvette disembarked and waited, like Tante Helene had told her.

There was a huge stump and other smaller ones, fresh wood chippings scattered all around which told her that someone had been there recently, signs of life. It was so quiet, and even the birdsong was unnerving her, imagining they were sending secret signals to one another, tweeting about her.

It felt like an age had passed, but after checking her watch it had only been five minutes when movement to her right made her start. She didn't see him at first, the face amongst the trees, but when he stepped forward and beckoned, Yvette did as she was told, heart pounding.

Pushing her bicycle, Yvette followed the man in silence, while part of her screamed danger, the other told her to trust. Hearing strange whistles, perhaps bird calls, Yvette swallowed down her unease, after all, Tante Helene had been there many times before and she had come to no harm. Deeper they went into the darkening forest where the pine trees seemed to squash closer to one another, their deep emerald branches vying for room and when Yvette thought they would go on forever she spotted movement up ahead. Before she had time to prepare or feel self-conscious, they emerged from the trees into another clearing where a group of men, their voices a low murmur, ceased talking and their heads turned, focusing on her.

A man rose from the fallen log he was seated upon and Yvette turned her attention to him as he strode towards her. He was tall and wearing the cloth cap favoured by men of the region, a leather jacket, military style, fastened tight against the cold, a woollen scarf tucked inside and pulled high around his chin and ears. All Yvette saw of him were grey eyes, not steel, but softer. His nose was long but slightly off-set towards the right, his high cheekbones were covered with smooth pale skin, protected around the jaw from the cold by a day or two of stubble. When he reached out his hand to shake it in a very British way, for a moment Yvette though he might be the SOE radio operator, until he spoke.

'I am Vincent, pleased to meet you. Would you like some wine or coffee? I suggest you take the wine.'

Breaking contact with his hand, Yvette replied. 'Yvette and yes please, wine.'

Vincent motioned that she should follow, and she watched as he took the cup from the log where he sat and poured white wine from a dirty green bottle. Yvette wondered if she should have chosen coffee which she presumed was in the steel jug that was resting on the embers of the fire.

Vincent passed the cup of wine and she nodded towards the flames. 'Is it not dangerous, lighting a fire? The smoke will be seen from the road.' Yvette was curious, taking in the makeshift wooden shelters that were scattered around the camp and what looked like straw bedding covered with blankets underneath. 'How many of you stay here?'

'Nine of us here but throughout the forest which stretches to the other side of the valley there are more, but it is safer in small pockets. These men are from my village. The Boche know that there are foresters at work, if they see smoke, they presume it's the old men, and if they did venture inside, we have lookouts, they will warn us.'

Yvette sipped her wine, still self-conscious and feeling the curious eyes of the others on her. 'I didn't see anyone.'

'You were not meant to. Now, do you have something for me?'

Remembering why she was there, Yvette flushed, wondering how the hell she was going to retrieve the note from her bra in full view of everyone. Instead she turned and took the parcel of food from the pannier on her bike. It was bound in one of Tante Helene's tablecloths which she carried over to the group of men seated on the ground. 'I must take this back but please, help yourselves to the food.'

The men fell upon the bundle and while they were eating,

she turned her back, undid the top button of her coat and desperately rummaged inside her clothing, pulling out the note which she handed to Vincent, praying that she wasn't blushing, ignoring too the slight smile on his lips.

'Come, we will go now. The operator is with another group, you can wait while the message is sent then I will escort you home.'

'No, there is no need, I will remember the way. It's dangerous and you should stay hidden, and you should eat, look, it will be all gone.'

Vincent appeared to ignore her and began to walk. 'It is fine, I am going to see my family, they live close to Helene so I will accompany you. My mother will be glad to feed me.'

Once they were on their way, they chatted easily as they followed a well-worn narrow footpath, the winter sun lighting the way when it managed to slip through the branches overhead.

Vincent told her he was the son of a dairy farmer, but he was a blacksmith and had learned the craft from his grandfather. His skills had been destined for the Nazi machine, which was why he'd fled and joined the Maquis. Yvette was curious to know how they managed to live out in the forest at this time of year.

'It is hard, but those who sympathise keep us fed. The winter is worse but when I am cold at night, I tell myself that I would be colder in the prison camps, because that is where I would be now. I will never work for them, the Boche, I would rather die.'

There were thousands like Vincent, spread across France, but they were becoming more organised, supplied with the tools of war by the Allies, aided by agents like Yvette. Vincent seemed glad of her involvement, saying that women could travel freely and whilst still under suspicion were more likely to pass through checkpoints and operate clandestinely and unhindered.

'From now on you will take any orders directly from me, is

that understood? We will work as a team, I need your skills and it is a pleasant change to see a pretty face, you have cheered me up today. Do you smoke?'

Taken aback slightly by his statement, Yvette answered the question. 'Yes, I do, and yes I understand.'

Vincent passed her a cigarette and they smoked as they walked, Yvette enjoying his company and trying hard not to take furtive glances at his profile or acknowledge how odd she felt inside.

'Is it not dangerous, visiting your family?'

Vincent took a drag of his cigarette then shrugged. 'Everything has its risks but I know this area better than the Boche, so they will have to be smart to catch me, but still, I am careful and I have a place in the woods. I stay there sometimes because I like to keep an eye on my family and my terrible sister.'

'What's wrong with your sister?'

'Pah, she is headstrong and has ideas, and is upset that the war has ruined her plans. My father cannot control her, and she fights with my mother all the time. The only person she listens to is me.'

Yvette was enjoying hearing about his family, in such bizarre and unfamiliar circumstances it was a moment of escape, and she liked his voice, deep and hoarse, probably the effects of outdoor living, strong cigarettes and wood smoke. There was a hint of humour too and in his next comment something else.

'I will take you to my place in the woods, it is easy to find by the stream and then if you ever need me, or time alone, you can go there. Polo knows where it is too, he brings me food and cigarettes.'

Not quite sure what to say, but knowing she was thrilled and terrified at the same time, Yvette asked about the radio operator instead.

Vincent explained it was imperative to relocate him

frequently because his safety was of paramount importance, the operator was their link to the Allies and a prize for the Boche if they caught him. He too had been parachuted in and now moved between the various groups along the line, it was safer that way.

'I expect you will be glad to meet one of your fellow agents, perhaps you will know him.'

Yvette thought it unlikely. 'I doubt it, my head was in such a spin during training I'm surprised I even remember who I am, let alone the face of another agent. But tell me, who was the little boy who brought the message?'

'Ah, my little shadow. That is Polo. His aunt owns the *chambre d'hotes* in the village, he is an orphan, and everyone has taken him under their wing. He is a good kid, and loyal too. You can trust him. I taught him to poach and he knows the woods near my home like this,' Vincent held up the back of his hand, 'and if you ever want rabbit stew, he is your man, or boy I suppose.'

Yvette smiled. 'I will remember, and I'll watch out for him too, while you are away.'

They had reached a wider track that split the forest in two, crossing over they disappeared once again into its depths where, by the time Vincent had asked her where she was from and she had abandoned any ideas of secrecy, enjoying telling him about her parents and home, they had reached another camp of many more men. After pleasantries were exchanged, they were guided to a dugout fortified by logs, and here Yvette met her fellow agent, code name Nelson, a man she'd never met before and who seemed arrogant and unfriendly. Aware of the rumours that radio operators had a short life expectancy due to the cat and mouse nature of a sometimes solitary existence, Yvette put it down to that. After the brusque manner with which he addressed her, Yvette hoped that the need to be in his company wouldn't arise again. They remained only minutes, she gave him her code name for the cipher so at least HQ would now know that Agent Nadine had survived the drop and was operational. Then Vincent and Yvette departed, she was glad to get away and spend the journey home in the company of a man infinitely more personable.

After that, Vincent would appear more frequently than Yvette thought he should, a whistle from across the farmyard would alert her to his presence and then they'd wander for a while across the field. Spending a few minutes smoking, he'd ask how she was, she'd enquire if he was warm enough or hungry. It was all very chaste, yet Yvette sensed that given the right signal the warm blood that ran through Vincent's veins would quickly bubble and boil. It was just over two months later that a spring evening during Yvette's first mission as a saboteur would mark a turning point in her life, for many reasons.

16

DIMENSIONS COLLIDE

CHÂTEAUBRIANT, 2005

They were back at the hotel, sitting in the peaceful courtyard garden at the rear. Dottie had made the call to the *mairie* and had been told he was still on holiday, but an appointment had been made and a new plan struck up. Dottie thought it would be nice to visit the sea, a day at La Baule was in order and while she paddled in the Atlantic, Maude could do a bit of painting or snap some photos, whatever she wished. They were on holiday after all, and Dottie was mindful not to turn the expedition into some kind of maudlin trudge in the mire, especially when the next part of her story, her happiness with Vincent aside, was about to head in that direction.

She watched as Maude scribbled in her journal, writing up the story so far. Dottie had cut her story short in the restaurant, knowing that it was not the place to fully reminisce and that her memories would ruin what had been an exceptionally good meal.

Oddly enough, after a starter of vegetable salad, the main course was rabbit, and had led to her explaining more about shy little Polo who in the absence of Vincent became her shadow, and would leave a gift of one on Tante Helene's doorstep and in return, she would make sure the pockets of her apron or coat held a sugary treat, in case she bumped into him as she frequently did. The black marketeers thrived during the war, and the town and city people who came foraging in the countryside were happy to swap an old hen for a tin of pastilles.

Noticing Maude click the top of her pen and relax into her deckchair, Dottie suggested they order some wine and make the most of the late afternoon sun.

'That's a nice idea. Oh look, there's the waiter, he must have read our minds.' Maude began waving to attract his attention and once their order was taken, settled down, speaking with her eyes closed. 'Are you going to tell me what happened next then? I got the impression that what happened on your mission wasn't pleasant?'

'Yes, but I also didn't want to discuss my love life over a dish of strawberries while that nosey woman earwigged. Did you see her, the American? This is why you *must* learn to speak French, Maude, it would come in very handy.'

'Yes, I did see her and yes it would, so I promise that as soon as I'm back from my travels I'll enrol on a course, or buy some CDs. Does that make you happy?'

'Why on earth would you do that when I could teach you?'

'Because, Grandmother dearest, I would rather stick my head in a bucket of poo than have you for a teacher, but you can help me practice, if you're good.' Maude opened one eye and smiled at Dottie whose attention was drawn by the arrival of the wine.

After it was poured, they chatted about the itinerary for the following days.

'I promise, I'm not doing it on purpose, stretching out the holiday and our time together. But it's lovely to change plans, go where the wind takes us, don't you think?'

'Yes, I do, that's sort of the vibe I was going for when I head to Oz, you know, wanderlust, go with the wind and all that.'

Dottie silently kicked herself in the foot, knowing what Maude was getting at. 'Mmm, I suppose so, it's just a pity you're going with...'

'Gran... stop! This is our precious time together so don't spoil it, okay?' Maude encouraged Dottie to continue with her story. 'Now, tell me more about Vincent because he sounds gorgeous, but a bit cheeky too, even though he was the mysterious leader of the Maquis.'

Dottie laughed. 'You make him sound like a film star, but I suppose to me he was. And even though we were living in an occupied zone, we still had feelings, hopes, and now and then, especially with Vincent, we allowed ourselves to have dreams.'

'Did you, what dreams?'

'Never mind, because you're getting ahead of yourself again, and without going into gory details, about good or bad things, I need to set the scene and explain how I remember it methodically, or in the bursts of memories as they pop up.'

Maude took a bowl of crisps from the table. 'Okey-dokey, well I'll sit here and listen quietly while you take me back in time, excuse the crunching noises.'

Dottie tutted and refilled her glass, and went back to a dark and eerie railway siding on the outskirts of the very town they were staying in. Suddenly the enormity of that moment shook her; the sense of two dimensions colliding. The same woman who crouched in the undergrowth, the worrying stench of fox shit close by, too terrified to move, about to commit a deadly sin, had no clue that many years later she would be back, seated across from her granddaughter, drinking wine, eating crisps and telling the tale.

17

THE DEADLIEST OF SINS

CHÂTEAUBRIANT, 1943

Yvette thought the blood pulsing through her heart was going to explode then shoot out of her ears up and her throat, or was she going to be sick? Yes, that was probably what it was. Never, even when the night monsters came to her bedroom as a child or when she jumped out of the plane into the abyss, had she been so utterly frozen and consumed by fear as she was now.

They had set off on foot earlier that day, lying low and trekking for hours along the outskirts of Châteaubriant until they reached their target; the bridge that spanned the railway line, running along the edge of the remote goods yard. The day had dragged, they were all tired and hungry, waiting for it to get dark before their work could begin. The explosives were to be laid under the track below the road bridge overhead. The following morning, a goods train was scheduled to leave the station at Châteaubriant, carrying supplies destined for the enemy. The moment it entered the short tunnel, passing over the trigger, the explosion would hopefully derail the train, damage its contents and the bridge. Their aim was to cause maximum destruction to the transport link that was used to ferry troops north, towards the Atlantic Wall along the heavily fortified section of the coast.

Yvette's eyes scanned the darkness, watching for a signal from the other side of the yard that the wires had been cut and access gained onto the track. The banking on each side of the bridge were inaccessible and intelligence said that the yard was disused.

Their comrades, Florian and Xavier, had gone first and once they saw the flashlight, she and Vincent would join them. Benoit, who was a few metres behind her, would remain as lookout. Yvette's role was to set the explosives that were in the sack by Vincent's side. When she heard a noise, a creaking, Yvette instantly knew it wasn't Xavier or Florian and to her horror this was confirmed when the door of one of the buildings in the sidings opened and a German soldier stepped out. They'd been told the place was deserted.

Three sets of eyes watched from the undergrowth. After the guard turned and spoke to someone inside, laughing before he made his way across the yard directly towards them, the Maquisards crouched lower. Yvette prayed and imagined Vincent and Benoit doing the same. The distance between their hiding place and the door was no more than five metres, so when the soldier, his rifle flicked onto his back, pulled down his zip, the stench of fox mingled with that of urine and Yvette gagged.

In the seconds that followed she saw it all play out in slow motion even though her brain recorded it in real time, allowing her to react instinctively.

While the soldier peed with his back to the fence, Yvette saw the three flashes of Florian's torch and she knew that when the soldier turned to go inside, he would see the next two, and they would be finished. Their information was flawed, and they had no clue how many more guards were inside the building –

perhaps there were just two, perhaps a whole division. She had to act. Vincent had a gun, too noisy, but she had a knife.

The zip went up. The soldier turned.

The torch flashed twice.

The soldier saw, stalled for a second, reached for his rifle.

Yvette leapt forward, took out her knife, and throwing her left arm around his neck, yanked his chin backwards and sliced with her right hand.

There was a thud and the sound of whistling in her ears as she looked down at the staring eyes of the soldier as he bled out. Then the sound of a voice: Vincent.

'Yvette, YVETTE!'

Startled, she responded, speechlessly holding out the knife that was covered in blood like her hands.

'Go to Florian now, hurry, here take the bag. I will check inside. If there are many we abandon, if not, wait until I arrive at the fence then we will proceed. Benoit, move the body, quickly. Take the gun and use it if necessary.'

Benoit emerged from the shadows as Vincent, his voice harsh and clear, urged Yvette on. 'Go now, hurry.'

Her mouth was dry and she knew her eyes stared, not blinking as they followed three more flashes from the torch, her legs moving with a will of their own. When she reached Florian and Xavier she collapsed in a heap onto her knees, dropping the knife and frantically wiping her hands on the grass, not caring which animal had left its waste there, it was better than the blood. She managed to mumble to the others what had happened and relate Vincent's orders, so they waited in silence for what felt like hours, listening for the sound of a hundred Nazi boots.

Two gunshots echoed through the darkness, then nothing, no German voices raising the alarm, and when they did hear boots running in their direction they belonged to a single figure:

Vincent. 'There were two more. Playing cards, drunk, incompetent. Now hurry, let's get this finished then we can go. Xavier, stay here. Florian, keep watch further down the bank, Benoit is over there in the trees. Yvette and I will do the rest.'

Standing, Yvette sucked in air and as Florian moved to hold back the wire, she caught Vincent's eye. Holding out her knife, clean of blood, he nodded, then inclined his head for her to go, and taking the knife and shoving it back into her pocket, she obeyed. She tried not to think about the scene at the sidings. Even though her hands were clean, she knew in her heart that they would always be stained, and on her mind, the unseeing eyes of the soldier she had killed would be imprinted forever.

Yvette didn't go back to Tante Helene's that night. The moonlit trek home during curfew hours was as treacherous as it was exhausting and when the group split up, saying weary *au revoir*s, Yvette was too tired to argue when Vincent took her hand and told her that she should stay with him in the woods. His cabin was sparse and made from scraps of timber but provided shelter from the wind and rain. Nestled within the elms it was camouflaged by leaves and branches. It was still dark, and they followed the stream, the numbing kiss of fatigue teasing the brain.

He guided her to the bed of straw and hemp sacking then when she lay down, more or less collapsing on top of it, he lay by her side and covered them with blankets, and held her in his arms. When she woke the next morning, Yvette couldn't even remember going to sleep and for a few disorientated moments, had no idea where she was. Then it came back, she'd been lying next to Vincent, who was now gone.

Kneeling by the stream with cupped hands, Yvette thirstily slurped the ice-cold water that trickled by. Then to her horror she noticed the remnants of her sin on her hands and clothes, so she discarded her coat and began frantically scrubbing at her fingernails, eradicating the dried blood and dirt that clung to them. After washing her face she still felt dirty so slipped off her clothes and splashed water on her body, shivering but at the same time welcoming the cleansing of her skin, even though her soul remained sullied.

Yvette was about to dress when she became aware of movement, the crunching of twigs and the rustling of leaves as someone approached. Standing as she tried to cover herself, Yvette looked up and saw Vincent.

'You are awake... I brought food from my mother and some coffee, we can boil water in the can.' Vincent was holding a small bundle to his chest which he placed on the floor at the door of the cabin, as his eyes glanced quickly at Yvette's partially covered body.

There was a shift in the dynamic between them, Yvette felt it, and it was as though the world around them was holding its breath, waiting. Stepping forward three swift paces, Yvette flung herself against him, clinging on to his sturdy body and feeling his strong arms wrap around her. When she found the courage to look up, Vincent's eyes met hers and taking her face in his hands, he kissed her gently, his lips soft on hers. But Yvette wanted more and when she responded, shyness was replaced by desire, and after breaking away, as breathless as she, Vincent took her hand in his and led her inside the cabin.

It was more than lust or young love, passion or thrill, that Yvette felt for Vincent. It was a combination of all those, along with admiration, awe, respect, and an immense desire to make him proud of her, to see her as his equal, have her stand beside him, a trusted member of the Maquis.

So far, she hadn't let him or anyone down, their network worked well and within the small group of Maquisard's that hid in the outlying hills, valleys and forests, she had formed an allegiance.

Perhaps it was borne of mutual respect that she spoke their language fluently, had risked her life to get there and continued to do so. And they seemed to like that she could hold her own, grudgingly impressed when she demonstrated the self-defence moves she'd been taught in Scotland, and she wasn't afraid to kill. Not that she was proud of this, but when it came to a choice between a sentry and her fellow fighters, her training and survival instinct kicked in.

In the summer it was harder to operate unseen and with more spare time, Yvette and Vincent had loved each other whenever the chance arose, lying in fields of maize with the sun on their skin, or on the bed of straw and jute seeping through the cracks in the roof of the cabin. Their snatched hours together were precious, sometimes hurried kisses in the farmyard, or when they parted and thought nobody was watching. Then there were whole nights of passion and laughter, when they would talk until the dawn broke and bathe in the stream, hungry but starved of nothing they really needed. Everyone knew, of course, but who could deny them their love or happiness?

But it was cold now, winter had them in its grip and whilst it made life hard for the Maquis who lived in the open air, darkness was their friend and kept them busy. While Vincent was away she got on with farm and village life and in between keeping an eye out for little Polo who, in the absence of his hero, gravitated towards Yvette, she attempted to make a friend of Béatrice, Vincent's sister. It was not a joyous task, simply because his wilful, vain sibling was not an easy person to warm to or get along with. Even her mama Lucille sometimes appeared to dislike her while her papa Raymonde sought an easy life and kept his head down.

But Yvette persevered for two reasons that, unfortunately, soon became three. The first was that spending time in the home where Vincent grew up and still lived before he joined the Resistance gave her great comfort. The second was that she missed and secretly yearned for her own family, so the Famille Matis provided surrogates even if she could have done without a sister. The third crept up unexpectedly and had Yvette not been in the right place at the right time, her observant eyes would have missed something that felt like a slap in the face.

It was a chilly December morning and they had been given a lift on the back of a hay cart to Châteaubriant. It was market day and Yvette had gone along with Béatrice because it broke the monotony of winter in the countryside and wasting hours hoping that Vincent would appear. It was also an opportunity for surveillance and once in town she made sure they took a stroll past the *mairie* that was now emblazoned with swastikas, and then up past the chateau to count the number of trucks and see how many soldiers marched by. She had been tasked with buying flour for Tante Helene, if there was any, and it was while she was standing in the queue she noticed that Béatrice, too bored and tired to wait with her, had wandered off. By the time Yvette had reached the front and secured her ration of flour, her feet were frozen, and she wasn't looking forward to the walk back to the village, regretting bringing bicycle-less Béatrice along.

At a loss where to start looking, Yvette retraced her steps thinking that maybe her fickle friend had set off home. The route took her back past the *mairie* and that's where she spotted Béatrice, halfway up one of the twisting alleyways that ran along and behind the ancient houses of the town, talking with a German soldier.

Immediately stepping back so she could not be seen, Yvette watched intently, reading the body language of both as they smoked and chatted, becoming more convinced by the second that this was not their first meeting and that something was greatly amiss. The way he touched the waves of Béatrice's yellow-blonde hair, then the stroke along the back of her hand. And she was too close, stepping nearer rather than recoiling from the unwanted advances of a cruel invader. Once their cigarettes were smoked it appeared the conversation was over and after he whispered in her ear, Béatrice giggled then gave him a coy wave before setting off towards the road. The soldier strutted off in the opposite direction. Rather than alert Béatrice to her presence, Yvette raced ahead and then slowed to a stroll, not caring if her flirtatious companion caught up, glad of the time to think.

Yvette heard Béatrice before she felt her hand on her shoulder and along with the whiff of cigarette smoke, caught the smug glint and hint of glee in her eyes and voice.

'Where did you get to, Yvette? I went to look at the church noticeboard and when I came back to the shop you were gone.'

Liar, thought Yvette as she continued to walk, too angry and astounded to look at Béatrice.

'I thought you were bored and had set off home without me, that's all.'

'Oh, I see. Did you get what you wanted?'

Yvette almost asked, *did you*? But bit her lip and instead merely nodded as a newly animated Béatrice chattered on about the dress she was going to make from some curtains she'd been given by her friend, Celeste. By the time they'd reached the village, Yvette had some kind of plan in her head.

She would say nothing to Béatrice, give her no hint of what

she had seen but, in the meantime and where possible, would watch her like a hawk and if this meant spending more time at Vincent's home then she would make excuses to pop by. The problem was that Yvette was needed for other things and she couldn't babysit Béatrice forever. What she could do was clip her wings and a word in her mother's ear might be enough to curtail the trips into town. Lucille worshipped the ground her son walked on and just a hint that her daughter's flirtations with the Boche might put Vincent in danger would be enough, Yvette was sure.

There would be no need to alert Vincent or Florian, not yet. The shame the brother would feel over his sister's betrayal was unthinkable, and when you loved someone you shielded them from everything, if you could. Yvette worshipped and adored the whole of Vincent and she would protect him to the last, of this she was avowed.

18

LOVE TRIANGLE

LA BAULE, 2005

They were ensconced at a quieter end of the beach and while Maude made sketches, Dottie forced herself to relax and take in the view. It was a gloriously sunny day and the flat pale-gold sand stretched languorously around the arced bay, white ripples from the Atlantic swell swishing in and out, making eager children squeal and paddling adults wince as it nipped their ankles.

Dottie thought she might chance dipping her toes later, but for now she was enjoying the shade of her parasol, the softness of the blanket on which she sat as it caressed her skin, while her feet poked off the end and wiggled in the sand. Her attention turned to Maude who was away with the fairies. Her eyes scanned the scene, then she gave a few strokes of her pencil before she returned to study shape and form, no doubt committing the colours and atmosphere to memory and added to the photos and video she'd taken earlier.

Lost in thoughts and memories of her own, Dottie had been trying to reconcile herself with one particular fact that she'd either buried on purpose, or that had somehow got lost in the maelstrom of hurt and confusion she'd felt after the war. Yes, she'd clung on to those nights of passion and how it felt to see Vincent's face and touch his skin, even the laughter of his voice could echo in her ears if she allowed it. But it was the plans for after she'd somehow managed to erase, or was it that in her obstinacy she'd also chosen to forget because to admit she was human, had feelings like lots of women of her time, would have rendered her weak.

Dottie had blotted out the nights they'd imagined after; what they would do, where they would live. They'd believed in victory and the day that Vincent would reopen the forge and she would live in the apartment above, as his wife and one day mother to his children. Yvette would have willingly given up her desk at the War Office and been content with visits to and from her family. She would have tended the garden, cooked Vincent's meals and washed his clothes, grateful to have survived, to be with the man she loved in a village she had come to call home.

This memory had actually rocked Dottie to the core when it had come to her whilst she was explaining to Maude all about Vincent, but she'd batted it away, only to be reminded later during those irritating hours when sleep evades you. By dawn, when the bedside clock returned to single figures, Dottie had intended telling Maude all about it, and perhaps would have cut her some slack over Lachlan had she not overheard a muted but very obvious row going on between them in the corridor.

She tried not to listen, but it was her grandmotherly duty to make sure Maude was okay so she pressed her ear to the door, only for a second or two, mind.

'Lachlan, what is your problem?'

A pause while Boomerang Boy explained.

'I can't keep ringing you every five minutes, it costs too much and I sent you a huge text last night telling you where we'd been so what more do you want?'

Dottie found it very frustrating to only be able to hear one side of the conversation.

'Well frankly, I'm shocked at how needy you're coming across. Seriously, I'm on holiday with my gran not romping round Ibiza with a bunch of sex mad uni mates.'

Well said, thought Dottie, pressing her ear harder against the door.

'No, I wouldn't rather be in Ibiza than with you... I am not being patronising... oh piss off, Lachlan.'

At this Dottie tittered and then scuttled as fast as she could to the bed where she pretended to be looking for something in her bag when Maude walked in.

'Stop trying to look innocent, Gran, I know you were listening.' Maude marched over to the dresser and grabbed her car keys before turning to face Dottie. 'Right, are you ready? We need to get going, and don't forget your glow sticks and vodka, just in case we decide to go to a rave and get wasted on the beach.'

Biting her bottom lip and trying not to laugh, Dottie picked up her bag and silently followed Maude out the door, resisting the urge to ask if linen trousers, hush puppies and a floaty blouse would pass the dress code, and if the bouncers would even let an octogenarian in?

Maude was packing up, so Dottie began setting out their picnic. It wasn't fancy, just some baguettes and fruit they'd bought from a supermarket on the way in and a couple of bottles of water. Nothing had been said about the argument on the phone and really there had been no point in asking, it was obvious that Lachlan was feeling neglected.

The thing was, Dottie found herself in a bit of a predicament because as much as she believed The Koala Kid was wrong for

Maude, her recent moment of lucidity had reminded her that when you are in love you do, say and feel things that to others seem crazy. All you want is to be with that person, forever, even if it is far away from your family, who love you too. How could she deny her dear Maude that? Even worse, could Dottie let her go?

Maude sauntered across, her long legs that protruded from cut-off shorts were slightly pink as were her arms, exposed in a vest top and adorned at the wrist by stacks of bangles. The straw cowboy hat perched on her head shielded Maude's eyes but after dumping her painting satchel on the sand, she flopped next to Dottie who scrutinised them, looking for signs of sadness. There were none. Actually, Maude was upbeat and as usual, curious and hungry.

'Ooh, sarnies. I'm starved... pass me the crisps, Gran, the chicken ones.' Maude accepted a bag and proceeded to open them. 'I've been thinking, you haven't told me how you met Hugh. You mentioned that you first spotted him in Scotland with Maude but you didn't know him properly then. And Uncle Konki, where does he fit into all of this?'

Dottie was repositioning the parasol. The sun was baking now and if it hadn't been for the brisk breeze, she'd have insisted they found somewhere more shaded, but for now she would survive. She was also thinking about Hugh and where he slotted into the story, definitely before Konstantin. Sometimes her head was such a jumble, like a ball of badly wound wool but all it took was a bit of patience, something Maude lacked, and eventually Dottie managed to straighten it all out.

'I thought I'd told you, but perhaps not... he's been there forever so I assume that everyone knows our story.'

Maude shook her head and stuffed crisps into her mouth, crunching loudly.

Dottie tutted, took a sip of water, and tucked a stray curly lock behind her right ear as she concentrated. 'Now let me think; oh yes, it was just before I met Maude again, in the spring, that's when he turned up and I must say I was very pleased to see a familiar face, you know, another agent. It reminded me that however tenuous, there was a link back to London, others like me were out there and knew how it felt to be away from home.'

'Was he pleased to see you? I bet he was, and how did he feel about Vincent, was he jealous?' Maude was unwrapping her baguette as she quizzed.

'I have no idea, Maude, but I will allow you your little fantasies about my imaginary love triangle–' Dottie was at this point interrupted by Maude.

'Well, technically it was a love square, if you think about it, because somewhere along the way Uncle Konki turns up and goes all gooey-eyed over you, too.' Maude chortled, then took a bite out of her baguette.

Ignoring the jibe, Dottie carried on. 'I was going to say that Hugh was and always has been a perfect gentleman and had he any romantic notions towards me he's managed to keep them to himself for all this time and proved to be a good friend. So no, there were no pistols at dawn or anything like that.'

'That's a bit boring, but go on, tell me what happened and then I want to know about Uncle Konki. And you said you met Maude again. I love hearing about her.'

The mood had been upbeat, yet Dottie felt a dip, knowing what was on the horizon of her story, and how she wished she'd seen it coming. Forcing a smile, Dottie then drank some water and while Maude picked the tomatoes out of her food, she got on with the tale, and went back to the day Hugh turned up, and she met Claude.

19

YVETTE AND CLAUDE

RENAZÉ, 1944

The Café des Amis was full. All the tables were taken, and the bar was lined with men; the stalwarts of the village barely visible through the swirl of smoke. Armand acknowledged Yvette when she entered and with an almost imperceptible flick of his head indicated she should go through to the back. Following the silent command, she pushed through the crowd leaving Polo at the door. He was as eager to see Vincent as she, but he wasn't allowed inside and had to go home to do his chores.

'Go now, otherwise your aunt will be cross. You can see him tomorrow, come to the farm and wait there.'

Polo hovered and seemed reluctant to go, staring past Yvette and scanning the faces of the men in the café. 'Okay, I will be there early. Say hello to him... see you tomorrow.'

Shoving one hand in the pocket of his shorts, Polo wandered off, his shoulders slightly hunched and his head low, leaving Yvette with mixed emotions; disappointment for him and giddy excitement for her because Vincent was waiting inside.

. . .

The corridor that led to the kitchen behind the bar was without a bulb and gloomy. The linoleum underfoot was worn, and she knew to her cost how easy it was to trip on one of the torn patches, so trod carefully despite her eagerness to reunite with Vincent. Her mind and heart were imagining a passionate embrace but when she turned the handle and entered the kitchen, her eyes immediately told her this would not be possible. At the table, wine glasses and the remnants of a meal scattered across its surface, sat four men. Florian with a cigarette flopping from his lips gave a nod, Benoit in his teashade glasses looked bashful but did the same, the other man had his back to the door. Naturally, Yvette's eyes were only seeking one face and when she found it, Vincent's eyes told her he was happy to see her. Sadly, it became immediately clear that this was business and when the unknown man stood and turned, the meeting suddenly turned serious.

Yvette recognised him instantly, it was the agent she'd played cards with in Scotland, the one Estelle had taken a dislike to, or harboured a grudge against or something, she couldn't quite remember but it was definitely him. Unfortunately, his face was one you wouldn't forget.

He held out his hand. 'At last, Agent Nadine, pleased to m-meet you.'

Yvette shook his hand and at the same time felt rather taken aback that he didn't remember her, but then logic took over, why would he? 'Call me Yvette. Did London send you?'

'Yes, m-my code name is Victor, but m-my cover name is Claude. London directed me to you. I'm to make my way to Normandy and need a place to s-stay while I await further orders. I can m-make myself useful here before I s-start to recruit again.' Claude's eyes flicked between Yvette and Vincent, as though he was trying to establish who was in charge of the group.

Vincent stepped into that role. 'It is fine, and I know where you can stay... there is a place on the edge of the village, I will take you there. We have curfew at 8pm so we need to hurry. Yvette, I will meet with you tomorrow.'

Claude seemed eager although his stammer slowed him down. 'I n-need to send word to London during your next transmission, can I meet with your radio operator?'

Vincent was abrupt in his reply. 'No. He has been moved to a safe house but I can get a message to him. There is no need for you to meet. It is too dangerous.'

'And your circuit leader, where is he?'

Vincent was once again to the point. 'Dead. The Gestapo executed him. For now, Yvette and I lead. We take our orders from London, now move.'

At this Claude gave a curt nod and then the group began to disperse, chairs scraped on the floor and three of the men made their way out of the back door which led to an alley. Vincent lingered, resting his hand on Yvette's arm suggesting she wait. There was no time other than for a fleeting kiss and as she pulled away, she spotted Claude watching from the doorway, turning away quickly and looking bashful. They said their goodbyes and hurriedly made their way in separate directions, Yvette sort of understanding how little Polo had felt earlier.

Movement was harder now with the curfew and lighter nights. Following a busy winter of sabotage, collecting and distributing supplies dropped by the RAF, moving evaders on to their next safe house under the cover of darkness, guided by the light of the moon, spring brought its own dangers. That's why she suspected Vincent was installing Claude in the old farmhouse rather than taking him to the forest or his own hut in the woods, but that was their special place. Once again, she would have to wait.

They had work to do and there was trouble on the horizon.

Eventually she would have to tell Vincent about Béatrice who was being more stubborn than ever since her mother had forbidden her to go into town. According to Lucille, Béatrice didn't take kindly to her 'imprisonment' and didn't need protecting from the lure of the Nazis. Nevertheless, that was the new rule and since it was imposed, life in the Matis household had been hell.

During the ride home, the clicking of the bicycle spokes the only sound on the isolated roads, Yvette resigned herself to another night alone in her bed and pondered on the errand that Vincent had in store for her. Tomorrow perhaps she would get to see Claude, maybe hear some news from home, until then she pedalled on, one eye on the rose-pink sky and the sun that was setting behind the hill, almost curfew.

Yvette did in fact see Claude again a few days later when she cycled to the old farm to drop off supplies, and he looked pleased to see her, no doubt bored, waiting for orders from London or Vincent. It was a sunny day and they sat behind the barn in the meadow of cowslips while he ate.

'Are you s-sure you can't take m-me to Vincent? I'm going insane here.'

'No, sorry. It's his way of protecting our circuit, in case one of us is taken. If he wants you, he will find you or send someone. Anyway, I'm here now, you can chat to me.' Yvette watched as Claude began to tear the bread, not looking particularly happy about his meagre meal.

'How long have you been here? I expect you've been busy, what've you been up to?' Claude began to eat, washing down a chunk of bread with watered-down wine.

'Just over a year. I could have gone back for a rest but I chose to stay and anyway it's dangerous, the journey home.

And yes, we've been busy with the usual stuff. What about you?'

Claude shrugged and smirked. 'The usual stuff, but my m-main job is recruiting, that's why I'm going n-north and you c-can't kid me. I think the real reason you stayed is your hand-some c-comrade.'

Yvette blushed crimson. 'I don't know what you mean.'

'N-no, of course you don't. So, if you're too shy to talk about lover boy tell m-me what it's like here, where you are billeted?'

Stretching her legs, Yvette told him about Tante Helene and how she made her feel welcome, and that she was taking a well-earned break from Resistance work now that Yvette was there. Instead, Tante Helene was focusing her attention on the black market and she was the person to go and see if you wanted a certain something from her contacts in the city.

'And the c-café, do you g-go there? Perhaps we can meet and drink some of this t-terrible wine. I take it the owner is a sympa-thiser and will give us a discount.' Claude winked and smiled.

He still seemed as shy as she remembered. Yvette also noticed his stammer but politely ignored it. When he'd spoken French the other day at the café, he appeared sure of himself in front of the men so maybe, when he was hiding behind a facade, another character, he felt more relaxed or confident than when he was boring old Hugh from England.

'Yes, Armand is a huge help, but no, we pay our way. He has a family to feed. Now, tell me about England, have you been back? You must have come here before me because I didn't see you at training again.' A rabbit darted from behind a discarded tractor wheel and as she waited for a reply she thought of Polo who would want it for a stew.

'I was dropped in October '42. S-so you came alone?'

'No, with another agent, Estelle, she was in Scotland with me, you might know her as Maude.' Yvette felt safe telling Hugh, he was one of theirs and anyway, it was good to talk openly for a change with someone you trusted, not in whispers and secrets.

Claude looked thoughtful then brightened. 'Ah, yes, I know who you mean, with the blonde hair... is she here in Renazé?'

At this Yvette felt the dip of sadness. 'No, she went to Nantes, that's all I know, and I haven't heard from her since.'

They both fell silent while Claude ate, and Yvette was lost in her imaginings of her friend until a spot of rain landed on her leg. 'Bugger, I'd best get going. I've left a whole line of sheets out. I might be back tomorrow, if I can. Vincent has been given orders and I'm off somewhere soon, so it could be Florian. Maybe they'll find you something to do, or blow up, or even steal; have a bit of fun with the Boche.'

Claude didn't comment at first and she thought he looked downcast, perhaps at being left alone, or was he jealous when she mentioned Vincent? But she pushed the idea from her mind; that he might have a small crush on her.

Claude stood and brushed crumbs off his trousers as he spoke. 'Okay, I'll wait, although I m-might have a scout around and get my bearings. Best to be prepared. Take c-care, wherever Vincent sends you and come and tell me all about it when you return, that's if I haven't gone stir-crazy or starved.'

Yvette tried to make light of his comments. 'Well you can do a bit of foraging while you are wandering or set a trap and use what they taught us in training. There's a rabbit around here somewhere just asking for trouble.'

It seemed to make him smile but as she pedalled away, she saw the shadow that crossed his face and the slow wave of his hand made her feel melancholy. *Poor Claude, his life on the road must be lonely.* Yvette felt rather blessed, having somewhere she could call home, her comrades and friends in the village and, of course, Vincent.

20

PLACE D'ARISTIDE

NANTES, 2005

They'd been driving around and around for over twenty minutes in rush hour traffic, trying to find somewhere to park and now Maude was losing the will to live. It was proving impossible to stay cool in the searing heat, especially when your Gran couldn't make her mind up if she wanted the air con on, the windows open, not the sunroof because it messed up her hair, the blower on her feet or face or both.

To make matters worse, Lachlan had gone into a sulk because apparently she was ignoring him. Well if he didn't watch his step, she would turn her phone off completely never mind leave it on silent. After an afternoon of swimming in the Atlantic and lazing on the sand, she'd glanced at her phone and spotted a list of messages which she'd ignored but simply by their existence, they had managed to put a dampener on her day.

And now, when Maude had envisaged a nice dinner in a seafront restaurant, her gran had suddenly decided she wanted to visit Nantes so she could tell the next part of her story. Not that it wasn't fascinating or anything, but the city was teeming with tourists and if they drove this circular route one more time, cathedral, chateau, quay, tram stop, cathedral, chateau... well Maude was going to scream.

It was obviously hugely important to Dottie that they came here, and Maude had a feeling that her gran's story was heading to a sad point, something bad was going to happen and maybe it occurred in Nantes. There was certainly no rushing her though, and Maude sensed that her gran was working her way through memories and putting them in order no matter how much it seemed to unsettle her. One thing that was for sure was Maude was completely in awe of Dottie and had had no idea how brave she'd been, not just in the work she'd done but leaving the life she knew behind, prepared to risk everything.

Over the past few nights, while her gran snored away, Maude had gone over her notes so far and tried to imagine what each of the characters might have looked like. She'd even googled images of Resistance fighters on her phone in the hope of capturing an essence of them; their clothes, background scenery, their faces and hair, anything really. Her scrolling had certainly achieved that because in every black-and-white photo she saw a Xavier as her gran described him, with his floppy cloth hat and neckerchief, or Vincent. Thierry in his white shirt tucked into trousers pulled high at the waist, braces and tatty jacket. Benoit in his round specs. Nearly all of them were wearing a beret or cap, rifles slung over shoulders, the odd cigarette dangling from a mouth like Florian. And in the women, skulking through streets bearing arms, standing side by side with the men, she saw her gran; fresh-faced and youthful, brave on the outside but terrified on the inside. Tante Helene wore a home-made dress, with tiny flowers, buttoned down the front. Through the photos Maude was starting to get it, most of all the camaraderie, the cause.

Maude thought it was sad that Dottie didn't have any actual photographs of her comrades, even Vincent, but then again knowing her gran she'd have locked them away in a box and refused to look at them like she'd refused to talk about the past for so long. At least now it was all tumbling out. She hoped it was helping and during texts had assured her mum that Dottie was doing okay, not overexerting herself or getting in a state, and it was true as far as Maude could see. This whole trip seemed to have invigorated her gran and yes, she was shattered in the evenings, but so was Maude, then in the morning, Dottie especially was raring to go.

Just as they were about to begin the circuit again, Dottie's arm stretched out and pointed, her forefinger bouncing up and down. 'There, there look, the red Fiat. Quick, quick, block the space so no other bugger can get in. Hurry, Maude, or we'll lose it.'

No intention of going round again, Maude zoomed forward and as soon as the Fiat moved out of the space, she manoeuvred the four-by-four, praying that it'd fit.

'Well done, Maudie, that was an excellent manoeuvre, now, let's check the sign and see how long we've got, then we can get on our way. I know where I'm going.'

Maude was reaching behind for her bag, beads of sweat along her hairline after her stressful mini-tour of the block, fifteen times! 'Are you sure, Gran? It's a long time since you've been here, what if it's all changed?'

A loud harrumph. 'Sometimes, Maude, you say the most stupid things. Have you seen this city?'

'No, Gran, just the same sodding streets for the last God knows how long, why?'

A raised eyebrow. 'Because it's ancient and that cathedral has been here forever and so have most of the buildings so, if we start off in the square just up there, it should lead us to where I want to go. Now stop dilly-dallying, some fresh air will do us both good – you look beautiful, if not a bit sweaty...'

At this remark Maude huffed then flicked up the visor, and after rummaging in her bag for some perfume which she sprayed liberally down her vest top and under her arms, did as she was told. Dottie read the street sign that told them they had two-hours free parking so once she'd replaced her sunglasses, she linked her arm through Maude's, and they set off up the street towards the Cathédrale St Pierre et St Paul, passing gift shops and art galleries, and busy restaurants and bars.

Dottie seemed determined and spritely as they dodged other pedestrians. 'Perhaps we can eat here tonight. What do you fancy for dinner? I know you wanted seafood, but we can go to Pornichet later in the week and have moules frittes.'

Maude knew the answer immediately but then had a question of her own. 'Pizza. A big fat massive one with everything on top... I deserve one after the trauma of city driving, but never mind that. When are you going to tell me why we are here and where we're going?'

There was a pause, Dottie had stopped on the pavement and was looking right and left, up at the buildings and street signs, as if she was getting her bearings before she finally answered.

'We're going to Maude's apartment so I can show you where she was living the last time I saw her, before we said goodbye.'

Dottie's words took Maude by surprise. She'd heard the sadness in them without even having to look into her gran's eyes, and when she did, they betrayed what was going on inside her heart. Not knowing what to say for the best Maude allowed herself to be guided along, curiosity overridden by concern for Dottie.

After a short walk they followed a narrower street, small terraced dwellings on either side and when Dottie stopped and asked a passer-by, Maude suspected they'd either taken a wrong turning or her memory wasn't that sharp. Nodding and thanking the man, Dottie pulled at Maude's arm and after no more than two or three minutes they took a right on to a wide road, separated down the middle by a pedestrian way, grassed on either side and dotted with wooden benches. The sign on the wall said 'Place d'Aristide'. The houses that lined the busy road were much grander than the ones they'd passed earlier, all with three or four, maybe five, storeys including attic windows, all of them encased in high walls with ornate iron railings on top.

Dottie was completely silent, scanning the houses on the opposite side of the road before setting off again, crossing quickly and coming to a stop by one of the benches on the grass. Maude remained quiet, giving her gran time alone with her thoughts.

Squeezing Maude's arm, Dottie pointed with the other towards a grey stone mansion that at a quick glance, and judging from the intercoms outside the huge double-fronted door, were now apartments.

'See that house there, number nine, with the balcony, the second one up to the left, that's where she was, waiting for me to arrive. I can picture her like it was yesterday, waving like crazy. She was so beautiful.'

Maude saw the tears that rolled down Dottie's cheeks and feeling her own eyes filling, sought to comfort her gran.

'Come on, let's sit here and then you can tell me all about her.' Maude stroked Dottie's arm and feeling her respond, they seated themselves more or less opposite the house.

While cars drove by and horns honked and city dwellers hurried home, Maude still heard her gran's intake of breath, perhaps gathering courage to tell her all about the original Maude, someone who had clearly touched Dottie's heart and soul.

21

REUNITED

NANTES, FRANCE, 1944

Y vette had never been so terrified but excited in her life. The train from Châteaubriant seemed to have stopped every five minutes at each rural station en route to Nantes. Locals piled on, heading for the city, mostly older passengers and women, some with children. The young men were nearly all gone now, only those who were needed remained, the other able-bodied citizens sent to Germany to slave for the enemy, or sent to prison camps for refusing while the others fled and joined the Resistance.

Suspicion was like an invisible force that lingered in the air, reflected in the eyes of the other passengers who, when they dared to make contact, looked away quickly, perhaps scared of what they would see or give away. This was why Yvette concentrated on the scenery outside. The once green pastures and fields of produce were now muted or barren; frigid, dormant squares of patchwork as far as her eyes could see. How she longed for spring, less than a month away. The winter had been harsh, not so much in temperature, more on the heart.

Their Historian Network still thrived but across the north of France the Nazis were making more raids, homing in on radio signals and capturing operators, dissembling the chain slowly but surely. Many of their comrades had been tortured then shot or sent to prison camps, their fate unknown. News filtered through via underground newspapers, or from one network to the other. Mistrust and paranoia ate at the core of their movement, everyone fearful of infiltrators and the gruesome methods of the Gestapo.

Yvette had thought that winter would be an ally, the darkness providing cover for their activities, yet in some ways, the barren landscape and trees left them more exposed and forced those who lived outdoors to seek out abandoned farm buildings or dig deeper, climb higher and stay out of sight. Life for the Maquis was hard, so she had welcomed the turn of spring. Each day she willed the trees to bud, the forest to blossom and then the verdant branches would provide benevolent protection and allow its human dwellers an easier existence.

Sometimes Vincent would be gone for days and she missed him so much, but she would rather that than he risk capture for the sake of a few hours together. It was enough just to see his face even for a second and she watched for him always, while she cycled to and fro from the village or as she hung the washing on the line, scanning the edge of the woods, listening for a whistle or an unfamiliar bird call.

In the meantime, her and Tante Helene listened to Radio Londres, dissembling the news, listening to the bizarre messages she knew were codes for the Resistance, praying that what else they heard was not just propaganda and jingoism. The tide had to turn soon, but in the meantime, Yvette continued in her role as courier, saboteur, guide, whatever was needed. Throughout they all remained vigilant, wary of newcomers, even the evaders they helped, trusting only their closest comrades.

This was why when Florian arrived with new orders given directly by Vincent, Yvette followed them without question. The detonators he delivered were to be sewn inside the front lining of her coat and taken to Nantes where she would meet with another agent, stay for two nights and only then return to the village. Yvette had no qualms whatsoever and when Florian handed over the package, she was eager to get on with the task.

Yvette listened intently as Florian spoke and smoked at the same time, his cigarette hanging from the corner of his mouth.

'Inside the package there is a map you must study then destroy and money for the return ticket. Once you reach Nantes, proceed directly to 9 Place d'Aristide and the agent there will take care of the rest. You do have a coat? Otherwise you will have to hide them in your luggage, it's a risk. Or maybe some other garment would do.' Florian raised an eyebrow and gave Yvette a cheeky smile.

It was a fair enough question because not everyone owned a full wardrobe of clothes. 'Yes, I have one, don't worry.'

'Good. We need you to take them all at once, not in separate journeys, it is too risky and slow otherwise.'

Yvette took the package wrapped in brown paper. 'But tell me, how is Vincent, are you together, is he close by?'

The look that flashed across Florian's face quickly made Yvette feel stupid and regret her question. If Vincent was close by then he would have come himself, she was sure of it, and the fact he hadn't meant he could be anywhere, not that Florian would tell her.

Changing the subject as her cheeks flushed, Yvette focused on her orders. 'Is it a man or a woman I'm meeting?'

'A woman, code name Simone. She goes by the name of Estelle but make sure you confirm both before you hand these over. Now I have to go. *Bon chance*, Yvette, and take care in the city. We will see you again soon.' And then he was gone, leaving the room filled with smoke and hope.

Yvette was sure his parting words held a deeper meaning,

but it was hearing the name of the agent she was to meet in Nantes that made her heart soar and her fingers sew faster.

The giant driving wheels of the steam train could not have turned quick enough for Yvette because soon she would be with her best friend again. It had been too much to imagine that somehow they would be thrown together. When they said goodbye that misty morning on a deserted road and went their separate ways, Yvette had hoped but never expected to be reunited, not in France anyway. It was like a dream come true, a reward, the most wonderful surprise.

Slightly nervous about her arrival in the city which she knew would be a world away from the deserted lanes where she lived, Yvette appraised her rather shabby appearance. Maude, *no Estelle*, wouldn't care, not one bit but she would definitely tease, that's why she loved her. Still, Yvette was so fed up of looking like she did; she was a young woman and longed to dress up and feel pretty again, despite what was going on around her.

She glanced down at her lace-up shoes, scuffed but clean, then at her bare and very goosebumpy legs, covered as much as possible by her coat, a hand-me-down from Polo's aunt and one that Yvette swore had never, ever been in fashion. She cringed. It was made from heavy cotton, a murky green colour that reminded Yvette of a mechanic's overall minus the grease and oil. The unnecessarily wide lapels were trimmed in black binding, as were the cuffs and it hung straight and shapeless, not quite a sack but it would have held a lot of potatoes.

It was of course made even more uncomfortable by the six detonators that were very tightly sewn on the inside – Yvette had been determined that none of them would fall off and give her away. For some reason, when she imagined what Estelle would think of her when they met, it made Yvette smile and hold down a giggle despite her feeling a complete frump; an enemy of fashion, never mind the Boche.

Passengers were beginning to gather their belongings, obviously used to the journey and familiar with their surroundings and once again, nerves fluttered inside. She'd already had her papers checked twice. Her mouth went dry both times and she'd felt perspiration in the pits of her arms as she stepped onto the platform to have her small handbag and basket searched by a clumsy-handed soldier. And then again by the steely-eyed Gestapo on board and now as the train neared Nantes, Yvette knew she'd have to endure the process once more. But she would stick to her story and try not to show nerves, because innocent people had nothing to fear, did they?

She was visiting her cousin who was expecting a baby, hence the knitted garments in her basket, along with the pomander of herbs and flowers from her aunt's garden, a gift. There were also two jars of home-made rabbit rillette. Amidst the mild panic, the sight of them had emboldened and amused Yvette, seeing the temptation and deliberation in the eyes of the soldiers. What would the jar really contain, was it worth removing black market goods so they could share them in the mess, or would the rillette be mixed with dog shit, or worse? It was a favourite trick of women resistors and the Boche had probably learned the hard way.

The queue was interminably long but Yvette waited as patiently as she could, keeping her eyes fixed ahead where she surreptitiously watched the three Gestapo who in turn, were scrutinising the passengers as they shuffled along. When it was her turn to show her tickets and identity papers, Yvette handed them over, looking at them and not into the eyes of the soldier. Defiance was not wise, it was best to act demure and appear respectful but never friendly, after all, the Boche were still the enemy, invaders. Only someone hoping to distract them would take this tack. This time the soldier merely flicked the cloth and quickly peered inside the basket before tapping Yvette's hand-bag, signalling that he wished to see inside. It was almost empty apart from her lipstick, a flattened stub of rouge and a compact that now contained a mirror and sponge, the powder long gone. With a dismissive wave of his hand the soldier allowed her through and Yvette slowly exhaled, her breath leaving her body gradually.

Following the crowd, Yvette made her way towards the street and once outside took a moment to acclimatise to the sights and sounds of a city. So many people, even more than on market day in Châteaubriant and cars and trucks everywhere, military, like dark grey elephants emblazoned with swastikas. Yvette suppressed a shudder and then pulled herself together. She didn't need a map because she had memorised the hand-drawn one that was wrapped around the francs she'd used to buy her tickets. By following the route in her head, Yvette would appear to be familiar with the city and hopefully avoid suspicion, so she strode purposefully onwards.

When she turned into Place d'Aristide, Yvette checked the numbers on the doors to her left and realised that the house she was looking for would be on the other side of the street. She scanned the grand pale-stone houses, with their ornate iron-work and elaborate sculpted columns aside beautifully carved doors. The road was wide and separated along the centre by a pedestrian walkway, grassed on either side. There was actually no need to look for number nine though, because her eye was caught by a figure standing on a second-floor balcony.

Dressed in sky blue, with one arm waving frantically above her head while the other poked at an angle, a cigarette holder dangling from her hand, the figure with the white-blonde hair that called out was unmistakable and Yvette would have known her anywhere. Almost racing across the street, she waved back just as enthusiastically, eager and desperate to reach the other side and her dear friend, Maude.

They met on the first landing, Yvette could hear Estelle's heels click-clacking down the stone stairs and when they finally stopped hugging, wiped their eyes and calmed down, they climbed upwards to the apartment. Once behind closed doors, one of them decided to be sensible and remind the other of some rules.

Despite it being second nature, in this instance it felt strange to speak only French, like being back in training but this time, their pretend life was for real.

Estelle's voice was barely a whisper. 'We must stick to French and our cover names for the whole time you are here. We cannot afford to slip up and as a precaution perhaps while we are in the apartment too. These clunking pipes and ancient floorboards have ears, so do doors, so we have to be vigilant.'

Yvette nodded.

'I am so glad Vincent allowed you to come, my pestering paid off.'

At this Yvette was astounded. 'What, you know Vincent? I don't understand, he never said a word, how, explain?'

Estelle lowered her voice further. 'Of course I know him, this is a safe house and he has collected evaders from here but it was only last time, when I asked if he'd heard or seen a red-headed agent, that the penny dropped. It was naughty of me, I know, asking, but I have been desperate for news of you.'

On hearing this Yvette was awash with love for her friend, for caring enough to push the boundaries and to Vincent too, for knowing how much it would mean to her. She had told him all about Maude and their bond, and this was like a gift, from Vincent to them both.

'I had no idea... just wait till I see him, but I'm so pleased you asked, you clever thing.'

Estelle winked. 'Well don't think you're off the hook because I want to know all the gory details because I can tell you are madly in love with him, and I saw the twinkle in his eye too.'

Yvette covered her burning cheeks with her hands, laughing but knowing only too well that Estelle would be true to her word. But for now, the moment had passed, and she was instead scrutinising Yvette's attire, a horrified look on her face.

'Now let me look at you... or perhaps not! My goodness what on earth are you wearing? Quickly take off that dreadful coat before it gives me a migraine and then I'm going to banish it for all eternity. The washerwoman will collect my things later so she can take this, too.' Estelle winked at Yvette as she helped her off with her contraband laden coat.

'Estelle, you are as bossy as I remembered, and even thinner! Surely you city dwellers don't starve? But anyway, Tante Helene has sent some of her famous rillette for you and look, a pomander too.'

'Pah, who needs food when there are cigarettes and wine but, sadly, no coffee? Not the real kind anyway, just that dreadful ersatz. It's like drinking a tree. But thank you for the rillette, I love it especially home-made. Now, what shall we do first, apart from burn that dress in the fire.'

Yvette stepped back in horror. 'No, this is my best one! I need it to travel home in.'

Estelle pursed her lips. 'All right, if you insist. So, what would you like to do? I know, let me pamper you and make you feel glamorous then we can go out, yes, let's do that. Come on, no time to waste. We have to pack as much as we can into our time together. I've been so looking forward to it.'

Yvette laughed because Estelle's *joie de vivre* was contagious and when she dragged her towards the bathroom, her heart was lighter than it had been for... ever.

Later, as Yvette languished on the bed, wrapped in a silk robe that made her look like she was resting in a field of flowers and peacocks, she watched as Estelle put on a record and then came to sit by her side. Undoing the jar of polish, she began to paint Yvette's nails a deep red, and for a moment appeared lost in thought. When she spoke it was in English, breaking her own rules as usual.

'If we speak quietly we'll be okay in here, the music will drown out our voices and I so long to speak English, I'm starting to think I may forget how... don't you miss it?'

Yvette nodded. 'Yes, and I don't think of myself as Dottie, fancy that. I even dream in French now, do you?'

Estelle's plucked and well-drawn eyebrows arched but she kept her eyes on the task. 'I don't dream, darling, not if I can help it.'

Yvette was curious. 'What do you mean? I love it if I dream of home. It makes me feel close to them.'

Estelle had finished one hand and signalled for Yvette to hold out the other. 'Well I envy you, because my dreams are more like nightmares, so I make sure that when my head hits the pillow I'm out for the count... thank God for cheap wine and the black market. I have some lovely cognac for later. That should knock me out.'

This disconcerted Yvette because rarely had Estelle shown weakness or admitted to fear of any kind but now she looked closer, there were dark rings of shadow under her friend's eyes, not quite concealed by powder. 'Estelle, that's awful. What are your nightmares about?'

As usual she attempted to bat away her concern. 'Oh, don't

mind me, enough of this, we should be jolly, not making one another feel miserable.'

Yvette persisted. 'No, you have to tell me. Who knows when we will see each other again and if I can help then I will.' It was then a thought occurred. 'Are you scared, Estelle?'

Apart from the dulcet tones of Charles Trenet playing on a scratchy seventy-eight, the room was enveloped in a hush. Estelle paused from her artistry, looked up and spoke, a great truth reflected in her eyes. 'Terrified, Yvette, I am absolutely terrified.'

There was a whoosh, pure shock delivering a sucker punch of panic and when it hit Yvette she reacted instantly by sitting up and enfolding Estelle in her arms, holding her tightly, eight red fingernails, two chipped and bare, splayed across her back. Right at that moment, Yvette didn't care about rules and training or Hitler because this was her friend, not an agent. And as she rocked her to and fro, and let her cry, she whispered in her ear.

'Me too, Maudie, me too.'

22

ESTELLE AND YVETTE

NANTES, 1944

They lay side by side on the bed. Estelle was indeed correct, and a glass of cognac did wonders, not just for sleep but the onset of panic, and now they were both more relaxed and found comfort in being with one another.

From the lumpy mattress, both were treated to a view of the beautifully moulded ceiling covings, stained by winter water leaks and adorned by cobwebs far too high to reach, had Estelle been remotely inclined to do so. The apartment was small, a lounge and bedroom combined, a slim galley kitchen with a two-ring stove and a sink, little else apart from empty cupboards stood next door to a tiny bathroom. It had elements of style, remnants of previous occupants with taste, like the walnut cabinet on which stood a gramophone player and three or four records in tattered sepia covers. The drapes were elegant but worn velvet, sagging in places due to missing hooks, their tasselled fringes faded by the sun.

Estelle told her that whoever had lived there before had left in a hurry, either that or they were taken by the Gestapo, their worldly possessions left behind. Sometimes she imagined they would just walk back in, make themselves at home and other times she felt their presence, like ghosts, an essence of them lingering on their belongings.

Yvette had thought that from outside, the apartment block appeared grand whereas once inside, the silence and shabby decor told another story. It was as though it had given up. The winding stone staircase was deserted and all the doors on each landing firmly closed. Not a sound emanating from within. While outside the city bustled and faked it, behind these walls she imagined the inhabitants were free to think and fear and hate, taking shelter like caged mice because out on the streets prowled the cats, ready to pounce, sly-eyed and hungry. It wasn't what Yvette had expected. She had mistakenly projected onto Nantes an image of London where despite its troubles, the spirit of freedom remained. Pray God it continued back home.

The record had come to an end and Yvette was relieved because she wanted peace. It was time to talk, like they had the night before they left England, in hushed tones that were laced with honesty.

'Tell me what it's like here, so I can imagine it when I'm back at Tante Helene's. It was so busy during the walk from the station and I was concentrating hard on finding the way and checking I wasn't being followed so I didn't have time to take it in properly.'

Estelle took a drag on her cigarette then passed it to Yvette. 'The best way I can describe it is like living in a twilight world where one has no concept of what's real. I suspect everyone, trust only a few. While people get on the best they can, making the most of their sorry lives, there is an undercurrent of hate and bitterness because the Boche behave as if this was their city now, but it isn't. Below the surface there are people like us, doing our best to rise up and take it back but with that comes risk. My role here is to provide a safe house while playing the socialite, make connections any way I can, gathering information to pass on, which I do. But I cannot describe the courage it takes for me to go out of that door, to paint on my mask and wear it in the sight of those who I despise, yet I am duty bound to consort with.'

'Do you sleep with them?' Yvette wasn't judging her friend, merely curious.

'No, never! I flirt, attempt to look good on their arms and flatter their pathetic egos but no, I will not sleep with them and anyway, if I did then I would lose my allure. It is best to keep them waiting, and in the meantime I sit and laugh and drink and listen, and watch.'

'Good, I would hate to think of you, you know, having to sleep with anyone you didn't want to although I am sure others do and they are far braver than I, and more self-sacrificing.' Yvette wasn't naïve enough to believe that other agents didn't end up as mistresses to the enemy and she was thankful for not having to play that role.

Estelle had a question. 'Do you love him, Vincent?'

'Yes, I do. It all happened so quickly, like I was grabbing happiness with both hands because I have no idea what the future holds or how long we have. I want to make every minute count just in case. Does that make sense?' Yvette passed the cigarette.

'Yes of course, perfect sense.'

Yvette thought for a moment about the Nazi officers Estelle fraternised with and wondered if perhaps amongst the Maquis there was anyone she was keen on.

Estelle was adamant in her response. 'No, nobody at all.'

'Have you ever been in love? I hadn't, not until now.' There was a lull, voices from the street below invading their privacy, then the sound of motorbikes racing past.

When Estelle answered her voice sounded quite matter of fact. 'Yes, I've been in love, a few times. I still am.'

'Who with? Is it some dishy earl or a prince, I bet it's an officer. Come on, you dark horse, tell all.'

'There's not much to tell because nothing can ever come of it, no matter how much I love them. They're from a different world than the one I live in and not only that, my parents, society, would never accept them. It takes Ma and Pa all their time to accept me, my rebellious streak has plagued them so my love, well it would tip them over the edge. It's how it is.'

'Oh no, that's so sad. Is it someone who works on your estate, one of the staff?' Yvette had heard all about *Lady Chatterley's Lover*.

Estelle reached over and took Yvette's hand in hers. 'It doesn't matter who it is, this world isn't ready to accept that some of us want to love whoever we want but maybe one day, when we've rid ourselves of the fascist Nazi devils, we can make a start on everyone else. Until then, I will be fine by myself, I promise. Now, shush, no more interrogation, you're like a terrier once you start digging,'

Yvette obeyed, aware that she may have touched a nerve, the sound of the needle spinning on the record was calming, slightly hypnotic. When Estelle stubbed out the cigarette and flipped onto her side, Yvette mimicked her actions.

Estelle's look was intense. 'Did you ever for one moment imagine it would be like this? I didn't. Not for a second, no matter what they drummed into us during training. To me it was like play-acting, a bit of a lark. I never thought I'd really jump out of a bloody plane or meet strangers in cafés and pass squares of paper containing coded messages. How stupid I was, please tell me you feel the same.'

Yvette reached out and tucked a lock of hair behind Estelle's ear and smiled. 'Yes, I am as stupid as you, and I feel the same, like I'm living in a film or a dark fairy tale.'

'Oh good. That's made me happy. Two buffoons together

who somehow managed to fool everyone and pass the course. I often think we should have failed on purpose and been sent to the cooler. Now that would have been a marvellous way to sit out the war, drinking whisky and doing the Highland fling with all the other inebriated no-hopers.'

At this they both laughed, but Yvette knew that despite her jokes, Estelle had wanted badly to succeed, to prove she could do it, they both had. 'Do you regret it? You know, doing what we do.'

'No, not for one second.' Estelle's voice sounded resolute. 'Dear Lord, can you imagine what it would have been like at home with mother? Rolling bandages in the village hall and being paired off with every suitable captain or officer of high rank that came home on leave. I only just survived the season in London and coming out, the war rescued me from one fate so I owe it a debt of gratitude, even if it might end in tears, or worse.'

'Is that what you're scared of, it ending in tears?'

Estelle nodded. 'Yes. The idea of facing a firing squad I have somehow managed to accept, or perhaps come to terms with by telling myself it will be quick. It's what comes before that haunts me; the torture, and worse, I suppose, not being able to hold out. They say if you can hang on for two days they give up, then that's it. The wall or a camp. I think I'd prefer the wall.'

Hearing Estelle speak like this, so unlike the gung-ho atti-tude she was known for, rattled Yvette, but if there was ever a time for truth, it was today. 'If it's any consolation I have the same fears, have considered the same fate, but you never know, that could be what keeps us alive. Once we realise we're not in a school play, the fear kicks in and the adrenalin spurs us on, making us more alert and effective. We should harness it and use it to our advantage, not allow it to eat us alive. What do you say?'

Estelle began to laugh, then cupped Yvette's face in her

hands and planted a kiss on her nose. 'Oh, you are a tonic, Dottie Doolittle, and I love you for it, I really do. In fact, you've given me an idea.'

'Oh no, why does that worry me slightly?' Yvette's heart had lifted simply because Estelle's mood had done the same.

Estelle tutted. 'If ever I am questioned by the Boche I'm going to give them all the names they desire, each and every one of my monstrous school-teachers, one by one. That should keep them occupied.'

Yvette brightened. 'And I'll work my way through the offices in Whitehall and start with all the really snooty miserable ones, I'll even give them descriptions. Send the Boche off on a wild goose chase.'

They both sniggered like schoolchildren and then Estelle brought them back to real life.

'But promise me you will be careful, darling. Use up all that adrenalin to stay safe because the Boche are getting twitchy now. Word has it that they are taking heavy losses and something big is planned on the Atlantic Wall, this is why we need to disrupt the troop movements and anything that the Nazis send that way.'

'I promise but I'm always careful, Estelle. Or is there something you're not telling me?'

Estelle twisted her fingers around Yvette's. 'No, it's nothing, just a feeling I can't shake, like something is creeping up on us, or we're running out of luck.'

'You told me you don't believe in luck so there has to be more to it, come on, tell.'

'I heard something that's all. I don't want to rattle you. We have enough to think about without rumours.'

Yvette gave Estelle a look that told her to get on with it. 'One of the girls in the brothel told me that she was entertaining a group of Gestapo officers and they were bragging about bringing the Maquis to heel. She said they didn't give away anything specific, but they sounded confident, as though they knew something.'

Despite the grip of dread that squeezed her heart, Yvette refused to give in to it. 'They will have been drunk and showing off and more than likely saying it on purpose, planting the seed and hoping the rumour would spread. The SS are evil and insidious, we know this and it's precisely the type of thing they'd do, propaganda, that's all.'

A loud persistent knocking at the door made both of them jump, and Estelle placed a finger over her lips before sliding off the bed and picking up Yvette's coat and dress along with two more that were draped over the armchair. Listening as she chatted and thanked the laundry woman, Yvette exhaled but remained hidden from view.

When Estelle returned Yvette sensed she wanted to forget about their conversation. 'Now that's taken care of what shall we do? I still haven't done your hair so let's start there and then we'll decide, but maybe we shouldn't stray too far tonight. I know a nice little bar that's not frequented by the Boche, we could go there and pick up some bread on the way home, to go with the rillette, does that sound okay to you?'

She was rifling through her drawer, pulling out combs and hairpins but Yvette was still curious. 'Why shouldn't we stray too far, is something wrong? You were going to show me the sights, remember.'

'Yes, yes I will, but tomorrow, when we can take a stroll along the river and not frequent places where the night monsters prowl. I'm not in the mood for making small talk with the enemy tonight and I'd rather them not see us together. They'll only ask questions and I don't want to put you in danger. If there is any chance they are onto me, we mustn't lead them to you and the circuit. Now come along, Miss Fifty Questions, get a wiggle on.'

Yvette knew her friend was speaking sense, but she couldn't shake off that feeling she was hiding something, not in a bad way, more shielding her from the unsavoury world beyond the apartment. Reminding herself that she was only allowed to stay for two nights, Yvette shuffled off the bed, determined not to allow the shadow of the night monsters to ruin her time with Estelle.

It had been the most wonderful two days that flew past. They made the most of every single second, getting outrageously drunk, hardly sleeping, dancing to the same songs over and over, laughing until they cried, sharing secrets that wouldn't have them tortured and when they gave in to exhaustion, clung on tight to each other beneath the eiderdown.

They had walked along the banks of the Loire River and enjoyed the fresh air, but little else, because Yvette found the sheer number of grey uniforms overwhelming and unsettling. They'd taken fake coffee in the same café where they'd lingered on the first night, before scurrying back to the apartment. Yvette had agreed that it was best to keep a low profile and, after all, they had so much to catch up on all they needed was each other, not the threat of prying eyes, even if it was their imagination, or a whiff of tension in the air.

Inside the apartment, Estelle had reverted to the vivacious and effervescent young woman who'd brightened everyone's Highland days and chivvied Yvette through the toughest tasks and homesickness. But even though she admired her dear friend's ability to act the part, she saw beneath the mask. It was killing them both, the imminent departure and inevitable goodbye.

It was with the heaviest of hearts that Yvette put on her shoes and the clean dress that had been returned that morning, the coat was not included in the neat pile that was passed through the door. When she emerged from the bathroom, she found Estelle fussing and folding clothes, keeping busy.

'Ah, there you are. Now, I want you to take these back with you, a few rather lovely bits and bobs to make you feel human again. And you can get dolled up for Vincent; he won't know what's hit him. I don't know what they wear out there in the sticks but if it's anything like that dreadful coat I really do fear for your sanity and sex life.'

Yvette laughed and made her way over to the bed, then touched the soft cotton of the pale-blue dress Estelle had been wearing the day Yvette had arrived and another, speckled with tiny polka dots. There was a skirt too in a soft lemon.

'They'll be far too long but you're a clever thing so you can take them up and here, have this lipstick and rouge, there's almost all the powder in the compact, I noticed yours had gone. What about some scent too, here take this.' She placed a small glass bottle in Yvette's hand, not catching her eye as she continued. 'Come along. Let's pack them away and I'll walk you to the station.' She maintained the mother hen routine, too bright, too cheerful.

Yvette let her have her way but not about the make-up. 'I can't take this. I know how hard it is to come by and you have more need of it than I do, so please, keep it.'

At this, Estelle placed a hand on her hip, then pulled open her draw with the other, motioning that Yvette should look. Seeing it was scattered with an assortment of lipsticks and other items required for adorning one's face, Yvette laughed and held up her hands in mock surrender. There was one more thing.

'Here, put this on.' Estelle held out a coat; brown wool with a huge belt and big wooden buttons, it was gorgeous.

Yvette held up both her hands in protest. 'No, I am not taking that under any circumstances. You'll need it more than me. The breeze along the river is harsh and I bet in winter it's freezing.'

Estelle merely gave her the look and within seconds the coat was on Yvette's body, the basket of clothes thrust into her hands before finding herself being bustled out of the door.

They walked in near silence to the station. Yvette struggled desperately for something to say but found no words, so instead listened to Estelle's voice when she occasionally spoke, instructions and observations, nothing deep or meaningful, *Let's cross here, oh look they're showing* J'accuse *again, how very dreary, stay close, you have your ticket*? Yvette just took everything in about her, the voice, her scent, her profile, committing Estelle, her Maudie, to memory, just in case.

Estelle was not permitted onto the platform, so their goodbyes were said behind the barbed wire barrier in full view of the stern soldier and ticket guard. Turning her back on them to prevent prying eyes, she removed a letter from her pocket which she gave to Yvette.

'This is for you to read when you are on the train... not now, we will both blub.'

Yvette took it and pushed it inside her deep pocket, eyes already misted and partially sighted.

'And I want you to have this too. Please don't say no. The letter will explain.' Uncurling her fist Estelle produced an antique silver ring set with an oval of diamonds and at the centre, one large amethyst.

Yvette's lips wouldn't work as her dear, tearful friend slid it on to the ring finger of her right hand. She wanted to protest but again, the pleading blue eyes of Estelle prevented any rebuke.

She then took control of the situation. 'Now off you go and

don't forget to write, once a month like we agreed, a nice jolly letter telling me all about carrots and beans and moo cows.'

Yvette sucked in the energy from her dearest, bravest friend and managed to respond.

'And you write back and tell me all about the theatre and...' but it was no good, her voice cracked. There would be no letters. It was too dangerous, but they still had make-believe. Nobody could take that from them.

Pulling her close, Estelle hugged Yvette and whispered in her ear, 'Goodbye, my darling Dottie Doolittle, take care until we meet again but if not, don't forget me and always remember that I love you.'

And then she was gone.

23

DEAREST D

They had followed the route that Dottie had taken all those years ago, along the quayside, letting the breeze from the river blow away the shadows that seeing the apartment had cast on the day. It was such a surreal experience revisiting a place that was littered with landmarks, like a roadmap of the mind, and even though they were camouflaged by progress and the trappings of modern-day life, they seemed to step forward, out of line and say, *Here I am, remember me? Don't walk past.* Dottie hadn't forgotten though, she'd simply filed them away. Those black-and-white images, that's how the world seemed back then, conflicting with the bright, vibrant city around her.

But wasn't that what they'd fought and hoped for? To be rid of the dour grey uniforms, the leather clad Gestapo in their trench coats who prowled and tormented, just like the flags, symbols of their occupation laying claim to a land that wasn't theirs. Dottie still hated those black swastikas laid on a blanket of blood as much as she'd hated those who saluted it. No, it was good to be free, to be able to walk in her old footsteps even though the Maude by her side now was not the friend she'd left behind. Had they not sacrificed so much, they might not be here at all.

'It's such a lovely city, isn't it? I'm glad we came and I've seen it like this.' Dottie was linking Maude's arm, she felt tired now and needed a rest and as much as it pained her to say so, it was time to call it a day.

'It is, and I'm glad that it hasn't upset you too much, telling me about your friend Maude. She sounds like the most wonderful woman. Honest, Gran, I could picture her in my mind... I don't suppose you have a photo, do you? I'd love to see what she looked like.'

Dottie shook her head. 'No, I don't. But I found a photograph online of her family, but it was of her as a child with her brothers and sisters. Their home is partially open to the public now and I have often been tempted to go, but then I think I'd rather remember her as she was, here and in Scotland and when she came to Mum and Dad's that time at New Year.'

Maude nodded her agreement. 'I know the ring you mentioned, you used to wear it all the time when I was little. I called it the princess ring, do you remember?'

A smile, picturing tiny Maude begging to wear the ring because it went with her dressing-up clothes but it was far too precious for that.

'Yes, I do. But it became too big for me and I didn't want to have it altered so I put it in the safe.'

Maude had another question. 'Did you keep Maude's letter. You didn't say what it said, or is that too private?'

'Yes, I kept it, folded up, hidden in the inside pocket of the coat she gave me. I kept it here, right next to my heart.' Dottie touched her left breast. 'I was terrified of losing it or leaving it behind at Tante Helene's so took it with me whenever I could. It actually survived the war, would you believe that? It was as battered and tatty as I was by the time I finally got home, and I kept it all these years. It's part of my gift to you, when I'm gone, it goes with the ring.'

A gasp. 'What, you're giving me the ring... but what about Mum, shouldn't she get it?'

Dottie reached over and with her free hand gave Maude's arm a squeeze. 'No, my darling, I want you to have it, I always have and that's the end of it.'

They walked along in silence then spotted the street where they'd parked the car. Maude made the next decision. 'I think we should head back now, Gran, I'm a bit weary so you must be too, you can tell me the rest later, about what happens to Maude, and I still need to know about Uncle Konki. I understand though, why you want to explain at your own pace and I have a feeling there's going to be more sadness so maybe another day, is that okay with you?'

A sigh escaped from Dottie. 'Oh yes, that's perfectly okay with me but I insist you have that big fat pizza so why don't we get a takeaway to eat in our room. And we can have a bottle of wine and watch some television, how does that sound?'

Maude pulled Dottie close and gave her a peck on the cheek. 'It sounds perfect, Gran, just like you.'

They crossed and headed towards their car, Dottie feeling relieved that they didn't have to sit and wait in a restaurant, the comfy seats of the four-by-four seemed like heaven.

'And I promise to tell you the rest of it... I'm almost at the end now and your dear Uncle Konki, as if by magic, is about to make an appearance.' Dottie waited patiently while Maude found her keys and after two yellow flashes, the doors clicked open and she was soon relaxing her aching bones and feet, flicking off her shoes and wiggling her toes.

As Maude began making her way out of the city, neither she nor her dozing gran had any idea that the story was nowhere near at its end, because by the end of the week everything that

Dottie knew, trusted and believed in would be turned on its head and some brand-new chapters would have to be written.

Maude had finished spraying deodorant around the room in an attempt to disguise the smell of two big fat pizzas, and even though the windows were wide open, the evidence of their illegal dinner hung in the air.

'Oh, leave it now, Maude, it will be gone by morning and you're making me restless so do relax. We've been on the go since we left London so I thought maybe tomorrow you could do some painting. You've been ferrying me around and writing notes like it's a field trip for grannies, so I want you to do whatever you feel like. I'll stay here and read my book or if you want some company I'll tag along, your call.'

Maude put the deodorant on the dressing table and did as she was told, climbing onto her bed and stretching her nicely browning legs. 'That would be good actually, to do some painting. I had tingly fingers today at the beach and again in Nantes. I thought it would be interesting to capture a street scene and then this idea pinged into my head, a before and after. One snapshot of now and another during the war. You've said a couple of times that when you think of London and here, the colours are muted. I wonder if I can translate that into paint, you know, how you felt back then.'

'Well, my darling, if anyone can do it you can. And you know what's really odd... when I think of the city, London or Nantes, and here in Châteaubriant, especially anywhere the Germans were, it's how I described it, dull, grey, smudgy. But where I lived with Tante Helene in the countryside, well in my mind's eye, the sun shone every day. The sky was so clear and blue, even in winter, and the fields were either vibrant green or yellow, tended or untended, nature found a way. In the autumn I see reds and golds, rich brown fields like fudge cake, winter was white and clear, the pine trees in the forest had emerald boughs and then there was the fire in the grate, yellow and orange, keeping me warm in a house where I felt safe.'

Maude had turned on her side, her prayer hands under her cheek as she listened. 'That's because you were happy and in love, despite everything. You had your comrades and Tante Helene and Vincent, that's the aura they omitted, it's like I can almost see it glow when you speak.'

That made Dottie feel happy, and Maude was right in her summations. 'What a lovely way of putting it, Maude, and fancy me having an aura. I always thought I was coated in steel.'

Maude laughed. 'No, Granny dearest, I can see right through you so no more putting on an act, okay? I like the soft, squashy version of you.'

A lull, the sound of mopeds outside, the little gang of teenagers that appeared to prowl the streets looking for mischief doing their rounds, and the church bell, striking nine.

'You okay, Gran? Do you want to get an early night, or shall we put the telly on, or the radio?'

Dottie was pulled from her thoughts, of the Gestapo prowling the streets, lurking in the shadows, looking for mischief. There was something she needed to say. Before she moved on with her story. 'I didn't understand, you know, about Maude, what she was trying to tell me. I do now and it hurts, a real pain like a stitch through the centre of my heart that I didn't get to tell her I understood, that no matter what, I would stand by her and be her friend. Oh, how I wish I could have told her.'

'What didn't you understand, Gran?'

'That she was in love with me, and that I was the person her parents would never accept. But worse than that, even if it wasn't me, whoever she loved it would have had to be in secret and she deserved better than that, my dear, brave, wonderful Maude.'

'Oh, Gran, that's so sad. Did she tell you in the letter?'

Dottie dabbed the tear that was about to leak from the corner of her eye, stopping it in its path. 'Yes, and I can remember every word, I've read it so many times, you see. It was in French obviously and addressed to My Dearest D. To anyone who found it, it would appear to be a love letter from a man to a woman, but it wasn't. I have a copy, I keep it in my address book, here, pass me my bag.'

Maude leapt off the bed and once she'd handed over the handbag, remained silent while her gran found the letter.

Removing it from the zipped section, Dottie unfolded it. 'It wasn't long, but enough. I'll translate it...'

Dearest D,

What a treat it was to see you again and I will be so desperately sad to see you go, the thought of it while I write breaks my heart. Please know that you are never far from my thoughts. The memories of the times we shared hold me up and give me something to cling on to, a glimmer of hope that we will be reunited again. Should this not come to pass, in case this is the last time, our last visit, our last letter, whilst I cannot bring myself to say them out loud, I am compelled to share my innermost thoughts like this, with you, my dearest one.

Since the day you walked into my life, you have filled each moment with happiness and bestowed upon me a gift of friendship, one so precious and wonderful, the kind I have never experienced or thought possible. Even though it seemed like the blink of an eye, I remember each and every day, cherishing those memories like treasure. I wish I had a photograph of you, an impossible notion, so I have committed everything about you to memory and I will hold this image of you close to my heart, to the last, whenever that may be.

Such fanciful ideas and wishes I have for the future, let me tell you so we may think of them separately and please God let them come true. Wherever you live I will find somewhere close by, I don't care where and I quite fancy a place near your parents' and dear Mémère. We will see each other every day and never be parted again. Don't you think that would be perfect, dearest one?

Please know that I am so glad you have found love, but even though your heart belongs to another please save a piece for me, a little corner of your life that I can slot into and be your flighty, unsuitable friend who blows in on the wind to shock your neighbours and spoil your children.

I shall never be permitted to love in the way or with whom I choose, dearest D. And you shall never love me the way I love you but that is fine, I understand and I hope with all my heart that you do too, and accept me, as you always have, for who I am.

I cannot bear to let you go tomorrow, but I will and I must. If I can I shall be brave and smile and be bossy, you know the drill. I have a gift for you, I hid it and brought it with me, naughty I know. Please wear the ring I will give you as a token of my esteem, friendship and love. Think of me often and forever, don't be afraid to laugh and live and be free, even if I am not there to do those things too.

Promise, dearest one, remember me always, and go on, for me.

Goodbye my friend,

Until we meet again,

With love, my love,

Your M x

Maude wiped her cheek. 'I know you're sad, Gran, but don't you see you made your Maude so happy, just having you in her life and that's precious. At least she knew what good friendship was. And I'm so glad you named me after her, I'm really proud to have that connection. I sort of feel like I'm linking you together, in her name and through your blood. Does that sound daft?'

A sniff before Dottie spoke. 'No, that's beautiful, Maude, and thank you, you've cheered me up, but would you make me a promise? Nothing too difficult and you can put your own spin on it.'

Maude nodded and even though Dottie couldn't see her she felt the movement.

'Will you do everything you can to be happy, live your life how you want to in the world we fought for. Don't be shackled by anything or anyone, or let prejudice or bigotry hold you back or taint your dreams. Live for Maude, take her magical spirit with you wherever you go and when you laugh, you'll hear her joining in. When you have a wicked thought, know she'd approve and when you love, love whoever you want with all your heart, whoever it turns out to be.'

Again, Maude wiped her eyes and cheeks, and when the knot in her throat relaxed, she replied. 'I promise, Gran, I promise I will.'

The moped crew came back for another reccie and the spell was broken with the toot toot of their horns and youthful calls to friends on the street.

'Shall I make us a nice cup of tea? And then I'm going to get on and tell you the rest of it. About Maude, and the last days with Vincent. I think I need to get it all over and done with, then we can move on, have some fun and once we've been to see the *maire*, I can say goodbye.'

'Yes, please, for the cup of tea and okay about moving on. I think it might make you feel better.'

Dottie swivelled off the bed as she spoke. 'You're right, and I need to tell you about Konstantin. That wicked man always lifts my spirits so I will explain about how he turned up here in

France. It's where our friendship began and once again out of all the badness, I found a soulmate, your naughty Uncle Konki.'

Maude attempted to insist she did the honours, but Dottie stood firm. A cup of tea and some biscuits usually helped put the world to rights, although what she was going to do about that stitch of sadness deep inside her chest was anyone's guess. Even Earl Grey and a digestive couldn't cure heartbreak.

24

THE RUSSIAN
RENAZÉ, FRANCE, 1944

Yvette had become used to the comings and goings of Vincent and the evaders he would produce from nowhere, arriving out of the blue with sometimes one, maybe more, dishevelled, displaced men. On the day she met her first Russian, she had only just said goodbye to Vincent who was escorting a Hungarian chap named Roberto, further up the line.

Yvette had taken to him instantly because he was full of life and stories of his travels across France, a free spirit who went where the mood and a story took him. He had fled Paris where he was studying photography and had since made himself useful within the Resistance. He'd holed up in the forest camp but before his departure, Yvette met him and some of the group on the outskirts of the village, high on the hill overlooking the hamlets below.

It was a good vantage point and for an hour or so it felt like they relaxed and in any other place and time, it would have looked like a gathering of friends at the end of a long day. Not a group of comrades armed with rifles, eyes and ears on alert, preparing to head off into the night to face whatever dangers awaited them. Florian, Benoit, Xavier, Thierry and Vincent were all in good spirits as they drank wine and ate whatever offerings the locals had donated, cured ham, eggs always, boiled potatoes in their skins, anything they could spare.

The sun was setting and as the last rays descended behind the trees, Roberto insisted he was going to take some photos of them all. The men suddenly became shy and scurried off, deciding to take a pee or have another smoke. Vincent, seated by Yvette's side, refused point blank, saying it was dangerous to have his face captured in case the Germans got their hands on the film but Yvette was thrilled to be asked, it was a bit of fun. While Vincent tutted, Roberto took the photo, making her laugh as she shielded her eyes from the sun, calling her his French Rita Hayworth, and promising to one day find a way to get the photo to her. She never expected for a second that he would keep his word.

As always, she shared a fleeting kiss with Vincent. It was becoming harder to say goodbye, for both of them. She saw the longing in his eyes, heard it in his voice and when he held her close it was never enough, Yvette wanted to stay like that forever. When he pulled away, Vincent told her to expect a new group of evaders. Florian would deliver them the following day and then he let go of her hand and left with Xavier and Roberto, while the others disappeared into the dusk, leaving only a trail of cigarette smoke behind them.

The following evening, just before dusk as arranged, Yvette was waiting at the rendezvous point for Florian who arrived in his smoky truck. In the back were three men covered in a pile of turnips and assorted rotting vegetables, not coal or in the case of more unfortunate evaders, pig shit. At least they were lying under a bed of food destined for the sties, not what they'd scraped off the floor.

It was a day she remembered well, not only because they'd taken in evaders, but because she got to spend a few moments with little Polo who she adored and liked to fuss over, and in return he would blush and avert his eyes but always wave like crazy when they said goodbye. He'd been riding up front with Florian but wasn't allowed to accompany her to the cave, as much as he wanted to. The risk of him knowing their hideout was too great because the Boche weren't averse to interrogating children, either.

The three rumpled men alighted from the truck, all of them looking tense, eyes darting everywhere. Polo, always fascinated by evaders, watched from the passenger seat, his eyes wide, talking everything in. Yvette knew what he was staring at and why.

They were dressed in what she imagined were their only set of clothes, either that or ones provided by the Maquis and they would all have blended into a crowd, apart from one. He was taller than the others, his hair covered by a cloth cap, blue-eyed and square of jaw but it was the angry red scar that ran just below his temple to underneath his cheekbone that set him apart. Trying not to stare, Yvette introduced herself and then said a quick hello and goodbye to Polo.

'Hello, little monkey, have you been good?'

Polo's eyes looked around Yvette and spoke in a whisper. 'I thought Vincent would be here and why has that man got a scar, do you think he is a pirate?'

Yvette laughed at his hushed question. 'Vincent is busy, and no, I don't think he is a pirate because he hasn't got a hook for a hand.'

At this Polo's eyes flicked to the evader's hands then back again. 'You are right, Yvette, but I don't like him. He is scary, and he talks funny.'

'He's just far from home and might be a bit scared himself,

who knows. Now let me speak with Florian.' She gave him a peck on the cheek at which he looked abashed, then motioned to Florian to join her.

In hurried conversation, she learned that the pirate was actually a Russian navigator who'd been moved from Nantes along with the other two young men, the ashen bespectacled chap was a Jewish doctor, the taller more assured man was an English pilot, both were needed back in England as soon as possible.

Some evaders took the southern route over the Pyrenees through Spain, these three were destined for the northern route. All being well, they would be delivered along the line to a pick-up point in Brittany and collected by a navy gunboat, once the coded signal from London came through. All being well, there would also be another evader added to the group, a Russian pilot, Anatoly, the brother of Konstantin.

Once she'd got the gist of things, Florian went back to the truck, the charcoal fumes catching in her throat as she waved at Polo whose head and half his body hung out the window as they drove away.

Turning to her charges, Yvette pointed towards the fields beyond the lane. 'Come, we need to get going, follow me.' Obeying, they followed closely behind as she set off.

The location of the hideout was a ten-minute walk away, along a narrow farmer's track that then led through unplanted fields of churned up earth and sprouting tufts of whatever seeds the wind had carried there. It was the Russian man with the scar who spoke first.

'Where are we going? We need to take cover; it is too exposed here.'

Yvette conceded. 'Yes, it is, but have patience and keep walking, we are nearly there.'

'Nearly where, another field? We have passed through three already and I see nowhere to hide.'

Choosing not to answer, she ignored her curious companion. Yvette kept to the thicket-lined edge of the field that was now sloping downwards and had the Russian looked behind him, he would have realised they were now out of sight of the track and the road. At the foot of the incline was a stream, running freely, and had she followed to the left, it would have brought her to Vincent's hut. Instead she turned right and walked on until their route appeared blocked by a copse of rowan and wild cherry trees, with the odd silver birch peeking above the rest. To skirt around it would mean getting your shoes soggy on the bank of the stream but instead, Yvette began pushing her way through the middle of the trees, holding back the branches for the Russian who did the same for the others until they were immersed, emerging on the other side at the base of the hill. There was a gap, a body's width, enough to squeeze along for a few paces where Yvette stopped in front of a three-metre-high entrance, braced by oak framework and covered by an iron grille. Taking a key from her pocket she unlocked the padlock that secured the chain before pushing it inwards, signalling that the men should move inside, then secured the grille behind them.

'It's dark but if you close your eyes and run your hands along the wall it's easier to walk, only about twenty metres and we will be there.'

They continued along the tunnel, the men crouching lower than Yvette who soon reached another door, this one solid oak and with her eyes closed – she always found it better that way – she felt for the keyhole with her fingers. The large iron key slotted in easily and hearing the click, she pushed open the door. Before entering the expanse of darkness before her, Yvette reached to her left and removed the dynamo torch hanging from the hook and clicked it on. Using its weak light she methodically moved along the wall and using the matches that were left there she began lighting the strategically placed candles, slowly illuminating a vast cave, casting a golden glow on the oak casks that were stored there. Once there was enough light to see, she returned to the men where the Russian had another question.

'What is this place?'

'It's one of many in the area, where the farmers keep their wine, and some grow mushrooms. We keep evaders safe in this one.'

The Russian nodded.

Yvette surveyed the group. 'You, what shall I call you?'

The tallest one with the mop of curly hair stepped forward when she nodded in his direction. 'Teddy, Miss.'

'Right, Teddy, can you carry on lighting these?' Yvette smiled when he responded immediately. She imagined they really were scared, and a little kindness in a harsh unknown world wouldn't go amiss. 'Now, you two, what shall I call you?'

'I'm Jakob.' The spectacled man replied.

Then the Russian. 'Konstantin.'

'Right, Jakob and Konstantin, it's not the most comfortable of places but you are safe here. It's impossible to be followed without seeing your pursuer and remote too.' Yvette made her way to the end of the cave and pointed to some folded blankets.

'Another good thing, it's dry down here and not too cold this time of year and before you ask, the barrels are empty, but I do have a treat for you.' Reaching behind one of the casks, she pulled out two bottles of wine. 'This should keep you a little warmer and tomorrow I will bring food but for tonight, you can help yourselves to the vegetables in the box over there, it's all we have, I'm afraid. It's just as dangerous bringing you food as moving you on. If I'm stopped, they'll want to know where I'm going so there is only so much I can carry, but I will do my best.'

Konstantin spoke next. 'I don't suppose you could get your hands on some vodka and perhaps a jar of caviar... that would be excellent.' His eyes creased at the corners, and his smile was infectious.

Yvette smiled, realising she had a cheeky one on her hands. 'Like I said, Konstantin, I'll see what I can do.'

Teddy had returned, the candles around the cave lit. Yvette had to leave soon, it would be getting dark and she couldn't use a torch, especially not the one hanging on the hook that had been salvaged from a downed plane.

'Now, rules, so listen. There are two spare keys here.' She picked up a set from the top of a barrel and showed them to her audience. 'They are solely for emergencies. If we are captured, and it is always a possibility, the last thing we want is for you to be trapped in here. These are only to be used if we have not visited you for more than five days. If this occurs, you will know something is wrong. The longer you can survive here the better, stay hidden, but then it will be up to you to decide what to do. Other than that, you are forbidden to go outside.' It was an ominous statement but important nevertheless.

'There is a bucket over there for the obvious, it can be emptied by one of you when we bring food. There is water in the bottles in the corner. It is from the stream and drinkable. It's up to you how many candles you light, please use them wisely. Do not open the door for anyone. We will let ourselves in. We have more keys. Now, are there any questions?'

Jakob said, 'How long will we be here?'

'I have no idea but when I get news, I will inform you.'

Teddy remained silent. Konstantin didn't. 'When will you bring my brother? I will not leave without him.'

'I'm sorry, Konstantin, but I don't know anything about your brother, but I will make enquiries. For now you should all rest, you look exhausted. I will be back tomorrow.' With that, Yvette turned and made her way to the door, locking it behind her as she left, retracing her steps. Once she exited the copse instead of making her way back over the fields and along the lanes, she took the path along the stream that led to Vincent, his bed and, if he was there, the safety of his arms.

25

LOVE'S YOUNG DREAM
RENAZÉ, 1944

I t was the following day when the wind changed, whipping up trouble, and Yvette had no idea that by the end of May a series of events, some out of her hands, other's not, would have a catastrophic effect on her life and change it forever. It began with Béatrice.

Yvette had called to the Matis home on the pretence of delivering the salt that Tante Helene had managed to lay her hands on, and as soon as she stepped foot inside, the atmosphere told her something was wrong. Raymonde looked sullen and barely nodded when he saw Yvette, concentrating instead on sucking the insides out of his cigarette. Lucille gasped a sigh of relief, then grabbed Yvette by the elbow and more or less dragged her from the room and into the tiny room they used as a cold store and larder.

Once the door was slammed shut, and as Yvette tried to ignore the stench of decomposing pheasants whose feathers tickled her hair, and the pungent aroma of whatever cheese lay under the cloth on the counter by her side, she listened to Lucille's lament.

'You must speak with Béatrice at once. She is out of control and our ploy to keep her away from the German has failed.'

Yvette asked why.

'Last night, and two times before, I have caught her creeping in after curfew. I heard the sound of a motorbike, too. I tried to stay awake, but I am so tired, Yvette, and eventually I fell asleep and Raymonde, pah, he is of no use because of the wine. She refuses to say where she has been, but I have seen the marks on her neck and I know what is going on – he has been coming here, the German.'

Yvette's stomach had started to churn. How could Béatrice be so stupid and naïve? The soldier would be out for what he could get and think of the shame if word got out. And worse, the danger the stupid girl was putting her brother in.

Yvette's mind was racing but maybe she could talk some sense into Béatrice, otherwise she would have to tell Vincent as much as Lucille tried to avoid it. 'Where is she now?'

'In her bedroom. Raymonde has threatened her with the belt, I threatened her with the priest and you, so she has refused to come out all day. Please speak with her, Yvette, because if Vincent finds out he will be so ashamed of her, like I already am.'

Yvette stroked Lucille's arm as she spoke. 'Do not worry, I will sort it out. Now go and rest, Lucille, you look exhausted.'

Nothing more was said, and the door was opened, Yvette sucking in less fetid air as she made her way through the cottage and up the stairs. It was clear which room belonged to Béatrice, it was the only one whose door was closed, so Yvette flung it open and strode in.

Béatrice was sitting on the chair, facing the mirror that stood on top of a chest of drawers, and didn't even bother to turn when she saw Yvette, instead she spoke to her reflection. 'What do you want? Has Maman sent you to warn me off?'

'Correct.'

Béatrice smirked and continued to file her nails. 'Well you are wasting your breath because Jörg and I are in love and I don't care who knows, even Vincent, so whatever you have come to threaten me with won't work.'

Surprised by the vehemence in her words and that Béatrice had pre-empted everyone's actions, Yvette chose a different tack. 'I don't want to threaten you, not at all. I thought that maybe we could talk this through, and you might listen to what I have to say, because what you are doing is dangerous. Do you know what the village will say about you, and how your brother and his comrades will feel?' Yvette noted the shrug so ploughed on.

'It's a betrayal, a slap in the face for everything we are fighting for and you're not stupid, Béatrice, you know what we do. You really can't trust this Jörg no matter how much he says he loves you; it could be a trap.'

At this, Béatrice whipped round, the effrontery of Yvette's remark written across her pretty face. 'How dare you! You know nothing of our feelings for one another. And I am not stupid; I would never tell him anything about Vincent, I have kept my brother out of things no matter how curious he is.'

The dawning of her words hit Yvette like a slap in the face and she could tell from the look on Béatrice's that she too had felt the sting.

Yvette's heart pounded in her chest and it was as though the walls were closing in or that the net was tightening around them all. Boche eyes could be watching them as she spoke, creeping forward through the field that surrounded the Matis home, about to strike. 'What do you mean, curious?'

'Nothing, I meant nothing.' Béatrice looked nervous now and her eyes wouldn't meet Yvette's as she stood and replaced her nail file in the pot, like everything was normal.

Yvette had no idea whether it was panic or anger that overcame her, or that her training was ingrained somewhere in her psyche as the action was involuntary, but when she leapt forward and grabbed Béatrice by the hair at the nape of her neck, then yanked her left arm up her back, the shock and pain was visible in the other woman's eyes.

'I am going to ask you one more time, why is he curious? And believe me, Béatrice, if you don't answer I will break your arm, or your neck... I'm not really bothered which.' Yvette jerked Béatrice's head back, knowing that the roots of her yellow-blonde hair would be straining, and her arm would feel like it was about to snap.

'He was asking about my family because we are going to be together after the war, so it is only right that he should know who they are... I didn't tell him about Vincent though, I swear.'

Yvette squeezed tighter and pushed higher, hearing a yelp from Béatrice, then she whispered in her ear, 'You stupid, stupid girl... do you really think he's going to marry you, or that you'll live happily ever after here, or in the Fatherland in the bosom of his Aryan family? No, Béatrice, he will use you and then go home to his other blonde girlfriend, from a good family not a poor farmer's daughter who gave him whatever he wanted in return for false promises and flattery.'

Béatrice's voice, when it came, was through gritted teeth and filled with hate. 'You are wrong, he loves me, he said so. And the Germans are going to win the war and run rats like you and the Jews and the communists into the sewer where they belong, and then France will be great again.'

A rage like she'd never felt before consumed Yvette. She let go of Béatrice's head and arm, and using all her might spun her around before slapping her hard across the face with the force of a punch. At the same time as her palm connected with her cheek, Lucille burst into the bedroom and while Béatrice grasped her face and sobbed, Yvette shook with rage as she spoke. Lucille remained silent and looked on.

'You will stop seeing Jörg immediately, do you understand, Béatrice? You need to give me your word or I will have no option but to tell Vincent and the rest of the Maquis, and if I do, I cannot guarantee your safety. You will be seen as a collaborator, and sometimes terrible things happen to them. Am I making myself clear?'

But Béatrice wasn't going to be cowed or blackmailed or shamed, it was clear the moment she opened her mouth. 'Do your worst, Yvette, go on, run to Vincent, and I will run straight to Jörg and tell him all about the strange woman who appeared one day at the home of her Tante Helene, who speaks very good French but isn't really one of us. Perhaps she's an agent, a spy. So off you go, go on, GO ON!' She was hysterical now. 'I don't care what you say or do because I have picked the winning side, not the silly little Maquis men who run around with their guns and hide like mice. At the end of the war, Jörg will take care of me but who will take care of you, Yvette? Who will save you when they have you in their cellars, taking you to pieces bit by bit?'

'Enough!' Lucille stepped forward, white with rage, the diminutive figure rising up against her child.

Yvette was immobile, pinned to the spot by Béatrice's cruel words and not so idle threats. *What to do? This is Vincent's sister; how can I give her up? But she is a traitor, if not yet in deed, then in thought.*

As if on cue, Raymonde then appeared at the door, a hammer in one hand, his other fist full of nails. When he strode defiantly across the room and began banging them into the frame, sealing the window shut, Yvette was sure the wail from Béatrice could be heard for miles.

'He will come for me, tomorrow or the day after, and when I don't show up, he will march straight to this door and demand to see me and then I will tell him everything... I hate you, I hate you all.'

Ignoring his daughter's threats, once the job was done, Raymonde left the room, averting his own angry eyes from the hateful ones of his irate child who screamed and swore her defiance. Yvette followed him out on to the landing and watched as Lucille retreated from the room and locked the door in her wake.

Turning to Yvette, her lips set in a thin line, tears of shame in her eyes, she gave a simple instruction. 'Go now, do what you have to do. Make sure everyone is safe. We will take care of things here.'

Still trembling, Yvette merely nodded and took the stairs quickly, desperate to get away from the sound of Béatrice kicking and pounding the door, the threats she issued through the wood ringing in everyone's ears.

Two days later, the body of a German soldier was found on the roadside, near to the bridge that led to the track that ran along the Matis property. It looked like a terrible accident. His motorbike had collided with a deer perhaps, his head injuries gruesome, but still, most of the villagers came out to look. Rumours were rife that the soldier had been meeting someone selling black market produce, everyone had their price and the Germans had the money for it, after all. There were cigarettes in his pocket, plenty, and there was a smashed bottle of pastis in the road so maybe he was drunk, that's what the doctor and the priest thought, anyway.

When the soldiers from the town came to investigate, a Gestapo officer in tow, the villagers reported that they heard and saw nothing. When they left, the rumours took another turn, to the fear of reprisals. What if the Boche suspected foul play, would they come for the villagers like they had in other places, dragging people off to the prison or putting them against a wall? The priest did his best to soothe his parishioners and assured them that the Gestapo had seemed convinced that it was an accident and if someone amongst them did know anything, they should keep it to themselves or share it in the confessional. There were no traitors in the village, he was sure, if they stood together and kept their counsel, everyone would be fine.

26

ZAYA

The late afternoon sun warmed Yvette's face as she sucked in great lungfuls of air, hoping too that the breeze would blow away the troubles in her mind. There had been such a terrible row before Vincent left for Nantes and she wished he'd taken her with him, if only so she could see Estelle and get away from the drama that his sister was creating. They had gone to his parents' home together to speak with Béatrice who had taken the news of Jörg's death badly to say the least.

Lucille had been at her wits' end and told them it was like living with a devil. A visit from Celeste, who innocently described in great detail the state of the dead soldier, hadn't helped. The absence of Béatrice was put down to a headache but she must have been listening on the stairs to her friend's animated description of brains and blood. Once Celeste left, all merry hell broke loose and Béatrice had been inconsolable ever since.

Vincent assured his tearful mother that now the soldier was gone the threat had receded and whatever Béatrice may or may not have let slip, would have died with him. He then left Yvette in the kitchen and went to speak to his sister who he hoped had learned her lesson and if she had, then the matter should be forgotten.

As he made his way upstairs, the clomping of his hobnail boots on the wood, Yvette wasn't in the least bit hopeful or reassured. She had seen the she-devil in action so hovered in the hallway, followed closely by Lucille who nervously wrung a dishcloth in her hands.

Vincent stepped forward and rapped on the closed bedroom door, then took a step back as he spoke.

'Béatrice, may I come in? I would like to speak with you. There is nothing to worry about, I just want us to sort this out.' Silence, a few seconds passed and then Vincent slowly unlocked the door and the banshee appeared.

From where they waited Yvette and Lucille witnessed the monster unleashed as she pounced on her brother, punching and scratching and pulling his face and hair as she screamed obscenities and vented her anger.

'You murderer, you cowardly murdering scum. You killed him and I hate you and I always will.' Béatrice kicked out with her feet and words.

Lucille took the stairs as fast as she could while Vincent defended himself and tried to tame his sister as she was prised away by Yvette who clung on tightly to her arms, his mother positioning herself between son and daughter.

'Stop this, Béatrice, in the name of God what is wrong with you? This is your brother; he is trying to protect you and this is how you treat him?' Lucille's voice trembled, a combination of shock and anger.

'And Jörg was my boyfriend and he killed him, and I will never forgive you, Vincent, ever. I hate you and I hope you die a worse death than him, now get out of my sight or I will kill you with these hands, I swear I will.' Her eyes were wild; Béatrice was not for taming.

Yvette saw the hurt wash over Vincent's face, pale against the blood on his cheek where his sister's nails had torn and gouged his skin. She thought he was going to say more, or maybe he was waiting for her to intervene, make things right, but Yvette knew whatever she said to Béatrice would probably make things even worse.

'Vincent, go downstairs, there is nothing you can do here, please, go.'

She saw him look at his sister one more time, great sadness etched across his face, or was it disappointment? Yvette couldn't tell. With a nod he did as she asked and once he was out of sight, footsteps receding, she released Béatrice from her grasp, not wanting to look at a face she fought hard not to slap. It was as she reached the top of the stairs Yvette heard the sound and felt the spit as it landed on the back of her dress.

Reining in every last ounce of self-control, Yvette made her way down the stairs, trying hard to ignore the parting threat from Béatrice.

'If either of you ever speak to me again, I'm going to turn you in, all of you. I hate you both. It wasn't an accident, I know you killed him, you killed him, you killed him!'

From behind, Yvette heard the sound of Lucille cajoling her hysterical daughter, shuffling feet then the door slam. When she reached the kitchen, Vincent was seated at the table, head in hands, blood smeared across his fingers from behind which he spoke.

'Do you think she means it?'

Yvette took the tea towel that was hanging from the range and went over to the sink, rinsing it under the water before going to Vincent. Lifting his chin with two fingers, she waited until he moved his hands and then began to clean his face. 'No, she is angry and upset but even Béatrice understands the cost of collaboration and no matter how crazy and riddled with grief she is right now, soon common sense will kick in.' Yvette silently prayed this was true.

'I am not so sure. She has always been wild, but I cannot believe she said those things.'

'Try not to worry. Your mother will keep an eye on her so even if she does escape and march all the way to town, I doubt she will have the guts to walk into the Gestapo headquarters, let alone turn her family in.' Yvette continued to clean his face, one she could gaze upon all day and in the moments when their eyes met, their longing for each other was mirrored.

By the time the job was done, Vincent's scratches looked red but not serious, Lucille returned to the kitchen and began to make coffee.

'She is sleeping now so please will you stay for lunch? I hardly see you, my son, and I would like the company of you both.' Lucille's eyes were raw from crying and she looked tired.

Yvette glanced at Vincent and willed him to say yes, relief relaxing her taut muscles when he smiled and agreed. It was a small thing, but meant the world to a mother, Yvette knew this. For now, Lucille's family and world was splintered and it would be hurting her deeply. The least they could do was try to heal the wound.

Vincent and Yvette were in the garden behind the house, he was smoking, and she was feeding the chickens with the scraps from lunch before they left. She could tell something was on his mind but presumed it was Béatrice, until he spoke.

'Will you stay with me tonight? I have to meet Claude first. He is going on reconnaissance, but I won't be long.'

Then Yvette knew. 'Of course. I will meet you later. Are you going away too?'

He nodded as he smoked, watching the chickens from the garden wall he sat on. 'Soon, maybe in the next day or two. To Nantes, to bring the Russian's brother.'

Yvette's head flipped around. 'Please let me go, Vincent, then I can see Estelle. Is he with her?'

Vincent stood and was about to answer when a noise alerted them and Lucille appeared at the back door, a parcel in her hand that Yvette knew would contain whatever food she could spare for her son.

'You must stay here and take care of our guests. We will talk later... I have to go.'

Yvette watched as he threw the cigarette butt into the field and after taking the parcel and kissing his mother goodbye, he made his way out of the gate and along the lane. They had parted many times before, never showing their feelings in front of others, but this time was different. Perhaps it was the incident with Béatrice that had set her nerves on edge, or the rumours amongst the Maquis of raids, reprisals and internments or the bulletins they heard on Radio Londres, saying the tide was turning against the Nazis. But Yvette felt unsettled, a tinge of panic, or was it the portent of change that hovered on the horizon? Whatever it was, something told her to make the most of it all, Vincent, Tante Helene, France, just in case it was all about to come to an end.

Pedalling faster now, aware of the sun on her pannier and knowing the food wrapped in cloth wouldn't fare well in the heat, even if it was covered by her coat which she never left at home, just in case. Her ears listened out for the sound of a vehicle, and if she heard one she would attempt to hide. There had been a marked increase in Boche activity and word along the line was that something big was on the cards, the Allies were gaining momentum, but how accurate that was she had no idea.

They listened with hope and fear in their hearts; the news via Radio Londres told of advances and victories, but the thumping of Boche fists on doors reminded them of the heavy price of being caught. They were getting nastier, if that was even possible, and the twitchy German presence was on high alert, poised for revenge. At this thought Yvette felt her heart lurch, knowing that if they did strike, the blood of many could be on her hands.

For now, the roads were clear. Yvette loved the countryside despite it being a shock to the system at first and to her surprise, she now preferred it to the city of her birth. Fancy that. London was loud, busy, exciting, with smoky exhausts, foggy smoggy mornings, dance halls and cinemas, fancy shops and hotels. But her part of France was like the painting she'd seen at the National Gallery back home. How strange it was that when she'd visited on a school trip, little Dottie Tanner had no idea how her life, or the world, for that matter, was going to pan out. And that one day, she'd be cycling past the fields of gold she once gazed at in awe.

It was also hard to imagine living anywhere else now and she'd spent many an hour lost in daydreams while tilling the earth in the vegetable patch, trying to conjure an image of free France and how life would be if she lived here with Vincent. It wasn't so far from England and Mémère Delphine for one would love to visit, even her parents, once the scourge had been defeated.

She adored the tranquil lanes, actually being able to hear the hum of insects and birdsong, and the church bells on the hour and the clip-clopping of hooves and voices on the wind. All this would be drowned out by the sound of London. Yes, life would be perfect once the Boche were gone.

Her mind then turned to another event, one surer than independence day, but nonetheless it caused Yvette's heart to constrict because hundreds of miles away, her family's thoughts would be on one thing, her twenty-fourth birthday. This was her second one away from home, and again there would be no knees-up in the pub, no home-made cake courtesy of her mum or her dad's tradition of a pie with a candle stuck in it, something he'd been doing for as long as she could remember.

It didn't matter about presents or material things because the best gift of all would be staying alive, seeing her family, and Vincent, if he would just hurry up, bring back Anatoly and some news of Estelle. That was all she wanted. And to spend more nights like they had before he'd left.

Despite the breeze, Yvette felt herself blush when she thought of how he looked at her when she appeared at the hut wearing the blue dress Estelle had given her, the ring on her finger, a touch of rouge on her cheeks and lips, scent dabbed on her wrist and behind her ears. She had wanted him to see her as a woman, at her best, alluring, beautiful even. He was used to seeing the countryside version, or the agent, relying on her like one of the men, crawling through mud, doing what they did. She would never forget the night in the wooden hut, how they made love like it was the last time, again and again until, as always, they had to say goodbye.

Forbidding any further thoughts of home or Vincent, Yvette cheered herself with the thought of seeing Konstantin. There was something about him that made her happy, his humour was dry but infectious. He was different, mysterious but in a storyteller kind of way and most of the time she wasn't quite sure if he was pulling her leg or being serious. It was clear from the time spent with him that his fellow evaders didn't trust him, or like him that much either, but she did, on both counts.

It would be another long night if Vincent didn't show, followed by another long day, so in the meantime her evaders could keep her company. Yvette felt her mood dipping. She was fine during the day when she pedalled freely in the sun but at night, all alone in her bed listening for noises, waiting for the Gestapo to pounce, her mind went into overdrive and fear kicked in. Yes, being in the cave while she waited was better.

During the time that Konstantin and the others had been there, Yvette had learned more about how they had ended up in France. Jakob was fleeing for the obvious reasons and Teddy had been shot down and needed to get back to his squadron. She was privately in awe of her Russian evader, and secretly thrilled that he had given her a nickname, Zaya.

He had used the term on her third visit, when she had brought them cheese, bread, sausage and wine, plus a treat for Konstantin, a bottle of eau de vie, the eye watering, cough inducing home-made apéritif favoured by the locals. It was the nearest he was going to get to vodka, for the foreseeable future anyway.

While the others concentrated on the food, Konstantin had savoured the first sip and then had taken a fortifying swig. 'Ah, my little Zaya, thank you for this, it is appreciated.'

Yvette gave him a quizzical look. 'Zaya?'

Konstantin smiled. 'Don't worry, it is a Russian form of endearment and it suits you, my little baby rabbit who scurries underground, my very own Zaychik.'

'Oh, I see. I like it. Zaya. I'll remember that. Now, why don't you eat, you need to keep your strength up in case we have to move you quickly.'

At this Konstantin shook his head. 'No, Zaya, I am going no further until they bring Anatoly. I only left him in the city because they promised to get him well and reunite us. I will take my chances and stay here and wait for him.'

'I don't understand. We are not told too many details about any of you. I, we, have to trust whoever you have stayed with before us, we just keep moving you on, so tell me, how did you get here, to France?'

Another sip from the bottle, and a moment of quiet as Yvette passed Konstantin some food and signalled that he should eat. Between mouthfuls, he explained the circumstances of his arrival in France, and all about Anatoly, his brother.

They had been en route to Alexandria in Egypt via the Atlantic, stopping off at Gibraltar then through the Med. Anatoly was a pilot and was a member of a special squadron, trained by the RAF in Scotland. The northern air route from Russia to England, through Europe was becoming too dangerous but the need for munitions and supplies was relentless, therefore a new southern air route was planned, via Algeria, Tripoli, Cairo, Tehran and on to Moscow. Anatoly was needed in Cairo, and so it seemed was Konstantin, in a more secret capacity.

They were being transported, along with two other pilots, by the navy when their small frigate was hit by a gunboat. None of the crew survived, Anatoly, Konstantin and one other pilot clung on to debris and managed to make it towards land, after being picked up by a fishing boat. The other pilot had terrible injuries and didn't make it, Anatoly had a broken leg, Konstantin was unscathed. They had been moved inland by the Maquis but Anatoly had been left behind, at a safe house in Nantes.

'Is he very sick, Anatoly?'

'He was when I left. They had fixed his leg but he got an infection so he couldn't be moved. I argued that I wanted to stay but they refused, and I understand why. The city is dangerous but here, I would have a better chance to survive. That is why I will stay and wait. You cannot make me go.'

Yvette said nothing about that and asked a question instead. 'Is he really your brother or is that what you call all your comrades?'

Konstantin looked affronted. 'Yes, of course he is my brother, younger by two years but the cleverer son. I am the wily black sheep.'

'So how did you end up together, if he was the dashing pilot and you a simple farm animal?'

This seemed to amuse Konstantin, his eyes creased and after a bite of sausage, then another swig to wash it down, he answered. 'It was my father pulling strings. He was a general in the old guard, it's how it works in Russia, so instead of being sent to the front, my resourcefulness was to be used in other ways and I found myself in Scotland. My relocation to Cairo was ordered by a higher authority, not my father.'

'Ah, I see. But Vincent told me you were a navigator... are you?'

'That was what it said on my papers, and I can read a map and use a compass, so yes, I suppose I am.' Konstantin did not meet Yvette's eyes, he chewed the bread instead.

'Well then, that means I'm a navigator too, fancy that.' Yvette's voice held a hint of sarcasm which Konstantin ignored.

While he ate, he watched Jakob and Teddy who were over in another corner, propped against the cave wall, sharing a bottle of wine. They didn't seem to warm to Konstantin.

'Do you not get on well with your fellow troglodytes?' Yvette gestured to the others and in response Konstantin shrugged, a lack of concern in his expression.

'I do not think they like my politics, Zaya, or my country of birth but it is of no consequence to me. I will never see them again once we get back to England, but I would hope to see you again, if our paths should ever cross.'

Yvette felt herself flush, and secretly acknowledged that she was pleased this wily and clearly very intelligent, ruggedly handsome man would want to look her up. 'Well that would be very nice, Konstantin, but let me ask you something… is that really your name?'

He tilted his head to one side and held her in his stare. 'Is Yvette your real name?'

Shaking her head, she laughed. 'Touché. Okay, here's another. Tell me how you got that scar on your cheek, I'd say it's not that old, and I bet it hurt, however you got it.'

Konstantin turned his body slightly as if to prevent the others from hearing and in a low voice, his accent more pronounced, he answered. 'This, I can tell you.'

Yvette felt her eyes widen and for a second, she felt rather naïve, like a child listening to a bedtime story but it was too late to cover it up. 'Go on then.'

'I had a fight with a huge brown bear. It lost.'

'No you didn't.'

'Are you saying I am liar? My heart is wounded. I mean it, Zaya, I was hunting in the woods near our home in Petropavlovsk and it came out of nowhere, the rest is a long but rather macho tale of me wrestling it to the ground. I won't bore you with the details, but he left me this memento.' Konstantin touched his scar.

Yvette raised her eyebrows. 'Okay, so saying I do believe you, what happened to the bear, did it escape, surely you didn't kill it?'

'Of course I killed it, Zaya, and my mother now has a wonderful winter coat and my father a fetching hat, the head of the bear is on the wall of his study, he is very proud of my trophy.' Konstantin then took another drink and stood, taking the bottle to Teddy and Jacob.

'Here, drink, save me from myself and put some hairs on your chest.'

After Teddy silently accepted the bottle, Konstantin returned to his place by Yvette who remained unconvinced by his bear story so chose another more intellectual topic. 'I'll need to go soon but before I do, tell me another tale about old Russia and the revolution.'

Konstantin sighed and looked wistful. 'You are like a taskmaster, Zaya, but I am happy to talk of my homeland, so I will tell you of my grandfather and his days in the Cheka, and about the troika, a Russian obsession with the number three. It may serve you well.'

At this Yvette curled her legs underneath her body.

Konstantin smiled. 'So, if you are sitting comfortably, I will begin.'

27

THE LAST DAY

RENAZÉ, 1944

Yvette was making her way down the tunnel of the cave, remembering how she'd repeated the bear story to Vincent and explained how revolutionaries used the troika system, of keeping their secrets in a triangle of three. Vincent was a big fan of Konstantin and drank in every word he said, admiring the Russian's conviction and cause, if not all of his politics, but the sound of raised voices snapped Yvette out of her thoughts.

A heated discussion was audible through the oak door and even the rattling of the key in the lock didn't interrupt them, but the sight of her standing in the doorway did. Yvette looked from one to the other, then quickly closed and locked the door behind her before demanding answers.

'What's going on? You know to keep your voices down. I could hear you from the tunnel.'

Teddy spoke next. 'Ha, that's the least of your worries because this idiot went outside, and he was gone ages. The bloody fool could have got us all killed, and he won't say where he's been either.'

Yvette could not believe what she was hearing and disappointment raged through her. Konstantin had shocked her and let her down. Keeping her voice as level as possible she focused her attention solely on him. 'Why did you go out and where have you been? Answer me, Konstantin, you know it's forbidden.'

At first Konstantin glowered at the other two men, but when he turned towards Yvette his face was softer and slightly bashful. 'Zaya, I am sorry. I only meant to be gone a few minutes. I took the bucket because it stank, but once I was outside, in the fresh air, I enjoyed the freedom a little too much. And then I had an idea... I am sorry.'

Yvette was not satisfied, sensing also that Teddy wanted to throttle Konstantin. 'I asked you where you went, and what idea, what are you talking about?'

Konstantin stepped forward and put his right hand inside his overcoat and for a second, her brain went onto alert and her blood ran cold. Before Yvette could react to the swift movement as he retracted his hand, Konstantin had produced a bunch of wild flowers; purple campion and white parsley, blue speedwell and yellow cowslip, bound together with wheatgrass.

'I wanted to give you something on your birthday. You told me it was today, so I went foraging. Here, for you, *s dnem rozhdeniya*, happy birthday, Zaya.' He held them out for her to take.

Yvette was stunned. Touched and humbled beyond compare, torn between duty and friendship, she was unable to speak and was, thankfully, saved by timid Jakob.

'Well no harm has been done so why don't we forget about it and, after all, it is Yvette's birthday so let's move on. Teddy, do you agree?' The bespectacled young man looked nervously from the pilot who merely shrugged, then to Yvette who answered.

'Yes, I agree as long as, Konstantin, you promise never to go out again. Is that a deal?'

The Russian nodded, surly and sulky in the face of the men,

smiling when he looked towards Yvette who then felt she should show a little gratitude.

'Thank you for these, Konstantin, they are lovely and the only gift I have received, so even though you almost gave me a heart attack, you have also given me something to smile about, too.'

Appearing to rally and abandon his pout, Konstantin clapped, making Yvette start.

'Well what is a birthday without excitement? So all we need now is wine, come, let us drink to your good health.' With that he moved towards the oak barrels and began picking up the empty bottles that stood there, shaking them to check their contents.

Yvette intervened. 'Konstantin, stop, I have brought wine and food so let's sit, you can eat, and I will open the bottle now we are all friends again.'

Silently the four of them moved to where the blankets lay on the floor and under a dripping candle, Yvette uncovered the basket and watched as they helped themselves to the eggs, cold boiled potatoes and bread that lay inside. Once she'd pulled the cork from the bottle, she took a drink and then passed it along, to Konstantin first.

'Thank you for my flowers, they really are lovely and when I get home, I'll put them in water.'

'Will your Tante Helene wonder where they are from? Perhaps she will inform Vincent that he has a rival and he will come and beat me to a pulp.' Konstantin's blue eyes laughed.

Yvette had told him about her life on the farm and back home in London. She suspected he enjoyed their trade of tales, his of the Revolution, hers of chickens and big red buses. She hadn't given away too much, but enough perhaps to take Konstantin's mind off living in a hole underground, just as talking to Teddy and Jakob about their families seemed to cheer them for a moment and remind them not to give in. The agent rule book would have advised against it but then again, whoever wrote it didn't live on the precipice of fear, miles from home, never knowing what tomorrow may bring.

'I am sure the bear killer of Petropavlovsk would have no trouble dealing with Vincent, now try to sleep. I will stay here tonight in case they arrive. Close your eyes because we will have a long journey ahead.'

For once the Russian did as he was told.

Yvette was huddled under the pile of sacking, Konstantin by her side. As always, once the sun set her thoughts skittered like beetles, remembering instructions, imagining their escape route should it be required, dreading the impending journey to the Atlantic Coast.

How she wished Vincent had sent her to Nantes instead of him, then she'd have been able to see Estelle. She had sent him with a message, in case Anatoly had been taken to her safe house, but he could be anywhere in the city. Yvette looked down at her ring and sighed as she touched the precious stones, like they connected her to Estelle.

The time seemed to crawl by as they waited for news. Surely soon they would hear from London via a message on the radio, Yvette knew what to listen for; 'The crow will sing three times in the morning'. But down there, in the candlelit cave below the fields there was no chance of hearing a bird sing, let alone a code. They had to move the evaders soon, they'd been there too long already.

Once more Yvette prayed for Vincent to arrive. She was worried about him and he made her feel safe because no matter how hard she tried to be strong and brave, self-preservation was getting harder each day.

The atmosphere had changed, she could feel it, a shift, ever since the death of Jörg. She feared reprisals were coming but in what form was anyone's guess. Bloody Béatrice, she had a lot to answer for and it felt as though because of her, the walls were closing in on them all.

And she felt sad too, because each time she'd left the house to take food to the men hiding in the caves she'd kissed Tante Helene goodbye, as though she was simply heading into town to get provisions. Deep down, both of them knew it might be for the last time because as soon as she got word from Florian or Vincent, Yvette would have to make the journey west with the evaders and it was riddled with danger. Even if she made it to the rendezvous with the navy boats, there was no guarantee she'd make it back to the village.

Yvette's identity papers were fastened inside one pocket of her coat that was wrapped around her for warmth, along with some francs folded around a note, one she couldn't bear to leave behind, and the gun Vincent had given her was in the other pocket. That's all she would take with her if and when they fled.

A shudder, not from cold, even though the cave wasn't the warmest place to be even in May, but that damn sense of dread that had been creeping up on her, ever since she'd left Nantes. It had been Estelle's cautionary tone, an uncharacteristic hint at danger that left Yvette with a sense of foreboding and then there was Jörg.

She didn't want to think of that anymore, it was counterproductive so instead she turned to check on Konstantin who had woken from his dozing and was also deep in thought.

'Are you okay, comrade?'

'I will be once Anatoly is here.' Konstantin pulled the sacking further over their bodies.

'It shouldn't be long now. The signal from London will come soon.'

Konstantin didn't comment, he focused on her instead. 'You

seem tense, Zaya, what is wrong? You are usually so cheerful, but today you are different.'

'Ah, you are always so intuitive, comrade, I can hide nothing from you, can I?' Yvette saw Konstantin smile. Her term of endearment always amused him. 'And yes, I am tense which I suppose means I have failed dismally because aren't agents supposed to be cool and collected, not jumpy and tetchy?'

'I really wouldn't know, Zaya. I am just a navigator for the Russian Air Force and have no special skills where espionage is concerned.' The skin around his eyes creased as he smiled, then he rested his head against the stone wall of the cave.

Yvette smiled too. 'Mmm, if you say so, but I do wonder if that's why Anatoly's plane crashed... either your navigating skills weren't up to scratch or perhaps you were just hitching a ride to Egypt, on business, so to speak. I did wonder what happened to your uniform along the way.'

Yvette heard him chuckling but didn't expect an answer, which was fine, secrets were secrets, but she attempted to interrogate him further, to pass the time if nothing else.

'What will you do when you get back to England or is that another mystery?'

Konstantin shrugged his shoulders. 'That I do not know, but I will be fine. Do not worry, Zaya.'

Yvette was about to ask him if Anatoly would be sent back to Russia when there was a sound beyond the inner door to the cave, one she recognised as the outer door being opened, causing her stomach to lurch and fear to trickle slowly down her spine.

Taking the gun from her pocket, Yvette scrambled to her feet and sped towards one of the large barrels and took cover, training the sight on the door. Konstantin had nudged Jakob and Teddy awake and immediately aware of danger, all three sought hiding places in the shadowy crevices and crannies, blowing out the candles as they ran. Yvette strained her ears and eyes as the only light was from one remaining candle by the doorway. There would be no footsteps, the path down to the cave was earth, and unless the next sound she heard was the voice of Vincent or Florian they were all doomed. Then it came.

Four taps on the door, then two. 'Yvette, it is me, Vincent.'

Joy and relief accompanied the sigh when Yvette exhaled, unaware she'd been holding her breath but despite that, rather than return to normal, her heartbeat pounded. Taking the key from her pocket, Yvette unlocked the door. He was there. Alone.

At first, she thought maybe Anatoly and the other refugee would be somewhere behind, maybe hobbling, so many thoughts rushed at once but when Vincent stepped inside and closed the door her fears returned.

Standing beside the candle, their faces illuminated by a flickering glow, Yvette and Vincent shared a moment, their lips an inch apart, the look in his eyes told her he'd missed her, then the trance was broken by footsteps emerging from the shadows.

Vincent turned to face Konstantin and the others, but it was Yvette who spoke first.

'Vincent, where are they, what has happened?'

His focus flicked from her to Konstantin and she could tell Vincent was stalling, and then she knew why. 'I am sorry, Konstantin, Yvette, but I have terrible news.'

When he had arrived in Nantes at the home of his contact Olivier, Vincent was met with a chaotic scene, grave news and a cache of documents. The members of the Choir Network were moving out, disbanding and heading south, panicked that they might only have hours, minutes to spare. Olivier suspected an informer had given them up, it was too much of a coincidence as they had been so careful.

At first Vincent didn't understand and the look of confusion on his face clearly warranted a fuller but hasty explanation. The documents were stolen from the Gestapo offices in the city, a daring raid co-ordinated by a close-knit team, one that Olivier trusted with his life. The information would be of great use to the Allies and Resistance alike, detailing troop and ammunition movements that were heading north, to the coast. It had clearly been a step too far and now the Boche were rounding people up like crazed animals and one of their own was amongst them.

Before he even spoke the words, Yvette knew who it was, the name Vincent would say would break her heart. That cold hand of dread ran its fingers all over her body and rested on her lips which froze, numb, too afraid to speak.

Vincent reached out and took her hands in his. 'I am sorry, Yvette, but they took Estelle.' Then he turned his head to Konstantin. 'And Anatoly.'

Yvette was aware of Teddy placing his hand on Konstantin's shoulders, her eyes meeting those of her devastated comrade. Neither of them spoke, leaving Vincent to fill the space.

'I didn't want to leave immediately, I hoped that maybe Olivier was wrong so I stayed, staking out the apartment, praying that they had got away or would be released after questioning, but I knew in my heart I was fooling only myself. I had to make a choice, and I knew there was nothing I could do for Estelle and Anatoly, but I could save us, so I came back. Someone must have given Estelle away, and now I fear that we too are in danger, we could be next even if she or Anatoly don't crack.'

That was it, the word, the image, the horror that Yvette could not bear to contemplate – what was happening to Estelle right now? Covering her mouth with her hand Yvette battled to hold in the scream because once it was out, she thought she would never stop. Her whole body trembled and even when Vincent pulled her to him, it didn't stop. Then it was Konstantin's turn to speak.

'Where did they take them?'

'To the prison. Someone saw them being put into the truck and followed by bicycle.'

A nod from Konstantin. 'What do we do now? You said your circuit is betrayed, what about us. Should we go on alone?'

Yvette was watching Konstantin through eyes that seemed not to blink, they just stared, disbelieving, while her brain processed what she was hearing. Konstantin looked like a man who had been punched in the face but refused to fall, expecting another blow and hardening himself before it hit. Although expressionless, his eyes were black pools of anger, the hate they reflected burning through the darkness of the cave.

'No, we will take you. We cannot remain here now.' Pushing Yvette gently away from his body he spoke to her first. 'Listen to me, Yvette. I want you to take everyone to the Chateau Motte Glain, you know where it is, we went there once, remember, to collect ammunition?'

He was willing her with his eyes to focus, she could tell. So she nodded, her voice still not found.

'There is a small track that leads alongside, it is marked by a large rock carved with a cross, follow it to the end and wait there by the shrine until Florian and I arrive. Do not go with anyone else, or show yourself, do you understand?'

'But where are you going? Why can't we all go now, together.'

Vincent took her by the shoulders and spoke softly. 'Because I have to warn the others, Xavier, Benoit, Claude, Thierry, Florian. They need to disappear quickly but once I have found them, I will come back then we will head for the coast.'

Yvette nodded, her voice when it came belied the fear she felt inside. 'Be quick, it must be getting dark outside.'

'Good, now come, we will leave together.'

Outside the cave, it would have been good to breathe fresh air had Yvette's chest not been constricted. The light was fading, and it was imperative they reached the chateau before nightfall. She knew her way during the day but with only the light of a half-moon it would be impossible.

It was time to go their separate ways and it took Yvette all of whatever strength she possessed not to crumble, that and pride. She could not let Vincent, or the others, see weakness. They were relying on her now.

When Vincent spoke, it was to all of them. 'If I am not there by midnight go without me. It is just over two hundred kilometres and should take you around two days on foot. Travel by night and be vigilant during the day. Do you remember the route I told you? There are two safe houses along the way, the home of Etienne in the village of Marcy and Davide in Anse. They will help you. London know that you are en route, our radio operator has already been moved but sent the message first. All you have to do is wait for the signal. Davide will do the rest.'

'But why are you saying this? You only have to go to the village, it won't take long, I don't understand.' Yvette was angry now, this wasn't the plan, they were going together, that was the end of it.

'Just in case I am delayed, Yvette, that is all. If you reach the coast before me wait there if it makes you feel better, there is a small beacon on the headland at Bonaparte Beach, you'll know it when you see it.' He gave Yvette a smile, one of courage, bestowing belief, like that a parent gives to a child. It did not convince the adult.

Turning, Vincent faced Konstantin, his voice lighter, faking levity in a dire situation. 'Konstantin, my friend, you can use your so-called navigational skills to assist Yvette, head in this direction, keep the moon to your left.' With his arm Vincent signalled the route.

Even though she could hear the words Yvette did not want to acknowledge them, especially the next, those meant solely for her. As Vincent pulled her to one side, the other three men averted their eyes.

Vincent's hands cupped Yvette's face as he spoke. 'I want you to go now and be brave and promise me you will not come back to find me if I am not there at midnight. Say it, Yvette, say you promise.'

Even though she was weeping inside, her body almost limp with despair, Yvette forced herself to be strong. 'I promise, and I won't let you down. I will see you soon. Here, take the gun, not that you will need it. Now hurry.' She pulled the firearm from her pocket and wordlessly Vincent placed it in the bag.

'I love you.' Her words were a whisper.

His identical. 'I love you too.'

Vincent's parting kiss was firm and lingered but not for long enough. He stepped away and quickly shook the hands of the others, and then he was gone.

28

BETRAYED

FRANCE, 1944

They heard the sound of a vehicle in the distance, and as it neared, Yvette held her breath. If it was Florian he would be driving slowly, turning on his headlight for a second only to light the way, but the chug of the engine would remain constant, the old bone shaker breaking through the silence of the night. Lights could be seen for miles around in the pitch darkness, so it was necessary to avoid detection like in the blackout at home. *No, don't go there.*

It was always a risk, going out during curfew but the chances of anyone being seen amongst the vast expanse of the Loire countryside was minimal, unless it was a Boche ambush, and then it was all over for them. When the chugging slowed Yvette scrambled from her hiding place behind the dense thicket and crouched. Sure enough a faint beam shone for a second and then was extinguished, a few seconds passed and again, a faint light. As the truck travelled further into the heavy woodland the lights stayed on, but still Yvette couldn't see who was driving or if there were one or two occupants. *Please God let there be two.*

Remembering Vincent's orders and wary of this being a trap, Yvette scurried back to the undergrowth and watched with the others as the truck passed by. Once it reached the shrine a few metres ahead, the engine stopped. Plunged into darkness they heard a door open, feet land on the ground and the strike of a match. A shadowy figure emerged from the other side of the truck and the cigarette smoke carried across the night air, as did the voice of Florian.

'Yvette.'

For a heartbeat she didn't respond, she couldn't see over the side panels of the truck and what if German soldiers lay there, waiting to pounce? Then another noise, a groan, male, and Florian ran to the back of the truck and simultaneously Yvette broke cover... Vincent. *My Vincent is injured.* She heard the others following but when she reached the truck it wasn't Vincent lying there it was Claude.

'Oh my God, what happened? Where is Vincent, where is he?' Yvette could hear the panic in her own voice and when she saw Florian rub a hand over his hair, unable to meet her eye, she snapped, grabbing his shoulders as she screamed, 'Tell me, Florian, where is Vincent?'

When the answer came the forest fell still, the world stopped and so did Yvette's heart.

'He is dead. I'm sorry, Yvette, but Vincent is dead.'

Florian had found Claude by the side of the road, his Solex in the ditch. There was blood gushing from the gunshot wound in his leg and after Florian tied a tourniquet to stem the flow, he managed to manoeuvre Claude to the back of the truck and here, the barely conscious man told him what happened.

As Florian repeated the tale, Yvette and the others listened in silence.

'Vincent arrived at the old farmhouse where Claude was hiding out. He'd only been there a few moments when the

Boche arrived. It was a Gestapo car, four men, all armed. Claude told Vincent to run but he ignored him and tried to shoot his way out. Claude managed to escape but took a bullet in the leg as he drove off... the last time he saw Vincent he was on the ground, the Boche stood over him, then a gunshot... they killed him, Yvette. The Gestapo chased Claude, but he took a back road and managed to lose them. He must have lost consciousness and control of the bike. That's when I found him.'

Yvette trembled; her body unable to stay still. It wasn't true, Claude was wrong, so she climbed onto the back of the van and began to shake the injured man awake.

'Claude, Claude, wake up, wake up.' How she managed not to slap his face when he moaned, she did not know, instead he lapsed in and out of consciousness. 'How do you know he's dead, Claude? You can't be sure, you can't be.'

When strong arms gripped her shoulders, Yvette desisted and listened to the voice that accompanied them.

Konstantin spoke firmly. 'Stop, Zaya, he is too sick to answer you and even if Vincent is still alive, they will have taken him... I'm sorry but you know this is true. Now come, we must make decisions and go. We have to leave; it is too dangerous to stay here.'

Feeling the fight leave her body as the words hit home, Yvette slumped against Konstantin and let Florian take the lead.

He began by agreeing with Konstantin. 'You are right, we leave now. If we follow this track it will lead us past the village. We can use the truck until it is light, hide, then continue until we run out of fuel. There is no way we can go all the way on foot, not with Claude in this condition, and we cannot leave him here, not now.'

Teddy usually remained silent, but his panicked voice cut through the darkness. 'Can't you find someone to care for him? He will slow us down!'

'No! They will start searching the houses at first light, I am sure, and whoever is found sheltering Claude will be punished. He is one of us and we do not leave him behind.' Florian sounded adamant.

Yvette spoke next. From her pit of grief, fuelled by anger she clawed her way out as adrenalin began to pump through her veins and a terrible rage engulfed her. 'We have been betrayed. Vincent was right, the network is falling apart. None of us can stay here now. Let's go, quickly. We will keep going until the fuel runs out, then we will walk, somehow, with Claude. Two of you can ride up front with Florian, one of you will have to stay here with me. I will not let the traitor end him like they ended Estelle and Vincent.'

'I will stay with Yvette.' Konstantin gave a jerk of the head, motioning to Teddy and Jakob that they should go to the cab. He remained on the flat bed and dragged Claude away from the back then settled himself into one corner while Yvette took her place in the other.

Once again, the truck moved slowly off into the night and as it creaked and rolled over the bumpy track, taking Yvette further away from the village she called home, she swallowed down tears as she thought of Tante Helene, Xavier, the others and, of course, little Polo. But the image that stayed with her for the whole of the journey and for many years to come was that of Vincent, the man she loved, lying in a pool of blood, murdered by the Gestapo and betrayed by one of their own.

The wind whipped across the headland, sand stinging Yvette's bare legs that were cut, scratched and filthy. Pulling her collar up to shield her ears before wrapping her arms around her body, she listened in the darkness for the sound of boats. The others were hiding in the dunes, waiting like her. Just as

Vincent had said, once they made contact with Davide he knew what to do which was fortunate because Yvette was lost in a pit of grief, the arms of a monster sucking her further and further with every passing hour. All she wanted now was for the boat to come, the evaders to be gone and then she could be alone and wait at the headland for Vincent, in body or spirit. He would come, he had to.

A noise carried on the Atlantic wind reached all their ears: an engine, then nothing. Then a light tapping out Morse code, then action. Davide broke cover first and led Konstantin, Jakob and Teddy to the shore, two of the local Maquis dragged Claude across the sand by his arms, a crude and no doubt painful movement, but speed was essential. He had survived the journey in agony, rambling and delirious for most of it, riddled with infection, but once he was in England he'd be fine. She had done her best for him, saved his life and not left him behind to suffer the fate of others. Her sprint across the sand, Florian close at heel, was not in order to board the dinghy that would take them to the gunboat, it was to say goodbye. They had already thanked her many times but until they were safely on their way, Yvette couldn't accept their words or relax.

She watched from the shore as they all boarded, following the orders of the black clad men. When Konstantin turned and held out his hand before he stepped into the shallow waves, she kept hers dug firmly in her pockets and met his eye with determination and resolve.

'I'm not coming, Konstantin, you need to go quickly, comrade.'

With a look of surprise, he stepped forward and tried to take her arm, but Yvette stood firm while he reasoned with her.

'Yvette, Zaya, you must. Do not be afraid, it is only a short crossing and we have come this far, we will be fine, trust me.'

The commando on the boat told them to move it, Yvette

ignored him. 'I'm not afraid but I'm not ready to go yet. Please, Konstantin, try to understand. Good luck and take care, comrade.'

Another order from the boat and she saw that Konstantin was battling with his conscience but maybe the set of her jaw, or the steel in her bones that would not be moved when he tried to pull her, told him he had lost.

'Where will you go? You must not go back to your village; it is too dangerous.'

'I won't. Go now, please, or they will leave without you.'

It was with a nod of the head that he told her he understood, respected her decision and then he turned and ran through the waves. The engine fired, nobody waved, Yvette kept her trembling hands in her pockets. Florian remained by her side and they watched as the mist swallowed the boat whole. Within seconds they were gone.

Once they'd climbed and descended the dunes, reaching the road, breathless, they paused and listened. There were patrols all along the coast and if they'd been alerted to the presence of a boat then soon the area would be swarming, they had to move fast.

Florian took the lead. 'Come, we will keep going until dawn then rest, we have a few hours before it is light. We can go to the house of my cousin, he is in Finistere but it's a good walk south. Are you okay, Yvette? You should have gone with them; you have done enough here.'

'You go, Florian. It will be safer alone. I want to stay here.'

'No, I will not leave you, Yvette. Vincent would never forgive me. Now come, stop being so stubborn it is sending me mad.'

At this Yvette managed a smile. 'Then you will go mad here, on this road because I am staying. Please, Florian, head south and be safe. You too have done plenty and I don't want you to be captured with me. Alone you have a chance.'

Florian patted his jacket pockets and looked angry when he remembered he had no cigarettes. 'Pah, why are you women so stubborn?'

'And why do men need to be told three times before they do as they are told? Please go, Florian... I cannot bear another goodbye so hurry, your cousin will have plenty of cigarettes, I am sure.' She smiled, willing him to go.

Another exasperated sound left Florian's lips and then he reached out and pulled her to him, kissing each cheek and then letting go. 'Good luck, Yvette, I am proud to have known you and maybe after the war you will come back, this is your home now too.'

Yvette only had time to answer quickly, there was a sound somewhere in the distance, a vehicle. 'You too, Florian, I will never forget you. *Vive la France, vive la Resistance.*'

The sound grew louder and after one last look they parted, taking different directions. Yvette darted into the field then ran along the road, throwing herself behind a hedgerow, where Florian went, she had no idea. She lay like that, huddled beneath her coat, legs tucked inside, head covered with her arms as the German jeep rolled by and once it passed, she remained where she was until morning knowing that once it was light she could begin her wait, for Vincent.

29

ALONE
CHÂTEAUBRIANT, 2005

Maude sniffed and wiped the tears that leaked and coursed down her cheeks while her gran fetched tissues from the bathroom. Darkness had fallen while Dottie told her tale uninterrupted, one that came out in a torrent of memories, faces, places, anger, love and hurt.

'Oh, Gran, that's so sad. It hurts my heart to think of you all alone like that. How long did you stay there, at the beach?'

Dottie came over to the bed and handed Maude a fist full of toilet paper, sitting beside her, then giving her a hug while she wiped her eyes and nose. She thought for a moment, gathering all the thoughts that after all these years demanded attention after being squashed into a box, the lid closed.

'You know I really can't be completely certain, days definitely. I found the beacon Vincent mentioned the next morning and hid in the dunes, watching and waiting for him. I remember feeling numb, even when I said goodbye to Konstantin and the others, even Florian. Something inside me had died, like a light switch being flicked off. I drank water from the trough on the lane, I ate nothing so maybe it was hunger that forced me to move on, or some part of my addled brain accepted that Vincent was really dead.'

'Where did you go? I can't believe you were on your own and stranded in the middle of occupied France.' Maude leant her head on Dottie's shoulder.

Dottie took Maude's hand as she spoke. 'I headed for St Malo, and don't forget, it was my choice to stay. I was selfish really because I should have thought about my parents and gone home but I couldn't. It was like I was stuck.'

'What do you mean?'

'It was as though I couldn't leave it all behind, France, the Resistance, my friends, Tante Helene and even the dead body I pictured on the floor of a barn. I wasn't ready and...' Dottie fell into silence.

As if sensing something, Maude lifted her head and pulled away from her gran but kept hold of her hand. 'What?'

'I had to keep my promise, didn't I? To Vincent. I swore I wouldn't go back to the village so even if I didn't go back to England, I had to move on.'

'He was trying to keep you safe, Gran, because he loved you so much and he was right. Look what happened to Claude and the others.'

Dottie nodded. 'Do you think that's why I refused to come to France again? Not being able to face what happened to the Maquis, those who were rounded up?'

'Probably. I think you buried everything deep inside and it all got jumbled up... but did you ever check that Vincent was really dead because can you imagine if he'd survived and was...'

Dottie placed her hand on Maude's leg, it silenced her immediately.

'Hugh checked for me, he offered and brought me a transcript of the coded message. The details were sparse, but they mentioned our circuit had been compromised and its leader was dead. That was that; Vincent was gone, no miracles or post-war reunions.'

'And what about Maude, Estelle, sorry I never know what to call her. Did you find out what happened to her? I know it can't be a happy ending so I'm sorry if the question upsets you more.'

Dottie smiled. 'It's okay, I'm going to have to tell you anyway. When I talk about the war, she's Estelle, a masquerade, but in my heart, she is and always will be Maude.'

Taking a deep breath, Dottie said the words she dreaded. 'Maude was tortured and then transported to Buchenwald concentration camp in Germany. They kept her there for a while and then she was executed by firing squad.'

Dottie couldn't cry, not for Maude because if she started she'd never stop, so instead she spoke her pain. 'When Hugh told me, many, many months after I went back to work, I thought I would go mad from the horror of it. That my Maude had endured our worst fear, survived it only to be murdered by those vile creatures. I wanted to run out on to the road at Whitehall and scream at the world, at all the stupid, ignorant people on the bus and on the pavement who were getting on with their lives when Maude was dead. I was so angry because they had no idea what we had done, what she had sacrificed for them. I was very bitter for a long time and that resentment was the only thing that kept me going. I had to for her.'

'Oh, Gran, I think that's so cruel and sad... and I'm starting to understand now why you've lived your life like you have and the decisions you've made. I think a lot of them are a result of this, what you're telling me.'

Dottie took a sip of cold tea before she spoke. 'You may well be right, because what I'm going to tell you now will probably prove your point.'

Maude gave Dottie a quick hug and then asked, 'So where did you go after the beach?'

'Well this is where it all goes completely crazy because I got it into my head that I should head to St Malo, to find Mémère Delphine's family, my uncle and his wife. The thing was, it took me over a week to get to the coast because the whole of the Atlantic Wall was riddled with Germans, so it was early June when I arrived in the port.'

'Did you find them, your family?'

'I found their farm, but they were gone. A neighbour told me my aunt had taken the children south to stay with relatives, my uncle, as you know, had been taken for forced labour. I stayed in their house a while, it was a roof over my head, and I knew they wouldn't have minded. Then I joined with a local Maquis group who were gearing up for the invasion. D-Day. Our forces landed on the beaches at Normandy on the sixth of June, the Allies were pushing south. The Germans were in a state of panic, so we did our very best to make their life even worse.'

'Bloody hell, Gran, you certainly were a sucker for punishment, weren't you? You could have been killed, did you have a death wish or something?' On speaking those words Maude fell silent and then her head snapped up, as though she'd realised something, a thought she passed on to her Gran. 'Oh my God, Gran, is that what you were doing... did you want to be killed so you could be with Vincent?'

Hearing the words that mirrored the thought that had only that second popped into her own head, Dottie stood. She needed a proper drink so took a bottle from the carrier bag on the floor, gesturing to Maude who nodded and watched while two glasses were filled. Passing one to Maude before she took a seat in the armchair by the window, Dottie pondered for a moment, relishing the soft breeze of a summer evening.

'I know that I didn't care if I lived or died. And that I hated the Germans with a passion so fierce that the rage in me could have killed with my bare hands. Yes, I took risks, and in those eight or so weeks I fought alongside the Maquis once again. I did as much as I could to avenge Vincent and Estelle, my Maude, and all the others who I feared had been taken or lost in Renazé.'

Maude sipped her wine. 'So how did it end for you, the war? Somehow you got back to England.'

Dottie flipped off her shoes and wiggled her toes and the sight of bare feet triggered an odd memory. 'There were around 8,000 German troops in St Malo, or so the Maquis reckoned, and they were determined to hold the town, but the Allies were just as determined to take it. The shelling began on August the sixth. I knew the date because it was my dad's birthday, and the only way I can describe the battle for St Malo was like hell on earth. A barrage of bombs rained from the sky, the attack hitting us from both sides when a German minesweeper shelled the cathedral wall, and allied shells hit the prison freeing those inside. The town was engulfed in an inferno of fire. I can still hear the noise now, and feel the heat on my face and everywhere was red and gold and the smoke and dust choked me. It was horrific and it lasted three days. We were trapped in the centre, a few of us, and when the order came to evacuate, I was running through the square when a shell hit, blowing me off my feet.'

Maude gasped. 'Oh my God.'

Dottie was lost in the past so carried on. 'When I came to there was a lull, no bombs. I was in an alleyway, covered in rubble. Someone must have dragged me there and when I finally managed to stand, I only had one shoe. I was so upset that I burst into tears, fancy that. I remember crying and crying and wandering around looking for my horrible black shoe that I hated anyway. I didn't notice at first that the soldier who guided me to a medic was American, not German, and that the man who cleaned and dressed my feet and told me not to worry about my shoe, didn't speak French. I still see snapshots of it, like flicking through an album of black-and-white photos, no colour, the red and gold had gone and all that surrounded me were grey bombed-out buildings, then white, clean white and a red cross, nurses with stern faces and kind English voices, and then I was home, with my family.'

'I bet they were so happy to see you.'

'Oh yes, they were overjoyed! Mum didn't stop crying for days, and Delphine sat by my bed and kept me company. She never left my side. I was in a bad way, you see.'

'Were you injured?'

'Not physically, apart from lots of bumps and bruises, but it was up here where the damage was done.' Dottie tapped her forehead. 'Today they'd called it PTSD, but back then the doctors put it down to exhaustion and shock, nothing that a good rest wouldn't sort out. They didn't know how I felt inside, and I'd never have told anyone.'

'And how did you feel, Gran?'

'Like I was going mad, that there was a scream lodged in my throat and I had to hold it in because if I started, I'd never stop. I was out of place, in the wrong bed. I wanted to be back in Renazé at Tante Helene's and hear the cockerel and the sound of the church bell strike. And I wanted Vincent.' A sob erupted from Dottie's throat that took her by surprise and once it was out, like the long held in scream, it flowed into tears.

Maude took her Gran in her arms and held her tightly as she sobbed quietly. Eventually Dottie calmed and pulled away slowly from the embrace.

'I'm sorry, Maude, I don't know what came over me and look at the time, you must be shattered, listening to me rattling on.' Dottie felt slightly foolish, she'd never cried in front of Maude ever.

'There's no need to apologise, Gran. I feel honoured that you've shared all this with me and I'm not tired at all. I think you needed to get all of this off your chest and I can tell it's been building up for a while, maybe even before we came to France. Do you feel better though, for telling me?'

Dottie didn't hesitate. She really did feel like a weight had lifted. 'Definitely, and you've been a wonderful listener, Maudie, and I'm so glad it was you I told all this to. I kept it locked away, waiting for the right person, and it was you.'

Maude gave Dottie a peck on the forehead. 'Well, I'm going to make us some hot chocolate and then we can get ready for bed. I'd still like to ask you some questions though, I didn't want to interrupt earlier.'

Dottie couldn't imagine what more there was to tell. 'I've told you everything now, we've caught up, really.'

'But how did you get better and end up at the Ministry of Defence, and how did you meet Hugh and Uncle Konki again?'

Maude was talking as she flicked on the kettle and poured the chocolate powder into cups.

'Hugh wrote to me and asked me to visit him at the convalescent home where he was recovering so he could thank me for saving his life, and he sounded rather lonely too. I didn't want to go at first, I didn't want to do anything, but it was Mémère who persuaded me. She was wise and suggested it would be good to connect with someone that understood. Slowly it dawned on me that Hugh was my only link to the Maquis and the idea of it spurred me on. Funny thing is, it's not like we sat there and chatted about the good old days because we didn't even mention the Resistance, those last days were too painful but it was as though we had a bond, and that was enough.'

Dottie stirred the hot chocolate that Maude handed her. 'He was more worried that he'd said something embarrassing while he was ill, you know, rambling because of the infection in his bullet wound, bless him, but I reassured him that he had been a complete gentleman. From what I remember he did seem confused, talking about traitors and documents, smatterings of German that Konstantin interpreted as gibberish.'

Maude was smiling now. 'I bet he thought he'd sworn undying love to you or something a bit rude. I told you he's always fancied you, that's why he made sure you were near him at work. Just think, you could have been Lady Dottie if you'd played your cards right and be living in that big posh house of his.'

'You need to get a grip of your imagination, Maude, there's never been any hint of that from Hugh, but you're right, he has always looked after me and was a huge support emotionally too. Like I said, he was the one who found out about Maude and Vincent; he had, still has, lots of contacts. Hugh was so sweet, and I knew I could confide in him because he'd been there at the time, so when I was ready, like he promised, he brought me the information. I had to see it with my own eyes, to believe they really were gone.'

'Well, he's lovely and I'm glad his shyness and, you know, his physical appearance didn't stop him from finding someone, even though he probably always held a torch for you.'

Dottie raised her eyebrows as she took a sip of her drink. 'Moving on to Konstantin, my other imaginary admirer, when he popped up again it certainly was a surprise.'

Maude put her cup on the bedside table then wriggled up the bed. 'Oh, I'm looking forward to this... go on, tell all.'

Laughing, Dottie followed suit. 'Don't start all that, you minx. Konstantin literally did just turn up one day. It was 1952, December to be precise, and I was on my way home from work, waiting for the bus and I heard a voice say, "Hello, my little Zaychik." I was so shocked... but genuinely thrilled to see him.'

'What was he doing in London?'

'Well, it was the start of the Cold War and he said he was working as a consular attaché at the embassy, but I've always known, well, suspected that he was KGB. Hugh wasn't pleased about our friendship, although he was gracious and thanked Konstantin for helping to get him to the boat. After that they remained guarded with each other but that was natural, owing to their work. It's always fun, though, when they spar with each other. The rest is history. Your Uncle Konki just became part of my life, disappearing for a while, then he'd be back, witty, wise and loyal as ever. I've been blessed really, having them both in my life, but my favourite has always been Konstantin.'

'Aw, I love Uncle Konki even though he still won't tell me how he really got that scar on his face and I've heard about a hundred different versions of that story, the big fibber.'

Dottie laughed. 'I learned a long time ago to take a lot of what he says with a pinch of salt but he's never let me down and I would trust him with my life, just not to cheat at poker.'

'I wonder why he never got married, do you think it's because of his job?'

Relieved that Maude didn't hint that it was because Konstantin was in love with her, Dottie related what she knew of his liaisons.

'Probably, but he was never short of admirers and kept himself busy with a number of affairs, from what I can gather. Right, I think I've told you everything and I'm glad we ended with the life and times of Uncle Konki, thinking of him has cheered me up. I might ring him tomorrow while you're painting a masterpiece. I'm going to get ready for bed now... it's late and all this talking is exhausting, and I bet your ears are aching from my ramblings.'

A loud yawn from Maude confirmed she was tired too. 'Not at all, Gran. It's been fascinating and I'll write it all down tomorrow but you're right it's late and I'm glad the last part was about Konki. I don't want you feeling sad before you sleep or having nightmares because we've talked about the past.'

'I'm not sad, so don't worry. It's done me good. Now go to sleep. I'll turn the light out when I've finished in the bathroom. Sleep well, my darling girl. Love you.'

'You too, Gran, night night. Love you too.'

Dottie watched as Maude turned over and snuggled down under the duvet, then she made her way to the bathroom and once inside, closed the door and her eyes on the past. There was only one more thing she needed to tell Maude, or did she? Perhaps the truth about George didn't need to be told, it would do no good and maybe it was better that the only tortured person was herself, that the images she had of him at home in agony and those of Maude in a Nazi cell, stayed exactly where they were, locked in her mind for eternity.

30

CAFÉ DES AMIS

RENAZÉ, 2005

They walked from the car, across the square, over cobbles that Dottie imagined still held her footprints, invisible, layers deep. She wouldn't say it out loud but in her deepest moments, she'd imagined that coming back would be like walking through a portal and she would feel and see just as she did back then, in a time and place that clung tightly to her heart. It hadn't happened yet because traffic still buzzed by, planes flew overhead, people crossed paths, connected to their phones, eyes focused on the screen, ears wired for sound. When she looked down at her feet, they still wore her Clarks sandals, not her black lace-up shoes, and the tarmac below told her she hadn't time-travelled. She was stuck in the here and now.

The café though, was just as she remembered it. The signage lifted her heart because it at least had stayed true although the lettering was a modern font. It welcomed them nonetheless with the words 'Café des Amis'.

Maude went first, opening door and stepping inside. Nearly all of the tables were full apart from one in the corner by the window, so they made their way over and took a seat while they waited for someone to appear. It wouldn't be Armand, maybe his grandson, how wonderful that would be. While reading the menu, Dottie took in the café.

Structurally nothing had changed, even the counter was in the same place, but the rest of the interior had been updated although it still had some quaint touches that reminded the diners of its heritage. Black-and-white reproduction photographs of the village, possibly in the 1800s adorned the walls; market day, the village square, the church and numerous scenic vistas that in truth could have been anywhere in France. The wooden bistro chairs had gone, and modern white replacements were arranged around Formica tables decorated with a single vase and plastic gerbera, along with the condiments and menu stand. It had a good ambience though, clean and cheerful as opposed to the dark, smoky den that had once been a favourite haunt of the villagers, a place to plot and whisper in corners.

From the back kitchen that Dottie knew well, appeared a young woman dressed in a white T-shirt and jeans, an apron protecting her from the waist down, and on seeing them she smiled broadly and approached their table.

'Hello, I'm sorry if I kept you waiting... I am alone today so doing the job of everyone. Would you like the *plat du jour*, we are serving rabbit? Or perhaps something lighter.'

Dottie spoke for herself, 'I would love the *plat du jour*,' and when Maude looked up from the menu and nodded, 'and so would my granddaughter but may she have a soft drink instead of wine?'

Maude asked for Coke if they had it.

'Yes, of course, I will bring your drinks in a moment. My name is Francine so if you need anything, just ask.'

With that, she scurried off into the back, leaving Dottie and Maude to listen to the hum of chatter from the curious diners who glanced occasionally in their direction.

'Do you think they know we are English? I can feel them staring at us.' Maude's voice was a whisper accompanied by a roll of her eyes in the direction of the other tables.

Dottie chuckled. 'They know we are strangers, that's enough. Maybe they can detect a hint of an accent in my French. In the old days it could have got me killed so let's be grateful for stares, not quite so dangerous.'

Maude's eyes widened at Dottie's comments before turning her head and gazing out of the window. The square was deserted as was the section of the hotel that looked as though it was having major reconstruction work. Dottie hoped it wasn't all going to be demolished because she knew how long it had been there. Maybe she would ask Francine later, if not the *maire* would know.

Dottie's mind then wandered to their upcoming meeting. What if it drew a blank and there were no living relatives of the Maquis members in the village? The next stop would have to be the priest at the church, surely he would know exactly where Vincent was buried? Failing that, Dottie would wander along every row in the cemetery until she found him. She was sure he'd be here. Please God let the Nazis have returned the bodies to their families.

Francine approaching with a tray of drinks and their starters interrupted Dottie's train of thought. Seeing the *croquette de crabe*, both accepted their drinks, bade goodbye to Francine and began tucking in to their food.

Dottie had been watching Francine closely. She was wiping the tabletops while they finished the last of their desserts. The bistro was empty, the farm workers had gone back to their labours and the other customers petered off slowly leaving the three of them alone.

Dottie thought Francine seemed distracted, constantly looking out through the window across the street to where the bulldozers had resumed work on the old *chamber d'hôte*. Following her gaze, Dottie spotted a solitary figure, seated in his wheelchair, staring at the building site. When Francine approached the table to take their plates curiosity finally got the better of Dottie, her question causing Maude to look up from her phone.

'Francine, I hope you don't mind me asking but do you know the gentleman by the shrine? I noticed him last time we were here, and I can't help wondering why he sits there. Did he used to own the hotel? It must be difficult to see where you lived being demolished.'

Maude sighed. 'Gran, don't be so nosey.'

Erring on the side of caution and knowing how private the French could be, Dottie took the hint from Maude. 'Yes, forgive me, but I'm rather intrigued and it is rather hot out there.' Dottie followed Francine's gaze and noticed a smile playing on the waitress's lips.

'Ah yes, that is my great uncle. For some reason he has taken to sitting there each day to watch the workmen. My mother usually wheels him across and collects him later but today I must take him home.'

Dottie's skin prickled and her heart beat a little faster so she pressed Francine further. 'I remember the people who had it during the war, I lived just outside the village for a while, maybe he will remember them.'

Francine looked taken aback. 'You were here, in France, during the war, Madame?'

'Yes, it's a long story really but I'm here to meet the mayor, we have an appointment at three. I'm hoping he can tell me if any of the villagers from that time are still around because I'd like to meet them.' Dottie noticed that Francine appeared somewhat flustered, her hand rested at her throat as if containing shock.

'Oh my goodness, this is wonderful news! You must come with me right now so I can introduce you to my uncle. He has always lived here, and the hotel was his home. I'm sure he would love to meet you. Perhaps he can help.'

With that Francine more or less gathered Dottie and Maude up and ushered them out of the café, not bothering to lock the door. As they hurried along the street, Francine talked quickly and filled them in a little on her great uncle.

'Now, you must understand that he isn't the chatty type and has suffered a stroke so has difficulty speaking sometimes, so don't be offended if he seems a bit shy. He's become even more peculiar since we told him about the renovations and insists we take him there every day. My mother is a bit concerned but we have got used to his odd ways now.'

They were approaching from the rear and as they neared the solitary figure, Dottie took in his shiny bald scalp and close-cropped, grey hair. He appeared tall and sat upright, motionless, his left hand gripping the arm of his wheelchair. Maude and Dottie lingered out of sight for a moment while Francine walked in front of her uncle, then bent and took his hand. As his head lifted to meet her eyes, she smiled kindly and brushed his forehead gently, as if to reassure him.

Dottie was touched by the affection Francine showed and averted her eyes which caught Maude's briefly. Both then listened as Francine spoke.

'Uncle Polo, I have a surprise for you. This lady has come all the way from England to visit our village and she is searching for people who might remember her, look, she would like to say hello.'

When Maude and Dottie heard Francine call her uncle by his name they gasped in unison and Dottie felt her body begin to tremble. Maude's hand shot out and rested on Dottie's arm, giving it a gentle squeeze. Polo held his niece's gaze for a second longer and then began to turn his head slowly.

Tears swam in Dottie's eyes which she wiped away quickly, determined to hold on to the moment and allow Polo to react before she spoke. At first, he just stared. Dottie watched him look into her eyes, there was a flicker of recognition maybe but still he didn't speak. Then he took in her hair and she thought he'd finally made the connection, so slowly she moved closer.

His right arm was still bent and paralysed, his long fingers twisted now. Letting go of Francine, Polo lifted his left hand towards Dottie's outstretched arm, taking her shaking hand in his. Still he was silent.

Crouching in front of the wheelchair, Dottie spoke softly, willing herself not to cry.

'Polo, my dearest Polo, oh I'm so pleased to see you. Do you remember, it's me, Yvette?'

Time stood still as Polo's eyes took in everything about Dottie and when he pulled his hand away her heart sank, lifting again when he reached out and touched her face.

'Yvette, is it you, is it really you?' Polo's hand trembled as he traced a face from the past.

Dottie nodded. 'Yes, my dear friend, it is me.' Her voice cracked and to her right she heard a sob from Maude.

'Yvette, my Yvette, you came back. You came back. I waited and waited, but now you are here. I knew you would return to make it right, I always knew.' And with that Polo reached out and wrapped his arm around Dottie and pulled her close.

Dottie clung on tightly as they both sobbed into the other's shoulder, whispering their happiness, sharing their joy at being reunited.

Francine was in tears also, even though she could have had no clue why the reunion meant so much or how they knew each other and was comforted by Maude who was similarly moved by the scene.

When Polo finally released Dottie she stood, knees creaking but holding tight to his hand. 'Please forgive me for not coming sooner but I thought you were... I thought you were among the ones they captured. I have been such a coward, Polo, so please forgive me, I am truly sorry.'

At this Polo seemed agitated and he stumbled over eager words as he tried to speak clearly. 'Yvette, you were never a coward, never. You are the bravest woman I know and if anyone should feel shame it is I.'

Polo lowered his head as his lip started to tremble, as did his body, which is when Francine stepped in, preventing Dottie from asking what he meant by shame.

'Now, now, Uncle Polo, don't upset yourself. This is a happy day because you have been reunited with your friend... shush now, it will all be fine. Why don't we get you home and I will make us all a cool drink?' Francine rubbed Polo's back as she looked towards Dottie and Maude. 'He gets like this sometimes, very distressed, talking about the past and secrets but mostly we don't understand. Would you like to come to meet my mother and then perhaps he will be calmer and you can talk? Do you have time before you see the *maire*?'

Dottie nodded. 'Of course, we will come. I don't want to leave him like this. Lead the way.'

With that they set off, Francine pushing Polo, his wheelchair juddering over the cobbles as they made their way across the square and out of the glare of the sun. Maude linked her arm through Dottie's and spoke softly as they walked.

'Are you okay? This must have been such a shock for you, seeing Polo. I couldn't believe it when Francine said his name and I swear my heart stopped for a second. The poor man probably felt the same, bless him,'

Dottie was in shock. So many thoughts and emotions to contend with and they'd knocked her for six, such was the force with which they hit. Realising Maude had asked a question she focused on a response.

'Yes, I'm fine, dear, please don't worry.'

Maude stared at Dottie. 'No, you're not. You look like you've seen a ghost and you're miles away, so come on, what's going on in that head of yours?'

'I should have had the courage to check properly... when I was back in England. I could have found out exactly who was taken but once I knew Vincent was dead, I couldn't bear to hear any more. Not after Maude. SOE told Hugh that all the Maquis from here had been captured and killed, that the chain had been broken, and I took their word for it.

'I used to imagine him, Polo, being imprisoned and then executed, the horror of it. They told me how many were arrested, and I assumed when they mentioned a young boy, it was him. I was tormented by nightmares and the faces of everyone, what they would have endured, what the Nazis did and all the time, little Polo was still alive, waiting for me to come back.'

'Stop now, Gran. Don't beat yourself up. You didn't know and we discussed this, you were in shock after losing Vincent and Maude, then what you saw on D-Day. Why would you even want to dig it all back up when you got back home? I understand, so when you explain to Polo, I'm sure he will too.'

Dottie clung on to Maude's hand. She had never felt like this, so utterly elated yet wretched at the same time. 'He was such a shy little boy, remember I told you, but fearsome and wily despite his problems. I adored Polo and so did Vincent. To see him now, so frail and clearly confused is breaking my heart, never mind all these wasted years. Oh, I'm so angry with myself, Maudie, I really am.'

'Well you shouldn't be, so please try to shake off thoughts

like that and focus on the present. Polo's face lit up when he realised it was you and now you can make up for lost time and, who knows, there might be more of your old friends still here. Let's see what he has to say.' Maude gave Dottie a peck on the cheek and received a weak smile in return.

Francine stopped at the gate of a modern bungalow and went to open it.

'Here we are, come inside and meet Maman.' Pushing Polo along the pathway through a well-tended garden, Francine concentrated on her uncle, reassuring him that they were home.

Taking a breath, Dottie followed, Maude in her wake. No matter what Polo said, right there and then she didn't feel brave, not at all. Well there would be no more of this nonsense that was for sure. She knew that running away wasn't the answer. Once they'd checked on Polo and met with the *maire* she would find out where Vincent was buried and if she could, every single one of her comrades.

Instead of circumnavigating painful memories and cherry-picking the bits she thought she could handle, Dottie was going to embrace it all, welcome in the ghosts and pay homage to the past. France, the village, the Resistance had been the most important period of her life. It made her who she was, the woman she became.

She'd thought by locking it away in a box marked private, containing the pain, resisting the urge to relive a time that had made her feel alive, vibrant and useful would help her survive. To some extent it had worked, there had been no going back, the only way had been forward in a world dominated by men.

But Dottie wasn't that young woman anymore, fighting for her independence, desperately wanting it to have been worth it. The things she'd done and seen, the miles she'd walked, and the fear she had known were like no other. She'd faced death and caused it, looked an evil regime in the eye, dodged bombs that rained from the sky and survived it all.

Suddenly, at last, Dottie wanted to soak up the memories, hold them to her heart and drown in her tears if need be. Maybe it was Estelle, calling out to her from that balcony in Nantes, demanding she be heard, forbidding Dottie to keep her captive any longer.

From the moment she'd set her mind on coming back, a key had been turned, she'd opened the box, tipped it upside down and shook free the snapshots held inside. Her story was far from over though, but at least Maude understood it so far and for that, and finding little Polo again, Dottie was glad.

31

THE MAIRE

RENAZÉ, 2005

W hen they got him inside it had been clear that Polo had taken a turn. Apart from grasping tightly on to Dottie's hand while Francine's mother, who she'd introduced as Martine, served coffee, he remained silent but at least not too distressed.

Filling in the blanks where she could, Martine explained that her Uncle Polo had lived with them since his cousin Mimi, the eldest daughter of Tante Elise, had passed away in the sixties and the hotel was sold. Dottie asked if there were any photographs of Tante Elise or the hotel during the war because while she remembered them so clearly, it would be wonderful to see their faces again if only in print. Martine had promised to get out the box of old photos and invited Dottie and Maude to return the following day.

Before they knew it, their appointment at the *mairie* beckoned so after promising Polo she would return soon, Dottie extracted her hand from his grip, and they said goodbye.

It had turned out to be a productive if not exhausting day because the *maire*, Monsieur Lasalle, was not only fascinated by Dottie's story, he was eager to help her track down any surviving villagers and convene a reunion whereby they could all share their memories. While the desk fan whirred, cooling the wood-panelled office that smelled of beeswax and aftershave, the *maire* scribbled furiously, noting her cover name, that of the network and those of the members of the Maquis she remembered.

Once this was complete, he then placed a call to one of the committee members, a chap named Gabriel who taught history at the local school and enlisted his help. There were many photographs and documents in their archives. Gabriel was their guardian and only too happy to dig them out for Dottie and Maude.

The more sensitive issue was the whereabouts of Vincent. Lasalle promised to make enquiries immediately and would personally check their records. It seemed that each *mairie* kept details of who was buried in the cemeteries within their boundaries so, if as Dottie suspected, Vincent would be in the graveyard in Renazé.

By the time they left, Dottie felt invigorated and rather touched by Monsieur Lasalle's commitment and enthusiasm, but she was exhausted and needed time to assimilate the day's events. Even Maude looked rather wiped out so resisting the temptation to take a drive around the area and reminisce, Dottie suggested they head back to the hotel.

Maude had opened the windows and a strong breeze wafted the curtains as they relaxed in their room. Both lay on their beds, eyes closed as the bustle of town life carried on regardless of the August heat. Dottie always found it comforting to be able to hear the murmurings of life outside one's window; the sound of the living connected her, she couldn't bear the thought of isolation that accompanied silence.

Maude spoke first, in a sleepy voice. 'I could just nod off now, my eyelids feel like lead, but I'll be awake all night if I do, and that'll mean listening to zoo noises from your side of the room. I think I'm going to write some notes in the journal. Today was too important to forget a single thing.'

Dottie heard the motion of Maude getting off the bed and then the sliding open of a drawer and her rummaging around inside.

'Well I don't think I could sleep a wink, there's far too much going on inside my head.'

Maude pushed the drawer closed and with her journal and pen, returned to the bed where she sat cross-legged. 'I'm not surprised, and I bet you can't wait to go back and see what Monsieur Lasalle has found out. It's a lovely little village and I'd like to spend some time there and maybe do some painting... or a landscape. I got tingly fingers again when we were in Francine's café and that's always a good sign.'

Dottie smiled. Ever since she was little Maude insisted that her fingers tingled when she wanted to draw, even if it was with crayons or very messy poster paints. As she got older, some of Maude's best pieces were a result of her affliction, imaginary or otherwise, and Dottie was heartened that the village had inspired her talented granddaughter.

'Well, why don't you take your things back tomorrow? I'm quite happy to have a wander while you do your thing, maybe I can keep Polo company.'

Maude opened the journal and flicked through the pages as she spoke. 'I think I will, I could make some sketches if nothing else. Now shush while I write some notes.'

There followed a period of silence as Maude scribbled and Dottie dozed until the sound of a phone ringing interrupted the peace. Once her eyes pinged open, Dottie realised it was hers so stretched across and answered. It was Monsieur Lasalle.

'Ah, Madame, I hope I am not disturbing you, but I have some news already.'

Dottie raised her eyebrows to Maude. 'No, of course not. I didn't expect to hear from you until tomorrow though so it's a bit of a surprise. What news do you have?'

Monsieur Lasalle proceeded to tell Dottie that he'd accessed their records and had located the burial place of Vincent Matis and not only that, but due to a stroke of luck, his secretary had made the connection between his surname and the dairy farm that had been in the Matis family for generations. It hadn't taken long to establish that after Vincent's death, his younger sister Béatrice had inherited everything and while she had married and changed her name, the farm was still owned and run by her son. The most exciting news was that Béatrice was still alive and if Dottie so wished, he was more than happy to arrange a meeting.

'I take it you know Béatrice, Madame?'

Dottie envisaged the *maire* smiling, most pleased with himself. However, her own face bore no resemblance to the one she imagined. There had been no love lost between herself and Béatrice and the mention of her name had reignited long repressed suspicions. Someone had betrayed the Maquis, Vincent and Estelle. Could the traitor have held a grudge, their head turned by a Nazi thug and fanciful notions, was this person Béatrice? Had she despised Vincent, her own brother, enough to seek revenge, or had she already given away information before her lover had been silenced?

'Yes, I remember Béatrice very well, Monsieur Lasalle, but I suspect that after all this time she may have forgotten me so please don't be surprised or disappointed if she turns you down.' It was all Dottie could think of at short notice because while she was confident that Béatrice would remember Yvette Giroux very well, she doubted very much that she would agree to a meeting.

'Perhaps, but it is worth a try so I will endeavour to speak to the Matis family as soon as possible and inform you of the outcome.'

Dottie could not fault Lasalle's dedication or enthusiasm so rather than rain on his parade, she told him she would await his instructions, then bade him farewell. After updating Maude on what she'd learned, Dottie became thoughtful. Plumping up her pillows she sat upright, occasionally glancing at her grand-daughter who was lost in concentration.

Dottie had only one thought running through her head. Would Béatrice remember? Of course she would, but Dottie doubted she would agree to meet, but there were things she needed to know. It was time to set the record straight even if it meant picking the scab that had grown over the past, obscuring the truths that lay beneath the surface. Somehow, Dottie had to speak to Béatrice, whether either of them really wanted to or not.

'Have you nearly finished, Maudie?'

Maude didn't look up at first and continued to write, then did a dramatic tap with her biro and clicked the button before closing the journal. 'I have now, why, are you bored?'

'No, I'm not bored but don't put your pen away just yet, I need to tell you something, just in case we do meet Béatrice.' Maude sat upright and focused on Dottie.

Dottie answered. 'Remember the other night, when I told you about killing the soldier at the goods yard? Well, he wasn't the only person I killed.'

Wide-eyed, Maude simply stared at Dottie, then found her voice. 'Uh-oh, I think I know what you're going to say. It was you, wasn't it, not Vincent, who killed Jörg?'

Dottie sighed. 'Yes, and that's why I am riddled with guilt and probably have the blood of so many brave men on my hands. Béatrice thought it was Vincent and she blamed him, and I've always wondered if in an act of revenge, she gave him up. I suspect she was the traitor, the one responsible for everyone being rounded up.'

Maude didn't speak for a second or two then picked up her pen and opened her journal. 'Right then, let's get this down on paper. You speak, I'll write. Oh and, Gran, before you start, please know that I won't judge you, it was war, I understand that.'

Dottie nodded, just about managing a weak smile and with her brow knitted in a frown, took them back to 1944.

32

DOTTIE'S CONFESSION

RENAZÉ, 1944

I t wasn't a decision Yvette took lightly, but it was one she made herself. The risk was too great, and she was terrified that Béatrice might carry out her threat and tell Jörg about the Maquis. While locking Béatrice in her room was necessary, she was already as mad as a cat in a box so Yvette could only imagine what being imprisoned and kept away from Jörg would do to her state of mind. She didn't want to involve anyone else because at the end of the day this was Vincent's sister and the ramifications of having a collaborator in the family was unthinkable. So was what the Maquis might do to Béatrice if they found out. That was why Yvette took it upon herself to remove Jörg from the equation.

Béatrice was sure that Jörg would visit soon, and Yvette knew that he would approach the farm from the direction of town as there was only one road into the village. Raymonde said he'd heard the sound of a motorbike when Béatrice had been sneaking about so Yvette hoped that when he did return, it would be by the same means. He turned up on the second night.

It was impossible to see the wire that ran from the tree, across the road and was wrapped loosely around the fence post opposite. Yvette hid in the ditch just before the bridge and the track that lead to the Matis farm and waited, her heart thudding, her lips numb and the sweat from her palms soaking into the rough cotton gloves she was wearing. She would only get one chance and she had to be quick because from memory, Jörg was tall and broad and no amount of SOE training could guarantee she would overpower him if need be. By her side was a bottle of pastis and the stave from an axe she'd found in the shed, it would serve her purpose better than her knife this time.

When she heard the engine noise in the distance her guts began to swirl and Yvette held down nausea, telling herself this is what she had trained for. The lives of many rested on her actions; she had to do it, she had to be strong. The headlights appeared on the bend and Yvette held her breath and pulled the wire so it was taut, then frantically wound it around and around the post to secure it as the motorbike approached fast. Jörg would not have seen the wire in the dark, or known what the hell happened when the handlebars of his motorbike connected with it, flipping him into the air while it skidded across the road, spinning before coming to a halt at the edge of the opposite ditch, a moment before its driver landed with a thud on the road.

Without a second's hesitation Yvette grabbed the stave and darted from her hiding place to where the soldier lay motionless on his side. The headlight of the motorbike still shone, casting a white glow across the surface of the road and onto the body. There was no way of knowing if he was already dead, but Yvette did at least know he was unconscious so when the blow connected with his skull and she heard the sickening crack, Jörg wouldn't have felt a thing. It had to look like an accident so Yvette flipped Jörg onto his back, the head wound would appear to be a result of it connecting with the road.

Then with trembling legs she raced to the fence post and

unwound the wire, rolling it around her arm as she headed for the tree where with equally trembling fingers, she untwisted it from the trunk. Next, she removed two packets of cigarettes from her coat pocket and stuffed them into one of Jörg's, then she retrieved the bottle of pastis, which with her eyes averted, she poured some down the front of the dead man's uniform, before smashing the bottle on the ground. Once she'd retrieved the stave, without looking back, Yvette left the scene and ran along the track at the back of Vincent's home and didn't stop running, or crying, until she reached Tante Helene's.

33

OUR SECRET

Dottie waited until Maude finished writing, unable to see her granddaughter's face throughout the time it had taken to confess, because that's what it felt like, a terribly cruel confession and now she needed to know how Maude felt about what she'd heard.

'So there you have it, the sorry truth. And how do you feel about me now? Be honest, Maude, it's important to me that you are.'

Maude looked up, a bemused expression on her face. 'Gran, stop it. I feel the same as I did before you told me about Jörg. You did what you had to do and while I do feel sad for him, had he been told to shoot you or your friends as they lined up for the firing squad, he'd have pulled the trigger, wouldn't he? It was his job, it was the war, and you did your job.'

On hearing this Dottie let out a huge sigh, then rested her head on the pillow. 'Oh, thank goodness for that. I don't think I could bear it if you thought I'd done the wrong thing.'

'Well I don't, and I'd never think badly of you, Gran, ever. One thing though, did you tell Vincent what you'd done?'

Dottie nodded. 'Yes, I had to. I didn't want to lie to him,

although if I'm sensible I know that he must have kept plenty from me, but I understand why. I told him I'd take the blame, so that Béatrice wouldn't hate him but he said there was no point, she was past caring who'd done it and would still have thought he was somehow involved. It was best kept between us.'

'I think he was right, it would probably have made her even more angry. So do you intend telling her, if you ever meet again?'

Dottie thought about it. 'Perhaps we should wait and see, decide at the time because she might still hold a grudge and even though sixty years have passed, Béatrice might still love Jörg the way I love Vincent. I would like her to know that her brother didn't kill him though. I owe her that and it would ease my conscience too.'

'You're right, Gran, play it by ear with Béatrice. You've done the hard bit now, getting stuff off your chest, so maybe have a break from the confessional, okay?'

Dottie didn't answer straight away, the temptation to share one last story with Maude was strong, another confession bubbling in her throat. Or was it absolution she sought? After coming so far on her journey, it felt like it was time, one final step.

'Maudie, you know you said there are different situations where killing someone is concerned and they should be taken into consideration before we judge, especially in war?'

The look and the nod from Maude confirmed this.

'Well what if I was to tell you I killed someone else, but it wasn't wartime and it was someone I cared deeply about?'

There was a heartbeat and then Maude answered. 'Then I'd listen, like I have to everything you've told me so far and take into account the circumstances, because if there's one thing I've learned through all this, it's that my gran might be many surprising things but she isn't evil or unkind. Okay?'

Dottie managed a weak smile. 'Then I need to tell you something that I have never told another soul and never will after today, but it has weighed me down for so long and I think that if I can just say it out loud it will free me, or at least loosen the chains.'

'Just tell me, Gran, and I promise, it will be our secret, okay? I can tell it's heavy on your heart so whatever it is, let it out, like everything else, it's time.'

Dottie knew that her granddaughter was correct, and Maude had understood acts of self-defence and self-preservation, all she could hope was that she also understood acts of mercy.

34

DOTTIE AND GEORGE

LONDON, 1950

George was so ill, worse, he was in agony and at the end of his days, which to her shame Dottie wished would come soon. She had insisted he come home where she could care for him herself and it had been a dreadful mistake. Not because of his nursing needs, the doctor had arranged for one to call twice a day and Dottie had been happy to sit with him through the night, until the screaming started. She simply couldn't bear to see him like this, lapsing in and out of consciousness, confused and in so much pain. Selfish, that's how she felt because he was the one suffering, but her mind was also playing tricks, taking her back to France and the place she feared most; the torture rooms of the Gestapo. That's where Maude had ended up. The sounds and images that had so far been kept at bay were impossible to suppress, they were there, plastered on the walls of the room, played on a loop.

George had been prescribed what old Doctor Platt had referred to as a Brompton Cocktail, a painkiller and sedative made from morphine, cocaine, gin, syrup and chloroform water which was to be strictly administered. There were moments of serenity once the cocktail took effect, and George was able to drift into sleep with Dottie holding tightly on to his hand, the strains of Duke Ellington filling the room. But he was getting worse and Dottie was becoming more horrified by the cruelty and unfairness of the situation which is when she took matters into her own hands.

Old Doctor Platt was most understanding when she rang him to explain how George had become agitated and knocked the bottle out of her hand while she'd attempted to administer a dose of the cocktail. He said he would drop some more off soon, he was passing that way. Being old school, after Doctor Platt checked his patient over and gave him a dose of the fresh cock-tail, he accepted a cup of tea during which time he assured Dottie that 'it wouldn't be long'. The empty bottle was on the kitchen dresser in full sight, which he saw but passed no comment. Whether he knew the truth or not, Dottie wasn't sure, although she expected that he understood as he bade her good-night before going on his way.

That evening, as raindrops from a summer storm patted on the window ledge outside, a warm breeze endeavoured to invade and freshen the room. Dottie told George how much she loved and adored him, and he should drink his medicine, all of it, from his favourite china cup that contained the first bottle of cocktail. Then she put on George's favourite song 'Summertime', slipped off her shoes and lay down next to him on the bed, holding him close while Ella sang him to sleep.

A hush settled on the room and the next voice that broke through the fog of silence and a million thoughts was Maude's.

'Would you like a hug, Gran?'

Dottie wiped her eyes in the darkness. 'No thank you, darling, I'm fine.'

'You did the right thing, Gran, for George. And I know you feel guilty because you were scared but that's only being human, and what you did for George was human too.'

'So, you don't think I'm a monster... taking a life, not in war or anger or hate or fear? I did it calmly, I planned it, Maude.'

'Because you loved him, Gran, so much that you took away his pain. Now please, no more. I never imagined that events from so long ago could have such a profound effect on someone. What you saw and did during the war, it changed you, made you take decisions, act so differently to how "before the war Dottie" would have acted. But you have to remember this, it was life or death, them or you and maybe all that horror and training, whatever, helped you when you needed it the most, to help George, for the right reasons.'

'Do you really think that, Maudie?'

A firm voice replied. 'Yes, without a doubt and you've been punishing yourself for years. Now I promised you I'd keep the secret so you have to promise to let it all go, or else I'll go and find a bloody priest and get him to chuck holy water over you, or make you say a million Hail Marys, anything to get you to stop.'

A pause, and Dottie knew Maude was giving her time to think and when she had, she gave Maude what she asked for, and what Dottie needed for herself. 'All right, cancel the priest and I promise, I promise I will let it go and try to forget.' And she meant it.

Maude checked her phone and rolled her eyes as she read the messages on the screen, then shoved it under her pillow as if hiding it would make Lachlan go away. 'Good. Now I'm going to put this journal away and have a nice soak in the bath and I think you should have one too, relax a bit. We have a nice day planned tomorrow with Polo and his family so let's focus on that.'

'Okay, I agree. And yes, I'd like a nice bubble bath so off you go, I'll ring Konstantin and when you've finished run me one, then you'd better put Lachlan out of his misery.'

Dottie spotted the look of surprise on Maude's face when for the first time she forgot to use one of her sarcastic monikers. *I must be going soft*, or maybe Dottie was starting to think differently, about lots of things and even, as much as it pained her, the very annoying Mr Didgeridoo.

35

LITTLE SHADOW

RENAZÉ, FRANCE, 2005

D ottie was seated on the wooden bench next to Polo. They observed the scene before them in companionable silence while the bulldozer scraped back the earth, leaving in its wake deep furrows of rubble as it moved back and forth. Dottie thought that watching someone else's toil and the rhythmic swing of the mechanical arm was mildly therapeutic, and understood why Polo liked to sit here, that and the fact the remaining section of the hotel used to be his childhood home.

Earlier, as they drove towards the village, Maude and Dottie had formulated a plan of action. Before they went to the churchyard, they would check on Polo because in Dottie's opinion the plight of the living was more urgent than paying a visit to the dead.

When Maude brought it up, Dottie had admitted she was still delaying the inevitable, gathering the courage to face facts. Once she saw his name on the gravestone it would be incontrovertible proof that all those years of silly daydreams and wishful thinking had been just that, a fantasy. Vincent hadn't somehow survived, that's why even now, he couldn't track her down and would never turn up at her door one sunny afternoon, wearing a smart suit with his unruly hair slicked back, a bunch of flowers in his hand. He would remain a ghost that lived only in her memory.

When they arrived, Polo had seemed much brighter and was waiting for them in the lounge but rather than look through the photos Martine had found, he insisted they went straight to the building site, alone. Seeing as Maude had brought along her bag of arty bits and bobs, she'd been quite happy to head off into the village and find a location where she could sketch. Martine was also happy to let Polo go, saying as she waved him and Dottie off that she hadn't seen him this enthusiastic for a long while.

However, as much as she enjoyed the ambience of the quaint village and people watching was a relaxing pastime, Dottie's patience wasn't the best. She was curious as to why Polo was so interested in the renovations and what he'd meant the previous day when he'd said he was waiting for her to make it right, and that he felt shame.

Dottie started with a gentle enquiry. 'It's sad isn't it, the hotel being demolished? Is that why you sit here, because it reminds you of the past?'

Polo continued to stare. 'Everything reminds me of the past, Yvette, this village has been my life, it holds the memories of everyone I have ever loved. It does not matter how many new houses they build, the new faces I see, for me, Renazé remains the same. That is why I stayed, it gives me comfort.'

Dottie's neck prickled every time Polo called her Yvette, but she didn't mind because to him, it's who she was and, really, part of her always would be.

'So you think of the old days often, living with your sister in the hotel and the terrible time during the occupation? I missed this place so much after the war, but I trained myself to lock it away, the memories were so vivid, but too painful. It was the only way to get on with life back then.'

Polo nodded.

There was one question that had been burning a hole in her head, but Dottie feared it might cause Polo distress, so she began tentatively. 'Sometimes I weakened and would spend hours imagining what became of everyone after I fled; who had survived, who betrayed us, what happened to the villagers when the Germans left. I've been too scared to ask, but I have to know… what happened to Tante Helene, did they take her?'

Dottie left that thought hanging in the air, hoping it would encourage Polo to talk. She was actually quite desperate for someone to fill in the gaps, describe the scene after she headed north with the evaders and Claude, to understand what happened in the days and weeks that followed.

It seemed strange after all this time to refer to Hugh as Claude, but that's who they were then, agents, fakes, resistors, living in plain sight or hiding in the shadows of a twilight, make-believe world. Maybe some real hard facts in the cold light of day would bring Dottie peace. So when Polo shook his head, and seemed quite animated, her heart held a shred of hope.

'No, Helene was lucky. She got Vincent's message and went to stay with her sister in Tours and came back after the war to sell the farm. We never heard of her again, but I like to think she had a good life elsewhere.'

Dottie sighed. 'Oh, I'm glad she got away… I did write to her, to let her know I was safe but now I understand why she didn't reply. Well that's one mystery solved, isn't it?'

There was a moment or two of silence and then Polo twisted slowly in his chair and looked straight at Dottie, his eyes penetrating, intense. 'This is what I need to tell you, Yvette, what happened when you left. I have kept a secret for too long because I did not know who to tell but now, you are here, and you can help me make it right.'

Lowering his voice slightly, he tapped his chest as he spoke. 'I know who betrayed us.'

Dottie couldn't quite believe what he was saying. Could a little boy have held the key all these years? But from the look on his face, her little Polo was going to tell her.

'Was it Béatrice?' Dottie heard the tremble of anger in her own voice.

Polo shook his head, his voice was louder, more agitated. 'No, Yvette, it was the man with the scary face. Remember I was frightened of him, and he talked funny.'

The second Polo said the words a cold dread ran through Dottie's bones. Pieces of what could be a nightmare were falling into place. No, it couldn't be. Her mouth went dry as her mind raced, a torrent of thoughts and memories engulfing her.

The man with the scary face, Konstantin had a scar, and Polo had thought he was a pirate, and his accent to a little boy would sound strange. And Konstantin had disappeared that day... was he really picking flowers or was he trying to make contact with someone, to pass on all the information I'd given him while we sat and chatted in the cave? I confided in him. Did I betray us with my loose lips? I told him about Estelle and Tante Helene and Armand in the café... I asked him what Claude was saying, in the truck, the German words, he said gibberish, but was it? Please God no, don't let it be Konstantin, he can't have betrayed us, it will kill me if Polo says his name.

But she had to ask even though the answer was unthinkable. 'Tell me, Polo...'

Gripping on to her hand, Polo said in almost a whisper, 'It was Claude. He shot Vincent. Claude was the traitor. He betrayed everyone.'

A gasp, followed by relief, then shock. *Claude, not Konstantin, thank God, thank God... but Claude?*

Dottie covered Polo's hand with hers. 'I'm confused, Polo, did you see the ambush? I thought the Gestapo shot Vincent and Claude.'

Polo looked anguished and vigorously shook his head. 'No, Yvette, it was not the Gestapo who shot Vincent. That is a lie.'

Dottie couldn't take it in. 'I don't understand… Claude was in a bad way when Florian brought him to the rendezvous but managed to tell us what happened. They were ambushed at the barn but managed to escape and were chased by the Gestapo, they were shot at. Vincent was hit and the Gestapo finished him off, Claude took a bullet in the leg. Claude was one of ours, an agent. It was a long time ago, perhaps you are mistaken.' Dottie was now praying that Polo was wrong, he'd been so young, it was late and dark and…

Again, Polo shook his head, his voice angry in response. 'No, it was HIM. The man with the spotty face, like holes. He scared me back then and I didn't like to look at him, and he made a funny sound when he spoke. I listened at the back door of the kitchen at the café that day when you told me to go home. I wanted to see Vincent and I peeped in. Then, when I saw him with the Gestapo I recognised him straight away. I have never forgotten, after all these years I remember everything.'

Dottie felt numb. She could see movement in the corner of her eye, and the cars that passed by and the woman across the road picking up what her dog had left behind, yet it seemed that someone had turned off the sound. Perhaps her brain needed silence for it to process the ramifications of Polo's revelations as a million thoughts exploded in her head like shards of glass, piercing her heart.

Hugh, Claude, one and the same, with his stammer and pockmarked face, the scars of teenage acne still visible even to that day. A man she had known for most of her life, who she had trusted, who she considered a good friend and admired immensely, was a traitor, worse, a murderer.

For some bizarre reason her head was now trying to work out if what he'd done was an act of war or a crime, a war crime maybe, or did it depend which side you were on. And whose side *was* he on? The answer to that at least was clear.

Polo interrupted. The sound came back on.

'Yvette, are you okay, you have gone white? I have upset you, I'm sorry.'

Taking a deep breath, Dottie closed her eyes and asked herself the same question. No, she wasn't okay but that didn't matter because all she cared about now were answers. She had to know the truth, exactly what happened that night after Vincent said goodbye. Touching her mouth she could almost feel his lips on hers, the strength in his body the last time he held her in his arms, his voice as he asked her to make a promise, one that she had kept.

When she opened her eyes, Dottie's vision was blurred by tears which she flicked away. This was no time for blubbing. Yvette would not have cried, she would have demanded answers, sought revenge, taken it with her bare hands if need be. Composing herself quickly, Dottie patted Polo's hand, forcing a weak smile to reassure him before she answered, then asked him another question.

'I am fine, Polo, please do not worry. I'm incredibly shocked but I still need to know it all, so will you explain, tell me everything about that night and then I promise you, I will put it right.'

Polo closed his eyes for a second, as though he was picturing the scene and relating what he could see. 'I had been setting new traps in the forest, for rabbits, so that Tante Elise could make stew. I had already caught two. That's when I heard the sound in the distance, a motorbike. From where I was, I could see the end of the lane that split the trees, where the tiny chapel is, there is a statue of an angel at the gate, do you know it?'

'Yes, I do, the angel was missing a wing.'

'At first, I thought it would be the Germans, so I kept out of sight, I didn't want them stealing my rabbits. Then, when it came into view, I realised it wasn't a motorbike, it was a Solex and I knew straight away it was Claude, he was the only person who had one. I watched as he pulled a brick from the back of the statue and take out a note then place another inside, then he jumped back on the Solex and rode off.'

Dottie imagined the scene, she knew the setting well. 'What did you do then?'

'I waited. I thought I should stay a while and guard the spot until someone came.'

Dottie smiled and raised her eyebrows, giving Polo a friendly nudge. 'Or you were being your usual inquisitive self and wanted to see who collected the note.' It felt good to laugh, just for a moment, in between the terribleness of Polo's revelation.

'Yes, I suppose you are correct, but really, Yvette, I did not expect what happened next.'

Dottie felt her chest tighten and held her breath for a second while Polo continued.

'I dozed off. It was warm and I was tired but I woke up when I heard the sound of a car. I was expecting a member of the Resistance, someone on a bicycle or maybe in a farm truck, not one of the Nazi staff cars. You remember them, the big black limousines that parked outside of the *mairie* in the town?'

A nod from Dottie preceded the rest of his tale.

'It pulled to a halt at the shrine and one of the black bats got out of the back. That's what I called the Gestapo, in their flappy leather coats and hats pulled down to their eyes. It was as though they knew everything and could hunt us down, even if they couldn't see. I was terrified of them.

'The man went over to the shrine, removed the brick and the note and then returned to the car and got inside. Then they drove away. I panicked. In my childish brain I thought at first that Claude would be in danger, but slowly I realised the truth. I realised our comrade was a traitor.'

Nodding, Dottie sighed. 'He was certainly that. But go on, what happened next?'

'I knew that Vincent was in Nantes but not when he would return so I ran to your aunt's farm. I was going to tell you instead, but you weren't there and she didn't know where you'd gone, naturally.'

Dottie's heart had quickened, it was as though she'd flown back in time, it felt too real. 'I had gone to wait with the evaders.'

Polo continued. 'After that I ran to the café and left a message there for you or Vincent. I told Armand I would wait for Vincent at the usual place, he would know where. I didn't tell anyone what I'd seen. I was too scared, and my trust was slipping away with each second.

'I ran and ran to Vincent's hut by the stream. It felt like my whole life passed by while I waited, that's how long it took until he arrived. I didn't go inside. I hid in the bushes and watched. It was dusk when he finally showed up.'

Dottie remembered the hut, with the simple bed made from logs, the earthen floor, and the nights she had shared with Vincent there. Polo's voice interrupted her thoughts.

'I was so glad to see him, so eager to tell him what I knew but from the second the words came out of my mouth everything went wrong. I started it. If I had kept quiet, he might be alive still. It is something I will never know but it has haunted me every day since.'

Dottie laid her hand on his arm. 'If there is one thing I have learned, Polo, it's that we cannot change the past, no matter how much it haunts us. We can only try to make sense of it and learn to live with our mistakes.'

Polo sighed. 'I suppose. But it is an easier thing to say than do.'

'It is, but we can work through it together now, whatever is troubling you, so tell me. What do you mean, you started it?' Dottie was eager to hear but didn't want to press Polo, he looked sad, and was quite frail too, so she waited patiently. When he pulled himself out of his gloom, they went back to the hut by the stream, to a night she remembered vividly.

36

POLO AND THE TRAITOR

FRANCE, 1944

Vincent looked exhausted. He told Polo, who was watching with wide eyes, that it had been a traumatic trip, the road from Nantes had been fraught with danger with patrols and road blocks everywhere. Vincent was agitated, speaking quickly, pacing, thinking, telling Polo about Estelle and that everyone was in danger. He'd gone back for the propaganda leaflets that he kept underneath the bed, saying he needed to burn them. They would bring trouble to the village if they were found. In his bag he had documents from Nantes, they had to get them to England.

The frantic nature of Vincent's words and actions were scaring Polo and hearing the word England sent a shockwave through his body. Claude was English, he was bad. Polo panicked and just blurted it out, stopping Vincent in his tracks.

'Vincent, I know who it is, the traitor. I saw him leave a note for the Boche.'

At first Vincent didn't speak, instead he sat down on the bed and said simply, 'Who was it? Tell me what you saw.'

While Polo explained what he had seen, Vincent remained still, his face ashen, eyes like dark angry holes. Once the tale was told, he dragged his hands across his face, pulling stubbled skin downwards, tired red-rimmed eyelids looking ghoulish in the half-light. Then he spoke.

'We are in more danger than I thought. Thank God I told the others to disband and Yvette to change her plans... but she needs to know about Claude.'

Polo was wide-eyed and frightened. 'Why are we in more danger, Vincent? I don't understand.'

'Because Claude has betrayed us to the Gestapo. He knew about Estelle and I fear that soon they will start to round us up, it could even begin tonight. He's met all of our group, I took him to the forest but thank God I never showed him the cave. Are you sure he didn't see you today, has he ever spotted you before, with me perhaps?'

Polo's mouth was dry, and his legs trembled. He had never seen Vincent like this. 'No, I am sure he doesn't know me. I only saw him once, when he met you in the café, but I was hiding round the back. I peeped through the window then listened at the door. I was scared of his spotty face.'

Vincent exhaled and ruffled Polo's hair. 'Good, this is good. But he knows me and Yvette. Florian had taken a message to Xavier and the others at the forest, if they do as they are told they should be long gone before they are raided but if they take one of us...' Vincent seemed to falter. 'Never mind that, I need you to do something for me, and you must hurry.'

Polo nodded even though he wasn't sure what he was agreeing to, but for Vincent, he would do anything. He watched in silence as his hero scrabbled in his bag and eventually pulled out a carpenter's pencil with a thick stubby nib. Taking one of the propaganda leaflets he wrote a message on the back then he folded it three times.

Vincent stood and held the squared piece of paper in front of Polo. 'I want to you to take this to La Motte Glain. You know, the shrine by the fountain that's in the chateau grounds? Yvette will be there with the evaders. She is waiting for Florian to bring the transport, he should go straight there after he has been to the forest. On your way do not speak of this with anyone. Once you have given Yvette the note, go home and stay there. She will know what to do. Do you understand, Polo?'

Polo gulped and nodded. Taking the note, he slipped it inside his boot, pushing it down as far as he could. Then he asked a question, dreading the answer. 'I understand, but what about you, where will you go, when will I see you again? I want to come with you, please don't leave me behind, Vincent.'

Vincent crouched in front of Polo and placed one hand on the boy's shoulder. 'I cannot take you with me this time, Polo, but once the danger is gone, I will come back. It might not be for a while, but you will see me again, I know it here.' Vincent's free hand tapped his heart.

But still Polo wasn't satisfied. 'But where will you go... south to the mountains, to Spain? I would like to see a new country and you will need food, let me bring some from Tante Elise and then we can go together. I will not slow you down, I promise.'

'No, Polo, it is too dangerous and I could not bear for anything to happen to you, and there is no time for food, my friend. And I am not going to Spain, so don't worry. There is something I must do first. Then I will hide.'

'What must you do? I can help.'

Vincent sighed. 'No, Polo. You must go, now. Time is running out. Yvette will be leaving soon and if you don't go now you will miss her.'

Tears welled and from deep inside, panic erupted. Polo stood firm, surprised by his own desperation. 'Tell me where are you going?'

Vincent didn't flinch. 'I am going to find Claude and then I am going to kill him.'

296

. . .

Polo was finding it hard to keep up with Vincent who seemed to be in a great hurry as he followed the track through the forest. Once or twice Polo had been forced to dart behind a tree when Vincent glanced behind him, but it was dark and almost impossible to see, the glow from the moon barely enough to light the way. Only those who were familiar with the trail would make it through without getting lost and the two bravehearts who took the challenge that night were exceptional trackers, emboldened by stealth and knowledge. Polo knew that if Vincent saw him, he would send him home, but this was his *métier* now, his one and only job, shadowing his idol, watching his every move and keeping him safe.

After saying goodbye to Vincent, Polo had only got as far as the top of the bank when he faltered. Tears blinded his eyes and his heart felt like it had a crack in it, the pain really, really hurt. Pausing for breath Polo had repeated over and over in his head what Vincent had told him. *Speak to no one, take the note to Yvette, then go home.* But why, why should he run to her? Vincent was in danger, too.

Claude did not know where Yvette was, she was safe, but Vincent was not. Polo had to protect their leader. He had his grandfather's pocketknife and would stab to death anyone who threatened Vincent. It was in his sock, where all fighting men kept their secret weapon. The decision made, Polo had crouched behind a tree and waited. Within moments Vincent appeared, then scrambled up the bank and headed in the opposite direction to Polo who had counted to ten and then followed.

. . .

The only sounds were of screeching foxes and Polo's own shallow breath that he fought to regulate; keeping pace with a grown man was exhausting. When, for no apparent reason Vincent came to a sudden halt, Polo froze, no time to dart, the sudden movement might catch his eye. So instead he stood stock-still and watched from the darkness as Vincent rested, or was he thinking, his right hand on the back of his head. Decision seeming to have been made, Vincent swiftly removed the hunting bag from across his shoulders then crouched beside a fallen trunk. He took something from inside and placed it on the ground then wedged the bag between the earth and the bark. He then snapped off smaller branches and covered the bag with a leafy blanket. He picked up the object from the ground and when he stuck it in the waistband of his trousers, behind his back, Polo knew it was a gun.

Vincent then continued at pace, finally breaking through the edge of the forest, he skirted along the final row of trees, keeping close to the hedgerows that bordered the farm. Ahead there was a small cottage, isolated and in darkness and Polo knew this was where Claude would be. Polo couldn't break cover so stayed put until Vincent was out of sight and then ran, desperate to catch up.

By the time he'd reached the barn Polo was wheezing, he had a terrible stitch too, but forced himself forward sucking in air and holding his side as he crept closer. Peering inside the barn Polo spotted the Solex belonging to Claude. Edging towards the door, that was open just wide enough to slip through, Polo listened and then heard a match strike, the whiff of cigarette smoke tickling his nostrils. Then a voice, Vincent's.

'Are you going somewhere? You seem to be in a hurry.'

Claude. 'Yes, I've been ordered to Paris, they need my help. Word has it that our allies are ready to strike. I can help co-ordinate things from there.'

Polo could see the traitor stuffing things into a rucksack, his face turned away from Vincent.

'Yes, it's probably best that you run, especially now Estelle and her group have been taken... in case the trail leads here. That'd be a coincidence, wouldn't it?'

Claude's head snapped around. 'Meaning?'

Vincent shrugged and continued to smoke his cigarette. Claude prevailed.

'How do you know they have been taken, are you sure?'

'Yes, very. Estelle passed on the documents that were stolen from the Gestapo before she was taken. They show troop movements and storage depots in the north, the Boche must be really pissed. She's being questioned along with the others, that's all I know, oh, apart from that we are all compromised. The chain is broken, and our cell could be the next target, so we have to disband. I have already given the order. All I have to do now is deliver the documents to England and deal with the person who informed on us.'

Polo took a step further inside the barn, and stealthily edged inch by inch towards a sodden pile of hay and tucked himself behind, well out of sight. From his vantage point only feet away Polo could see both men clearly and when Claude lit a cigarette, bringing the match close to his face, the golden flame illuminated his pockmarked skin.

Exhaling a cloud of smoke, he sounded composed yet impatient. 'I can take the documents to Paris. Did you bring them? As for the traitor, whenever you find them give them a bullet from me.'

'Oh, I will.' Vincent looked angry and took a drag of his own cigarette as he watched Claude pace.

Polo knew that expression and it made him nervous. It also seemed to make Claude shout.

'I asked you a question, did you bring them?'

Vincent merely stared and folded his arms. It reminded Polo of when one of his cousins were being awkward. Dumb insolence was the expression her maman often used.

Finally, he spoke and when the words came out, Vincent was the one asking questions. 'And what if I did? Do you think I would be stupid enough to hand them over to you?'

Claude did not respond at first, apart from the smirk which Polo spotted just before he turned his back on Vincent.

In his dreams, the scream was always silent, the moment when Polo saw Claude slide his hand inside his jacket, when he knew the traitor was reaching for a gun, drawing it faster than Vincent who realised his mistake too late.

Perhaps Polo hadn't screamed at all, it was merely his brain crying out against the horror his eyes were about to see. Claude spun around, his elbow resting on his hip, a gun pointed at Vincent who had only managed to get a hand to the one tucked inside the back of his trousers.

Time froze. So did Polo and Vincent, but Claude's mouth moved, twisting into a grin, then two shots, bang, bang. The noise cut through the air and sliced Polo's eardrums, his heart felt like it stopped twice with each blast while his eyes stared in horror as Vincent staggered backwards and slumped to the floor, motionless. His gun lay useless at the end of an outstretched arm. Claude stared at Vincent's body for a moment and then turned to the haystack and collected his bag, placing his gun inside his jacket, not even looking back at the bleeding body as he headed towards the barn door.

Polo was numb with fear, his eyes fixated on Vincent who he willed to be alive so when there was a slight movement, Polo's heart danced with joy. The lift of a shoulder, a twitch of a finger and a hand that scratched in the dirt for his gun, and then a bullet speeding through the air followed by another which pinged off the Solex mudguard. Polo's head whipped in the other direction and saw that Claude had been hit, he was grasping the back of his leg, staggering the final step to the bike. Polo sucked in air. What would Claude do, would he go back and finish Vincent off or would he flee? When Polo dragged his eyes back to where Vincent lay he found his answer, there was no point, it was over.

37

GOODBYE, VINCENT

RENAZÉ, 2005

D ottie gasped. Double tap, it was the method all SOE agents were taught to kill. Point and aim, shoot from the hip, two shots to be sure. Nausea swirled inside her stomach, rising slowly upwards causing Dottie to pinch the bridge of her nose and breathe deeply. To distract her brain from the images in her mind, she focused on Polo, or more precisely, the little seven-year-old boy who had just seen his hero shot dead, executed by a traitor.

'My dear Polo, you must have been so scared, you poor thing.' Dottie held his hand tightly.

'Yes, Yvette, I was. And I am ashamed to say I didn't use my knife. I was frozen to the spot and hid in the hay, watching as Claude limped to the motorbike, blood pouring from his leg. I didn't think he would be able to ride it because he howled in pain as he kicked the stand and started the engine, but he did and then sped away. I listened until the sound faded then broke cover and ran to Vincent.'

Dottie wanted to interrupt, to stop Polo from describing a scene she'd imagined for so long, knowing his words would make them real. Then she noticed that rather than being distressed by his memories, Polo looked eager and determined. His back was straight, and he leant forward, anger in his eyes, jaw set firm and she knew he had more to say. He'd waited over sixty years to tell his tale so gathering her courage, she squeezed his hand and took a deep breath.

'Go on, Polo.'

'When I reached Vincent, I knelt by his side and called his name, I was crying and shouting. I pushed his chest to try to wake him. There was blood all over the floor, spilling from underneath him and I cried and cried, saying his name over and over. Then his eyes opened.'

On hearing this Dottie's heart skipped a beat, it was ridiculous but that simple notion of Vincent being alive filled her heart with joy, even though she knew that it would soon be shattered again, all hope lost.

'He smiled when he saw me, for a second, and it made me so happy and I thought he would be okay. Then he tried to speak so I leant close and turned my head to listen.'

Dottie felt her chest tighten as she imagined a little boy and his hero, their last moments together, huddled close on an earthen floor swimming in blood.

Vincent's breath was rasping as he spoke, his voice barely a whisper. 'My little shadow... I should have known.'

'Please don't be angry with me for disobeying.' Polo sniffed and rubbed away the tears and snot from his face.

'I'm not angry... I promise... Polo, Polo, did you see where I hid the bag?'

Polo nodded and Vincent gave a weak smile.

'Good boy. Listen. Keep it hidden. The contents are

dangerous for you.' Vincent winced in pain and his skin was damp and a funny colour.

Polo desperately tried to right his wrong. 'What about Yvette, I could give it to her?'

'It is too late now, I think she will be gone. Please God let her be gone.' Vincent's breath was laboured, a tiny hand held his.

Polo pleaded. 'Don't speak anymore. I will get help. I will bring the doctor.'

'No, no time. It is over for me but not for you. They will come soon, you must hide, do not let them take you.' Vincent closed his eyes, the blood oozed from the wounds in his chest.

They were both silent. Polo's heart was breaking, terror flooding his veins. He had never seen anyone die but he knew that the moment was coming so before it was too late, he spoke to his hero for the last time.

'What will I do without you, Vincent?'

Vincent's eyelids fluttered and his voice rasped. 'You will be brave like always, my little shadow. You will be brave and one day you will be free.'

When Vincent's eyes closed and his grip loosened, Polo hung on tightly and sobbed, remaining on his knees in the dirt and blood, by the side of his friend, his hero.

When Polo's resolve crumbled so did Dottie's, knowing she had witnessed through the words of an old man and the eyes of a little boy, the last moments of her true love's life.

They cried silently for a moment. Polo recovered first.

'I stayed with him until morning, too scared to venture outside of the barn, listening all the time for vehicles or the march of boots but there was nothing. I didn't want to leave Vincent lying there in the cold, so I dragged the sheet from the top of the hay and covered him with it and said goodbye. Then I took the gun and ran.'

Dottie pulled a tissue from her bag and passed it to Polo and then took one for herself before dabbing her eyes and blowing her nose.

'He must have been so comforted to have you there, his little shadow, faithful to the last.' She saw Polo give a faint smile.

It felt so odd, surreal, to be talking about the past when the here and now was going on all around. The mother pushing her baby in the pram, fussing with the sunshade, and the man who'd popped into the *tabac* and out again with a packet of cigarettes, a newspaper under his arm, the foreman of the site on his phone while watching his workers. Their lives seemed so simple, uncluttered whereas hers, in the space of a few moments had become littered by Polo's revelations and the sheer magnitude of them.

'Where did you go afterwards? Vincent was right, we were waiting, ready to go. I was so spooked and devastated about Estelle, and terrified for the others so we left as soon as Florian arrived, and, oh my God, I took that traitor with me. I saved his life when I should have thrown him over a cliff or into the sea and held him under until he drowned.'

It all made sense now. The pieces were starting to fit together, and Dottie could see that night in a whole different light, the things Hugh said, the ramblings about documents, smatterings of German, not professions of undying love like Maude had intimated.

To Dottie, the man she had refused to leave behind for fear of what he would endure at the hands of his enemy, who would in reality have been cared for by his Nazi friends, was no longer Claude. He did not deserve the name of a French man, in fact there was only one title befitting him.

Polo patted her hand. 'It was not your fault, Yvette, you did not know but thank goodness Vincent told you to go, because any later you might have walked straight into an ambush.'

'Yes, with Hugh by my side. Wouldn't that have been interesting? I believed everything he said when Florian brought him to me, why wouldn't I?'

'You had no reason to doubt him, Yvette.'

The anger was building inside Dottie and worse, she felt foolish for being duped and not seeing through the lies, not putting two and two together. But then a voice reminded her of the fear she'd felt that night, lip numbing terror, desperate to flee while her heart ached for Vincent, willing him to show up. It had been hard to think straight under those circumstances, yet one brave man had managed to work it out, do the right thing, send his brigade to safety then confront a traitor, sacrificing himself for the cause and paying the ultimate price. Right up to the end her Vincent was thinking of others.

The words tumbled from her mouth, intent on getting things straight in her mind. Dottie's mind began racing ahead; charting her history that involved Hugh until suddenly she realised that Polo had not finished his tale.

'Forgive me, Polo, for rambling on. We need to take things a step at a time and you haven't told me about where you went after you left Vincent.'

'It is fine, Yvette, I know this has been a great shock to you but for me, I have had plenty of time to think it through.'

Dottie slumped against the back of the bench, already exhausted by his words, but preparing for more. 'Please, go on. Tell me about afterwards.'

Polo took a cursory glance at the site and then back to Dottie before he began the rest of his story. It began with a frightened little boy, racing through the woods on a dewy May morning.

38

POLO'S HIDING PLACE

RENAZÉ, 1944

The first thing Polo did was to retrieve Vincent's bag. Then he placed the gun inside, along with the folded leaflet which he slipped between the documents, after which he slung the bag across his chest and raced back towards the village. But even before he emerged from the trees Polo heard a sound that filled him with dread – the rumble of trucks as they made their way into the marketplace, then the sound of boots on the ground. Terror coursed through Polo's veins as he scrambled up a tree and watched from within its boughs. He was far enough away to remain undetected but close enough to see and hear what was going on.

The soldiers swarmed like grey beetles, women and children were ordered at gunpoint on to the street where they could only stand and watch as their homes were searched and ransacked. The priest ran from his church that was being invaded then began protesting to the officer who merely laughed in his face. Next, they went inside the hotel and when he saw his aunt dragged into the courtyard Polo thought his chest would explode from the pressure of his wildly beating heart, his bones had turned to stone. Paralysed he watched as she was flung to the floor, an officer shouting, demanding answers and then a kick to her stomach.

After more searching, the beetles scurrying out of sight up side streets, they returned with Armand and from another corner of the square they brought two more men, the grandfather and crippled uncle of his best friend, Louie. Polo watched as the officer barked more orders and had the three men loaded onto the truck, his attention drawn away from Tante Elise.

Polo hated going to church but today he prayed with the priest who had now given up protesting and pleading with the officer and instead, pleaded with God. Polo fervently made the sign of the cross then prayed. *Please do not take my aunt, please do not let them hurt her, I will be good, I will never forget to feed the chickens, I will work hard at school, I will go to mass every Sunday forever, please, God, hear my prayer.*

When the officer gave the instruction and the truck started to drive away, Polo allowed himself to breathe. But instead of all the soldiers departing, some of them stayed, making their presence known like a sullen, watchful threat. A few stomped around the square, guns pointed, flicking the butt towards doors and ordering everyone inside while others lounged and smoked, laughing amongst themselves.

There was no way Polo could risk going back to the hotel, so he slid down the tree and made his way further into the forest. He was used to foraging and would easily survive, he knew the tracks well and could hide for days if need be. It would be cold at night, but he couldn't risk sleeping in Vincent's hut. Instead he took the blanket from his bed and squirreled himself away. Once the Germans left, he would find someone to trust, then he could tell them about the bag and that Claude was a traitor and Vincent was a hero.

. . .

Polo emerged from hiding four days later, cold, starving and smelly. He'd managed on berries and mushrooms and water from the stream, sleeping deep in the forest and only venturing to his lookout tree once a day. He watched the Germans leave on the third day, but waited for another twenty-four hours, just in case.

When he crept around the back of the hotel at day-break, Polo crouched in the garden until it was light, watching the windows, checking for signs that a stray beetle hadn't stayed behind waiting for him to return. By mid-morning his stomach and heart could bear it no longer, so he took off Vincent's bag and hid it behind the chicken coop then tentatively made his way to the back door and listened. Somebody was crying, Tante Elise. Slowly Polo pushed open the door and as it creaked, the crying ceased for a second until their eyes met. As her chair tumbled to the floor in the rush to hug him, Elise began to sob uncontrollably, holding him tightly while thanking Mother Mary and God and the angels and the saints for bringing him back.

Polo allowed her to kiss his greasy hair and filthy face and for a while, he was happy again as she called upstairs for his cousins. Once bleary-eyed Nicole and Mimi stumbled into the kitchen, they took over fussing him while Tante Elise hurriedly made breakfast. But his bread and comfiture had barely touched the sides before Polo's world descended into despair once again.

The Germans had wreaked havoc, rounding up those who were suspected of being partisans and along with the three men from their village, more from the surrounding areas had been arrested. Elise was sure that the rest of the Maquis had got away but their shared relief at their escape was tainted by the thought of never seeing their friends again, or at least until the war was over. The rest of her tears were for the twenty-seven poor souls who had been imprisoned in the camp at Châteaubriant, questioned and tortured, and then sentenced to death. They would be shot the following day in reparation for attacks on German supply stores, the death of the young soldier and a daring robbery in Nantes.

Polo felt his world tip upside down. He thought he might pass out from the terror of it all. Never had he imagined that people he knew, harmless old men and a boy aged only seventeen, were going to be executed. Fear ravaged his soul and his mind wandered to the bag lying behind the chicken coop. Whatever was inside it was dangerous, Vincent had said so, and the traitor wanted it. Polo knew he had to go as soon as possible in case the Germans or Claude came back. But where?

His aunt ordered him to take a bath and while Polo scrubbed the dirt from his skin and fingernails, downstairs she was washing Vincent's blood from his clothes. The bag and its contents felt like a weight around his neck, a death sentence for them all if it was discovered. Vincent said to hide it, this time he would not disobey.

Later that evening as his family slept, Polo crept downstairs and into the garden from where he retrieved Vincent's bag. He knew exactly where it would be safe; somewhere the Nazis would never find it.

Dottie was drained yet curious, in awe of the little boy she remembered as she imagined him scurrying about in the darkness, riddled with fear but determined to keep his promise to Vincent.

'So where did you put it, the bag?'

Polo turned away from her and with his left arm he pointed to the hotel and building site. 'In there.'

Dottie followed his gaze. 'Inside the hotel?'

Polo shook his head. 'Do you remember the cave in the cellar?'

'Yes, of course, that's where we hid one of the evaders, only for a night but I collected him and took him to the next safe house.' Dottie could picture the low roofed room where all manner of things were stored and a young chap huddled in the corner, a pilot desperate to get home to England.

Polo looked pleased she remembered. 'On the far wall there was a range, the chimney was blocked, and nobody had used it for years. I took the bag and Uncle Xavier's ladder and climbed onto the sloping roof, it wasn't hard. I was nimble in those days.

'I made my way to the chimney and threw the bag inside. The bricks around the edge were loose so I pulled them free and dropped them on top, the mortar came away easily, so I kept scraping and throwing until I thought the bag was covered. Nobody heard. Aunt Elise and my cousins slept at the other end of the house. Afterwards, I slid back down the roof and put the ladder away. It was done. I kept my promise to Vincent.'

Dottie was mesmerised by the images of a seven-year-old child standing on a roof, under a jet-black sky lit only by stars and a watery moon, keeping his family safe, honouring his best friend's last command.

'Oh, Polo, you really were such a brave little boy. Vincent will be so proud of you. I'm proud of you.' Dottie wanted to hug him but didn't get a chance because Polo had more to say.

'I watched the chimney for years as it crumbled, knowing that the bag was hidden deep inside its grave. Of course, back then I was glad that it was gone. To me it symbolised death, it was the reason Vincent was gone and why they took your friend Estelle and the others. Its existence threatened my family. I hated it. Then as I got older, I wondered what was inside that was so important. I became curious and many times, during my teenage years I went down to the cave and wondered if I moved the range, I could find it. But it was trapped, somewhere deep inside the chimney and after a while I forgot about it. I left the past where it was, amongst the rubble.' Polo sighed and continued to stare at the remains of his home.

'Now I am beginning to understand why you sit here. Are you hoping they will find it amongst the debris?'

'Perhaps. I did wonder if someone would spot it. Knowing it has been there for so long and will be dug up like a body, well, it made me uneasy so I thought I should sit here and wait, just in case.

'I am also watching my memories being dismantled bit by bit. I have seen them blast through the walls of our bedrooms and Tante Elise's salon that she loved so much. The kitchen and guest rooms will be gone soon, then the scullery with the cave below.'

Dottie's heartbeat quickened. 'But we must ask them to keep an eye out for the bag. They are almost down to the lower walls and once they take away the chimney, they might uncover it. Don't you think it's worth a try?'

Polo wiped his brow that was dotted with sweat. 'They would think we are crazy if we go over there, and surely it will be in a terrible state now, after sixty years.'

'Yes, it could be, but Vincent's bag was made of leather and some of the papers in there could have survived... they are part of our history, Polo, and I for one would love to see them. And I bet you'd like to get the bag back. It's Vincent's, after all.'

Polo sat forward in his chair and looked from the site back to Dottie. 'Do you think we could get it, Yvette? That we should ask, will they take us seriously?'

Dottie shrugged, but before she answered, someone caught her eye, serendipity in the form of Monsieur Lasalle, the *maire*. 'No, possibly not. But we both know a man who they will listen to and he's coming our way.'

Raising her hand to attract the attention of the *maire*, Dottie smiled sweetly then beckoned him over. She had already decided, from the moment she knew of the whereabouts of Vincent's bag that even if she had to dig with her bare hands, she would retrieve it for posterity, for Polo and for herself.

Dottie was overwhelmed by the desire to touch something that belonged to the man who had never really left her side since the day they'd said goodbye. She'd read about work being halted when archaeological remains were discovered and as far as she was concerned, Vincent's bag was far more precious than an old bone, or a fragment of pot. So while she had breath in her body, Dottie was going to do her best to get it back.

39

BÉATRICE

RENAZÉ, 2005

Maude parked the car outside one of the grander houses in the village of Chaze Henry. Both Dottie and Maude looked up at the double-fronted house with freshly painted cream walls and deep blue shutters, open on the ground floor but firmly closed on the two above, keeping out the heat in preparation for the evening. Dottie always thought it looked so unwelcoming from the outside and knew from experience how dreary it made the house look inside, but it was the continental way and a sensible precaution.

She remembered the searing heat of the summer during the war and the exertion of cycling or walking everywhere, from village to village, covering miles just to deliver a note or make a rendezvous. Dottie marvelled at how fit and healthy she must have been, and probably sweaty too, but nobody seemed to mind how you looked back then, or how tatty and old your clothes were. In a way it helped you blend in, or in the case of visiting Nantes and Estelle, stand out like a sore thumb, as a yokel.

Dottie once again pushed those memories away, it would confuse the issue because the main topic of today's agenda was telling Béatrice about Vincent and maybe, if she was brave enough, making amends for her own actions.

'Are you sure you'll be okay on your own, Gran? I don't mind coming in with you and from the looks of that house I'm sure there's somewhere I can wait while you talk.'

Dottie leant across and patted Maude's leg. 'I'll be fine, I promise.'

'But what if she's nasty to you? She might still bear a grudge and let's be honest sometimes your generation don't exactly mellow with age!'

For that remark Maude received a tap on the leg, which was followed by a chuckle from Dottie. 'Cheeky... I'll have you know we're not all like the grumpy old buggers at the bridge club. I am the delightfully chilled-out exception to the rule.'

Maude's guffaws were then ignored as Dottie picked up her handbag from the footwell and pulled the door handle. 'Right, you head off and scout some locations. I'll ring you when I'm ready to be collected but don't rush. I can always take a stroll around the village, or down memory lane.'

'So you've been here before?' Maude sounded unsurprised, more curious.

'Oh yes, I don't think there's a village for miles around that I haven't spent time in, or passed through. This one is no different, in fact, remind me to tell you about this house later, with the wardrobe with a hole in the bottom that dropped you into the barn below... very useful for moving evaders when the Boche came to call.' With that, Dottie winked and left a wide-eyed Maude to find her own way out of the village.

The walk up the gravel pathway that split a garden bursting with deep pink rhododendrons and a border of yellow roses, was overshadowed by the notion of being watched. Dottie held her nerve and summoned a bit of the grit and determination that had waned over the years. Thankfully it hadn't totally expired and only needed a good kick up the bum, the after-effects urging her to ring the doorbell, which she did, quite forcibly.

When the door opened, a much younger woman than Dottie had expected stood before her.

'Bonjour, Madame, I am Arlette, the daughter of Béatrice. We are expecting you, please come in.' Standing aside, the friendly woman gestured with her arm and once Dottie was inside, the door was closed firmly on the mid-morning heat. 'Please would you come with me, Maman is waiting in the salon.'

Dottie hadn't time to say anything apart from hello, and followed Arlette along a dark corridor, her heels tapping on the tiled floor below. It was hard to take everything in but from what Dottie could see of the polished central staircase and tastefully decorated walls covered in elegant flock, the ornate covings above and the delicate china vase festooned with summer flowers, Béatrice had done well.

At the second door along, a large crucifix hovering above the frame, Arlette stopped. 'Maman is in here, would you like coffee or tea, she will take tea?'

'Tea would be lovely, with milk and sugar please.' Dottie liked the forthright approach from Arlette so responded accordingly.

Nodding, Arlette gave a polite smile and opened the door then went inside. 'Maman, your guest is here.'

Dottie could not see beyond the door, and for a second courage failed her until curiosity won out so she stepped forward to meet Béatrice; another face from the past.

She was waiting by double doors, slightly ajar, that led on to a terrace. The sun was streaming into the room, bathing its waiting occupant in a rather surreal shard of light. Dottie took Béatrice in, from top to toe in seconds. She stood erect, slightly to one side as though admiring her garden while awaiting her guest. She wore a pale grey crepe dress, high at the neck, three-quarter sleeved, belted at the waist then flowing to her calf. Black patent shoes, an unfortunate choice and too hot for the season, but they gave her height. Her arms were bent, hands clasped at the waist, not in a nervous way, it was a confident stance and when she turned her head the eyes that bore into Dottie's held a hint of defiance like always. That was the only similarity to the Béatrice she remembered.

Gone was the voluptuous shape, her womanly wiles reduced to the simplicity of a stick figure, still handsome though, but the waves of blonde hair that used to cascade down her back were ice white and scraped into a tight chignon, as pinched as her face. A small but visible crucifix rested on her dress, apart from wedding finger rings, Béatrice's only adornment.

The room screamed elegance and family history, with its oil paintings, dull neo-classics that Maude would hate. Another crucifix hung in the alcove. The furniture was a melange of styles, the chaise was probably Empire, the armoires she'd guess at Regency and the rest good reproductions but tasteful none-theless. Dottie silently applauded Béatrice; she had set the stage well.

Still, there could only be one leading lady in this act and today, Dottie was in no mood for playing understudy so stepped forward, held out her hand and opened the scene.

'Béatrice, it's been a long time. You look remarkably well. Thank you so much for seeing me. To hear you still lived in the area was a pleasant surprise.' Dottie shook the cool and delicate hand that accepted hers, and then waited.

'You may be even more surprised to hear that I am very glad you are here. My Arlette heard the rumours about Vincent's bag and when I realised it was you she was talking about, an English woman with red hair, I had to speak with you.'

At this Dottie was wrong-footed. Béatrice's tone was soft, not sullen or confrontational like she remembered, but caution was still called for. Maybe the sting was yet to come once the prey was off guard. That was how the Béatrice of old would have played it.

'Well, as always news travels fast in these parts but I had already asked the *maire* if there were any relatives of the Maquis still living in the area and his secretary remembered your son, so I would have tracked you down eventually. There are things we need to discuss and I'd rather you hear what I've discovered about Vincent from me, not via wagging tongues.' Without meaning to, Dottie had issued a veiled threat and that wasn't her intention, nevertheless her words had an effect on Béatrice who had visibly paled and shrank slightly.

Stepping to the side and casting her eyes towards two sofas that stood either side of the marble fireplace, Béatrice gestured that they should sit, just as Arlette arrived bearing a tray. She placed it on the table in the centre, then asked Béatrice if she needed anything else before leaving the room.

The tea was poured and had her eighty years not been a factor, Dottie would have said Béatrice's hands trembled as she did so. But she hadn't come here to ignite old battles and in her next sentence, it became clear that neither had Béatrice.

'It is hard, is it not, to know where to begin? I am sure there is so much we could tell each other about our lives since the last time we met... husbands, children.'

The first cup was passed across the table and while doing so, Béatrice glanced at the wedding ring on Dottie's hand. It was the one from her second husband, not her third or fourth. *Yes, I'm sure we both have many tales to tell*, thought Dottie but listened in silence as her host continued and poured a cup for herself.

'But there is something more important I need to say than all that idle chit-chat. It has weighed heavily on my mind since the day Vincent died, a truth that I could not share with the priest because even my confession to him would not alleviate the guilt and shame I feel. No matter how many Hail Marys I say.' Béatrice looked momentarily at Dottie before replacing the teapot and hanging her head.

Dottie felt duty bound to intercede, suspecting that Béatrice was alluding to the terrible argument and now, knowing that it was Claude who betrayed them, not Vincent's own sister, felt her own shame.

'Béatrice, please, I think I know what you are going to say and there is no need. It was the war, we were different people then and you were so young, and perhaps in those days we were all naïve, in our own foolish ways. We did and said things that we regret. I certainly do, so I am sorry that you have felt this burden, I truly am.' There, that sounded okay, and Dottie assumed it would stem the tide of sorrow and allow her to explain about Vincent and Claude, but Béatrice had other ideas.

When she straightened and looked Dottie in the eye, there was a flicker of the young Béatrice, arms folded across her chest, meeting the challenge of an older brother, a mother, a priest, the threat of her father's belt and even the whiplash of harsh words and home truths. When she spoke, however, there was no trace of the young impetuous woman. The voice Dottie heard held the wisdom of years, the measure of calm a parent needs when dealing with a crisis, the steel of a wife when she is determined to get her way.

'I can only imagine the burdens you have carried, Yvette, and the sins that you committed. But I swear to you, had I the power to absolve you I would, because now I understand why you and the Maquis did what you did. It all became so clear the day they brought Vincent home. As I helped my mother bathe his blood-soaked body, and touched the two holes that pierced his skin, I too was bathed in shame. I was invaded by hate and despair and such terrible fear. In that moment I realised what I had done, and my life changed forever.'

Once Vincent was buried and the bodies of those executed by the Nazis had been returned and also laid to rest, another level of fear permeated the village. The Maquis who roamed the hills and forests and hovered on the periphery of their lives were gone. These shadowy fighters had been a symbol of hope, something to cling on to, pride personified in those who were still prepared to lay down their lives for France, resistors who encouraged resistance in everyone. No matter how small the act of defiance, they made even the most timid believe that to spit in the coffee or put dog shit under the door handle of a Boche car was worth it. The fight was still on. But then the Nazis played their hand and showed their might and the depths of pure evil they would stoop to if anyone dared to rise up. The executions touched everyone.

News still came of daring raids, sabotage of train lines and the like, maybe at the hands of their brave boys and men who had spread far and wide. With them gone, who would protect the village now? Morale was low and rumours and mistrust were rife, but life had to go on, a slow plod, a grind. When slowly, news began to filter through that the Allies had landed in the north and the Nazis were capitulating, pulses quickened and hearts felt hope. Then it came. D-Day. And like a house of cards their regime came tumbling down.

As joy swept the nation, liberation was the word on everyone's lips, but along with the relief came fervour, the need for revenge and that wasn't limited to the Nazis. There were those amongst them who had collaborated and they too had to be punished. Women were easy targets and those who were accused of *collaboration horizontale* faced *les tondeurs*; head-shavers. Béatrice lived in perpetual fear of them.

On a sunny morning in late August, she had cycled to Châteaubriant where she hoped to pick up provisions for her mother and it was here that Béatrice came across a rowdy crowd of jeering men and women. Her arrival coincided with some sort of parade she couldn't see at first. When it came into view, six or seven women were being jostled towards the main square, all of them spat upon and called the most dreadful of names. Béatrice was pushed forward by the crowd and unsure of what was happening, asked a woman standing close by.

'They are *des putes*, whores, and about to receive their punishment for sleeping with the enemy. Watch.' The angry-faced woman then smirked as she flicked her head in the direction of the procession.

Béatrice could only stare in horror, petrified to the spot as the women were handled roughly, punched and slapped, then forced to sit as one by one *les tondeurs* got to work, hacking off hair in great chunks while others set it on fire, the stench filling the air. Béatrice could only bear to watch the first two women meet their fate. One sobbed throughout while the other stared defiantly into the crowd, or maybe she was in shock.

Whatever it was, Béatrice was consumed by her own terror. Her bowels rumbled and her stomach swirled, and she knew that soon, this fear would be evacuated from her body, one end or the other, so she had to move, quickly. On legs that felt like marrow, Béatrice pushed her bicycle away from the square and she thanked it for holding her up. Talking to a bicycle was a sign of madness, as mad as consorting with the enemy, madder than the people chopping off hair and beating women in the street.

Béatrice was finding it hard to breath. She could feel perspiration leaking from her body, yet she was consumed by cold dread, a cool hand squeezing a heart that somehow pumped, forcing her limbs to move. Her brain was riddled with panic and screamed that she should get away from the crowd, go home to her maman. When she reached the cobbled alleyway below the chateau walls, Béatrice let her bicycle crash to the floor, as did her own body that spewed its terror onto the ancient stones.

Once it was done, she wiped her mouth and dragged her trembling body to its feet, then mounted her bicycle. Béatrice didn't care about the stares from those she passed as she sped away from the town, tears coursing down her face, drying on the wind only to be replaced by more and more. All she could think of was home, Maman, and Vincent. All she could say were her prayers, begging God for forgiveness, asking for his mercy, promising to be a good girl forever as long as he kept her safe and *les tondeurs* away.

God kept his promise and so did Béatrice. For months she lived in fear, stayed at home or obsessively tended her brother's grave. She became a perfect daughter who helped her mother, went to church twice a day, swept it, picked flowers for the altar – whatever Béatrice thought The Almighty required.

The hair hackers stayed away, but Béatrice never wanted to feel terror and shame again so married the first young man who proposed. She became a God-fearing, dutiful wife, mother and daughter. A more upright, well thought of citizen and valued member of the community you couldn't find for miles around.

But when Arlette came home from her exercise class at the village hall and told her mother all about the hoo-ha over in Renazé, and the red-haired woman who had returned from England, the walls closed in on Béatrice. She was back in that square once again and this time, the most fearsome hair-hacker of all was coming for her.

40

BÉATRICE AND CLAUDE

RENAZÉ, 2005

Béatrice paused and took a sip of her tea. Her face had taken on a troubled frown, brow furrowed, and her eyes seemed to be far away, lost somewhere. Dottie brought her home.

Placing her cup onto the saucer, she transferred both to the tray as she spoke. 'It makes me sad to hear that you have carried this for so long, Béatrice, but you have to let it go now.'

A snap of the head, then watery eyes focused on Dottie. 'I cannot, no matter how I try. The images never leave me. They are imprinted into my brain. Do you know what happened once the war was over, and a new kind of normality returned? Well I will tell you... madness moved in. Twenty-thousand women had their heads shaved and for what?'

Béatrice stood and walked to the glass doors, she seemed agitated. 'Maybe they were simply easy targets on which to take out their temper, or were accused by those who wished to divert attention from their own indiscretions. Not all collaborators were evil traitors. Some slept with the enemy to feed their children, for some it was their job; others were forced to take officers into their homes but were punished afterwards for merely obeying orders, or cleaning their offices for heaven's sake.

'I accept that there were those who believed it was all over and that France would soon be ruled by the Reich so they gave in and reserved themselves an officer before others cottoned on. And then there were girls like me, young fools who fell in love with blond-haired, blue-eyed boys who were far away from home and looking for comfort. I didn't see Jörg as the enemy; to me he was beautiful, kind... different.'

Béatrice stroked the voile that hung at the windows, straightening the folds as she spoke. 'I was so full of hate back then, first for the Germans when they invaded, then for Vincent when he killed Jörg, then for the Germans again when they killed my beloved brother and the others... but the person I hated most was me.'

'I know all this, Béatrice, I remember so well our conversation about Jörg and how in love you were but you have to listen, there are things you should know about...' Dottie was unable to finish.

'Please don't be kind, Yvette, I don't deserve it. I said the most terrible things to Vincent before he died, and I never had chance to say sorry. But on that night, when I washed his body, I realised what he was fighting for, what his comrades had died for and that it was my lust that killed him.'

'What do you mean your lust killed him?' The hairs on the back of Dottie's neck stood on end and her spine became rigid. Had she been right all along, did Béatrice betray Vincent?

Béatrice turned and came back and slumped onto the sofa. Her shoulders sagged like the cushions she leant on, nervously fiddling with her rings as she spoke. 'Because of me, Vincent killed Jörg, and then the Nazi reprisals began. He told me they would, and that my brother had been foolish, and his mistake would cost others dear. But Vincent was only protecting me, like any good *frère* would, I see that now.'

Dottie felt the creep of unease as it made its way over her skin, and she was forced to ask a question she probably knew the answer to. 'Who said the mistake would cost others, who told you that Vincent was a fool?'

Béatrice looked up from her fingers. 'Your comrade, you know the one with the terrible skin. I felt sorry for him, I suppose. He was shy so I always took time to chat with him, and he was always kind and gave me chocolate... Claude. Yes, that was his name.'

Dottie closed her eyes for a second and sucked in air, and when she had composed herself asked Béatrice to tell her everything.

It was two days after Jörg died, Vincent had disappeared and Béatrice's maman was cross because she refused to come out of her room. She'd threatened to bring the *curé* if Béatrice didn't get out of bed soon, or the doctor, even both! How could Béatrice tell her maman that where she wished to be, was in a hole next to dear Jörg.

The house and her bedroom were becoming a prison of her own making and Béatrice was tired of hearing her mother's voice outside the door, so before she went mad or died from heartbreak, she decided to go out. The nails had been removed from the window and her door was now left unlocked.

It was dusk and her mother was in the salon, darning or something equally boring while listening to the radio. Her papa was asleep in his chair. After creeping down the stairs, taking a bottle of wine from the cave and closing the door to the outhouse behind her, Béatrice raced through the garden and vegetable patch, then into the lane that ran behind the house and towards the bridge where she used to meet her lover. Here, she slumped behind the wall and proceeded to drink the whole bottle of her father's home-made wine.

If she popped her head over the wall Béatrice could see the spot where Jörg died and imagine the pool of blood that oozed from his head, his blank sightless eyes that would ever again look into hers. And the rage inside, it swelled like dough, rising slowly, but the only thing Béatrice wished to punch and kneed was Vincent's head, see how he liked it.

By the time darkness had fallen like a blanket over the countryside, cheerful birdsong had been thankfully replaced by the night prowlers who rustled leaves or cried out to their mate. Béatrice had no more tears to cry, she had used them all up, but in their place, hate swirled deep inside, round and round, whipping up a storm. She took another swig from the bottle and once the wine was gone, craved more, or perhaps it was oblivion she sought. But rather than go back home, Béatrice decided to walk into the village and seek sustenance from Armand at the café.

Béatrice wasn't scared of the dark and knew the road well. Only minutes away from Café des Amis, she realised she had no money so rummaged around in her coat pocket, desperate to find a few francs. Furious with herself she stamped her foot, knowing she couldn't ask for credit and was about to turn for home when something caught her eyes. A shadow emerged from the trees by the church wall; the yellow glow from a match illuminated a familiar face that was now making its way towards her. Claude waved so Béatrice lingered, throwing off the thought that he was always doing that, appearing from nowhere, smug already that she would get her drink, bought by a man her so-called brother approved of.

Almost thirty minutes and two glasses of pastis later, Béatrice knew she was very drunk and as much as it irked her, silently agreed with Armand when he suggested to Claude that he should see her home. Anyway, she was bored and had run out of small talk which was why she knocked back her last drink and staggered to her feet, allowing Claude to take her arm.

'Come along, I'll see you home. It's very dark now and I don't want you falling into a ditch.'

Béatrice fought the urge to snatch her arm away, wanting no man to touch her other than Jörg, and to tell Claude that she was quite capable of finding her own way, but she was still in control of her pickled brain which suggested she accept the offer. 'Are we going on your motorbike, my legs are tired.'

'No, n-not tonight, I have n-no petrol, but I am happy to walk with you. I think the fresh air will help to s-sober you up.' Claude guided her through the door and onto the street where they made their way across the cobbles, steadying Béatrice when she stumbled.

They continued in silence for most of the way, Claude offered her a cigarette which she accepted even though she hated smoking, but it made her feel grown-up, and it also annoyed Vincent. The moon was a perfect semi-circle, misted very slightly now and then by a passing cloud. There were no stars to wish upon for which Béatrice was glad, it would be a fool's errand as they never came true, just like prayers. Dragging on the cigarette, she blew the smoke into the darkness and listened to Claude who was now in a chatty mood.

'I hope that Vincent won't be annoyed with you when you get home. Perhaps you c-can sneak in unnoticed.'

This notion received a huff of derision from Béatrice. 'He is not there and if he was, I would stomp up the stairs like a herd of beasts, just to annoy him. Vincent is not my keeper and I don't care what he says, anyway.'

At this Claude sounded surprised. 'Oh, I didn't k-know he was away... where has he gone?'

Béatrice shrugged her shoulders and, sick of the taste of tobacco, bad-temperedly threw the cigarette into the bushes. 'How should I know... I am just his stupid sister who isn't allowed a life or will of her own, so I hope he stays in Nantes and never comes back.'

'I thought you said you didn't k-know where he was.'

'I don't, well not exactly, I heard him talking with the wonderful Yvette about it. They were whispering in the garden; they are always whispering, when they are not having sex in the barn. She is another person I despise because she told Vincent about Jörg. I hope her friend in Nantes gets bombed by the Germans or shot. They can all go to hell.'

At this Claude slowed his pace but Béatrice just wanted to get home. She was tired and felt queasy. They were approaching the low bridge that crossed the stream and realising they were at the spot where Jörg was murdered Béatrice came to an abrupt halt, while Claude asked more questions. She was starting to think he was annoying rather than kind, especially as he'd already told her in the café that he had no more stockings, or real coffee like last time they'd chatted.

'Let's s-sit for a while. You can't go home in this mood and your mother will know you are drunk.'

Béatrice responded petulantly. 'I'm not sitting here, are you mad, don't you know what happened right there?' She pointed to a spot in the road, not quite sure if it was accurate. 'And how can you ask me to sit with you... it is improper, especially as I am recently bereaved.' After her outburst she stormed off, Claude trotting by her side as he apologised.

'Mademoiselle, please forgive me if I have offended you in any way b-because that was n-not my intention. But I'm slightly c-confused, has someone died? I've been in Mayenne for a few days and had n-no idea. Please accept my c-condolences.'

Béatrice kept walking as she spoke. 'Yes, someone has died,

no, actually, he was murdered by your comrade, Vincent, my brother and jailor. And don't look so shocked. I know what you all get up to with your stupid resistance.'

This seemed to quieten Claude for a moment, and it made Béatrice feel quite smug and powerful, if only with words as her weapon.

'But who was killed, someone from the village?'

'No, it was a soldier, killed on this very spot. They all think it was an accident, a deer knocked him off his bike, but I'm not stupid, it was them, the Maquis and my brother!' There she'd said it and didn't regret it at all because it was true.

Claude looked shocked. 'N-no, I don't believe you, why would he?'

'Are you stupid or something? Because the soldier was my lover and my self-righteous brother couldn't bear the thought that I was going to marry a German because once this stupid war is over that's what I'm going to do. Jörg told me he'd take me to Berlin, and we would meet his parents and I'd never have to see this pitiful village or my annoying family ever again.' It was as her words cut through the haze of alcohol that was misting her brain, the ridiculousness of them hit hard. Jörg was dead. She was going nowhere.

When the tears returned and she began to sob, just like most men Claude withered and seemed unable to deal with or comfort a woman in distress, not that she wanted him to anyway. His whole demeanour had changed, and she knew why. He was closing ranks, unwilling to denounce his leader and, after all, he hated the Nazis and would be glad one of them was dead. Before he had the opportunity to skulk away and leave her feeling like a pathetic snivelling woman, she took the upper hand, pulling herself together quickly she began to walk away.

'You can go now, Claude. Go on, scurry off to your comrades and celebrate another of your pathetic victories... I will be fine. I can find my way home from here.' As she expected Claude didn't object, he simply stared for a second longer, then nodded and in the same way he had appeared earlier, melted into the darkness.

It wasn't until morning that along with a terrible headache and a chamber pot full of vomit came realisation. She had told Claude about Jörg and while she knew he would not be the least bit bothered about his callous murder, what if he told everyone that she was a Boche lover? She would be shunned, an outcast, her parents shamed and although she hated Vincent, she did not wish the wrath of the village to fall on her maman and papa.

What should she do? How could she put things right? Had she not been so terrified, Béatrice would have given in to the hysteria that was building in her chest, but it was not the time for panic, no, she had to think. Claude was the key and she had to find him and persuade him to keep her secret, but how? He was the one with the chocolate and stockings, Béatrice had nothing to barter with. Feeling her guts grumble, she stood, and on unsteady legs made her way to the lavatory, passing the mirror as she did. The glimpse of her red camisole, the one that Jörg had given her, and her breasts that swelled above the lace, gave Béatrice an idea. Wincing at the sight of her puffy eyes and dishevelled hair she ignored them and focused on her best assets. Shame flooded her veins, cheeks aflame at the thought of what she must do. Her body was all she had to trade for silence and if that's what it took, so be it. There was no time to ponder the situation further because her stomach heaved and before she made a mess of her camisole, Béatrice sprinted to the bathroom.

She found Claude later that day at the old abandoned farm she had once visited as a teenager, ghost hunting with her friends.

Béatrice watched him for a while as he tinkered with the engine on his Solex, hands covered in black grease, his head bent in concentration. When she spoke, it made him jump and for a moment it amused her, his startled look that quickly altered to one of curiosity. He was obviously wondering why she had walked to such a remote spot all alone, but when she showed her hand too soon, nerves getting the better of her, his look became knowing and for a second, mocking.

'Béatrice, what brings you here? Have you a m-message from Vincent, is he back?'

Swallowing down nerves, for this really was virgin territory, Béatrice feigned confidence and failed miserably. 'No, Vincent hasn't sent me. I wanted to apologise for my behaviour last night because I was rude and ungrateful, and to ask you a favour.'

Claude was wiping his hands that were still smeared with grease, a faint smile playing on his lips. He seemed different today, not friendly, like the times he'd given her a lift on his motorbike or sprang from nowhere to take time to chat and show interest in her day. There was a haughtiness about him, or was it indifference?

'It's fine, you were drunk and emotional, it's forgotten.' He turned and began to put away his spanners as he continued. 'But what is this favour you ask?'

Béatrice stepped forward and around his motorbike so he could see her face, and she his. It was then that she caught a slight smirk, or was it her imagination? 'The things I told you, about Jörg, please, I beg of you, don't tell anyone else. It is bad enough that Vincent knows but gossip and rumours, well, they are dangerous for everyone.'

If Béatrice expected Claude to fall over himself giving her assurances she was to be disappointed because instead of setting her mind at rest, he fell silent, as if pondering her request.

'There is coffee inside. If you would like some, we can

continue our conversation there.' Claude threw down the rag he was holding and walked towards the door of the barn, not waiting for her answer.

It was then that she realised what she was going to have to do. This Claude was not the shy man who had offered her a friendly ear, who she could flirt with and bat her eyelids at to get an extra slice of *jambon* like the man at the market. Claude was just like all the rest, he'd seen his chance and was going to take it.

Béatrice could feel the prick of tears in her eyes and the flush of her cheeks, and as her pride evaporated like a puddle in the sun, she meekly followed Claude into the house.

41

REVELATIONS

RENAZÉ, 2005

Béatrice wiped away a tear that had leaked from the corner of her eye. She had ceased picking at the tassel on one of the cushions that were scattered along the sofa and raised her eyes to meet Dottie's.

'So now do you understand? I'm sure there is no need for me to go into detail about what happened in the farmhouse, but Claude made it clear that to ensure his silence I would be required to, shall we say, be nice. Not only did he take my virginity, for a while he took away my sanity and plunged me into the depths of fear and shame. He said that Vincent had put everyone in danger by killing Jörg and if the other members of the brigade found out there would be trouble. He told me he would try to keep me safe from them but if the Boche came, they would have no mercy. They always said they'd take ten lives for one of theirs. I thought I would die from the sheer terror.

'Afterwards, I cried all the way home and once I had changed and thrown away the oil-stained camisole, I cycled to the edge of the village, praying that Vincent would use the main road from Nantes. I wanted to apologise, say I forgave him and warn him of the danger. I would have told him to turn around and go somewhere safe. For the next two days I got up at dawn and waited until it was pitch black. It rained, it was cold, but I did not care. In the end I missed him. I should have known he would sneak back unnoticed and not simply drive around in plain sight, but I had to try, I had to do something. I never saw my brother again, not until they brought his body home. And I have lived with that image, and the guilt that has eaten me like a cancer, ever since.'

On hearing this Dottie stood. She had had enough and couldn't bear for Béatrice to suffer any longer. The chasm between them had always been wide, ever since they'd met, but now was the time to close the gap and offer each other comfort, and in her case, the gift of truth and understanding. Moving to the sofa Dottie sat beside Béatrice and took her hand as she spoke.

'Béatrice, it is now my turn to speak and there are things I need to tell you, and they will be hard to hear, but once I am done I hope you can forgive me as you would have forgiven Vincent. I cannot allow you to torment yourself for one day longer and if you need to direct your hate and anger towards anyone, it should be at me and Claude.'

At this Béatrice looked confused but did not remove her hand.

Dottie gave an ironic smile, knowing that in the next few seconds most of what Béatrice thought and said would change. 'You see it wasn't Vincent who killed Jörg, it was me. And it wasn't the Boche that killed your brother, it was Claude.'

When Béatrice gasped and snatched her hand away, her face hardened, and her eyes bore into Dottie's. She didn't say a word. It was as though she'd been stunned into silence, so seizing the moment Dottie spoke hastily.

'Please, let me explain. I know you are shocked but there is so much I have to tell you.'

Béatrice gave an almost unperceivable nod of the head.

Feeling like a rabbit trapped in the glare of a spotlight, expecting a bullet from the shotgun, Dottie took a deep breath and told her the truth about Vincent and Jörg, and Polo; about everything.

Dottie felt like she'd been talking forever but it could only have been a few minutes, and Béatrice had remained silent throughout. Her confession had ended with Polo's revelation about Vincent's bag.

'Your brother didn't even know about my plan to kill Jörg, but after your threats I couldn't risk you passing on information. I acted entirely alone. It was self-preservation, although it did solve two problems at once. That sounds harsh but it's true.'

There was still no response from Béatrice.

'When I told Vincent what I'd done, I offered to tell you the truth that day we came to see you, but he forbade me. You know the rest now, the sequence of events which followed.'

Béatrice was ashen. Dottie was the opposite. Flushed from her confession she wished that her confessor and spiritual judge would speak. Her wish was eventually granted.

In a voice barely a whisper, tears rolling down her cheeks, Béatrice spoke. 'But in the end, I still betrayed Vincent. I told Claude he'd killed Jörg. He would have told the Boche and that's why they rounded everyone up. I'd even given away that Vincent was in Nantes. Claude was always digging, I see that now. What a pathetic fool I was.'

'You didn't know Claude was working for the Germans, none of us did. You thought you were talking to a patriot not a traitor. So did I when I told him about Estelle, my friend in Nantes. He knew exactly what she looked like so would have given them a description. The SS or Gestapo would have tracked her down.'

At this Béatrice merely blinked.

335

'And remember, it was my actions that brought on the reprisals. I killed one of theirs. They would have come for us eventually with or without the death of Jörg because Claude had been gathering information for a long time. He'd already betrayed the group in Nantes and probably others, and then my dearest friend was arrested, tortured and died in a camp in Germany.' Just the thought of Maude threatened to break Dottie, so she forced her mind elsewhere and listened to the woman by her side.

'Was it quick, for Jörg?' Béatrice sounded weary, sad.

'Yes, I promise.' Dottie could hear the thud, see the blood-stained stave even now.

'And the traitor... is he still alive, do you think?'

'Yes, I know for a fact that he is still alive.' Such injustice was not lost on Dottie.

'What will happen to him?'

'He will be punished. I will make sure.' Of this Dottie was certain.

'Good.'

Silence fell between them and Dottie watched as Béatrice bent her head and slowly turned the rings on her finger. When she looked up and spoke to Dottie there was softness in her voice, she sounded calm.

'Thank you for telling me the truth, Yvette. It took great courage and cannot have been easy.' She reached over and took Dottie's hand in hers.

The response was simple and sincere. 'As did yours, Béatrice.'

Both women allowed themselves a smile.

'I forgive you, for Jörg. It was war and you were a soldier, as was he. I have no doubt that had his life been threatened by you, then we would not be having this conversation today.'

Dottie felt a great lump form in her throat so coughed gently in order to disperse it. 'Thank you, Béatrice, that means a great deal. But I did not come here for forgiveness. I didn't expect it for one moment nor feel I deserve it, although I did want to set the record straight.'

'Well you have succeeded in your task and I think you have been incredibly honourable, not to mention brave. I expect you were prepared to face the monstrous Béatrice of the past, and all you found was a silly old grandmother haunted by secrets of her own.'

'I was actually quite looking forward to sparring with young Béatrice again, you always did give everyone a run for their money, but I have to say, I think I prefer the mature version.'

Béatrice smiled. 'And I was expecting a fiery redhead to come marching in and read me the riot act, so I too am relieved to see a calmer Yvette. We make quite a pair, don't we? Fancy that.'

At this they both laughed. It was good to feel some of the tension leave the room. But there were still things they needed to discuss, and Dottie brought up one of them, Claude.

'It rocked my world, you know, when Polo told me about Claude because I trusted him, we all did. So many things have clicked into place, like one of those impossible Japanese puzzles, and now a huge part of my life feels like a sham. I am sure that had I not spirited him away that night he would have stayed behind and caused even more mayhem. You and your family could have been interned. Either that or he would have carried on dangling you on a string, the vile creature that he is.'

'Either scenario fills me with horror. But tell me, how do you know he is still alive, you seem very certain?'

'Ah, well, this is what I mean about my life being a sham because the Claude that we knew then did very well after the war and took me under his wing, or so I thought. Now I suspect he was keeping me close, just in case I ever made contact with what remained of the Maquis. I think Claude was afraid that he would be identified because as you said, many of the Resistance wanted revenge and someone may have discovered who the traitor was.'

Béatrice was inquisitive. 'So Claude, he is still your friend?'

Dottie nodded. 'Yes, he is. All these years I have been proud to call him that and all the while he was duping me, again.'

'What do you intend to do with this information? Can he be punished? Even now, when he is an old man?'

The answer to this was not going to be simple, mainly because Dottie hadn't decided what her next step would be. 'Oh yes, he can be punished, he will be punished, but I haven't worked out the best way to go about it yet, so for now, I would like Polo's secret to remain between us, and our families of course. The less people know the better and then I can use the element of surprise to our advantage.'

'Like one last mission.'

Smiling, Dottie took Béatrice's hand. 'Yes, exactly. It will be our final mission to avenge our comrades. One way or another, the traitor will pay. But before that, I would like to spend some time with you and Polo, perhaps arrange a reunion for anyone from the old days... what do you think?'

Béatrice looked delighted and squeezed Dottie's hands. 'I think that is a wonderful idea and I will help. I know many of the families hereabouts and we can spread the word through the church, or perhaps we should go to the post office and tell them there, that usually does the trick.' Béatrice winked and chuckled.

She was back, that cheeky young woman Dottie remembered so well, like the click of a shutter, transporting them back through time. It was this thought that gave rise to another. For a second Dottie held back, perhaps wary of disappointment or lacking the courage she required to look directly at the past. But she had come this far so she asked Béatrice a question.

'I wonder, do you have a photo of Vincent? I have survived for so long on my memories of him and I know we didn't take many in those days, but perhaps you have some of him as a child, anything really.' Those damn tears were welling again so Dottie forced them away, chiding her lack of control.

'Of course, I have some, not many like you say, and they are quite faded, but I will bring them at once. And I'll ask Arlette to fetch more refreshments. Would like you to stay for lunch so that we may talk more? I feel like I never want to let you go.'

'That's exactly how I feel, Béatrice, and of course I will stay, but could I ask my granddaughter? She's here with me and I would love you both to meet.'

'Of course, please tell her to come at once. I cannot say how my heart has lifted. For the first time since I can't remember, it feels like a feather. I shall go and find Arlette while you make your call. I will be back soon with the photos.' With that, Béatrice gave Dottie's hands another squeeze before she stood and hurried from the room.

Placing her palms on her cheeks in the hope of cooling them down, Dottie closed her eyes and smiled, relief flooding her body. After taking a moment to have a word with herself, she got on with ringing Maude and then waited patiently for Béatrice to return.

The breeze from the double doors brushed Dottie's face as she took in the paintings on the wall, and after being thoroughly depressed by all of them she hoped that now she had exorcised the past, Béatrice might reconsider her choice of art. Really, there was only so much penance one could pay and she really didn't deserve so many scenes of crucifixion, gutted fish and the all-knowing eyes of Mother Mary. Perhaps Maude might donate one of her oils, or failing that, they could go to IKEA and buy some jolly prints, anything was better than this.

She was dragged away from her critique by the return of

Béatrice bearing a photo album, the sight of which made Dottie's heart flutter.

'Here I am, and I have told Arlette to listen for Maude and to bring her through as soon as she arrives.' Positioning herself on the sofa, Béatrice opened the album and flicked over the pages until she found what she was looking for, then slid out a photograph before silently handing it to Dottie.

With an uncharacteristic trembling of the hand, Dottie looked upon the image of a smartly dressed young man seated, perhaps in a photographer's studio. He sat bolt upright and wore a suit, the colour indistinguishable, with a white shirt under a waistcoat, his tie appeared too tight, or was it the collar that pinched his neck? Despite the unfamiliar garb, Dottie would have known the face anywhere, even with his unruly hair scraped back and held in place by barber's wax. Vincent. The square set of his jaw and long, slightly bent to the side nose, deep, dark eyes meeting the challenge of the camera just as he met everything, with determination and, yes, a haughty look of pride. Dottie could not speak but her lips trembled, and she wondered how it was possible for your heart to break yet sing with joy all at once.

'It was taken on his twenty-first birthday, almost ten years before you met him. Doesn't he look handsome? Here, I have another, taken at La Baule. I think this is more how you remember him. It was a family day out and Papa had borrowed my uncle's camera.' Béatrice passed the album over and placed it on Dottie's knee then pointed to the young man on the beach, leaning against some rocks, legs outstretched and arms crossed, laying in his lap. The unruly mop of hair was untamed and fell upon his forehead above laughing eyes. Vincent was smiling into the camera; happy, carefree and alive.

Sliding out the photo Béatrice passed it to Dottie. 'We will have copies made of any that you like. Look, here is one of me.'

Dottie flicked away her tears, glad of the diversion from Vincent's face. There she was, that young woman who sashayed along the street, attracting admiring glances. Béatrice was a character that was for sure, a handful before the war, a liability during it, but she had such spirit back then, a *joie de vivre* that even Hitler couldn't tame. In the photo she was leaning against the gate of the farm, her lips formed to a pout, her hair ironed into curls, her eyes full of mischief and as Dottie looked up, at the face of now Béatrice, her heart felt sad.

Not only had this beautiful young woman been plunged into a life of occupation, she had been terrorised and shamed, the legacy of which formed the rest of her life. Without even having to ask, Dottie knew why Béatrice had transformed herself into the dutiful wife and mother, devoted supplicant. The fight had left Béatrice the day they brought her brother's body home. Resistance was futile, so she gave in and became the opposite of everything she'd once strove to avoid. Dottie hoped that the truth would set Béatrice free and for the remainder of her life, a little bit of that *joie de vivre*, her spirit of resistance, would return. Béatrice deserved that.

They continued to peruse the album for a while longer, laughing at the photos within, pointing and remembering some of the faded faces and places, a black-and-white homage to the past.

They had reached the last page when Béatrice looked up, wearing a startled expression. 'I have just realised something.'

Dottie responded with a quizzical look but allowed her to continue.

'I know you as Yvette, that's how I have always thought of you, but it has suddenly occurred to me that this cannot be your real name... so please forgive me if you are upset in any way by my use of it.'

Dottie waved away Béatrice's worries. 'There is no need to

apologise, in fact I am enjoying being twenty-four again, if only in our memories and I love my French name, and my code name too, I always have.'

Béatrice sighed and looked relieved. 'I didn't even know you had a code name, thank God. What was it, you can tell me now?'

'Nadine. That's how London knew it was me sending them messages.'

'Mmm, I like it. But tell me, what is your real name? I must say I would have been confused if I'd had so many and my stupid young self would have definitely made a mistake.'

Dottie gave Béatrice a gentle nudge. 'You must stop putting yourself down, from this moment on, I insist. Like I said, they were harsh, terrible times. You have punished yourself enough.'

Béatrice's smile lit up her face that had colour in it at last, fewer lines, the tension easing. 'All right, I will try. So what is it, your real name?'

'Dorothy but everyone calls me Dottie.'

Béatrice was most perplexed by this. 'Oh no, Dottie does not seem right at all. To me you are Yvette. Can I still call you that? It makes me feel warm inside.' She touched her heart as she spoke.

At this Dottie laughed and mimicked the action. 'You know something, Béatrice, in here I think I will always be Yvette, so it's fine.'

The sound of the door handle turning, and the appearance of Arlette and Maude interrupted the laughter that filled the room. As more introductions were made, a thought crossed Dottie's mind. After spending more than half of her life running away from the past, now she had returned it was bathing her in happiness. Slowly, step by step, she was wading through the sadness and hurt, making sense of it all.

There was another chapter of the story to be written down, and after Béatrice's part was committed to Maude's journal, the final scenes would have to be played out. In the meantime, Dottie wanted to wallow, walk in her own faded footsteps, and touch the hands of those who had survived, whose misty faces often appeared in her memory.

The man who invaded her dreams, well, he was gone forever but at least she had a photo, and until they met again, she would hold on tightly to the hands of his family. That would see her through, it was enough for now.

42

VINCENT'S LETTER

RENAZÉ, 2005

There were six of them seated around the table in the boardroom, all of them awaiting the *maire* who, as Francine had sarcastically predicted, would want to make a grand entrance. She was correct. When the door opened and the receptionist-cum-secretary stood to one side for Monsieur Lasalle to enter, Martine, Béatrice, Dottie, Maude, Arlette and, grudgingly, Francine got to their feet while Polo remained in his wheelchair.

Dottie focused on the clay splattered cement sack that he was carrying like he'd baked a cake. She couldn't see what was on it because it was covered by plastic and she thought it was kind that the builders had sought to protect it.

They had been drinking coffee on the lawn at Béatrice's when Dottie took the call to say that the builders had uncovered Vincent's bag, and they should come to the *maire*'s office at once. Dottie couldn't believe that after all the hours Polo had actually waited there, he'd been at the dentist and had missed the big moment, such was Sod's law. The foreman had delivered the bag to the *maire*'s immediately, the importance of the find lost on the builders, who wanted only to get on unhindered by treasure seekers.

Once he'd walked to the head of the table, Monsieur Lasalle looked at each of them one by one and said, 'Are we ready?' at which point Dottie saw the eye roll from Francine as they all muttered or nodded their agreement.

Carefully and respectfully, he removed the top layer and there it was, the leather poacher's bag that Vincent always wore slung across his body. Dottie felt it, a tangible connection between her and the bag, a link to the past. The leather was faded to a murky grey, aged by damp and whatever rain had managed to trickle its way through and beneath layers and layers of brick rubble. It was covered in dust, the thick stitching eroded, the buckles rusted, but still firmly fastened since the last time Polo had touched it, sixty years ago.

'Monsieur, Mesdames.' The *maire* looked from Polo to Dottie to Béatrice. 'Would one of you like to open it, or shall I?'

The bag by rights belonged to Béatrice, but they had all agreed that the secret about Claude the traitor belonged to all of them and for now it should stay that way. The pact was made before Monsieur Lasalle had entered the room. It was a family secret, and the note from Vincent was from him to Yvette, they had agreed this also.

Béatrice spoke. 'You do it, Yvette.'

Nodding, Dottie pulled the bag towards her, cringing slightly when clay and dust smeared the polished tabletop. There was a hush in the room as she unfastened the stiff buckles, and she took care to slide the leather straps carefully so as not to damage them.

Again, she gently turned the flap and widened the opening to reveal the documents Vincent had placed there. Sliding them out she heard a chorus of gasps because despite the ageing of the musty paper, the leather bag had preserved its contents well and there for everyone to see was the emblem of the Nazis, the eagle. Everyone remained silent as Dottie removed the next item, pulling it carefully, not knowing if the bullets Vincent had fired at Claude were the last ones in the gun, before laying it on the table, barrel facing away from all of them.

'It's best if nobody touches this and we will need to have it checked... there might still be bullets in the chamber.'

Next, she felt inside and found the flat carpenter's pencil just as Polo had described, and some francs and a wad of propaganda leaflets. That was all, no note. Seconds of silence stretched while the weight of disappointment hung heavy in Dottie's heart, broken abruptly by the entrance of the secretary who summoned the *maire* to an important call. Now the contents had been revealed Monsieur Lasalle appeared content to obey, the moment of drama had passed and it wasn't until the door closed firmly that Polo spoke.

'Yvette, the note is inside the papers. Unfold them, it will be there, I know it.'

The relief in the air was palpable, but none more so than that in Dottie's heart. Doing as Polo said, she carefully unfolded the documents that on first glance were stamped with the word *klassifiziert* which she presumed meant classified, and one by one began to part each sheet. The note was between the third and fourth, still folded, waiting to be read. She felt rather foolish that her hand trembled as she picked it up and slowly, so as not to rip the delicate paper emblazoned with faded French propaganda, began to unfold it. On the inside, in his sprawling handwriting so typical of the French, were Vincent's final words to her.

Dottie swallowed and kept her eyes on the paper as she read them, the first time to herself and the second time to everyone else, her voice cracking now, eyes misty, cheeks wet.

Yvette, my love.
You must go quickly. Do not come back. Keep your promise.
Too dangerous. We are betrayed.
The traitor is Claude Rayon. Agent Victor.
My little shadow saw him exchange messages with the Gestapo
Get a message to London.
If I do not see you soon, my love, be happy.
I will love you forever.
Vincent x

Nobody spoke. Polo and Béatrice wept, and Maude came quickly to her gran's aid as did Arlette and Francine to their kin. When Monsieur Lasalle burst through the door once again he appeared embarrassed to see such an emotive scene, so excused himself on the pretence of bringing refreshments, giving everyone time to compose themselves and for Dottie to refold the letter and place it inside her diary. By the time he returned, an aide in his wake, eyes had been wiped and noses blown, and they all accepted a glass of wine and listened patiently to his suggestions.

'If you prefer to take the bag with you, I understand perfectly as it belongs to you, Béatrice, but should you prefer to leave it in my care I can assure you of its safety. I have contacts at the *musee* in Derval, and I am sure they would be delighted to see this. The contents are of great historic importance and they will be fascinated, and the gun will need to be inspected by the gendarmes and disarmed, I can arrange this also.'

Béatrice looked around the room, the decision fell to her. 'With regards to the gun I think that is the most sensible option for now, Monsieur, but I would like to have the bag at home for a while. The *musee* can take it later, does everyone agree?'

Six nodding heads confirmed this and once he'd drained his glass of wine, *le maire* excused himself to make some calls.

347

When he'd gone there was a collective sigh of relief and then Béatrice spoke up.

'Are you all right, Yvette? You looked rather shaken when you read Vincent's words, but I hope they gave you comfort.'

Dottie smiled and reached out her hand which Béatrice took. 'Yes, they did, and I only wish that you could have received some too, but how brave he was and how proud you should be of him.'

Béatrice merely nodded, clearly moved. The next to speak was Francine.

'So what will you do with the letter, Yvette, are you going to expose the traitor? Maybe everyone should know because there are families in these parts who lost their loved ones thanks to him.'

Before Dottie could speak Béatrice interrupted. 'No, for now it must remain our secret and it will do no good, stirring up the past, causing ill will. I say we let Yvette deal with the traitor her own way and when she is ready, when we are all ready, the story can be told. I trust Yvette to do the right thing, she has never let us down before.'

A smile passed between the two women and Dottie could have wept at the words of forgiveness and support from her old enemy. Polo spoke next.

'I agree with Béatrice. Yvette will make the traitor pay and as long as those in this room know the truth, that is what counts and, yes, one day it can be shared but for now it stays between us.'

They all nodded in silent unison as they heard voices in the hallway and footsteps approaching, causing Béatrice to roll her eyes, lightening the mood when they all laughed.

'Come, let us leave *le maire* to his arrangements and glory, I think it is time I took Dottie to see Vincent, would you like that, my friend?' Béatrice's eyes were kind as she waited for the answer.

Dottie's heart thudded, the final hurdle approached but she had to do it, she had to face one more truth. 'Of course, I would like to see where he is and tell him I kept my promise, and then I broke it and finally came back, but I think he will forgive me, don't you?'

Béatrice smiled and nodded before standing, then held out her hand, leading the way, taking Yvette to see Vincent.

43

MAUDE'S SURPRISE

RENAZÉ, 2005

Maude was waiting outside the gates of the churchyard while Dottie had another chat with Vincent and said *à bientôt*, not goodbye, for she would be returning soon to stay with Béatrice. It had all turned out so well for her gran who was something of a local celebrity and had spent the last week being feted by the locals, welcomed with open arms by the village and wider community.

It was with sadness that they'd discovered that she, Polo and Béatrice were the only survivors from the Maquis but their descendants had taken great delight in attending the reunion hosted by *le maire*. And now Maude had a stash of photographs she'd copied, the black-and-white faces of the Resistance, her gran's friends and comrades. Not only that, she had sketches galore and a whole roll of film just waiting to be processed, inspiration for a new collection of paintings that would pay tribute to the Resistance and the surrounding area.

Maude adored it here and while Dottie-Yvette, as she'd taken to calling her gran, spent time with her old and new friends, she'd had a painting and sketching frenzy, the tingliest fingers ever. The thing was, owing to her gran's sudden change of heart over Lachlan, some kind of benevolent epiphany, it looked like she wouldn't have too much time to put a collection together, not if she was heading to Australia.

It had knocked Maude for six, the little chat they'd had the previous evening as they packed their cases and chatted about their plans. She hadn't expected it, and now, if she was honest, wasn't too sure if she wanted to accept her gran's very lovely offer.

Dottie was stuffing her clothes into the case which drove Maude mad and she forced her to remove the lot and begin folding them neatly in a pile while her gran took a rest, looking suspiciously pleased with herself.

'All you had to do was ask and I'd have packed for you, not made a complete hash of it on purpose. Honestly, Gran, it looks like a five-year-old has folded these.'

Dottie tutted loudly. 'Oh, do stop fussing, Maudie, and anyway, there's something I want to tell you before we meet the others. I've come to a decision and I have a surprise.'

Maude paused and raised her eyebrow. 'Why don't I like the sound of this already, what are you up to?'

'Charming... now please stop folding and listen, I want you to go to Australia with Lachlan as soon as you can or want to. I'll pay for your ticket and give you plenty of spending money, you won't even have to work as a kangaroo shearer or koala farmer, or whatever it is they do over there, how does that sound?'

Caught utterly and completely off guard, for a moment Maude could only stand and stare. 'But why the change of heart? I don't get it, especially as you are basically sending me off with your arch enemy.'

A huffing noise preceded Dottie's answer. 'Because if this trip has taught me one thing it's that I have to let you go, to be the Maude you want to be not the woman I expect you to be. You have to live your life how you want to, and I have to let you go just like my mum and mémère let their children go. I have no right to connive and guilt you into staying, and it's wrong of me to judge Lachlan even though he does irritate the...' Dottie paused before continuing.

'What I'm trying to say is that if I can be fooled by a man I've known and trusted for sixty years, how can I be trusted to judge the character of one I've only known for a few months. I have to let you make your own mistakes and claim your own successes but if you go, I'd rather you do it the easy way. Life shouldn't always be a struggle, Maude, or a battle, I see that now. If you are in love, I am happy for you, if you want to paint deserts, then do it; be a wife, a mother, a hippy with sand in her knickers. I'd forgotten that I would have given everything up for the man I truly loved, so I'm saying to you what Vincent said to me, *be happy.*'

Maude put down the blouse she was folding and rushed to hug her gran, completely in awe of how this bloody contrary woman always seemed to come up trumps and work it out in the end. It would have taken a lot for her gran to say those words, her mind must have been spinning, laying all her thoughts out and putting them in order, again. Taking a breath, Maude accepted, not wanting to throw back the gesture.

'Thank you, Gran. It's a very generous gift and I accept, and I won't ever forget what you just said, or this brilliant adventure we've been on together. It was meant to be, I'm sure of it. But now I want you to promise me something.' Maude let go and eyed Dottie who looked suspicious.

'Go on... what is it?'

Maude placed her hands on her hips. 'I want you to tell

Mum how you feel, you know, say some of those lovely things about being proud of her because I know it would mean a lot and it won't be the same if she hears it from me.'

At this Dottie smiled, and for once conceded defeat easily. 'Okay, I promise. Now give me another hug, you wonderful girl.'

Feeling Dottie give her a squeeze and then a gentle tap on the back, Maude let go and heaved her gran upwards. 'Come on, let's get our glad rags on, they'll be there before us at this rate.'

Dottie wandered over to the wardrobe. 'Now where's my linen dress with the big daisies on, oh bloody hell, Maude, you've put it in the case and look, it's all scrunched up. Honestly, you just can't get the staff these days...'

Maude placed her hand on her hip and shook her head, laughing as Dottie-Yvette huffed and plugged in the iron, knowing she was only kidding and that she was one in a million, and she wouldn't swap her for the world.

Maude saw her gran on approach and noted she had a spring in her step as she waved through the window of the *tabac* at the owner Louis, who she was now on first name terms with. They were heading north-west, first to Bonaparte Beach where Yvette had waited for Vincent, and then on up to St Malo to see where Mémère Delphine and her family lived. Dottie also wanted to make sure they'd mended the city after the bombs and destruction. She said it was proving to be a positive experience, seeing things in colour.

When the door opened and Dottie was finally buckled in, had found her bonbons and sunglasses and the map, Maude sucked in a great gulp of patience and asked if she was ready to go.

'Oh yes, let's move on out. I don't feel one teeny bit sad about going because I'm coming back for Christmas, maybe before, once we've sorted the traitor out.'

Maude started the engine. 'I'm surprised that Uncle Konki took it so well, you know, kept calm. Hugh was responsible for the death of his brother and I can't imagine that even after all this time Konki would be able to forgive or forget that, I know I wouldn't.'

Dottie was trying to undo the tape from around a tin of sweets, picking at an invisible line with her nails. 'Oh I assure you Konstantin will do neither and I wouldn't want to be Hugh once we've decided what to do, that's for sure. He's got it coming. Ah, got the little beggar... why do they make things so fiddly? Ooh look, there's Francine, give her a pip as we pass.'

They both waved enthusiastically as they passed, receiving a two-handed wave from Francine as she waited on tables inside Café des Amis.

'Gran, what do you mean? I thought you were just going to expose him and basically ruin his life and reputation, what do you have to decide? It sounds like you're plotting to pop him off! Please don't go getting carried away because this is NOT the war and I don't want you to end up in prison, okay?' Maude sometimes felt it necessary to state the obvious with her gran in order to curb her enthusiasm or in this case, dramatic tendencies.

Dottie laughed as she searched through the tin of sweets for a pink one. 'But don't forget, Maude, that all the things I have done were for a reason; self-defence, self-preservation and mercy.'

'And what reason do you have this time, for what you are going to do?' As soon as the words were out of her mouth Maude knew exactly what her gran was going to say.

Dottie held a pink sweet between her fingers and answered before popping it in her mouth.

'Revenge, my darling Maude, revenge.'

44

DOTTIE, KONSTANTIN AND HUGH

LONDON, 2005

T he interior of the black limousine was warm, unlike outside where heavy rain splattered the windows and the streets of London, forcing sodden commuters to hurry and seek shelter or pull up their collars and tough it out. It was a dreary late-December day, dull and oppressively gloomy and even though it was only 4pm the light was beginning to fade. They had purposely chosen this time of day in order to give their target little time to react to Dottie's unscheduled arrival. And once she left, they'd have all evening to worry. A sleepless night would no doubt be on the cards for the recipient of a very special gift.

From the back seat of the car they could see the lights were on and according to Konstantin's associates, the person Dottie was going to pay a surprise visit was in residence. Turning in her seat she saw that Konstantin was watching the house intently, huddled against the door, his thoughts she could only imagine. The glass partition that separated them from the driver afforded privacy while they spoke.

'I think it's time. This weather isn't going to stop, and I don't want to be here all night.' Dottie checked her coat was buttoned up tightly, her woollen scarf tucked inside. The matching cloche hat she pulled a bit further down, covering her ears, knowing she was going to get soaked.

'Are you sure you don't want me to come with you? I would like to look him in the eyes one more time and see him squirm.' Konstantin's voice was level, he rarely showed anger.

Dottie shook her head. 'No, I prefer to do this myself and anyway what makes you think he will squirm? Maybe he will brazen it out like he has for the past sixty years.'

Konstantin ignored her remark while his eyes never left the house. 'Remember to keep your gloves on and bring the box back.'

Dottie followed the line of Konstantin's glare. 'I'll remember, don't worry. Do you think he'll do it or run?'

There was a pause and then a reply. 'Either way I do not care. He deserves to die, and he deserves to be shamed. I would like him to know the latter before the former occurs, but we can at least give him the option. Anyway, it would be interesting to see how strong his spine is and where he goes if he runs, like the coward I know him to be.'

'Will you definitely follow him, if he runs? We can't let him get away with it, Konstantin, not after all this time. He has to pay one way or another.' Dottie felt a swell of anger that was calmed by the touch of a hand when Konstantin reached over and patted hers.

'Have no fear, Zaya. This fox is too old to go chasing after a traitor, but I have plenty of willing young cubs who are eager and very capable, so leave it to me. Now, go. The rain has slowed. I will wait here.'

'You will be on camera? They are probably everywhere on this road look, and the houses too.'

A wicked smile lit Konstantin's face. 'We have discussed this, Zaya, so do not worry. What harm is there in one good friend giving another a lift to see their old comrade. It isn't against the law that I am, in many ways, above. It will be fine; we will be fine. I promise.'

Dottie sighed. 'I'm glad that it's us, you and me together, two old soldiers on our last mission. And of all the ones I took part in, out of everything I ever did, this is the most important one of all. I'll see you soon, keep warm.'

Not another word was spoken as Dottie opened the door and stepped onto the pavement. Closing it firmly behind her, she imagined Konstantin giving her a farewell nod from behind the blackened windows before she headed towards the home of Hugh Grosvenor-Townshend, traitor and enemy of the state.

While Dottie waited for the butler to inform Lord Grosvenor that he had an unexpected guest, she kept her eyes trained on the door, aware that she may be being observed by hidden cameras, or not, depending on how comfortable Hugh had become in his life and lie. Konstantin had assured her that while the anterior rooms and corridors were likely to have surveillance it was unlikely that Hugh's study would be the same. Whatever he discussed in person and via the telephone would probably remain private. Dottie would be able to determine the accuracy of Konstantin's summation during her conversation with Hugh.

The interior of his lavish home was as she remembered it: an affluent example of Georgian architecture more than likely furnished in the main by deceased relatives and the more recent assistance of an interior designer, or maybe blood money. Nothing would surprise her now.

Dottie felt not a tremor of nerves thanks mainly to a deep sense of calm that had pervaded her entire body, leaving her in what she could only describe as a serene state. To have control of one's emotions was essential at times like these, and her current mood reminded her somewhat of Konstantin's reaction when she returned from France and told him everything she had learned about Hugh. As he dissembled the information, she had noticed the pallor of his skin change as his whole face tensed. The eyes that twinkled with kindness and shone when his wicked sense of humour made them both roar with laughter, had hardened like ice.

They had been thwarted in their intent to confront him sooner by Hugh's month-long stay in the Bahamas on a luxury island owned by one of his billionaire friends. Then Konstantin had business to attend to in Mother Russia so in the meantime, Dottie had waited patiently and collated all the information that would be handed over to the press. Hugh's file of shame.

Snapped from her thoughts by the click of polished shoes on black-and-white marble, Dottie watched the butler as he approached.

'Lord Grosvenor will see you now.'

Barely acknowledging his remark, Dottie followed, her feet making their moves on the chessboard below.

The butler swung open the panelled door and there he was, seated in a leather winged-back chair behind his writing desk. A portrait of someone she assumed would be one of Hugh's scurrilous relatives peered down on them while a fire burned in the grate. The room smelled of smoke, cigars and polish, similar to a library, faintly musty but well-cared-for.

Hugh spoke first. 'Dottie, what a m-magnificent surprise. Please forgive me for not getting out of this b-blasted chair but the old gout is playing up and cooler weather plays havoc with m-my leg. Do sit, would you like some tea or p-perhaps something stronger?'

Motioning with her hand that his chair bound predicament

was fine, Dottie seated herself before speaking. 'Nothing to drink for me, and I must apologise for springing my visit on you like this, but I'm off on holiday so needed to pop in before left. I have a Christmas gift for you.'

Hugh silently dismissed his butler with a nod before replying. 'Oh r-really, that's very kind and unexpected. I don't think I've ever received a Christmas p-present from you before. Have I done s-something to deserve special treatment?'

Dottie's laugh tinkled, sounding as false as it felt. 'You could say that.'

Hugh left it a heartbeat, appearing to consider her comment then diverted. 'S-so where and when are you off?'

'Next week. I'm returning to France. I spent some time there in August, as it happens, in the village where we were based during the war, and I've been invited to stay with old friends for the festivities. Maude has jetted off to Australia so I'm at a loose end and have a yearning to go back.' Dottie watched him so closely that she thought her eyes would pop from the sockets with the strain. Nothing, not even the merest flicker.

'France, my, my. After all these years you finally s-succumbed. What made you decide to go back? You always seemed set against a trip down m-memory lane. Our m-mutual avoidance of that particular period in our lives seemed like self-preservation, so I'm surprised to say the least.' Hugh rested his elbows on the arms of the chair and made a pyramid shape with his index fingers, fixing Dottie with a stare.

He hadn't changed a bit, not really. Completely bald on top with fine wisps of grey hair at the sides, although he was thinner of face, sagging around the jowls, his giveaway pockmarked skin sallow. It was the eyes though that gave him away. For years Dottie would have described them as watchful or intelligent, but she realised they were neither. They were sly and belonged to a snake who'd shed his skin and reinvented himself, fooling them all.

'True, but I felt it was time, you know, to lay some ghosts to rest and I wanted Maude to know all about my work there, so we set off an adventure and I must say, we got much more than we bargained for.'

There it was. She saw it; a twitch in the corner of his eye and a loss of concentration if only for a second, but now he was back, scrutinising her. Slowly she untucked her scarf from inside her coat, the warmth from the fire having an effect. Her gloves stayed on.

'Oh r-really, in what way?' Hugh's demeanour feigned composure while his plummy voice betrayed great interest.

'Quite by chance we stumbled upon a face from the past and after that, well, it was like a domino effect. We discovered survivors of the Hun invasion and relatives of our network still living in the area, so we had a jolly good get-together in the *salle de fête*. It was marvellous to talk about the past and piece things together, especially about what happened after you and I left, and what happened before, actually.' She hoped the word Hun had stung, she'd been tempted to use worse.

'Oh, I s-see.'

Dottie fixed Hugh with her eyes, waited two beats then allowed herself a smile which he caught. 'And there were two people in particular who had lots of memories that they were eager to share. It seemed like my return triggered them off and so many things came flooding back; the pieces of a puzzle coming together.'

'A p-puzzle, how very intriguing, although I wasn't aware there was one to s-solve.' Hugh shifted in his seat, lowering his arms to his stomach, hands still clasped.

'Neither did I but it seems, to cut a long story short, the

information we received about the network being betrayed and who got rounded up was slightly inaccurate.'

'Well, Dottie, that was to be expected r-really. You k-know how hard it was to gather information especially on the run up to D-Day, more so when our r-radio operators were being discovered left, r-right and centre. No wonder some m-messages were unreliable, passed on verbally in m-many cases, like Chinese whispers.'

'Oh, I agree, Hugh. We relied greatly on the integrity of intelligence passed down the line and trust played a huge part in the network too. It was so hard to know who to share our secrets with, which was why the gradual round-up of our fighters hit hard and we suspected there was a traitor in our midst. But I'm running away with myself. I need to tell you about the faces from the past, one of them I wrongly assumed was amongst those shot.' Not giving Hugh time to reply Dottie sped on.

'Do you remember the reports that said the men from the village were taken?' She paused but received no response. 'And when I heard a young boy was amongst them, I immediately thought it was Polo.'

At this Hugh pulled a face, miming confusion and ignorance. 'P-polo, no, I don't think I remember him. But I moved around a lot and m-met so many fighters. It's impossible to r-remember them all.'

'Oh, but this one remembered you so well. He described you to a T, in fact.' Dottie watched as Hugh paled, then reddened slightly, which gave her satisfaction. Facial muscles can in some part be controlled but the rush of blood, well, that had a will of its own.

'You'll have t-to enlighten me.' Hugh's voice was clipped, less relaxed.

Dottie smiled, fully prepared to do so. 'Polo was seven at the time but wise beyond his years and an excellent foil for the Hun.

They never once suspected him of carrying messages. In their eyes people like him were only fit for the gas chamber so he was largely ignored or looked down upon.' Dottie hoped repeatedly referring to Hugh's real comrades in a derogatory way made him wince inside, on the outer he didn't flinch.

'He had a withered, paralysed arm, bent at the elbow, and fingers that didn't work so well but he was an excellent runner, a little whippet, in fact, who knew the area like the back of his hand. Polo idolised Vincent and used to follow him everywhere. He used to call Polo his *petit ombre*.'

Hugh shook his head. 'Little shadow? N-no, he still doesn't ring a bell.'

'And then there was Béatrice, now you must remember her... very pretty girl, a bit headstrong, Vincent's sister.' Dottie let the words settle. She was glad she'd never played poker with Hugh.

'Yes, of course I r-remember Béatrice, is she well?'

'She is in excellent health, fully compos mentis. We didn't get on during the war, but we were able to put all that behind us and talk frankly, you know, about what we knew and endured... that type of thing. Slowly we were able to unravel some knots and discovered certain things about ourselves, and others.'

The crack when it came was like lightning, his words were preceded by an irritated sigh. 'Is there a p-point to all this, Dottie, because I have rather a lot on. You said you had a gift, but I see nothing that would indicate that.'

Yes, the tide had turned, and Dottie knew he was rattled. 'Oh yes, the gift. Silly me.' She opened the clasp on her handbag and removed a box, no bigger than one that would contain a ring, decorated with a small red bow. She placed the package on her knee, clicked the bag shut and continued. 'Now, where was I? Ah, Béatrice... but never mind her for now, let's go back to Polo, the little boy you've forgotten but who remembers you very clearly. He can describe you in great detail, you know, and one night in particular has remained in his memory for all these years.'

'I s-suppose you're going to tell m-me which night.'

Dottie waited, held his gaze and noticed the beads of perspiration on his bald pate and how he'd swallowed, quite a gulp. There was a ticking clock somewhere in the room, behind her she thought, and she liked the dramatic effect it added to the moment. Tick, tick, tick, one more tick, then she spoke.

'Yes, Hugh, or should I call you Claude, or your code name, Victor... it doesn't matter really because you probably had another name known to the Hun. One I wish I'd known on the night you murdered Vincent.'

45

THE TRAITOR

LONDON, 2005

I t was as though the air had left the room. Dottie suspected she had inhaled some of it as she waited for Hugh to react and when he did, she wished that the carbon dioxide that rushed from her lungs was red hot flames. Then she could have burned him alive and sent him to hell.

The slow clapping, like four sarcastic slaps in the face, for a moment managed to cut Dottie to the quick. His irreverence in the face of such a revelation made her thankful Konstantin was not in the room because she was sure that by now Hugh's brains would be splattered across the wall behind him.

'Well it seems that congratulations are in order. You finally worked it out but s-sadly, there is n-no way of proving anything. I take it the cripple is your only w-witness.'

And there he was, the real Hugh who'd given her the closest thing to a confession. It also proved another point, that as Konstantin had suspected, the room wasn't bugged which meant that Dottie could finish what she had started, just as they'd planned.

'Correct. He related the scene in great detail, but apart from that, I do have written evidence of your treachery and trust me, it is enough to prove you are a murderer and a collaborator.' Dottie's heart was beating so fast she thanked her doctor very quickly for prescribing a variety of preventative medications that she had fortuitously taken that morning.

'And what do you plan to do with this so-called evidence, drag m-me off to the tower, have m-me hung for treason? Seriously, Dottie, do you think The Hague will r-regard me as a war criminal? Hardly. So why don't you get it off your chest, whatever it is you've c-come here to say and then go. This little trip down m-memory lane is proving m-most tiresome.'

'Why... that's what I want to know. I suspect from looking into your family history that somewhere along the line their fascist tendencies and support of the Blackshirts evaded detection by SOE and you slithered your way in. Your father's connection to Lord Rothermere and his propaganda machine at *The Daily Mail* also slipped under the net, am I correct?'

Hugh replied with a smirk. Dottie had more questions but also had a feeling they would go unanswered.

'Maude never liked you and I wondered at the time why she'd taken against a vague acquaintance she'd spotted across a dining hall, but now I know why. She was always intuitive and from your social circle too, so I'm sure that's why she was suspicious. Is that why you betrayed her? Or was she just the Abwehr equivalent of cannon fodder?'

When Hugh ignored the remark and flicked his wrist and checked the time a surge of rage coursed through Dottie's body.

'How dare you behave like this, Hugh, with such disdain and disrespect. I'm starting to believe you are inhuman and I am ashamed that I've regarded you as a friend for all these years. I have nothing left for you but hate and disgust. Those people you gave up, betrayed, they thought they were your brothers in arms. They trusted you and yet you sent them all to their deaths, for what? A lost cause, a twisted ideology because that's what the

Reich was, a failed, sick, perverted regime that you wanted to be a part of.'

A smirk played on Hugh's lips as he spoke. 'It was war, Dottie, and we both picked a t-team. Yours won, but p-people on both sides died and we both killed. Neither of us are without blood on our hands so p-please desist with the holier than thou routine. We are both murderers, Dottie. It's as simple as that.'

'No! I will never fall into the same category as you, Hugh, ever, so don't even try to manoeuvre me that way. Yes, I have blood on my hands, but my acts were carried out in the pursuance of freedom, ending the war not perpetuating a warped, hateful despot's sick dream.'

Hugh shrugged 'On that we will have to agree to differ.'

'Why did you remain my friend? Was it out of guilt or so you could keep an eye on me, control me like a puppet master?' Hugh's wry smile answered her question. 'I see. You're a fake. I despise you.'

Silence descended.

Dottie had had enough and felt sick to her stomach. Hugh would give nothing up, he had no remorse either. She knew that now.

'You asked me what I intend to do with the information. Well it's very simple, Hugh. I am going to expose you, take apart your whole life and watch it crumble. All this,' she gestured with her hand, 'is built on a lie. Just like your reputation. The books you've received accolades for will be derided. Your peers and learned colleagues will feel the stain of acquaintance, and then there's your family, the muck will stick to them too. Once everything I know is handed over to the press you will be hounded, and when you seek shelter, doors will be slammed in your face.'

The explosion of anger made Dottie start inwardly, on the outside she remained like stone.

'You have no proof!' Hugh's voice was riddled with anger and his face tinged with panic.

'Oh, I don't need proof, Hugh. All I need is to cast enough doubt, lots of circumstantial evidence and eye witness accounts. The night you murdered Vincent, you asked him if he had the documents from Estelle. Why did you want them so badly, Hugh? When he arrived in Nantes, Vincent was told of Estelle's capture and that her network had been betrayed. You asked Béatrice where Vincent had gone, and she told you after eavesdropping on our conversation. You must have informed the Hun, after all, I more or less told you where Estelle was and I bet you hoped Vincent would be caught too. Polo saw you pick up a message and leave one for the SS officers; he was there at the chapel. Did the note tell you about the robbery in Nantes, what the documents contained? I think that's why you wanted them back.'

Hugh remained silent, his eyes wild, like a hungry animal waiting to pounce. Dottie taunted him, live bait.

'When Polo told Vincent what he'd seen everything must have fallen into place. Vincent wrote me a message, telling me who the traitor was. Polo was supposed to deliver it but instead he followed Vincent and watched him hide the bag containing the documents in the woods, then he followed him to the barn and witnessed his murder.'

'It's s-still his word against mine. That isn't proof, it's rumour, a folk s-story at best.'

Now it was Dottie's turn to smirk. 'Not when you have the bag, a gun, the note and the stolen documents, a good old-fashioned paper trail that can be scientifically aged and verified. Oh, and a cover name, one that can be traced right back to the SOE archives and matched with an agent's code name. Claude Rayon, Victor, Hugh Grosvenor, you.'

Hugh appeared dumbstruck. The pulse in his temple was

throbbing, almost keeping time with Dottie's heart while she waited for him to react. So, when she saw him glance at the box, she knew it was time to give him his gift.

'I forgot to say, Konstantin is waiting outside. He doesn't send his regards, not now he knows you were responsible for his brother's death. You may not know or care that Anatoly died in a prisoner of war camp, not the same one where they executed Estelle, by the way. Both of them died because of your actions so this gift is actually from me and Konstantin, on behalf of his brother and my beloved Maude. I'm the courier on one last mission.' Dottie removed the lid of the box and took out the sealed inch-square bag that contained a small pill. Holding it between her gloved fingers she placed it on the desk before her, and then put the gift box back inside her bag.

'I take it you know what it is. We weren't sure if you had your own supply so thought it polite to provide you with a means of escape, should you wish it, from the public humiliation and scandal you are about to face. Russian-grade cyanide, quick by all accounts. No need to thank us, by the way. It really is our pleasure.'

Once again, the room was plunged into silence and this time the clock seemed to tick faster. Hugh's voice brought Dottie back to reality. 'What m-makes you think I haven't planned for this eventuality and therefore have no need of your gifts, or the use of my own supply?'

'And what makes you think Konstantin hasn't pre-empted your reaction? As you know he enjoys a game of chess, so I think it's your move.' Dottie rewound her scarf and tucked it inside her coat.

When Hugh spoke his voice betrayed nothing. 'How long have I got?'

Dottie stood and looked upon her ex-friend for the last time. 'Longer than Anatoly, Maude and Vincent had before the bullet left the gun. Forty-eight hours and then it's Konstantin's move. I'll see myself out. Goodbye, Hugh.'

Their eyes met briefly and in his she saw nothing that would make her regret this last mission, so she turned and walked away, her shoes muffled by the rug. Once she pulled open the door and strode across the chessboard hallway, the sound of her heels clicking marked time, eleven seconds until she was outside and on the pavement, sucking in fresh air and heading towards where Konstantin was waiting.

The driver was out of the car and opening the passenger door before she arrived, and once she was seated and it was closed behind her, she heard the comforting voice of a true friend.

'It is done?'

Dottie nodded. 'It is done.'

'Good. For you it is finished, Zaya, now leave the rest to me.' Konstantin gave a curt nod and his driver, watching through the rear-view mirror, obeyed.

As the car glided past the home of the traitor neither occupant turned their heads to look, instead they focused on the road ahead and in Dottie's case, the future.

46

DOTTIE'S BIG BIRTHDAY

RENAZÉ, MAY 2020

D ottie was tired, weary was how she'd described it to Maude earlier, before she popped out to the Super U to get some supplies for the weekend. Maude always shopped in the evening, when the light faded and her studio up in the attic caught too many shadows.

Shadows, now there was a word that never failed to conjure a memory. Dottie spent a lot of time with her memories now and she liked to surround herself with her bits and bobs, her photograph album that she spent hours poring over, touching the face of her precious ones, reminding herself, chuckling and sometimes having a little chat with them. It didn't matter that she looked a bit potty. Maude called her dotty Dottie, it made them both smile.

There had been so much of that since they both moved to France permanently ten years ago, once Maude had returned from her failed travels and got on with the serious business of being an artist. Dottie delighted in reciting to anyone who would listen, especially after a few red wines, the last part of the text message she'd received late one night from Maude.

. . .

Dear Gran, letting you know that me and Lachlan are over. Try not to look too pleased. Long story but basically, he has no intention of travelling anywhere so I'm heading off without him. Met up with two great girls who have wanderlust like me. Will stick with them and be home in January. Told the parents, Mum freaked, Dad's okay, have a word with Mum, will you? I'll keep you updated by email. Hope you are okay and have a brill time in France with the Maquis. Love you, Maude.

PS Thank you for funding this trip and giving me the opportunity to prove you right about Kangaroo Boy ;)

When Maude returned from Oz, the first thing she did was dig out her sketches from France and throw herself into her work. Her first collection, shown at a trendy gallery in Soho, sold out and from then on she was inundated with commissions. The paintings, beautiful landscapes, were eclipsed by her second collection of past and present representations of towns and villages, modern-day life overlaid by ghosts of those who walked the streets before them. Soon her work was in great demand.

Maude and Dottie made frequent visits to France where the artist would gather inspiration and the grandmother would while away her time in Renazé with her friends. Maude continued to sell her work through a prestigious gallery in London so the permanent move had seemed a sensible option and had worked well for both of them. Even Jean didn't mind, not after Dottie bunged her a few quid in an early inheritance cheque so she and Ralph could bugger off to Portugal to play golf in the sun.

Dottie checked the time, almost seven, Maude would be home soon. She was such a darling and had left the radio on, playing jazz nice and quietly in the corner, and there was a G&T, with lemon not lime, to see her through until dinner. The light was fading in the lounge but as always Maude had left the wall lights on, lighting up the two portraits which hung in the alcoves on either side of the fire. Feeling chilly, Dottie pulled the blanket from the back of the sofa where she lay, covered herself, then lifted the photo album from the table by her side. Before she opened it, she glanced up and smiled at the portraits.

Maude was so clever. From the photo Béatrice had given Dottie of Vincent on the beach, and using the one that Roberto had taken of her that day on the hill, she'd reunited two lovers through oil on canvas. Side by side, Dottie's arm rested against that of Vincent and both of them were smiling into the camera. Anyone who didn't know the truth would imagine that was exactly how the original scene had played out.

Her eyes then moved to the left, to the portrait opposite of her beautiful Lady Mary Eliza Balfour, Maude to her friends. Young Maude had made it her mission to find a photograph of Old Maude as they now referred to her. After following an online paper trail that led to a second cousin, she was rewarded with two family photos, one of baby Maude and her siblings, and one of her just after her coming out in London. It was the epitome of the vibrant beauty with ironed blonde hair that rolled in waves, her rose complexion and laughing blues eyes smiled along with rosebud lips. The only alteration to the original was that she was wearing pale green, like the first time Dottie ever saw her. A vision of loveliness.

Dottie had wept when Maude presented her with the one of Vincent and next the one of Old Maude. Konstantin had made them all laugh when he asked Maude to immortalise him too, in his youth, but he wanted to be wrestling a bear. In the end he settled for an image of him sitting on a bench by the side of the Thames, wrapped up warm in his black Crombie overcoat and trilby hat, looking moody and mysterious with a folded newspaper by his side. Konstantin loved that painting and after his death it came to Dottie and was hung in the hallway, keeping an eye on anyone who entered the house. Turning the pages, knowing exactly where to find her old friend, Dottie sighed when she reached the homage to their years together. *Oh, I do miss you, Konstantin.*

They were all in the album, those who had gone before. Konstantin had succumbed first, he might have fought bears and tsars, but he couldn't beat a dodgy ticker. Béatrice went next and two years previously Polo, the little shadow. They were never far away though, in her thoughts and by talking of them constantly she kept them alive in her mind, like when she used to go to the schools thereabouts and chat to the children about VE Day. She'd become quite a celebrity once the story of Hugh the Traitor broke and Vincent's bag went on display.

VE Day was always an important one in France, and it was such a blasted shame that the seventy-fifth celebrations had been ruined by that confounded disease that had swept across the world, an invisible enemy. Not that Dottie could have got out to celebrate like years before, apparently she was too frail and hated that bloody wheelchair so spent much of her time indoors. Had she been able to get up and at 'em, Dottie told Maude she'd have looked that enemy in the eye, unafraid, like she had the last invisible infiltrator.

She rarely gave Hugh or his fate the time of day, but the train of thoughts took her there. He'd run, like Konstantin had expected, before the story broke of a British traitor, a peer of the realm, respected government advisor, political commentator and esteemed author. While the press went wild, the old Russian fox sent his cubs on a mission, tracking Hugh to Cuba, observing him and his odd band of wrinkly evaders with fake names and secrets to hide. And then one night, Hugh the Traitor had an unfortunate accident, falling off the hotel balcony, then the cubs went home to Papa. Hugh's funeral wasn't well attended, nobody wanted to be guilty by association, and his legacy was left for Wikipedia to document his shame.

Dottie couldn't be bothered with *him*, so took a sip of her G&T, yawning as she placed the glass on the table. She felt ever so tired all of a sudden, but she put that down to the excitement of the day before. They'd had lots of champagne during her birthday lunch, she and Maude on Zoom toasting her special birthday with Jean and Ralph over in Portugal. Then there was the big socially-distanced surprise, a ring on the doorbell and Maude insisting she came to the door. Realising that something had been planned, Dottie humoured her eager granddaughter, but it took ages to get there using her stick, nobody was going to see her with that wheelie-walker thing.

When Maude flung open the door to a large (and against regulations) crowd, comprising of the children from the school, Gabriel the mayor and so many of the villagers, Dottie actually felt her lips wobble as they all sang happy birthday. The path was strewn with flowers and gifts and after the hip, hip, she could barely manage a simple thank you, so overwhelmed was she by the gesture.

Dottie loved her life in France and had felt at home in the house she'd bought for Maude ever since they moved in. She didn't even miss the Hackney house although she dreamt of it sometimes, took a wander along the halls and popped her head into the rooms that were no doubt transformed by the students from The Slade who rented it. Maude hadn't wanted to sell up and Dottie was glad, it would have seemed too final, the end of an era.

She'd passed the photos of her parents and Mémère, George and Eddie the Beagle, so many happy photos of Young Maudie and then to her ragtag friends of the Maquis, images gathered by Maude from relatives still living. She touched their faces one by one, and lingered over Polo the shadow, taken after the war, her brave little Maquisard.

The final page was dedicated to Vincent and although there were only a few and no matter how faded, they were her treasure and his face shone like a diamond. Maybe it was her tired eyes playing tricks but in this light, tonight, it seemed to glow and move on the page, his flesh real and his eyes warm, and yes, he looked happy.

Enough of this you silly old woman, Dottie closed the album and stretched to place it on the table, then snuggled down. She would close her eyes for a while and then Maude would be home, and dinner would be ready. The radio was playing something she recognised... oh yes, it was the song she danced to with Old Maude in Nantes and as her eyes turned from the painting of her friend, in the last moments it rested on the face of a handsome young man. Dottie smiled and reached out her hand, taking his. After all this time of waiting, he was here at last, her one true love, Vincent.

EPILOGUE

E veryone was gathered in the packed lobby of the *mairie*. As the eager reporters vied for a front row position the correspondent from the local news channel won the fight. Gabriel stood on one side of the huge frame that was resting on a plinth, covered by a white sheet, while Maude stood on the other. She was suddenly nervous, being centre of attention in front of the crowd who were eager to see what lay underneath.

On the table by the office door stood a pile of books, guarded closely by Francine who was in charge of selling them once Maude had signed them later. Dottie's biography had been translated into French and due to the furore that the traitor had whipped up many years before, it was already a huge hit in England. There were omissions though, Maude had thought it prudent not to mention certain revelations, some secrets had died with her grandmother.

Maude still couldn't believe Dottie was gone and found it hard to contemplate a life without her gran in it. If her mind wandered to that evening when she'd come home from the supermarket to find Dottie taking her final nap, Maude cheered herself with the notion that the stubborn old bugger made sure she stayed *just* long enough to celebrate her big birthday.

It was time for the unveiling now everyone had shuffled and squeezed in and Gabriel was making a short speech, explaining the origins and inspiration of the painting, blinking now and then at the flash from the reporters' cameras. Maude listened intently, understanding most of it now she could speak French and after her grandmother's insistence. Maude smiled, thinking, *That woman always, always got her way.*

Then Gabriel gestured with his hand that Maude should do the honours so after stepping forward and with a flourish, more to get it over with than anything, she pulled away the sheet and revealed the painting. There was a gasp from the crowd and then a round of applause as the scene Maude knew so well was uncovered.

On a hilltop overlooking the village of Renazé below, stood the members of the Maquis. Above, in a cobalt-blue sky streaked by clouds edged in grey, flew two spitfires, a lone parachute on its descent into occupied territory, an homage to the evaders they helped to escape, or perhaps the agents and the moon squadrons who leapt into the abyss.

In the forefront, some clutching rifles, all wearing proud expressions, were the brave and defiant men and women who had resisted. Florian, his habitual cigarette hanging from his mouth, Benoit in teashade spectacles, Xavier in his floppy beret, Armand in his white apron, Thierry with his short trousers and braces, Tante Helene in her best flowery dress, and next to his hero, the little shadow Polo holding a brace of rabbits. At the centre, stood side by side was their leader Vincent and his comrade Yvette. But if the voyeur looked closely at the pair, they would see that their hands touched and one of their fingers entwined the other, telling you they were more than just comrades. They were soulmates, parted for a while but now immortalised in oil on canvas and somewhere, together for eternity.

Underneath the painting, attached to the oak frame was a gold plaque bearing the names of each member of the Maquis. Once the applause died down, Gabriel asked for silence and read them out, one by one. When he came to the last, Maude fought hard to hold it together because finally, the moment had come. It had taken seventy-five years, but today they would all hear the name of the woman who jumped into the abyss, who risked her life, who resisted, who fought for freedom and, in so many ways, won.

She was Dorothy 'Dottie' Tanner, alias Yvette Giroux, code name Nadine, but to Maude, that brave, wonderful, beautiful young woman in the painting, would always and forever be known as Gran.

The End

AFTERWORD

The last letter of the young communist militant, Guy Môquet, who was executed by the Germans on 22 October 1941.

My darling Mummy, my adored brother, my much loved Daddy, I am going to die! What I ask of you, especially you, Mummy, is to be brave. I am, and I want to be, as brave as all those who have gone before me. Of course, I would have preferred to live. But what I wish with all my heart is that my death serves a purpose. I didn't have time to embrace Jean. I embraced my two brothers Roger and Rino (1). As for my real brother, I cannot embrace him, alas! I hope all my clothes will be sent back to you. They might be of use to Serge, I trust he will be proud to wear them one day. To you, my Daddy to whom I have given many worries, as well as to my Mummy, I say goodbye for the last time. Know that I did my best to follow the path that you laid out for me. A last adieu to all my friends, to my brother whom I love very much. May he study hard to become a man later on. Seventeen and a half years, my life has been short, I have no regrets, if only that of leaving you all. I am going to die with Tintin, Michels. Mummy, what I ask you, what I want you to promise me, is to be brave and to overcome your sorrow. I cannot put any more. I am leaving you all, Mummy, Serge, Daddy, I embrace you with all my child's heart. Be brave! Your Guy who loves you.

1. Brothers in arms

A NOTE FROM THE AUTHOR

Some of you may have recognised the black Cross of Lorraine at the front of the book, it's the symbol of the French Resistance, but perhaps you also wondered why we used the swallow on the cover. I wanted something meaningful, like a secret code, a message. Swallows symbolise many things to different cultures, working class pride is one, and while the Maquis was made up of fighters from all walks of life, many of them were working class men and women. Fighters often have tattoos of swallows on their knuckles, it's a mark of strength and swiftness in battle. Swallows are also associated with passion, unity, love, a journey and most importantly, freedom.

All of these values and sentiments form the basis of my book and the little swallow on the cover is also sending a final message, one of thanks from me to you.

ACKNOWLEDGEMENTS

Hello and thank you for reading *Resistance*. I hope you enjoyed it because I loved writing it for you.

I've had this story in my head for such a long time, ever since I saw the tragically sad letter from Guy Môquet to his parents. The idea was further embellished after visiting the home of one of our French friends and just as I mention in the book, upstairs there is an old wardrobe with the floor cut out and below is the stables. The house was used to hide evaders during the war and that evening, as I looked across the great swathes of land that stretched to the horizon, my mind was captured by the brave Maquis who roamed the countryside and hid in the pine forests. I began to feel their presence, and I looked out for the Cross of Lorraine on buildings, the symbol of the Free French that you see at the start of the book.

I also wanted to tell the story of a young British agent in a different way, how her service left a mark and what her life would have been like far away from home, operating undercover in a climate of oppression and fear. I hope you fell in love with Dottie like I did, and her wonderful friend Maude, they were both so much fun to write, and little Polo too.

During the story I have used places, towns and villages close to my home in France, it helped me to picture the scene and describe it to you. Café des Amis is actually a painting that hangs over my fireplace and I had to include it. I knew that's where the Maquis would meet, in a smoky bar, whispering secret plans.

I was also thrilled to discover the existence of a British agent who operated in the area, so my first thanks go to Musée de la Résistance de Châteaubriant who were so helpful and kindly sent me lots of information and the name of Agent Nadine.

As always, I want to thank #TeamTrish, my fabulous ARC readers who diligently read and report back on their early copy. Every book journey is made more fun having you all along for the ride. Special thanks go to Tina Jackson and Josephine Bilton for your speedy beta-reading and feather-smoothing feedback.

To Keri Beevis, for being my cheerleader, motivational guru and all-round star. And for making me laugh so much I sometimes really do cry!

My Anita, perfectionist personified who must have said, 'Get on with it, Dixon' about a hundred times during the writing of this book. Love you, Waller.

Next, the brilliant team at Bloodhound Books – Betsy, Fred, Alexina, Tara and Heather. You make work fun and I'm so proud to be one of your authors.

Many thanks to my editors Emily and Abbie for polishing my book and making it shine, and to the publicity team for getting my book out there.

And to you, the reader, for choosing *Resistance* and if you've read any of my others, for sticking with me.

Finally, as always, I want to thank my family. Brian, Amy, Mark, Owen, Jess and Harry.

I love you all so much and remember, *vous êtes mon monde et mon tout*.

Take care and stay safe everyone, *à bientôt* x

Printed in Great Britain
by Amazon